"Jump," his father told him

"I don't want to jump

crackle.

"You are meant to."

Dusk had never left the tree. "May I go back to the nest?" he asked.

"No."

Dusk felt his throat tighten. More than anything he wanted to wriggle down into the deep furrow where he slept, feel the tree's soft, fragrant bark around him.

"It's time," his father said. Though his voice was calm, Dusk sensed there would be no more discussion. "Are you ready?"

"I can't remember all the things you told me," Dusk said in a panic.

"It doesn't matter," his father replied.

"Tell me once more, please!"

His father nuzzled him gently, then shoved him off the branch.

Dusk gave a cry, as much in amazement as terror, and twisted around, clutching for something, anything. But the branch was already out of reach and he was falling, headfirst now. Wind filled his ears. Branches rushed past; the world swelled below him. His entire body trembled, his stomach slewing inside him. Instinctively he stretched his arms and kicked out his leg, spreading his sails wide.

Also by Kenneth Oppel

Airborn
Skybreaker
Dead Water Zone

THE SILVERWING TRILOGY
Silverwing
Sunwing
Firewing

DARKWING

KENNETH OPPEL

Illustrated by KEITH THOMPSON

An Imprint of HarperCollins *Publishers*

Eos is an imprint of HarperCollins Publishers.

Darkwing

Text copyright © 2007 by Firewing Productions Inc.

Illustrations copyright © 2007 by Keith Thompson

www.harpercollinschildrens.com

Library of Congress Cataloging-in-Publication Data

Oppel, Kenneth.

Darkwing / Kenneth Oppel.— 1st ed.

p.   cm.

Summary: Dusk, the world's first bat, must lead his colony to safety in a time of changing
species.

ISBN 978-0-06-085056-2 (pbk.)

1. Bats—Juvenile fiction. [1. Bats—Fiction. 2. Prehistoric animals—Fiction. 3. Survival—
Fiction.] I. Title.

PZ10.3.O555Dar 2007   2007007432

[Fic]—dc22   CIP

                                                                                                          AC

Typography by Hilary Zarycky

❖

First paperback edition, 2008

To Philippa, Sophia, Nathaniel, and Julia

CONTENTS

PART I

The
ISLAND

CHAPTER 1

Jump

THE TREE HAD never seemed so high.

Dusk labored up the trunk of the giant sequoia, sinking his claws into the soft, reddish bark. Pale lichen grew along the ridges; here and there, pitch glistened dully in the furrows. Warmed by the dawn's heat, the tree steamed, releasing its heady fragrance. All around Dusk, insects sparkled and whirred, but he wasn't interested in them just now.

His father, Icaron, climbed beside him and, though old, he moved more swiftly than his son. Dusk hurried to keep up. He'd been born with only two claws on each hand, instead of three, and hauling himself up the trunk was hard work.

"Will my other claws ever grow in?" he asked his father.

"They may."

"If they don't?"

"You'll have less to grip and pull with," Icaron said. "But you have unusually strong chest and shoulder muscles."

Dusk said nothing, pleased.

"That will help make up for your weak legs," his father added matter-of-factly.

"Oh," Dusk said, casting a surprised backward glance. He hadn't realized he had weak legs, but his father had obviously noticed. Maybe that helped explain why climbing was such tiring work.

Just four weeks ago he'd been born, rump first and three seconds behind his sister Sylph. Blind and naked like all newborn chiropters, he had crawled up his mother's belly and started nursing immediately. Within days his vision cleared and focused. Fur grew over his body, and he gained weight. He ate insects his mother had caught and chewed for him.

And this morning his father had roused him in the nest and told him it was time to climb the tree. They'd set off, just the two of them. Even though he'd been nervous, Dusk still loved the way everyone looked at him, the youngest son of the colony's leader.

"Am I odd-looking?" Dusk asked now. He was merely repeating what he'd overheard from others—including from his own mother, when she thought he was asleep.

Icaron looked back at him. "You are rather odd-looking, yes."

The answer disappointed him, even though he knew very well it was the truth. Watching the other newborns, he could tell he was different. His chest and shoulders were bulkier than normal, giving him a slightly top-heavy appearance. His ears were large and stuck out too much. And, most mortifying of all, even at four weeks, no fur had yet grown across his arms and sails, making him feel childishly naked. He wished at least his sails were like his father's.

"Dad, what's it like being leader?"

His father reached back with a rear foot and fondly tousled the fur on Dusk's head. "It's a lot of responsibility, trying to take care of everyone. It's a great deal to think about."

"Like what?"

"Well, we've been very fortunate here. Food is plentiful. There are no predators. I hope things stay that way. But if they change, I might have to make hard decisions."

Dusk nodded, trying to look solemn, not really having any idea what his father was talking about.

"Will I be leader one day?" he asked.

"I very much doubt it."

"Why?" Dusk asked indignantly.

"When a leader dies, his firstborn son becomes the new leader."

"That would be Auster," Dusk said glumly. He scarcely knew his eldest brother. Auster was eighteen years older than Dusk and had a mate and many children. Most of his children had children. Dusk was uncle to dozens of nieces and nephews, and great-uncle to hundreds more— and he was younger than practically any of them. It got very confusing, very quickly.

"But," Icaron continued, "if by some dreadful chance the firstborn is already dead, then the next oldest son would assume the leadership, and so on."

"Borasco, Shamal, Vardar . . ." Dusk felt proud he knew the names of his eight older brothers, even though he'd only ever exchanged a few words with most of them.

"And if there are no sons," Icaron continued, "only then would it pass to the daughters."

"So Sylph might be leader one day?" he asked in alarm.

"A frightening thought, I agree," his dad said. "Of course, her seven older sisters would have to die before her. So it's even more unlikely than you becoming leader as my ninth-born son."

"I see," Dusk said, feeling this was all outrageously unfair.

He paused to catch his breath. High overhead, through the redwood's vast canopy, he caught small glimpses of the sky. Sleek feathered creatures darted through the air. The sight of their beating wings made his stomach swirl excitedly.

"Are we related to birds?" he asked his father.

"Of course not," he replied. "We have no feathers. We're not hatched from eggs. And we can't fly."

Dusk peered up, hoping to see more birds. He loved the way they lifted so effortlessly.

"How much higher will we go?" he asked.

Surely his father wasn't planning on taking him all the way to the tree's summit. That was where the birds perched, and the newborns were always told to stay clear. The flyers were fiercely protective of their territory, especially when rearing their hatchlings. Luckily the sequoia was over three hundred feet high, and big enough for all of them. Dusk and all the other chiropters lived in the tree's middle reaches. Among the profusion of mighty limbs, they nested in the bark's endless network of deep furrows.

"Not much higher now," Icaron told him.

Despite the effort of the climb, Dusk was not eager to reach their destination. He knew what awaited him there, and though he and the other newborns had chattered endlessly about it, Dusk could not help feeling afraid.

"Is this the tallest tree in the forest?" he asked. He wanted to talk.

"I've never seen a taller one."

"How old is it?"

"Very old. Thousands of years."

"Are you old?" he asked his father.

His father gave a surprised laugh. "Not quite that old. But old enough to have had many sons and daughters."

"Seventeen including me and Sylph," Dusk said.

"That's right. But you two, I think, will be my last."

Dusk was alarmed. "Are you going to die soon?"

"Certainly not. But everyone reaches an age when it's no longer possible to have more offspring."

Icaron stopped suddenly. "This is the Upper Spar," he said, sidestepping from the trunk to an enormous broad branch that projected out over the clearing. "This is as far as we chiropters go. Remember it. Above this, the tree belongs to the birds."

Dusk looked at the branch, memorizing its outline.

"This way now," Icaron said, and started walking on all fours out along the Upper Spar.

Dusk faltered a moment, limbs shaky.

"There's nothing to fear," his father said, turning to his son and waiting.

Dusk came to him. They continued along the branch side by side, and then single file down a thinner branch, luxuriant with needlelike leaves and pinecones, some almost as big as Dusk. Near the branch's tip they stopped. It drooped slightly with their weight. The cicadas' drone ceased suddenly, then resumed with renewed intensity.

Dusk looked down and down, through the branches, to the forest floor, impossibly far away. He urinated noisily against the bark.

"Are you ready?" his father asked.

Dusk said nothing.

"Jump," his father told him.

"I don't want to jump." His voice was an unfamiliar crackle.

"You are meant to."

Dusk had never left the tree. "May I go back to the nest?" he asked.

"No."

Dusk felt his throat tighten. More than anything he wanted to wriggle down into the deep furrow where he slept, feel the tree's soft, fragrant bark around him.

"It's time," his father said. Though his voice was calm, Dusk sensed there would be no more discussion. "Are you ready?"

"I can't remember all the things you told me," Dusk said in panic.

"It doesn't matter," his father replied.

"Tell me once more, please!"

His father nuzzled him gently, then shoved him off the branch.

Dusk gave a cry, as much in amazement as terror, and twisted around, clutching for something, anything. But the branch was already out of reach and he was falling, headfirst now. Wind filled his ears. Branches rushed past; the world swelled below him. His entire body trembled, his stomach slewing inside him. Instinctively he stretched his arms and kicked out his legs, spreading his sails wide.

"That's it!" cried Icaron, suddenly alongside him, flaring his own furred sails.

Bizarrely Dusk felt an overwhelming urge to flap.

"Stop that!" his father shouted. "You are not a bird! Stretch them out! Farther! As far as they'll go! That's it! Hold them straight! You're gliding now!"

Air flowed around Dusk's sails and filled them. His shoulders and head lifted as he came out of his nosedive. He breathed in little gulps. He felt as though he'd been struck by lightning. He was soaring away from the sequoia, his home, out across the great clearing, toward the other giant redwoods on the far side. Moths and flies whirled past him.

He was sailing too fast, slanting down too sharply. Whenever he'd watched the other chiropters gliding, they always seemed to be moving so serenely, hardly losing height at all. He felt barely in control.

"Slow down!" he heard his father shout.

"How?" he cried.

"Are your sails all the way out?"

Dusk stretched as far and wide as he could, and he did slow a little, but still felt he was dropping too fast. He watched with alarm as he neared the trees across the clearing.

"Slow down, Dusk!" his father shouted again.

"I'm trying!"

"We're going to turn now," Icaron called out. "Just tilt a bit to the left. Use your legs as well as your fingers and arms. Good! A bit more! Keep your sails straight! Don't fold them! Here we go!"

Dusk made a fast, jerky turn, wobbling, the forest spinning as he pointed himself back at the sequoia. Seeing it made him feel better. Below him he could make out the familiar branches of their nests and hunting perches. Crisscrossing the clearing were the graceful shapes of chiropters, hunting insects. He straightened out and felt a small thrill of accomplishment.

"We're going to land," Icaron said, pulling ahead of him. "You follow me, and do what I do!"

Dusk tried to match his father's glide path, but he was still falling too quickly.

"Dad!" he called out, as he sank below his father.

Icaron glanced back and angled his sails for a steeper dive.

"Keep your sails flat, Dusk!"

He *was* keeping his sails flat, but it didn't seem to help any. He kept his eyes locked on his father, who he knew was making a much steeper landing approach than normal.

"When you're almost at the branch, flare your sails!" Icaron shouted back to him. "Angle them up and dump all the air out of them and you'll stop. Here we go!"

Dusk watched intently as his father neared a nice broad branch, sticking far out over the clearing. Icaron leveled off effortlessly, flared his sails sharply, and touched down with his rear claws. Then he furled his sails and set himself down on all fours. He whirled around to watch Dusk.

"Slowly now!" he called out. "As slowly as you can!"

Dusk saw the branch heaving toward him and knew he was coming in too fast and steep.

"Level off! Level off!" Icaron shouted.

Once again, the urge to flap was overpowering, and Dusk started chopping the air with his sails.

"No!" Icaron yelled at him. "That's not helping. Stop it! Flare your sails now!"

Dusk flared his sails, and decelerated so sharply he felt he'd been yanked backward. Pain jolted through his arms and shoulders. He stalled in midair and dropped hard toward the branch, instinctively flapping. He landed in a heap on top of his father.

"Sorry," gasped Dusk as they untangled themselves.

"Are you all right?" Icaron asked.

"I think so." Dusk's flanks heaved as he caught his breath.

He flexed all his limbs to make sure nothing was broken, then looked at his father sternly. "You pushed me!"

"I push all my children," his father replied with a chuckle. "Believe me, no one wants to make their first jump."

Dusk felt better. "Even Sylph?"

"Even Sylph."

Yesterday, his father had taken Sylph up for her first gliding lesson, and she hadn't said anything about having to be pushed.

"How did I do?" Dusk asked. He was still trembling.

"I've never had anyone try to flap before."

"Sorry," said Dusk sheepishly. "It just seemed like the thing to do."

"Your sails are made for gliding, not flying. Remember that."

Dusk nodded dutifully.

"You did well," said his father. "A bit fast. I'm wondering if it's because your sails are furless. Less to catch the air." Dad peered at him. "And your shoulders and chest make you a bit heavier up front. Might explain why you tend to pitch forward. You'll certainly be a fast glider. A ferocious hunter. Those sphinx moths won't have a chance! But you'll really have to work on that landing of yours."

"I will, I promise."

"Ready to go again?"

Dusk's heart thundered. "Yes," he said instantly.

CHAPTER 2

Dusk

SIX MONTHS LATER

HIDDEN BEHIND LEAVES, motionless against the bark, Dusk peered up at the bird. Only a few feet above him, it perched on a branch, head tipping from side to side, occasionally answering the calls of other birds in the forest. Dusk admired its lines, the way every part of it seemed designed for a life aloft.

The bird rustled its wings, and Dusk's eyes widened expectantly. But then the creature merely refolded its wings, took a few steps, and pecked at something on the branch. Dusk exhaled silently. He wanted to see the bird fly.

It had taken him a long time to reach the Upper Spar, and it was no easy climb. His legs were stronger than they used to be, but his missing claws had never materialized. In fact, he was as odd-looking as ever. Far below him, the other chiropters were slanting across the clearing, busy hunting. No one knew he was up here. It was his secret.

It was hard to see birds properly unless you came this high. Though they often flitted down through the trees to forage on the ground, they never lingered near the chiropter perches. And they passed so quickly Dusk hardly ever had time to get a good look. Here, on the Upper Spar, on the very border between chiropter and bird territory, it was much easier to study them. This wasn't the first time Dusk had come. He couldn't quite explain what it was that drew him—and he'd certainly never told anyone. What would his father say?

It wasn't the birds themselves he was interested in. Flying was what he yearned to see, especially those first few moments when the birds flapped and lifted into the air. Every time he saw this, Dusk felt a strange ache in the center of his chest. He wanted to understand how it was done.

He was starting to think this particular bird was completely useless. It was just standing there, doing nothing. Why wouldn't it fly? He'd been watching for almost fifteen minutes now. His stomach rumbled. He really should be hunting. But first he wanted to see at least one proper takeoff. Unfortunately the bird had decided this was an excellent moment to fluff and groom its plumage.

Silently Dusk sucked air through his nostrils, and then—

"Fly!" he shouted with all his might.

The bird instinctively leaped from its perch, spreading its wings and battering the air. Dusk leaned forward eagerly, watching everything, noting the flex of the wings, counting the number of strokes. And then the bird was gone, lost in the tree's dense foliage as it beat its way into the midday sky.

"Fantastic," Dusk mumbled, his heart still pounding.

He backed out of his hiding place and found a wider spot along the branch. He unfurled his sails, still virtually furless. The bird had made it look so easy, hardly beating its wings as it rose quickly and gracefully. Four flaps. Dusk looked all around to make sure no one was watching. He crouched and sprang straight up, spreading his sails and beating them hard, one flap, two, three—

And landed on the branch in a heap. He ground his teeth in frustration—and shame.

You are not a bird.

His father had told him that during his very first gliding lesson—and a few times afterward, until Dusk taught himself never to flap, no matter how strong the urge. But the urge had never left him altogether. Some stubborn part of him still believed that if he could just flap, he would lift.

Chiropters only glided down, never up. But maybe, if they learned the secrets of the birds, they *could* go up. He couldn't be the only chiropter in history to think this. But no one else seemed at all interested in wings, or how they were used.

Was he doing something wrong? Flapping was hard work, but maybe he needed to do it faster than the birds, at least to get him airborne. He closed his eyes, trying to remember exactly how the bird had launched itself, crouched, and—

"What're you doing?"

He jerked around to see his sister Sylph climbing out along the Upper Spar with two other newborns, Aeolus and Jib. Jib's great-aunt was Nova, one of the colony elders. Dusk wondered how much they'd seen.

"Oh, hello," Dusk said, casually folding his sails. "I was just about to hunt."

"You don't usually come so high." Sylph looked at him strangely. She knew how much he hated climbing.

"Gives me a longer glide," Dusk said. "And it's less crowded up here."

"He doesn't kill as many chiropters that way," Jib sneered.

"I haven't killed anyone in days," Dusk said, stealing Jib's laughter. "Anyway, the number of deaths has been exaggerated. If everyone would just sail a little faster, there'd be plenty of room."

Dusk had earned a reputation as a breakneck and somewhat dangerous glider. Over the past six months he'd tried hard to learn how to slow down—with minimal success. His sails, his entire body, simply would not cooperate. There'd been several collisions with other chiropters, including a much-talked-about midair landing on Jib's head, not so long ago.

"I've been looking everywhere for you," Sylph said, nuzzling Dusk in greeting. "Have you been up here long?"

"What are you three doing on the Spar anyway?" Dusk asked, eager to change the subject. Jib and Aeolus, he noticed, glanced quickly at one another, as if reluctant to answer.

"We're having a contest!" Sylph said excitedly. "Here to the Lower Reach. Interested?"

"Sounds fun," said Dusk. "I like winning."

"It's not a race," said Aeolus, a bit sharply. "It's a hunting contest. Whoever catches the most on the glide."

"Ah," said Dusk.

All the newborns knew he was fast, but also that his speed worked against him when hunting. Because he fell faster, he had less time to target and intercept prey.

"Well, why not?" he said. He was just glad none of them had seen him flapping. He could imagine what they'd say.

Always been a little odd, and now this.

Thinks he can fly.

Birdbrain.

"I'm not sure it's a good idea," Jib said, flicking a sail at Dusk. "If he crashes into someone, we all get in trouble."

"I'll be on my best behavior," said Dusk. He hated Jib's barbs, and only hoped he didn't let it show.

"You're just worried he'll beat you," Sylph said to Jib.

Jib snorted.

"Dusk's the only newborn to catch a sphinx moth," Sylph reminded him.

Dusk looked fondly at his sister. She was amazingly loyal when they were around the other newborns. When it was just the two of them, she was not nearly so considerate—but then again, neither was he.

"So are we ready to go?" Sylph asked impatiently.

Sylph was loud. She had a big voice and tended to shout.

Their mother said she'd been born shouting, and really hadn't stopped since. She was always getting shushed by Mom and Dad. Sometimes Dusk wanted to tell her to shush, too, but what he loved was her laughter.

When Sylph laughed, she laughed with her whole body. It wasn't enough for her just to laugh from her mouth; her entire body jerked and lurched and she'd often throw herself around a bit until she ended up splayed on the branch. It was quite something to watch.

"I'm in," said Jib. "Let's go."

The four of them lined up along the edge of the Upper Spar.

"You haven't got a chance," Sylph murmured to Dusk.

"Against Jib?" he whispered back.

"Against me," she said. In her normal voice she shouted, "Everyone ready? Launch!"

Dusk threw himself off the branch, unfurled, and within seconds was well ahead of the others. His hairless sails cut the air unhindered. It was this speed that had enabled him to catch a sphinx moth, the very fastest of bugs. But Sylph, over-all, was a much better hunter. There hadn't been many days when his tally of prey was greater than hers. Dusk had little hope of beating her. He just didn't want to disgrace himself completely.

He caught sight of a snipe fly, and unleashed a barrage of hunting clicks. The returning echoes told him everything he needed to know: the fly's distance, its heading, its speed. Dusk tipped a sail, kicked out his left leg, and banked sharply to match his prey's trajectory. Then he dumped some air and plunged upon the fly's tapered black-and-gold body, dragging it into his mouth, wings and all.

He scarcely had time to savor its pleasantly sour tang before he had to wheel to avoid the trees at the clearing's far side. The sun set alight drifting spores, dust motes, and the myriad insects flitting through the air.

It was important to focus, to not get distracted by all the choices. A few times he was too ambitious, and missed his prey because he overshot it. *Slow down*, he urged himself. He caught a few more insects. Below him, in the prime hunting ground, hundreds of darkly furred chiropters glided between the giant redwoods. He'd be in the thick of them soon.

He sighted a blue dasher dragonfly, strafed it with clicks, and set his course of attack. A flick of a finger to angle his sail, and the spicy dragonfly was thrashing its translucent double wings against his teeth as he bit down and swallowed.

"Watch where you're going, newborn!" someone shouted after him.

Dusk careened through the crowds, doing his best to stay out of everyone's way.

"Slow down!" one of his older brothers barked. It was either Diablo or Norther. Dusk always got them mixed up. "You're going to kill someone!"

"Sorry!" Dusk called back, and seconds later snagged a fairy moth in his jaws.

"Hey, that was my food!"

Dusk gulped down the cloying moth and glanced back sheepishly to see yet another chiropter glaring at him.

"Are we related?" Dusk said.

"Unfortunately," said the chiropter.

Dusk couldn't tell which cousin it was—after all, he had something like three hundred.

"Sorry," he chirruped again, then looked higher to check on the others. There was Sylph! It looked like she'd just got herself a hover fly. He couldn't see Aeolus or Jib.

Below the crowds he got lucky, very lucky indeed. Hovering near a tree was a haze of newly hatched insects. He made a quick turn, took aim, and skimmed through, taking six small bugs into his mouth at once, and spitting out a seventh when he started to gag. Not even their stingy, bitter taste could temper his glee—this just might put him in the lead.

He didn't want to get lazy, though. He figured he had about twenty-five more seconds, and he planned to make each one count. His eyes and ears, brain and body worked together seamlessly. He caught a soldier fly, then a marsh moth.

There was the Lower Reach looming below him—the great branch that marked the end of the chiropters' territory. They were forbidden from going down any farther. Dusk sighted a wood nymph, fluttering for the shade of the forest. He decided he had enough time before having to land.

He timed his attack perfectly. His mouth was just opening to snatch up the moth's dark thorax when he felt a gust of heat against his belly. It pushed him up into the air and spun him off to one side so that his right sail collapsed. He tumbled for a half second before managing to level off. He was startled, but not afraid. He knew he'd just hit a thermal, one of the columns of hot air that sometimes rose from the ground at midday. This one was surprisingly strong.

He circled tightly and cast about for the wood nymph. It was already above him. There'd be no catching it now. Chiropters could only glide down, never up. His ears twitched in irritation.

The Lower Reach was before him, and he glided in to make a sturdy if not exactly elegant landing. With practice, his technique had improved over the months. He reviewed his prey count. He could scarcely believe it. It was strong. Very strong. Would have been one stronger if he hadn't hit that thermal. He wondered how Sylph and the others had done.

As he waited, he peered down to the forest floor. Fifty feet below was a dense tangle of tea and laurel shrubs, ferns and horsetails. He tasted the air with his tongue: a humid funk of leaves and flowers, rotting vegetation, sunbaked mud, and urine. He'd never set claw down there. All sorts of four-legged groundlings lived amid the undergrowth, foraging and burrowing. According to his father, they were mostly harmless, though a few weren't very friendly. Luckily none of them could climb trees. If you listened you could hear them scuffling and snuffling, and occasionally he'd make out their dark furtive shapes.

Aeolus came in to land, quickly followed by Sylph and Jib.

"How did everyone do?" Dusk asked cheerfully.

"Not good," said Aeolus. "Just eight."

"Thirteen," said Sylph, preening. It was an excellent count.

"Twelve," muttered Jib.

Dusk waited a delicious moment. "Fifteen," he said.

"What?" Aeolus exclaimed.

"You did not get fifteen!" Jib said.

"My brother doesn't lie," Sylph said, and Dusk saw the fur lifting on the back of her neck.

"It was pure luck," said Dusk, trying to avoid a scrap. Sylph could be combustible. "There was a cloud of something just hatched. I glided right through it and took six all at once! They were tiny."

"Count it as one, then," grumbled Jib.

Dusk said nothing, but refused to break Jib's angry stare.

"It counts as six," Sylph said firmly. "It's fair."

Jib hunched his shoulders at Dusk. "If you weren't the leader's son, you'd probably have ended up like Cassandra."

"The newborn who died?" Sylph asked. "What're you talking about, Jib?"

"Didn't you ever see her? She looked even weirder than Dusk. Her mother stopped nursing her."

"Why?" Dusk asked, horrified.

"She was a freak," said Jib with a shrug. "Her body was all wrong. They took her down to the dying branch and left her."

Dusk felt chilled through his fur and skin. The dying branch was a place he'd never visited. It jutted out low down, from the shady side of the tree, and was half veiled by hanging moss. It was where the sick or very old went when they knew they were going to die.

"They say you can still see her bones," Jib said, looking straight at Dusk. "Want to go see?"

"Are you saying there's something wrong with Dusk?" Sylph shouted at Jib.

"No," Jib muttered, taking a step back from Sylph. "But I heard he probably would've been driven out of the colony, because of his sails and—"

"You are such a bad loser, Jib," Sylph said in disgust. "Get lost."

Jib snorted. "Congratulations on your lucky win, furless. Come on, Aeolus, let's go."

Dusk watched the two newborns begin the long climb back to their hunting perches.

"Why are you friends with him?" Dusk asked his sister.

"He's not usually so unpleasant."

"Not to you maybe. Hey, you don't think Mom and Dad were tempted to abandon me, do you?"

"Of course not!"

"Jib just hates me because he'll never be leader."

"Dusk, you're never going to be leader."

"I could!"

"Well, I could, too. I'd just have to kill off the rest of you first."

Side by side on the branch, the two of them absently set about grooming each other.

"You are really filthy," remarked Sylph with interest. "Don't you ever comb your fur?"

"Of course I do," said Dusk indignantly. "Why? What's in there?"

"Just a whole colony of mites," she mumbled, happily eating them off his back.

"I have been pretty itchy there," Dusk confessed.

"I always know I can get a decent meal off you."

Dusk grunted, hoping to find something incriminating in his sister's fur. But aside from a few spores and a single aphid,

Sylph was, as usual, extremely well groomed.

"Did you really get fifteen?" she asked sweetly.

"Sylph!"

"Just making sure."

"You just can't believe I beat you!"

"Well, it probably won't happen again," she said cockily. "Want to race back to the perch?"

"Not really," he said.

"Afraid you'll lose?"

He knew he would lose. In the air he was fast, but on bark, his missing claws and weak legs doomed him to be among the slowest. He hated the climb back up. It was always so discouraging. He took a deep breath of the scented air, and his eyes strayed to the sun-bathed clearing. Insects soared effortlessly in the thermals.

"I'll even give you a head start," Sylph said, "how's that?"

"Don't need one," he said.

She looked at him strangely, then gave a laugh. "You really think you can beat me?"

"I think so," he replied boldly.

"All right then. See you up there!"

Sylph darted up the trunk; for a moment Dusk watched her go, envying her agility and speed. Then, after only a moment's hesitation, he hurled himself off the branch, sails unfurling.

"What're you doing?" he heard Sylph call out to him.

Chiropters only went down, never up, Dusk thought. But maybe he could change that. Glancing about, he tried to find the thermal he'd encountered earlier. Where was it?

"You're really going to lose now!" Sylph shouted.

He had no idea if his plan would even work. He'd slipped below the Lower Reach now, and with every second was falling more. Dusk looked down in alarm. He'd never been so close to the forest floor. He saw something dark shift in the undergrowth and disappear. Too risky. He decided to abandon his plan. What a waste. Now he'd have an even longer climb back to the perch.

As he glided back toward the sequoia, warmth grazed his chest and he was suddenly weightless. He bounced up half a foot before tumbling to one side. Eagerly he circled, and slid back into the thermal, this time angling his sails to anchor himself in midair.

He wobbled, but managed to hold on, and with an unexpected surge, the hot air lifted him. He felt it pushing against his sails, wafting past his chin and snout. He could not restrain his whoop of delight as he was propelled upward.

Chiropters *could* go up!

It might not be flying, but it was the next best thing.

Rising higher, he caught sight of Sylph diligently hurrying up the redwood's trunk.

"See you up there!" he called out.

She turned and stared as he floated past, her face blank with confusion.

"Don't slow down," Dusk told her, hoping he'd remember her expression his entire life.

"What're you doing?" she bellowed.

"Just riding some hot air."

"But . . . you . . . you're cheating!"

"How am I cheating?" he asked calmly, rising higher all the while.

"You're not climbing!"

"Who said anything about climbing? You just said it was a race."

"That isn't fair!" she howled in outrage.

For a moment she glared at him, shoulders hunched, sides heaving.

"Show me how to do it!" she demanded.

"Maybe some other time," Dusk said.

"I want to know how!" And she threw herself off the tree and sailed out into the clearing, already well below him. "Dusk, show me!"

For a moment he did nothing, just watched her fierce upturned face below him. A few chiropters glided past, hunting, and stared at them in bewilderment.

"Please!" Sylph begged.

Dusk sighed. This was getting embarrassing. "Find the column of hot air," he told her. "It should be right underneath me."

He watched as she sought out the thermal, and then lurched straight through it.

"Brace yourself with your sails!" he told her. "You've got to stay on top of it."

It took her three tries before she succeeded. Listing from side to side, she held tight and came bobbing up after him. He worried she might steal his lift, but there seemed enough for both of them.

Sylph's delighted laughter carried through the clearing. Her whole body rocked so wildly with mirth that Dusk worried she'd laugh herself right out of the thermal. Somehow she managed to hold on.

"Oh! This is good, Dusk! Very good!"

"Hi, Jib! Hi, Aeolus!" Dusk called out.

Trudging up the redwood's bark, the two newborns stopped and stared, Aeolus with bafflement, and Jib with undisguised envy.

"What are you doing?" Jib demanded.

"Just going back to the perch," Sylph said smugly.

"Watch out, everyone!" Dusk shouted. "We're coming up!"

They were rising through the prime hunting grounds now, and chiropters had to swerve around them to avoid a collision.

"Nuisances!" someone called out. Dusk was pretty sure it was Levantera, one of his sisters. She was only two years older, and when he was born, she'd still been sharing his parents' nest. He'd been very fond of her, but two months ago she'd found a mate, and now had her own nest in another part of the tree. She was too grown up and important to speak to him and Sylph anymore—unless she was reprimanding them for something or other.

Dusk saw a few other chiropters watching, amused, but most looked suspicious and even disapproving before they sniffed and turned away. Dusk couldn't believe that more of them didn't want to try catching a thermal on their own. Weren't they at all curious? Didn't they see how much easier and faster it would be to get back to their perches?

Dusk looked down at Sylph's spread sails—luxuriant silver-streaked black fur, the three claws on each hand—and wondered how she and he could be so different, born from the same mother within seconds. He didn't like the way his arm and finger bones always showed beneath his own taut, hairless sails.

From the sequoia's mighty limbs grew thinner branches that drooped down slightly over the clearing. It was mostly these that the chiropters used as their hunting perches, for they made excellent vantage points for sighting prey and launching. A good perch was jealously held, and once chiropters were old enough to find mates, they were expected to claim their own perch and use it for the rest of their lives. Dusk and Sylph were still allowed to use their parents' perch. Dusk could see it coming into view now.

He didn't feel quite so jaunty anymore. He started looking around for his father. At first he'd desperately wanted Dad to see him floating and know how clever his son was. But now, after all the stern looks he'd received, he wondered how his father would react. No one had ever told him *not* to ride thermals. No one had said anything about it at all. He couldn't spot his father or mother anywhere. Maybe it was for the best.

He checked on Sylph. She was still there below him, doing fine. He'd sort of hoped she'd slip off the thermal, so he alone would gloriously rise past the perch.

"You know, little brother," Sylph commented, "you look particularly odd from this angle."

"You know, big sister," said Dusk, glancing down at her, "from this angle it would be particularly unfortunate if I had to pee."

"Don't you dare!" Sylph said.

"I won by the way," he told her. "First to the perch."

"You didn't reach the perch," she said. "We've actually floated right *past* the perch. The winner has to be *on* the perch. And since I'm well below you, it seems I've got the lead."

"But I've got the speed," Dusk countered.

"Not that much speed."

He knew she was right. She'd probably beat him to the perch.

"You go ahead, then," he told her. "The thermal's still strong. I'm not done flying."

He heard Sylph's mocking laugh, and instantly regretted his choice of words.

"After all," she said, "you always did want to be a bird."

It was a joke in their family—and outside it, thanks to Sylph. Dad liked to tell the story of how Dusk tried to flap during his first gliding lesson. And when Sylph wanted to be particularly irritating, she'd start flailing her sails, saying, "Oh, I think I'm getting somewhere! I'm getting liftoff! Just a bit more!" Dusk had learned his lesson quickly, and he never told anyone about his secret visits to the Upper Spar. He was deeply ashamed of his abnormal impulses, but seemed powerless to prevent them.

"Hey, do you think this'll take us above the treetops?" Sylph asked.

"I don't know," Dusk said. "Anyway, we're almost at the Upper Spar."

"So?"

"Dad said—"

"You don't always have to do what Dad says," Sylph said impatiently. "Don't be such a newborn."

"Well, we *are* actually newborns until we turn one."

"Don't you want to see above the treetops?"

"That's bird territory," he said.

"Well, you're practically a bird, aren't you?" she replied with a chuckle.

"The birds won't like it," he said.

"But they fly through our territory all the time," Sylph pointed out. "To get to the ground. We don't mind."

"Right," Dusk agreed, not wanting to seem meek. "It's not like we're landing on their roosts."

"We're just passing through," said Sylph.

"Just to the canopy, to get a better view of the sky," Dusk added.

Sylph's confidence made him feel bolder. But he heard his father in his head, telling him not to go beyond the spar. Dusk was not a rule breaker by nature. Sylph was the rule breaker. He tried to do everything he could to please his father. But he was truly curious to see a proper view of the sky—and the birds who inhabited it. They were level with the Upper Spar now, and Dusk swallowed nervously as they rose past it.

The sequoia's branches were shorter here as the tree narrowed toward its peak. The clearing opened wider. Birds traversed the sky, and the sun was just starting its slow descent to the west. Before long they'd be almost as high as the sequoia.

Dusk followed the birds' speedy flight paths with eager eyes, marveling at how their wing strokes carried them effortlessly higher. A large flock suddenly wheeled in unison and streaked out of sight. In their wake, a strange shadow appeared in the sky, just emerging from the sun's glare, its outline blurred.

"What is that?" Dusk asked Sylph, directing her gaze skyward.

To him it looked like a tree uprooted, sailing on its side, boughs thrashing. Once free of the sun's glare, the object became clearer, and with alarm Dusk realized it was coming toward them.

He'd never seen anything so large in the air.

A long crested head.

Jagged wings that spanned forty feet.

"It's some kind of bird!" Sylph said, her voice constricted with fear.

Dusk saw its massive wings arch sharply and push down in a halfhearted stroke.

"But it has no feathers," he muttered.

The thermal, which had been giving them such a delightful ride, was now carrying them heedlessly closer to this thing. Dusk angled his sails and pulled away, shouting for Sylph to do the same. Free, they began a hasty descent. Dusk kept looking back.

The creature slewed through the air, heading unmistakably for their clearing. No wonder the birds had beat a frantic retreat! Had this thing seen him and Sylph? Dusk angled his sails more sharply, hastening his fall. Sylph led the way, past bird territory, past the Upper Spar.

He heard the thing coming, bringing the sound of a sudden

squall. Wind pushed against his tail and back. Turning, he saw the long head slanting up to a bony crest. He saw a long beak—or jaws, he wasn't sure which. One wing was half collapsed against the body, the other snapping and billowing, its tip grazing branches as the creature started its ferocious slantwise plunge into the clearing. He had to warn the colony.

"Look out!" Dusk bellowed, for there were still hundreds of chiropters hunting between the trees. "Get out of the way!"

They must have heard him, for he saw the chiropters scatter to the safety of the redwood branches.

But Dusk did not know which way to fly to escape it. The creature was huge, and its wings spanned nearly the whole clearing.

"Land!" he shouted to Sylph, who was well below him.

"Where?"

"Anywhere!"

Sylph swerved to the left and landed hard on the sequoia, scuttling in toward the safety of the trunk.

Dusk hurtled on, afraid to bank because the creature was so close behind him now. He careened through the deserted hunting grounds, and could see the forest floor rushing toward him. Surely the creature would have to pull up!

He glanced back and at that moment the thing thundered over him, its hot, rank turbulence sucking Dusk after it, head over tail. The forest whirled. He heard the creature's wings crackling against branches, snapping wood.

Dusk untangled his sails and managed to right himself, but

could not wrench himself free of the creature's wake. Tree trunks loomed. He expected the creature to pull up and veer, but instead it piled straight into the redwoods. Digging in with his sails, Dusk braked desperately. He collided with some part of the creature's leathery tail, spun off stunned, and flailed down through branches. He crashed against bark and dug in with all his claws, shaking so badly he could barely hold on.

All was silent. No birds sang; no insects trilled. The forest held its breath.

Dusk looked up into the redwood and saw the creature tangled in the branches directly above him. Its huge body lay crookedly, the great wings pierced and crumpled. Its long head lolled over a branch, the sharp beak hanging not ten feet from Dusk's head. He followed the fearsome bony rails of its jaws, up to its nostrils—the slits big enough for him to crawl into. There seemed no light behind the creature's huge black eyes.

Dusk was afraid to move. Was it dead or just unconscious? A bough splintered and Dusk flinched. But the creature itself did not stir. Dusk was overwhelmed by its sheer size. It had no feathers, so it couldn't be a bird—but its jaws did look a lot like a long beak. He wasn't sure what it was.

He glanced down and realized with a start he was mere feet from the forest floor. His heart thumped. Unless he meant to crawl along the ground, he would have to climb higher in this tree in order to glide to another.

Sound began to return to the forest. He gazed up hopefully

into the clearing, searching for his father, or some of the other chiropters. But he saw no one.

He looked back at the creature. Its body was as wide as the tree. A branch creaked ominously under the stress. Dusk could not stay here. For all he knew, this thing could come crashing down on top of him. He would have to crawl up past it. He plotted a course with his eyes. It was possible, but would take him perilously close to the creature's head.

Surely it was dead after a crash like that. Its crest was cracked. It must have collided headfirst with the trunk. That would kill anything.

Gingerly Dusk walked splay-legged toward the trunk. The prick of his claws into the wood sounded deafening to him. Part of the creature's wing hung down over the branch, and as Dusk sidled past he looked at the thick leathery hide.

He hesitated. It had no feathers, yet it flew. He hadn't thought it was possible. The creature's skin was stretched over a long spar of bone. There were no other fingers.

Though the skin was much thicker than his own, he couldn't help thinking the creature's wings looked a bit like his own furless sails. It was a disturbing, even distasteful thought, and he quickly banished it.

At the redwood's trunk he began his climb. The creature's body hung over him, dark and brooding as a storm cloud. Its humid heat washed over him and his nostrils narrowed at the odor. He wanted to groom himself.

Why had it crashed in the first place? What had made it fly so erratically?

From the leading edge of its right wing extended a cluster of three claws, each one twice the length of Dusk. He took a breath and hurriedly ducked beneath them. He felt no bigger than a twig alongside this giant. He did not want to look at it anymore; he only wanted to get past it, to glide away to the sequoia and climb back to his nest.

And yet, his eyes kept straying to the wing, its shape, the fine covering—he could see it now—of hair, or was it some kind of feather after all? Across the wing membrane were strange blooms of rotted skin. Maybe the creature was diseased; maybe that was why it had flown so poorly.

Dusk climbed hurriedly, now parallel with the creature's lolling head. The branches creaked. He felt a stirring of wind. Slowly Dusk looked back over his shoulder. The creature's left wingtip twitched, making the membrane rustle.

He waited no longer. He moved with all speed, not caring if he was noisy now. The creature flinched. The head shifted. If Dusk could only get past the jaws, past the head, and up to the next branch, he could launch himself across the clearing.

Now he was alongside the creature's left eye. It was as big as he was, this eye, black and impenetrable. With a start, Dusk saw himself reflected in it, just as he sometimes saw himself in pools of still water in the sequoia's bark. He stared, transfixed. Then the eye became eerily translucent; light shifted within and Dusk saw his reflection dissolve. The creature's head tilted toward him.

Dusk could only stare back. The creature's jaws parted, and a great gust of reeking air washed over him. But mingled with this exhalation was something else, something that sounded to Dusk like language, though a kind he'd never heard. One more sour gust of breath escaped the creature's throat, and its head thudded against the branch as the last echo of life faded from its eye.

CHAPTER 3

Carnassial

IN THE SHALLOW depression were two eggs, long and narrow, nestled amid a thick mulch of fruit and mud and leaves. The rotting vegetation sent up a rich stink, and a surprising amount of heat, which Carnassial knew was meant to keep the eggs warm. He'd seen many saurian nests like this one.

"How did you know it was here?" Panthera asked, amazed.

His eyes flashed triumphantly. "I could smell it. Now, take cover."

They quickly backed up into the tall grass, and pressed their bodies flat against the earth. The nest was unguarded, and though this was not unusual, it still made Carnassial nervous. Something might be returning, or watching.

He could remember times when he'd found a whole colony of nests, twelve or more, guarded by at least one saurian, while the others were off hunting. The mothers would walk among the eggs, patrolling them. Sometimes they would lie down beside them to help keep them warm. They were too large and heavy to actually sit atop them, as birds did. But in the past two years, he'd seen only lone nests, and ever fewer at that.

Where was the mother? Or the father, for that matter? It was possible they'd both gone off to hunt, trusting that their nest was well camouflaged. And so it was, tucked into the tall grass at the edge of the cliff. Carnassial might have missed it altogether if it hadn't been for the nest's characteristic smell— over the years, he'd become very familiar with it.

Carnassial's tall ears, so sharply tapered they might have been horns, swiveled: one to the east, one to the west. He heard the wind against the cliff, the sea breaking along the shore; he heard the tread of some small gnawer not far distant—but he picked up nothing that might have been the sound of a returning saurian. His belly against the earth felt no vibrations of approaching footsteps. The leathery eggs themselves did not tell him what kind of creature they contained, though the elevated location of the nest made Carnassial suspect they were flyers. He turned his gold-flecked eyes skyward. Nothing but birds.

He forced himself to wait just a moment longer, his impatient heart thumping against his ribs. Saliva flooded his mouth. He kept his long, bushy tail very still. The breeze rustled his whiskers. He pressed himself even closer to the earth, rump tensed, ready. His eyes, huge in his lean face, were locked on the eggs, as though he could bore right through them, and see his prey within.

"Now," he said.

Carnassial sprang forward, grass against his belly, taking fast, slinking strides. He leaped into the nest among the eggs. They were the same size as him. He and Panthera each chose one and set to work. His jaws would not open wide enough to crush the shell. Putting his head against the egg, he rolled it to the edge of the nest, against the raised mud rim, so it could not wobble away from him. He put his shoulder to the shell, and extended his four claws. They were stout and strong, with curved hooks at the end.

With his left claws he held the egg; with his right he cut four parallel swaths into the shell. Fluid oozed through the cracks, and with it a delicious smell. He wrenched his claws free and dug the tips into a single crack, pulling. A leathery shard ripped off, then another and another, until Carnassial had torn a large opening in the side of the egg. He put his eye to it. Within, through the torn membrane, he saw the pale glimmer of the hatchling, trembling slightly.

He looked over to see how Panthera was faring. A skilled hunter, she too had gashed a hole in her egg. His ears pricked and swiveled; he looked all about him once more, high into the skies, without seeing any sign of saurians. Then he returned to his prey.

The hatchling was far along, close to being born. Carnassial

was delighted. If the eggs were new, there was little more than the yolk, but with this one there would be plenty of tender flesh. He thrust his snout into the opening, his gaping jaws cracking the shell even more. Teeth gnashing, he gorged himself on the hatchling without even bothering to drag it from its egg.

For two days he had eaten little except grubs and nuts and fruit, and his feeding now was so savage, he barely remembered to note what manner of saurian he devoured. Patriofelis would want to know when Carnassial returned to the prowl. Their leader was a great keeper of such facts. He pulled back and cast an eye over the remains. The hatchling's elongated arm bones told him all he needed to know. He'd guessed right. It was a flyer. A quetzal, by the looks of it.

Its bony wings and the cartilage of its crest and bill were the only parts he rejected. Sated, Carnassial fell back, licking the remaining fluid from his muzzle and paws. Panthera was watching him. Like most of the other hunters, she had savaged the shell, lapped up the yolk, but left the hatchling to die.

"You do not want the meat?" he asked her.

She gave a shake, and stepped back, inviting Carnassial to feed. As he ate, he felt her watching him curiously, her stripeless gray tail whisking back and forth in agitation. Meat was not a typical part of the felid diet. But years ago, Carnassial had discovered that his rear teeth allowed him to shear meat from bones—not something all other felids could do, he learned. He sometimes wondered if his craving for meat had been with him since birth, or whether the eggs had given him the appetite. He glanced again at Panthera.

"Will you eat nothing?" he said.

"No."

She watched him almost warily, as though he might turn his shearing teeth on her.

Carnassial gazed skyward, watching for the mother saurian. Maybe she was already dead. With every year he'd found fewer and fewer nests, many of them abandoned as their parents fell victim to the disease that bloomed on their skins. Likely these two eggs were all that was left. Still, it was best he and Panthera take cover quickly. The quetzals could dive down from the sky with lightning speed.

Before leaving, he lifted his hind leg and triumphantly sprayed the nest with urine. It was *his* territory now.

"Maybe these were the very last," Panthera said, as they bounded through the tall grass.

Carnassial licked his teeth thoughtfully. He'd developed a liking for eggs over the years, especially those that contained tender flesh. He would miss them. But the thought that he might be responsible for destroying the last nest—that was very pleasing. Of all the hunting parties stalking the earth, he had sniffed it out. It was the kind of honor that would one day make him leader of the prowl.

The last saurian eggs.

The completion of the Pact.

CHAPTER 4

The Pact

DUSK HEARD HIS father calling his name, and looked up into the clearing to see him gliding down with a dozen other chiropters, including the three elders and Sylph.

"I'm here!" he shouted. "Down here!"

He scrambled out farther along the branch so they could see him.

"Come away from it, Dusk!" Icaron shouted.

"It's all right. It's dead."

Just to make sure, he looked back at the creature's inert body. Already flies were beginning to settle around its eyes and nostrils. It certainly seemed dead. His father and the others landed cautiously on the branch.

"Are you all right?" his father asked, hurrying up and nuzzling him in concern.

"Just a bit sore," he said, only now thinking about his aching body.

In silence, they all stared intently at the creature. Then his father looked at Barat, one of the elders, and nodded.

"What is it?" Dusk asked in a whisper.

"A winged saurian," his father replied.

"A saurian!" Dusk exclaimed. Just speaking the word made his fur bristle. "But . . . they're all dead!"

His father made no reply.

Everyone had heard stories about saurians, the fantastical creatures that had once roamed and ruled the earth. Many times Dusk had imagined these great scaly monsters, tall as redwoods, with vast jaws and mountain ranges of teeth. They were voracious hunters, feeding on virtually every other creature, large and small, including chiropters. But they had disappeared from the world before Dusk was even born. At least that's what they'd always been told.

"Tell me what happened," Icaron said to Dusk.

Dusk couldn't help being pleased he'd been asked rather than Sylph. He was afraid to tell his father how he and Sylph had been riding thermals, so he only mentioned how they'd spotted the creature in the sky, and been swept into its wake, and how he'd tried to climb past it after it crashed.

"I think it spoke to me," he added.

"Why would it speak to you?" Sylph asked.

"It sounded like talking." His legs were shaking, and he clenched tight, willing them to stop. "But I didn't understand."

"That's all right," said his father. "Why would you understand a saurian language? Do you think you can make it back to the nest?"

"Yes, but—"

"Go then," his father said, gently but firmly. "You too, Sylph."

Dusk gazed enviously at the other chiropters, especially his eldest brother, Auster. He'd probably be the colony's next leader. He even looked a bit like Dad. He nodded smugly at Dusk, as if wanting to hurry him along. It wasn't fair that Auster got to stay when it was Dusk who'd seen the saurian up close.

"Why can't we stay?" Sylph asked, echoing his thoughts.

"We need to examine the creature."

"Well, we can help," Dusk said. "I was pretty close—"

"Go now," said Dad. "And don't speak of this to anyone but your mother. Do you hear? I'll call an assembly of the four families when we're ready."

Dusk nodded. Icaron was not simply his father right now; he was leader of the colony, and Dusk dared not question him. He began to climb. He didn't have the heart to try and catch a thermal this time. Somehow, the thermal and the saurian were all bundled together in his confused thoughts, and he felt one might have caused the other. Anyway, the sun had passed over the clearing now, and he doubted the warm air had enough power to lift him back to the perch.

It would be a very long climb.

Sylph, infuriatingly, streaked ahead up the tree so she could be the first to tell their mother the news. When Dusk finally hauled himself up to the nest, Mistral made a terrible fuss of him. What seemed to horrify her most was that the saurian had breathed all over him. She made him bathe in a pool of rainwater on the branch, rolling him over and over until his fur was completely sodden. Then she groomed him, head to tail—because she didn't trust Dusk to do it properly himself— while Sylph made helpful suggestions.

"I'd double-check his armpits, Mom. I found an entire mealworm there once."

"Thank you, Sylph, I'm sure I can manage."

"Also, his lower back is usually *teeming* with something. I think he has trouble combing back there."

"That's enough, Sylph," their mother said. "I suggest you groom yourself. You're looking a bit mangy after the long climb."

Dusk sent his sister a smirk through his matted hair.

"Now, both of you," Mistral said sternly, "have behaved very foolishly today. I heard many complaints that you were riding thermals in the clearing and making a great nuisance of yourselves."

"Who said we were a nuisance?" Sylph demanded loudly.

"It doesn't matter who said it. What matters is you did it. Riding thermals is not something chiropters do."

Dusk said nothing; he knew he could rely on Sylph to do the protesting.

"Well, no one ever told us!" she shouted.

"Shush, Sylph," said their mother. "It should be obvious. Have you ever seen others doing such a thing? Were you *taught* to do it?"

"No," Sylph said, "but does that mean—"

"Was this your idea?" their mother asked.

Sylph hesitated, then replied, "Yes."

Startled, Dusk spoke up. "It was my idea, Mom."

"It was mine!" Sylph yelled. "I figured out how to ride the thermals and taught Dusk."

Dusk was bewildered. Sylph was a loyal sister, but this was going too far. Was she trying to protect him—or just steal credit for his discovery? Either way, he couldn't let her get away with it.

His mother looked over at him impatiently. "Dusk, is this true?"

"No. It was my idea, Mom. I didn't want to climb the tree, and I was tired, and I wondered if the hot air could lift me, and it did."

Mistral nodded. "It was very resourceful of you, Dusk," she said.

He didn't dare glance over at Sylph, but he heard her groan of exasperation and could just imagine the delicious look of indignation on her face.

"But," his mother continued swiftly, "I don't want to see you ever doing it again. We have sails so we can glide. That is how we use them. And for no other purpose. Don't make yourself more different than you already are, Dusk. Difference can be severely punished in a colony."

"Will Dusk be punished?" Sylph piped up with great interest.

"Not this time," Mistral said.

"Dusk never gets punished," Sylph grumbled.

"But remember what I say, both of you," their mother continued. "Behave like the colony, or risk being shunned by the colony."

Dusk swallowed. "Mom," he began uncertainly, "why did they stop feeding Cassandra? Was it just because she looked different?"

The fur on his mother's forehead furrowed. She came closer and nuzzled him. "No, Dusk, she was very sick. She would never have been able to glide or hunt or feed herself. She couldn't have survived. It wasn't because she looked different."

"Oh," said Dusk. He felt relieved, but it still seemed cruel to stop feeding her.

"Who's been talking to you about that poor creature?" Mom asked.

"Jib," Sylph told her. "He said it's lucky Dusk was the leader's son, or he would've been driven out of the colony."

"That newborn should watch what he says!" said Mom, her eyes flashing.

"I knew he was just trying to scare me," Dusk sniffed. "I know things like that don't happen."

When his mother made no reply he felt a jolt of panic. "Mom? They don't, do they?"

"Of course not, Dusk," she said gently. "We'd never allow such a thing."

"You mean, they *wanted* to, but—"

"I mean, it doesn't happen," she told him firmly. "Now listen, don't change the subject. I'm not quite finished with you two yet. I also heard reports you went beyond the Upper Spar. You know you're never to trespass in bird territory. And *that* you have been taught. Never do it again. Do you understand?"

"Yes, Mom," said Dusk, hanging his head. "Sorry."

"Sylph?" Mistral said.

"Sorry!" she said loudly.

"Good. Now, here comes your father," she said. "And if I'm not mistaken he'll be calling an assembly soon."

Dusk's colony numbered in the hundreds, and was made up of four families who had lived on the sequoia for twenty years. An elder governed each family. There was Sol, Barat, Nova, and Icaron, who was both an elder and leader of the entire colony.

All four families had been mating with one another for many years, so practically everyone was related, if you cared to figure out how. Dusk would sooner have tried to count raindrops.

In the day's dying light, all the chiropters gathered along the sequoia's mighty branches, anxious to hear about the winged creature that had hurtled through the clearing. Most had seen its terrifying dive; certainly all had heard it. Some had narrowly avoided being pulverized by it.

Crouching atop a large bulge in the redwood's trunk, where all the assembled chiropters could see them, were Icaron and the three elders. The birds' dusk chorus had faded away, and cricket song was beginning to pulse across the forest.

Dusk rested beside Sylph and his mother, waiting expectantly. He was exhausted by his long climb and the ordeal with the saurian, but now, looking up at his father, his fatigue evaporated. Even though Icaron was far away, he seemed bigger than usual, and more powerful. Dusk hoped Dad could see him from way up there. He lifted a sail to catch his father's attention, and was delighted when Dad returned the gesture. Dusk glanced around to see if any of the newborns had seen their exchange. Sure enough, a few were stealing glimpses at him and whispering, no doubt boiling with jealousy that their fathers weren't leader. He tried to find Jib in the crowd, but couldn't.

Dusk had never known such a gathering. Assemblies were only called on occasions of great importance. Before this, all he'd witnessed were minor disputes about hunting perches or mates. The chiropters normally didn't need meetings. Anything they needed to know was passed from branch to branch, family to family, parent to child. There was not much to know, really.

Until now the colony's life had been uneventful. The chiropters strayed hardly at all from the great redwoods ringing the clearing. They never ventured onto the ground, so they saw virtually no other animals except birds, high in the trees and in the skies. Dusk had heard many say their world was perfect. It was always warm. There was food and water, and good perches—and no predators. They could hunt and breed in complete safety.

Dusk couldn't help feeling that this saurian attack (if he could even call it that) was the most momentous occasion in his life—and he was pleased he had some small part in it. But he was also a bit nervous to see his father looking so grave, and all the hundreds of chiropters—normally so noisy and active—still and quiet now as Icaron began to speak, describing what had happened earlier in the day.

"Will there be others?" someone called out, when Icaron had finished.

"Unlikely," Icaron replied. "This is the first I've seen in almost twenty years."

Dusk twitched his sails in surprise. His father had never said anything to him about seeing a saurian *ever*. They were supposed to be long gone.

"If there's one, how do we know there aren't more?" someone else asked.

"This one was old," Barat replied, "and nearly blind. It had cataracts."

Dusk remembered the cloudy moon in its eye.

"My son Dusk saw it crash," Icaron told the assembly. "He said it was flying erratically. Indeed, its wings had the rot that killed many of the saurians."

Dusk grinned at Sylph, pleased to be mentioned at the meeting. For a moment he imagined himself up there. Leader. Why not? It was possible. But the thought was complicated and unpleasant, because it meant the death of his father, and all his brothers, and he could think of nothing more terrible than that.

"Maybe if your newborns hadn't been playing in the air,

the creature wouldn't have spotted them and made the clearing its target."

The reproachful words were spoken by Nova, the sole female elder, and addressed to Icaron.

"Many of us might have been killed," she said.

Dusk ground his teeth. That wasn't fair at all.

"The saurian wasn't hunting," Icaron told her. "I believe it was in its death throes."

"Who's to say there isn't a nest nearby?" Nova continued.

Even though she was almost as old as his father, Nova still had a thick coat of fiery copper fur, undulled by age. Her fur matched her temperament: the few times Dusk had seen her speak to other chiropters, she was often contrary and argumentative—much like her great-nephew Jib, he thought with a sniff. Dusk always had the feeling Nova didn't like his father, though Dad never seemed to bear her any ill will.

Icaron nodded. "Even so, these flyers pose little threat to us. They're called quetzals," he told the assembly. "The largest of the winged saurians. They pick fish from the shallows and creatures from the mud. Or they strafe the plains for prey. They can't hunt over the forest. The canopy hides us and keeps us safe."

Dusk was amazed at how knowledgeable his father sounded. Just how much experience had he had with these creatures?

"But we were not safe today," Nova persisted. "It was only a matter of time before this happened. For every saurian we see, there are hundreds more unseen. This is what comes of shirking our obligations."

Obligations? Dusk glanced at his mother and saw her stiffen. What was Nova talking about?

Icaron exchanged looks with Barat and Sol, silent for a moment.

"This is not a matter that needs to be discussed here," Sol told Nova angrily.

"Oh, I believe it is," said Nova. "And it should have been done years ago. This saurian in our forest is proof of that!"

Barat shook his gray head. "Nova, you speak without care!"

"Do not let her speak again!" Sol implored Icaron.

"Silence her!" Barat agreed heatedly.

"Silence—that is the problem precisely!" cried Nova. "There has been too much silence for too long."

"Enough!" shouted Icaron, and Dusk flinched.

All eyes were on the leader, waiting.

"Nova, you have spoken recklessly, and without my consent." He paused, glowering at the other chiropter. "But perhaps you are right," he went on more calmly. "We should explain what happened in the past. There's nothing shameful in it, and much to be proud of."

At this Nova gave a quick snort. Dusk would have liked to bite her ear.

Barat and Sol looked at Icaron, waiting for him to begin.

Icaron's voice carried out to the entire tree. "You've all heard something of the saurians. Thousands of years ago they were the undisputed rulers of the earth. Some of them were plant eaters; many were flesh eaters. Some walked erect on two legs. Others lumbered on four. A few could fly. They hunted one another, but also fed on the beasts, including chiropters. Like all beasts, our agility and relatively small size helped keep us safe. We could hide. We often took refuge in the trees, since most saurians were poor climbers."

Dusk listened with rapt attention. A few of these things he'd heard before, but in less detail. Closing his eyes made it easier to concentrate, and he could let his head fill with images.

"The saurians were rapacious. They ate and bred and flourished. And we watched and waited, knowing they couldn't survive forever. They were huge and strong, but without vast amounts of food they would starve; without the sun they couldn't even warm themselves. On cool mornings they were sluggish until the sunlight heated their scaly skin. And yet they reigned and reigned until, thousands of years ago, the sky changed and they were all but wiped out. Some say part of the sky collapsed, and crashed to earth, and the dust that rose blotted out the sun."

Dusk shuddered as he imagined the sky thickening, coagulating with darkness.

"It became very cold. Anything that needed the sun suffered. Plants died first, then the saurians that ate the plants, and finally the flesh eaters who fed on them. But we were able to survive. We were small and quick, and we needed little. As the world grew cold, the saurians grew cold with it, and died. Within our fur, we kept warm, and hibernated if need be. We weathered the long, cold night, eating insects and grubs and seeds. When it was over, the saurians' giant carcasses were strewn across the earth. Still, some survived."

Icaron paused, and then began a story that Dusk had never heard.

"It was then the beasts saw their chance. The saurians were weaker than they'd ever been; many were diseased, their scales rotting. But for all we knew, they would become strong again unless we did something. So, centuries ago, the beasts formed the Pact."

Again Icaron hesitated, as though telling this story were not altogether easy for him. A pact, Dusk thought excitedly. It sounded secret and daring.

"The beasts knew they could never hope to defeat the saurians in battle. They were far too powerful. But the beasts could attack them in another way. Under the terms of the Pact, all the beasts agreed never to harm one another. They would work together to seek out saurian nests and destroy the eggs. They would prevent a new generation of saurians from rising. It would take centuries, but eventually they would wipe the saurians out entirely."

In the silence that followed, Dusk shivered. He did not know what to think. Truly it was an ingenious plan—chillingly ruthless too. But how else could small creatures ever hope to defeat such large ones? For a long, uncomfortable moment Dusk imagined all those helpless saurian hatchlings growing inside their eggs, and then having their shells ripped apart around them.

"The Pact was an act of genius," Nova told all the chiropters forcefully. "It was a triumph of our intelligence over the sluggish might of the saurians."

"It was barbaric," Icaron replied evenly. "Especially since many of the saurians weren't even meat eaters. They posed no threat to us, but we destroyed their eggs nonetheless."

"The eggs looked the same, regardless of the type of saurian they contained," Nova countered. "So we needed to destroy them all. It was a matter of survival."

"It was extermination," stated Icaron.

"Call it what you will," said Nova. "The beasts used to live in daily fear—"

"Fear, yes," Icaron interrupted, "but every creature fears its predators. That is the way of things. The Pact was something unnatural. The Pact was a deliberate decision to rid the earth of the saurians so the beasts might reign in their place!"

Dusk had never seen his father so impassioned, and he looked anxiously at Nova, wondering how she could reply. He felt almost ill, for this kind of verbal battle was unknown to him. His father's control was remarkable, the way his words never faltered, his voice never shook. But Nova too was commanding, Dusk had to admit.

"The saurians' time was over anyway," she said. "The Pact simply sped up the inevitable. It was what needed to be done. There was no alternative."

"Of course there was," Icaron scolded her. "And we chose that alternative."

"Tell them, then," Nova urged him, with more than a hint of mockery in her voice. "Tell them of this noble choice."

Dusk was astonished by Nova's insolence. Why did his father not silence her? Why did he not sink his teeth into her fur to reprimand her?

Instead, Icaron turned his full attention to the four families assembled along the branches. His chest swelled as he took a deep breath. "For hundreds of years, the chiropters took part in the Pact. When I was younger, I too performed my duties hunting saurian eggs."

Dusk glanced at Sylph, stunned, scarcely aware of the excited chittering that swept through the colony, echoing his own surprise. He'd been led to believe the saurians had died out hundreds of years ago. But they weren't creatures of ancient times at all, they had populated the world of his own father! And he had hunted them!

"More and more," Icaron was saying, "I felt misgivings about what I was doing. And I wasn't alone. Sol and Barat felt the same—and so did your father, Nova."

"My father's opinions are not my own," she retorted.

"There were twenty-six of us in total who decided we could no longer hunt and destroy saurian eggs," Icaron continued. "So we rejected the Pact. It was not an easy thing to do. It didn't mean just breaking with our colony. In some cases it meant breaking with our own parents and siblings and even children. It was very painful for all of us. We earned the contempt of the other beasts. We were deserters. Cowards. Our colony drove us out. We had to find a new home. We wanted somewhere remote, someplace where we could live harmoniously with other creatures, and raise our families in safety. We were extremely lucky to find this island. It has been the birthplace to practically all of you."

"All we did was ignore the problem," Nova told the assembly. "We didn't solve anything. We just left others to do the work. There were no saurians on this island, but there were many back on the mainland, feasting on our fellow chiropters while we enjoyed our splendid isolation. It was selfish."

Dusk looked worriedly back at his father, wondering how he would respond. Nova's words were very persuasive, and he wanted his father to say something that would prove her wrong, and crush her defiance.

"It was a simple matter of conscience," Icaron said. "We chose to avoid the slaughter."

"It was the wrong choice!" Nova shouted.

"Nova, silence!" said Sol, enraged.

"Only the leader can silence me!" spat Nova. "If we had done our part in the Pact, we might have been completely free of the saurians by now. As it is, we may now have them on our beloved island."

Dusk moved closer to his mother, seeking out her solid warmth. The world suddenly seemed a much larger and more frightening place than it had just hours before.

"You are fear-mongering, Nova," said Icaron severely. He tipped back onto his legs, and his sails unfurled forcefully.

"We should all heed this saurian as a warning," Nova said, spreading her own sails, as if in response to a challenge. "We can't live in isolation any longer. Now is the time to take up our obligations to the Pact once more. If this was a she-saurian, there will be a nest. A nest means eggs. I suggest we send a group to the mainland to confer with other colonies."

"What happens on the mainland is not our concern," said Icaron. "A crossing would be extremely dangerous. Have you forgotten?" He paused and Dusk thought his eyes strayed to him and Sylph. "Nonetheless, to reassure us that we and all our children are safe, tomorrow I will organize an expedition, to see if there is another saurian or a nest on the island."

"It is highly unlikely," Sol told the assembly.

"That is a start at least," said Nova. "But what of going to the mainland?"

"No," said Icaron. "There is no need."

Barat and Sol nodded their agreement.

"And if we should find eggs here on the island," Nova asked, "what will your course of action be?"

"There will be no eggs. But if we were to find any, you know my answer. Saurian eggs are not to be harmed."

"Even in our own home, our own forest, you would allow these eggs to hatch?"

"We are here because we made a vow to abstain from the destruction of the eggs," Icaron said. "To destroy the eggs now would be a terrible hypocrisy. I will not tolerate it."

"That is not the decision of a leader."

Dusk's eyes widened as his father reared back, chest thrown out, and pounded the air with his sails, battering Nova with a wind that made her fall back, cringing.

"I have allowed you to speak your mind, Nova," he shouted. "Do not make the mistake of thinking your words carry any authority! I will decide what is best for the colony and will continue to do so until the day I die."

Dusk stuck close to his father the rest of the evening. He felt safer that way. Moving about their nest as they prepared for sleep, he shadowed Icaron so tightly that his father almost tripped over him. Icaron looked at him sharply, but the annoyance in his face quickly faded.

"Everything's all right, Dusk," he said.

"Are we really safe?" he asked.

"Stop being feeble," Sylph said, but he noticed she too was watching their father, waiting for reassurance.

"Yes, we're all very safe," Icaron said. "This was the first saurian I've seen since leaving the mainland. I doubt we will ever see another."

Though his father no longer stood upon his leader's perch, Dusk was aware of his power and authority as never before. While he felt protected within its aura, he was also a bit afraid, because he'd never seen Dad so angry and fierce. He hoped that temper would never be turned on him. He had a question, as insistent as an itch he couldn't scratch, but he almost couldn't work up the courage to ask.

"Dad? I'm just wondering . . ." His voice faltered.

His father settled down beside him. "Go on."

"Why didn't you ever tell us about the Pact?"

Icaron looked briefly at Mistral and sighed. "So many reasons," he said. "When we came to this island, we truly felt we'd found some kind of paradise. There were no saurians, and it seemed we might never see any again. Why did our children need to know about the old world, with all its dangers and sordid history? We wanted to keep our children safe here."

Mistral nodded. "The heads of the four families all vowed to keep it secret," she said. "If we'd talked about the Pact, there would've always been a few fiery-tempered chiropters who wanted to go back to the mainland and see the saurians, and maybe hunt them. But no one wants to see their own children harmed or killed. Even Nova, you'll notice, has chosen to spend her life on the island. And until tonight, she kept her vow of silence."

"Why did Nova even come?" Dusk wanted to know. "If she thought the Pact was such a good thing."

"She wasn't elder when we left the mainland," Mistral explained. "It was her father, Proteus, who made the decision."

"And it cost him dearly," Icaron said. "It destroyed his family. None of his sons would come with him."

"But Nova could've stayed behind too," Sylph said.

Icaron grunted. "Better for all of us if she had. But Proteus wanted her to come and she was obedient to his wishes."

Dusk found it hard to believe that Nova could ever have been obedient to anyone but herself.

"It wasn't simply a matter of obedience," said Mistral. "Nova's mate had just been killed by saurians while hunting eggs, and she was grief-stricken. She wanted to escape from the saurians forever, and the island was a haven."

"Her father was an excellent elder," said Icaron, "and I admired him very much. But Proteus was the oldest of our group, and not strong, and he died after only two months on the island. Then Nova became elder."

"I always wondered how it happened!" Sylph said to Dusk. "No grubby sons hanging around, and she was the eldest daughter! It's probably the only time there's ever been a female elder."

"But she never did find another mate," said Mistral. "Maybe if she had, her hatred of the saurians wouldn't have grown so fierce and vengeful."

"Over the years she's talked a great deal about returning to the mainland," Icaron said, "and rejoining the Pact, but Barat and Sol and I never agreed with her. I think the quetzal today reignited all her old anger and fear, and she broke her vow of secrecy. It was a vow meant to keep everyone safe. Sometimes ignorance is preferable to knowledge."

Dusk nodded. He wasn't sure he quite understood, but he trusted his father and knew he must be right.

"You really hunted eggs?"

Icaron nodded. "We both did."

Dusk turned to his mother in amazement. "You too?"

"Of course," Mistral said.

"This is so incredible," Sylph said to Dusk, her eyes bright with excitement.

"She was the better hunter," Icaron admitted. "Stealthier, with a superior sense of—"

Dusk saw his mother shoot Dad a warning glance.

"—much better senses," Icaron finished. "She was excellent at scouting out nests."

"So you saw saurians close up?" Sylph asked their mother.

"Well, we tried to wait until the adults were far from the nests. But yes, sometimes we came very close to them."

Sylph nuzzled her mother's shoulder admiringly. "I wish I'd hunted saurian eggs like you, sneaking up on—"

"Don't say such things," Icaron snapped. "They're offensive to me."

All the exhilaration flew from Sylph's face and was instantly replaced by astonishment and hurt.

Mistral looked at Icaron. "She's young and excited," she

told her mate quietly. "You're too severe with her."

"She should know better, especially after what she's just heard me say. I expect more from my own daughter. These are not things to boast about."

Sylph said nothing, and in her dark, hooded eyes, Dusk saw a simmering resentment. This was hardly the first time their father had spoken sharply to her. Some days it seemed that Sylph did nothing but irritate him. She was too loud. She shouted and argued and objected. Things were boring or stupid or unfair. Dusk pressed closer to his sister, hoping to comfort her, but she wouldn't look at him. The dogged set to her face made him anxious.

"But what's wrong," she began, "with protecting the colony from saurian nests?"

"Sylph . . ." her mother said warningly.

"I think if I found saurian eggs near us, I'd be like Nova and want to—"

Icaron's teeth clashed mere inches from her left shoulder. Sylph recoiled with a cry, and Dusk let out a loud, startled exhalation. Sylph scuttled behind their mother, whimpering. Dusk looked from his father to his mother, expecting her to rebuke Icaron, but she said nothing, just hung her head sadly.

"Learn your place," Icaron told Sylph. "And learn some sense as well."

No one spoke as the four of them settled down into their deep furrows in the bark. Sylph stuck close to her mother, refusing to go near Icaron or even glance in his direction. Dusk was happy enough to lie beside his dad. He didn't like to see his father so angry, but Sylph *had* been exasperating—goading him almost. Dusk happily breathed in the familiar scents of the tree and the night, of his parents and sister around him.

He scarcely knew which of his many questions to ask his parents next; he was so overwhelmed by their new identities.

Slayers of saurians.

Breakers of the Pact.

"How did you cross to the island?" Dusk asked suddenly.

"It wasn't easy," said Icaron. "We watched for a long time, and twice each day the water briefly drew back from the mainland and left a narrow path of sand to the island. The coast of the mainland is high, and we climbed to the tallest trees overlooking the water. We chose a day when the wind was behind us. We waited until the water had pulled back, and we launched ourselves toward the island. Some of us managed to glide across the whole way. Some landed on the sand and walked the rest of the way. Some landed on the water and drowned. Twenty of us made it across to start new lives."

Dusk shuddered, glad that he'd never had to make such a perilous journey. And yet he couldn't help envying his parents their early adventures. He wondered if he would ever have any of his own.

"Can Sylph and I come tomorrow on the expedition?" he asked.

"Certainly not," said his mother. "All newborns will stay behind."

"But—"Sylph began to object loudly, but their mother just

gave a sharp grunt and Sylph fell silent. Dusk almost chuckled, amazed at his sister's boldness. There was no keeping her down for long.

"To sleep now," said Icaron.

Dusk dreamed he was examining the saurian, studying its massive, featherless wings. He touched the taut skin. It felt like his own.

The saurian stirred and opened its eye. It turned its head toward him and breathed upon him.

"I give you my wings," it said.

Dusk opened his eyes, feeling alarmed and excited and guilty all at once. He'd felt such delight at the idea that he could fly. But dreams weren't true, he knew that well enough. How many times had he dreamed he was flying only to wake up crouched against the bark? He remembered his mother's words: he should try to be like the other chiropters. But was he really even like them? He closed his eyes again, but sleep would not come.

Judging by the silence shrouding the tree, the rest of the colony seemed to have little trouble sleeping, as if this were any other night and they hadn't just heard their own momentous history for the first time.

Quietly, so as not to disturb his family, Dusk left the roost and crept a ways down the branch, around the nests of other sleeping chiropters. At the tip of the branch, near his family's hunting perch, he crouched. The moon had not risen yet, and the clearing and forest beyond were hidden by a great veil of darkness. Down near the earth, sprawled dead among the low branches, was the winged saurian.

A quetzal, his father had called it. It had spoken to him as it died.

Here on the branch, he felt poised on the very edge of night. Before and below, it stretched out, endlessly deep. The darkness did not frighten him; it never had. He knew it scared many of the newborns, and adults too. They gladly retreated to their nests when night came. But for some reason, he never minded it when he woke up alone at night, with no company but the crickets and the stars.

A firefly briefly sparked the darkness, and instinctively Dusk sent out a barrage of hunting clicks.

In his mind's eye, the firefly and its trajectory gleamed, and then—

His breath jerked out in surprise.

Silvery light bloomed from the firefly, like ripples spreading through a pool of water, revealing a constellation of other insects—and beyond them the weave of branches on the far side of the clearing. The light slowly faded and Dusk was left staring at the blackness.

Like all chiropters, he'd always used his hunting clicks to target prey.

But he'd never known they could bring light to the dark.

Tentatively he sent forth another stream of clicks. His ears pricked high and swiveled to catch the returning echoes. Once more, within his head, the world appeared etched in silver. The thousands of flying insects appeared as streaks of light against the stillness of the great redwood trunks and branches. Did anyone know there were so many insects active at night: moths and beetles and mosquitoes, enough to feed an entire colony of chiropters!

The world faded to black again and Dusk inhaled deeply.

He could see in the dark!

Why hadn't anyone told him? Did Sylph already know, and was she just keeping it to herself? He wouldn't put it past her. Or maybe no one had realized. During the day, it would be hard to notice, since the world was already illuminated. And that was the only time they hunted and used their clicks anyway.

How far, he wondered, could he see? He angled his head down in the direction of the redwood that held the dead saurian. It was a long way. He fired out hunting clicks.

His echoes illuminated more airborne insects, but this time, evaporated before they brought him back any image of the faraway tree. It seemed to be beyond his range. He wasn't ready to give up though. He took a breath, opened his mouth wider, and sang out an aria of stronger and longer hunting clicks.

He didn't even see the insects this time, only darkness. But just as he was about to give up, the distant lower branches of the redwood bloomed in his mind's eye. And there, toward the trunk, he caught sight of the saurian's head and sagging wing, lit by echo light.

This was incredible! Not only could he see in the dark, but he could see things up close or far away—in a quick blossom of light, or a slow flare, depending on how he shaped his clicks.

He tried again, studying the saurian's outline.

"Dusk?"

He started at the sound of his sister's voice beside him. After the brightness of his sonic images, she seemed dim in the starlight.

"Hi," he said. "Can't sleep either?"

She shook her head. "What are you doing?"

"Just looking around."

She stared at him strangely. "Looking at what? It's pitch black."

Dusk was delighted. "You don't know? You really don't know! You can use your hunting clicks!"

"To see in the dark?" she said.

He nodded. "I don't know why they never told us. It's really amazing. Try it. You can see it all in your head."

Sylph turned to the clearing, and Dusk saw her throat and jaw vibrate as she made her clicks. He waited expectantly for her face to lift with delight.

"Well?" he said after a moment.

"I think I saw a bug or two."

"That's it?"

"Yeah."

"But there's hundreds of bugs out there!"

"Maybe. But I just saw a few that were fairly close."

"Try again. You can send out stronger clicks."

"How do I do that?" she demanded loudly.

"Shush," he said, "you'll wake everyone!"

"Don't shush me, Dusk," she whispered dangerously. "I've

been shushed quite enough already."

"Sorry. All right, make stronger clicks . . ." How could he explain it? With him it had come instinctively. "Just concentrate on casting your clicks farther, with an extra kick at the end. Does that make sense? We'll do it together. Oh, and try closing your eyes. It makes it easier to concentrate. Ready?"

Sylph cleared her throat and barked out some hunting clicks alongside Dusk's.

"Nothing," she said after a moment. "This is a joke, isn't it?"

"You didn't see the trees across the clearing?"

"No. Why, did you?"

Dusk did not know what to say.

"Tell me," Sylph insisted, sounding almost angry. "What did you see?"

"Just a bit of a tree."

"You're lying. What else?"

"The trunks and the branches too, all silvery but very clear. I could see knotholes and grooves in the bark. Their leaves shimmered, because the wind moves them, I guess. It's really pretty, how they dance and glow. And around the branches there's a million bugs, like shooting stars, and deeper into the trees there's a kind of glow, a hum, of everything just living and moving."

When he finished speaking, Sylph said nothing for a moment, then, "You saw all that with your eyes closed?"

He nodded eagerly.

"This is so unfair," she muttered. "You just discovered you could do this?"

"I never tried it at night before," he said. "Maybe lots of us can do it."

"No one ever told us chiropters could see in the dark."

"You think I'm the only one who can do this?" he asked. He couldn't help feeling pleased at the idea he had a special skill. "Maybe I should ask Mom if she's ever done it."

Sylph snorted. "She'll just tell you to stop being different."

Dusk started to feel anxious. "I don't want Dad to think I'm a freak."

His father had always seemed patient with his other differences—his strange, furless wings, his missing claws, weak legs, and too-big ears—but maybe this new thing would be too much. He remembered the fury in his father's face when he snapped at Sylph. Dusk never wanted to have that directed at him.

"Don't worry," said Sylph, "you've always been Dad's favorite anyway."

"That's not true," Dusk said uncomfortably.

"He never gets angry with you. It's always me. He just thinks I'm noisy."

"Well, you are sometimes."

"If I were a male he wouldn't care. It's because I'm female. Dad doesn't think much of females."

"No, Sylph!" Dusk was astounded. He'd never even thought about this before. Hadn't Dad always treated Mom well?

"You wouldn't notice because you're male. Males get to name their families. Males get to be leaders and elders."

"Nova's an elder, and she's female!"

"And it drives Dad mad. Look how he treated her at the assembly."

"She deserved it!"

"Did she? What if she's right?"

"Sylph! Dad's right."

"Yeah, Dad thinks so too." His sister sniffed. "All the time."

"Dad knows better than all of us," Dusk reminded her. "He's older, and he's been leader for twenty years."

"Then ask him about seeing in the dark," Sylph said, a bit sulkily. "And see what he says."

Dusk wasn't sure anymore. Tomorrow there was to be an expedition to search the island for saurian nests, and his father would be distracted and busy.

"I just hope I'm not the only one," Dusk said.

Sylph gave a noncommittal grunt. "I'm going to sleep now. Coming?"

"I'll be back soon."

Alone once more, Dusk settled down on the branch and sent his sonic gaze toward the dead saurian. The outline of its massive wing flared in his mind's eye, furless, stretched taut over bone—not so unlike his own sails really. It was not a comfortable thought. He let the image quickly dissolve in his mind. He could still smell its rank dying breath in his nostrils. *I give you my wings.* He realized he was shaking. He felt like the saurian had cracked the sky of his world wide open.

CHAPTER 5

The Prowl

From the top of the hill Carnassial saw the familiar profile of his forest. His strides lengthened, Panthera keeping pace at his side. The day's heat was at its most intense now, but he was impatient to be home after so many days of traveling. His fur was matted with sweat and dust, and his breath came in ragged bursts.

Entering the dense cover of trees and ferns, Carnassial felt a great wave of relief and well-being wash over him. The light softened, filtered through the high canopies. His pupils dilated. His pelt cooled, and he stood, panting, to better absorb the beloved smells of the forest.

With Panthera, he navigated the scent trails that their prowl had marked along the forest floor. All around him, he was aware of other felids stirring from their midday slumber or grooming quietly, curled on the ground or in the low branches. Carnassial felt eyes following him, and heard his name whispered, at first soft as a breeze, and then more loudly, as many felid voices took up the chant.

"Carnassial . . . It's Carnassial . . . Carnassial's back!"

Many pairs of felid hunters had set out on this last hunt, and he and Panthera had been sent farthest. They'd been gone a full month, and he was fairly certain they were the last to return. As they neared the poisonwood tree that marked the heart of the prowl, there were now hundreds of felids keeping pace with them through the trees and on the ground. Carnassial could smell their expectation.

He stopped at the base of the poisonwood and looked up into its branches. These trees were common in the forest, and had long been favorites with the felids, for the touch of their leaves caused a fast and maddening rash on many animals, including the saurians. The felids were immune, however, and so the trees were safe havens for them.

Patriofelis, the leader of the prowl, walked out along the lowest branch, limping slightly on his aged legs. His pale brown fur was shot through with gray.

"Carnassial! And Panthera! Welcome home!"

He jumped nimbly enough to the ground, and sniffed both Carnassial and Panthera fondly in greeting.

"You are the last to return," Patriofelis said. "Some began

to worry, but not me. Nothing could harm our two finest hunters."

"And the others?" Carnassial asked eagerly. "What did they find?"

"Nothing. Not even one nest. And you?"

"A single quetzal nest with two eggs. There was no sign of the mother or father. I believe them dead. We destroyed the eggs."

"The last eggs, then," Patriofelis said hoarsely. "Carnassial and Panthera have destroyed the last nest!"

He arched his back, stretched his jaws wide to reveal his black gums and still-sharp teeth, and shrieked his jubilation to the sky. His cry was taken up by the entire prowl, thousands of other felids.

Patriofelis swiftly clawed his way up to the poisonwood's lower branch, and the ecstatic screams of the prowl faded as its leader spoke.

"Three days ago, we had reports from the other beast kingdoms. The tree runners, the paramys, the chiropters, and dozens more. None of their hunting parties has discovered a nest in more than a month. This can mean only one thing. We have triumphed. The Pact has succeeded."

More roars of approval rose from the prowl.

"Without our brave hunters, this would not have been possible," Patriofelis said. "All the beasts have worked hard, but none harder and longer than the felids! I will dispatch emissaries to the other kingdoms to tell them of Carnassial and Panthera's glorious and final victory. The battle is won. The saurians are gone; and we have inherited the earth!"

Carnassial felt the heat and scent of the prowl's praise rise like an intoxicating musk. It made him roar himself; he felt sleek and strong and ready to fight and feed.

After grooming himself thoroughly, Carnassial fed. Scouring the forest, he found ample fruit and roots, grubs and other insects—but he could not forget the taste of saurian flesh, and the memory made his meal lackluster and unsatisfying.

Insects formed the bulk of the traditional felid diet, mostly the enormous hard-backed beetles that could be unearthed beneath rocks or fallen branches. They were speedy on their many legs, but flip them over, and their soft bellies were defenseless. Their flesh, however, was cold and bloodless.

To distract himself, he paced through the prowl, basking in the felids' admiring glances. He had always enjoyed a lofty status, but it had never been higher than now. The prowl seemed to have grown considerably in the month he'd been away. As the saurians had died out, the felids began leading a privileged life, with virtually no predators. There were countless newborns gamboling about, their mothers watching over them, smugly tired.

He lazily imagined the life ahead. He would mate with Panthera; she would be glad to bear his many children. And what exquisite hunters and fighters their offspring would be.

His brow furrowed. As the prowl's numbers continued to swell, they would all have to forage farther to find enough food. And if the other beast kingdoms enjoyed the same prosperity, would there not come a time—all too soon, perhaps—

when scarcity would become their new enemy? Unless . . .

As Carnassial sprawled on a broad branch, licking his paws meditatively, Patriofelis joined him. Carnassial stood deferentially and allowed his leader to settle himself. For some time, Carnassial had known he was a special favorite of Patriofelis, prized for his prowess as a hunter. He had served the prowl well over the years, defending its territory, tirelessly seeking out the saurian eggs. He'd even heard talk that he was being groomed as the next leader. Carnassial wondered how much longer Patriofelis would live.

"You must be weary," Patriofelis said.

"Never," Carnassial replied.

"An excellent reply," said the leader, and for a few moments, they lounged side by side in companionable silence.

"We are many now," said Carnassial, looking at his fellow felids stalking the undergrowth.

"We are indeed," Patriofelis purred contentedly.

Carnassial paused for a moment before replying, "Perhaps too many."

"What do you mean?"

Carnassial wondered if he was being rash, but with his new glory still hovering about him, would there be a time when his words would be better received?

"We've been successful, yes," he said, "but the more numerous we become, the harder it will be to feed us all."

Patriofelis licked his tail complacently. "There has always been enough food in the forest for us."

"But we share the forest with many other beasts. And with

the saurians gone, they will flourish too," Carnassial pointed out. "We all feed on the same things. Before long there will not be enough."

Patriofelis looked thoughtful. "The world is wide. We can increase our feeding grounds."

"Of course," said Carnassial, making himself pause respectfully.

Patriofelis batted Carnassial fondly with a paw. "The world is at peace now; even the best hunter must allow himself to rest."

"Ah, but who will hunt us next? That is the question."

"The birds are of little consequence, if that's what you're thinking."

"No, I was thinking of the other beasts."

"It's never been the way of beasts to hunt one another."

"If we were wise, we would be the first to do so." Carnassial had turned to his leader and lowered his voice. His ears flattened against his head.

"What are you saying, Carnassial?" Patriofelis growled softly.

"It's as you said. With the saurians gone, all the beasts will inherit the earth. Someone must emerge as the new rulers. Let it be us."

Patriofelis stroked the graying fur of this throat with his claws. "How would you achieve this?"

"We must find more food for ourselves, better food."

"And where would we find such food?"

Carnassial lowered his voice further still. "I have only to

cast my eyes around this forest."

"You are suggesting we eat other beasts?" Patriofelis said, appalled.

Carnassial swallowed. It was too late to turn back now. "Let us be the hunters, not the hunted."

"And what of the Pact?"

"The Pact is completed. Its work is done. This is a new world now."

"These creatures were our allies against the saurians."

Carnassial sniffed. "I did not see so many of them. They were feeble allies at best. Their resolve was not as strong as ours. Who worked harder than us? The felids were the ones who made the earth safe for them."

"Felids do not feed on other beasts!" Patriofelis snarled.

"All of us have eaten flesh," Carnassial reminded him.

"Only from beasts that had already died. We may eat carrion, yes. We may scavenge. But we have never hunted live prey. That is not our way."

"The world has changed and we must change with it."

"We are not flesh eaters."

"I am," Carnassial said.

"Our teeth do not shear," Patriofelis said sternly.

"Mine do!" As he said it, he could taste the rich dark flavor of the saurian flesh and blood in his mouth. Saliva rushed over his teeth.

In his outrage, Patriofelis had risen on all fours. His pupils narrowed to slits.

"The Pact honed our hunting instincts," Carnassial said, letting his head drop in deference to his leader. "Many of the beasts ate the eggs, at least the yolk, for strength, and some of us surely developed a taste for newborn saurian flesh. Some of us crave more."

"I forbid it." Patriofelis's voice crackled with anger.

Carnassial felt all his strength seep away.

"If you have these appetites," said Patriofelis, "you must correct them."

Carnassial tried, and with each day his resentment grew. His appetites were not wrong: they were the ones he had been given. He moved through the forest, and when he should have been searching for grubs and insects and fruit, his eyes strayed to the other beasts.

He longed to confide in Panthera. If she were to be his mate, she'd have to know his cravings, and perhaps even share them. But he was too afraid that she, like Patriofelis, would condemn him. He remembered the way she had looked at him when he'd devoured the hatchlings.

He saw the chiropters, gliding from trunk to trunk, and a coryphodon on the ground, using its stocky limbs to dig and grub for roots and tubers. Sharp-snouted ptiloduses scampered from trunk to forest floor, devouring seeds. From time to time he had seen them hunting saurian eggs, but what they had done paled in comparison to the felids' efforts. The chiropters, he imagined, were particularly useless, their sails making it difficult for them to creep quickly and unsuspectingly along the ground toward the nests.

The other beasts barely noticed Carnassial. He was a denizen of the forest, like they were, and they did not fear him.

It would be so easy.

Stalking along branches, he followed a bushy-tailed para-mus as it rustled through the leaves on the forest floor. Carnassial's lithe feet padded softly; he slowed his breathing so he could not even hear it himself. He watched. He became a silent part of the forest. The paramus, its back to him, was busy eating some seeds it had found.

He felt suddenly sick with uncertainty. Never had he hunted down his own food. He forced his eyes shut.

Go away, he silently urged the paramus. *When I open my eyes, be gone, so I will not be tempted.*

He breathed ten times slowly, opened his eyes, and the paramus was still there, foraging. Oblivious.

Saliva moistened his teeth. Carnassial tried to turn himself around on the branch, but his muscles clenched in rebellion. He blinked and felt faint, his vision contracting. And in that moment, he knew.

Carnassial knew exactly what he was about to do, and that once done, things would never be the same.

He looked all around. No one was watching.

He sprang. Landing upon the paramus, he smothered it beneath the weight of his body, driving its face into the dirt to muffle its shrieks. Instinctively he sank his claws into its body to hold it in place, then clamped his jaws around the creature's neck and squeezed.

The paramus gave a violent shake, trembled for a moment, and then was still.

Carnassial's pulse jolted his whole body. He had done it. He had killed. He drew back his head to look at the creature, its eyes wide. Had anyone seen? He quickly dragged the paramus into a laurel bush. He tore into the soft flesh of its belly. The meat and entrails steamed and came away easily in his teeth.

He fed hungrily. It tasted much different from saurian meat, warmer and richer with blood. It was intoxicating. He ate and ate.

Finally sated, he kicked leaves over the carcass and peered through the undergrowth before reemerging. His feasting had made him thirsty, and he slunk down to the edge of the stream. The still water reflected his face. His muzzle was matted with blood.

He had killed a fellow beast. He had eaten its flesh and thrilled at the taste.

He quickly dipped his face into the water so he would not have to look at himself.

CHAPTER 6

The Expedition

DUSK WATCHED ENVIOUSLY as his mother's search party glided off into the forest. The sun had scarcely cleared the horizon and Dad's group had already left, along with more than a dozen others, radiating out through the trees, each bound for a different part of the coastline.

Earlier that morning, Dusk had made one final plea to be taken along, reminding his father that he'd said there were no saurian nests on the island anyway, so it was perfectly safe, and why couldn't he and Sylph come too? He'd thought it was a pretty good argument, as did Sylph, especially since she'd come up with it.

But his father had just said no again, and his mother told him and Sylph to behave themselves, and stay at the tree until they returned that night. Bruba, an older sister Dusk scarcely knew, was supposed to be keeping an eye on them.

"This was probably our one and only chance to see a live saurian," Sylph said as the two of them sailed through the clearing, hunting halfheartedly.

"We've already seen one," Dusk reminded her.

"That one was dead," said Sylph. "Or practically dead."

Far below, Dusk could smell the quetzal, already beginning to rot in the trees. For some reason he didn't like to think of it getting eaten by insects and scavengers, its body and wings stripped to sinew and bone.

"Don't you want to see a nest, though?" Sylph said. "Saurian eggs!"

"There's probably nothing," Dusk said.

"But there might be." Sylph looked at him. "What do you think?"

"What?"

"Let's go have a look ourselves."

"We'd get lost," said Dusk, but he was already interested.

"We'd follow them," said Sylph, jerking her head in the direction of the last search party, just launching from the branch.

Dusk noted their heading. "We'd have to stay well back," he whispered. "If we got caught—"

"We won't," said Sylph. "We just follow them, and hide and watch while they search the coastline."

"What about Bruba?" Dusk asked.

"She's got about two dozen newborns to take care of, plus her own two. She's barely glanced at us. Anyway, I don't think she can even tell us apart. She's called me three different names this morning."

Dusk chuckled nervously. He didn't want to get into trouble. Sylph was used to being in trouble, but he wasn't. And he liked it that way. His physical appearance attracted enough attention, and he didn't think it would be smart to test the patience of the colony, or even his own parents. Jib's taunt about being driven away still haunted him.

And yet he wanted to go with Sylph. He doubted they'd see a saurian, or even a nest, but he would see the island's coastline, and the open sky—and more birds in flight.

"Yes," he said. "Let's do it."

Sneaking off was amazingly easy.

They glided among a big group of newborns for a few minutes, and then, when Bruba wasn't looking, simply veered into the forest. They sailed until they were certain they could no longer be seen from the clearing, and then landed, breathless with excitement.

In the distance, Dusk could make out a few of the chiropters from the search party, sailing on ahead. He turned back in the direction of the sequoia, and felt an odd contraction in his throat. Every day he left the tree's embrace to hunt, but never for very long, and he'd certainly never lost sight of it. He glanced down at the bark beneath his claws. It was smooth and scaly, not sequoia bark. He caught Sylph

86

glancing backward too, but if she was feeling any doubts about their adventure, she wasn't saying anything. Neither would he.

"Come on," she said.

They headed off after the other chiropters. It suddenly occurred to Dusk that all he'd ever done was glide back and forth across the clearing. Now, for the first time, he was actually going somewhere. He had a destination beyond his gaze.

With each glide, he and Sylph tried to cover as much distance as possible. It was difficult, for the forest was dense and cluttered, and they often had to swerve or dip around branches. When they'd fallen as close to the ground as they dared, they landed and made the arduous climb up the trunk to find another launching perch. Dusk knew he had a long and tiring journey ahead of him.

"Can't you climb any faster?" Sylph asked him impatiently.

"No," he panted, "I can't."

He cursed his missing claws and his weak legs. He looked about, hoping for a shaft of strong sunlight that might ignite a thermal current to lift him. But the forest was far darker here, the sky almost entirely blocked by trees and vegetation.

Sylph slowed down so she could climb alongside him.

"It's amazing to think Mom and Dad were saurian hunters," she said.

Dusk nodded his agreement. He could scarcely believe it himself. Even though he knew the Pact was wrong, he still felt proud imagining his father as a brave hunter of saurian eggs. Imagine creeping into a nest, maybe one guarded by fierce saurians. Maybe his father watched from the trees, and when no one was looking, sailed noiselessly down, right into the nest, and destroyed the eggs without ever being seen. Still, getting out of the nest would have been the most dangerous bit. You couldn't just glide away. You'd have to crawl out, scuttling along the ground, and that would be slow and dangerous. His father and mother must have been awfully clever and brave.

"I bet I would've been good at it," Sylph said.

"You'd have to be very quiet," Dusk said good-naturedly.

"I can be quiet when I want. Just imagine, if things were different and we'd never left the mainland. It would've been so exciting."

"Lots of chiropters probably died doing it."

"Not me, though," said Sylph. "I'd be like Mom. And everyone would think I was stealthy and amazing. Even Dad."

Dusk said nothing, not wanting to ruin Sylph's fantasy.

They walked out along a high branch, looking for a good launching perch.

"Oh no," Sylph said in dismay. "We've lost them already."

Dusk peered into the murky forest and couldn't see the other chiropters."You're too slow," Sylph complained.

"The shadows are just so deep in here," Dusk protested, and then he had an idea.

He closed his eyes, breathed deeply, and slung out a long volley of clicks. He waited, and watched within his mind as his echoes returned to him. The first to come back revealed a tangle of branches and trunks, and then, moments later, came a bright flare of outspread sails, glimmering slightly.

"I see them!" he told Sylph, opening his eyes.

"With your echoes?"

He nodded. "They're just up ahead."

She shut her eyes and released a barrage of clicks, then frowned and shook her head. "I don't understand how you do it. Did you ask Mom or Dad about it?"

"There wasn't time."

Sylph grunted. "Well, it's pretty useful for us right now."

They sailed off after the other chiropters. A bird flitted past, heading skyward, and Dusk watched it go with the same wistfulness he always felt.

"Do you ever," he began tentatively, "dream about flying?"

He'd never mentioned his dreams to anyone because they made him feel guilty. But maybe he was being foolish, and everyone had them sometimes.

Sylph looked across at him. "No," she said.

"Really? Never?" He was disappointed.

"Never. Do you?"

"Once or twice," he lied. He was sorry he'd brought it up. Sylph made no reply.

"You think I'm a freak, don't you?" Dusk said miserably.

"Not a freak. You're just . . . different."

"I *feel* different," he admitted. He could talk more honestly away from their tree, in the middle of the forest. "Or at least I think I do. It's hard to tell what's normal. Do you feel normal?"

"I think so," said Sylph.

Dusk struggled for the right words. "You never feel you should be something else?"

"What are you talking about?" Sylph said, exasperated.

"Don't you ever wish—" Dusk lost his nerve and trailed off.

"What?" She was almost shouting, and Dusk worried the other chiropters would hear them. "Tell me!"

"All right, all right," he whispered. "Don't you ever wish you could fly?"

He watched her face carefully.

"That's impossible," she said.

"But do you ever wish it?" he persisted.

"Yes, sure. But we can't fly, so why waste time thinking about it?"

Dusk said nothing. Sylph sounded like Mom, and it surprised him.

"You're different, Dusk, but you're not *that* different. You think you can fly now?"

"No, no," he said hastily. He'd never told her about his secret attempts at the Upper Spar.

"I wouldn't go telling anyone else this," she said. "It's like saying you wish you were a bird."

"I don't want to be a bird," he insisted. "It's just, when I saw that saurian—"

Sylph gasped. "You want to be a saurian?"

"No! But its wings looked sort of like mine, and I couldn't help wondering: If it can fly, why can't I?"

"Don't you want to be a chiropter?"

"Of course I do. I just wish I could fly too."

They traveled on in silence. Glide. Climb. Glide. Below them, groundlings scuffled through the undergrowth. Dusk felt sorry for them; they must get awfully dusty always grubbing in the dirt. He studied the trees. He saw new kinds, some with broad leaves that rustled in the light wind. He saw foreign mosses and lichens clinging to bark, and flowers he'd never seen before. He didn't know any of their names. It struck him how little he knew, how little he'd seen. The winged saurian and his father's stories of the past had made him painfully aware of that. He lived in a tree in a clearing in a forest on an island, with the entire world stretching out unseen all around him. The thought of it made him feel excited and frightened all at once.

Crouched on a branch, resting after a long climb, Dusk noticed that up ahead light shafted between the trees.

"Must be a clearing," said Sylph.

"Not a clearing," Dusk exclaimed, throwing himself off the branch and calling back to his sister. "The coast!"

A breeze played against his fur, and it carried a fragrance he wasn't used to. He couldn't see the other chiropters up ahead, and he guessed they must have reached the coastline and already be searching. Just to be sure, he veered away from the course they'd been following, keeping a careful watch. He didn't want to sail right into them.

As they approached the last line of trees, the light made Dusk squint. It was almost blinding after the gloom of the forest. He managed to pick out a branch with lots of leaves to hide them, and they landed. With Sylph at his side, he shuffled along the branch to find a good vantage point.

Then he just stared.

All his life he'd been surrounded by trees and branches and leaves. The vast view before him now felt like a weight against his chest. Wind rustled the fur of his face. His breath came fast and shallow. He had to turn himself around and stare back into the forest to calm his heart. It was too much.

"You all right?" Sylph asked. She too was panting, he noticed.

"It's a lot to look at," Dusk said, his voice hoarse.

"Yeah, it is a lot," his sister agreed.

He slowly turned back. The ground sloped away gently for several yards before falling off sharply into the water. Until now, the most water he'd ever seen was pooled in a big furrow in a branch of the sequoia. Here the water spread out from the coast and kept going and going until it reached the sky. He took a deep breath. This was the salty smell he'd noticed earlier, more pungent now. The water's surface glittered brightly, forcing Dusk to lift his gaze away. He'd never seen such a soaring expanse of sky either. It made him want to press himself against the branch and hold on.

He stared at his claws against the bark for a moment. Then he looked right and left along the coast, but saw no sign of any search parties.

"How do they do their searches?" Dusk whispered to his sister, just in case there were other chiropters nearby.

"Don't they just do it from the trees?"

Dusk looked down into the tangle of shrubs and grasses and shadows. It would be easy to miss something. "Wouldn't they need to go down on the ground?" he said. "To see properly?"

The thought made him shudder. Chiropters were hardly fast on their feet. And on the ground, there could be no quick launch into a glide. You were trapped. It was hard to believe his parents had taken such dreadful risks during their years as saurian hunters.

"Let's just look from up here," Sylph suggested.

"We should keep an eye open for other chiropters too," Dusk reminded her.

"What would a nest even look like?"

Dusk sniffed at their ignorance. They'd come all this way without any clear idea what they'd be looking for.

"Must be like a bird's nest, don't you think?" he said. "But on the ground. Round, made of leaves and sticks and twigs." This seemed fairly logical.

"Everything sort of blends together down there," said Sylph.

Dusk had an idea. He closed his eyes and sent out sound. His echoes penetrated the shadows and the muddle of colors and brought back an incredibly sharp image.

"Are you using your hunting clicks?" he heard Sylph ask.

He nodded, still studying the terrain with sound:

Grass.

A laurel branchlet.

Rocks.

A tea shrub.

A ridge of mulched leaves . . .

He let his echoes linger over this. It was more than just a ridge. It was a circle of leaves—and right in the middle of it rested something egg-shaped.

Dusk's eyes snapped open, his heart kicking hard.

"There's a nest!" he wheezed.

Now that he'd found one, he felt completely unprepared. Terrified, he looked all around. Where were the saurian parents? Would they come from the sky, like the quetzal, or from the ground. Or from the trees?

"Where? Where is it?" Sylph demanded.

He directed her gaze with a nod. "There."

"You think so?" Sylph sounded unsure.

Dusk stared. It wasn't nearly so clear with just his eyes. The egg was certainly larger than a bird's—he'd seen a broken one once, fallen on the ground. This one was bigger and rougher, and pointier at the ends. It lay lopsided on the mulch.

"We should tell someone," said Dusk.

"We tell them, we get in huge trouble for sneaking off," said Sylph.

Dusk thought of their father's temper at the assembly.

"But what if it's a real nest!" he said.

"We'd better be sure, Dusk."

"How should I know what a saurian egg looks like? It's not like Mom or Dad ever talked about them!"

"We'd know if it was real," Sylph said with absurd confidence.

Dusk ground his teeth in indecision. He feared his father's wrath. But he couldn't bear the thought of doing nothing when it *might* be a real saurian nest. "I better go closer."

"No, I'll go," said Sylph. "I'm older."

"Three seconds older!"

"I'm faster on the ground. You've got weak legs."

Dusk was startled to see a hunter's craving in her eyes.

"No," he said quickly. "I saw it first. And one of us needs to stay up here and keep watch."

"You're afraid I'll destroy the egg, aren't you," Sylph demanded.

Dusk didn't want to get into an argument with her, so before she could object he launched himself off the branch and sailed out into the open. He landed as close to the nest as he could manage. The moment he touched down, he knew he'd made a terrible mistake. He'd never in his life set foot on the ground. He looked back over his shoulder at the trees— they seemed very far away. He caught sight of Sylph hunched forward on a branch, looking down at him. He wanted to hurry back to her, but wouldn't allow himself to be so cowardly.

Weak legs pushing, he dragged himself through the wiry undergrowth. He reached the nest and clambered up onto the shallow hump of the rim. The nest sloped away into an irregularly shaped hollow.

Lying across the bottom, not more than a few inches away from him, was the egg.

Dusk cringed, glancing fearfully all around. What had possessed him to come down here, and make himself so vulnerable? There might be an adult nearby. And what about the egg itself? Was it close to hatching, or just newly laid? At any moment it might shudder and start to splinter. Even a newborn saurian would be bigger than him, and would barely need to chew before swallowing him down.

But was it a real egg? He needed to go closer still. He

sucked in a breath, held it, and then rushed closer until his nose was against the shell. He sniffed. It smelled of the earth. He touched it with his claw. It was not at all warm—shouldn't it be warm?—and as he pulled his claw back, confused, a bit of the egg's surface flaked away. He grunted in surprise.

It wasn't shell that had broken loose. It was hardened mud.

He looked back at the egg, and where the mud had flaked off, saw what was underneath.

It was just a giant pinecone, coated in mud!

He laughed in relief. He wanted to let Sylph know he was all right, but didn't want to call out, in case any of his colony was nearby. Lifting his sails, he waved up at her. His stomach gave a sickening lurch as he realized that she was flapping her own sails in a frenzy.

Something rustled in the undergrowth.

Dusk jerked around. The rim of the nest was just high enough to block his view of whatever was on the ground beyond. The noise was very close, and sounded like something big. Was it a saurian? His heart shuddered.

He made a frenzied scramble up the rim; the noise was getting louder, branches crackling. In his peripheral vision he saw some leaves fly up. A dreadful weakness swept through him. He was stuck on the ground, so slow. He was helpless.

There was more loud rustling, closer than ever. If he did not act, he would be eaten. The sudden, scalding will to survive overcame his weakness.

Before he even knew what he was doing, he had sprung into the air and was flapping his sails, fast. A strength he had never known coursed from his chest to his shoulders, down his arms, and radiated out along his fingers like forked lightning. His breathing quickened; his heart purred furiously. The pauses between his upstrokes and downstrokes dissolved until he could not tell one from the other, and was only aware of his arms and sails in perpetual motion.

He was rising.

The ground shrank below him. One foot, two, three! There was no thermal helping him this time. It was all his own power. He was free of the earth! No predator could get him now. He kept looking from side to side, seeing the blur of his sails, scarcely understanding how this was possible. It was as if all his past, thwarted impulses to flap had finally been explosively unleashed.

Below him, something with wings thrashed out from the undergrowth and into the air, its beak filled with twigs.

It was only a bird, foraging for its nest! That was what had scared him half to death. It had sounded so huge on the ground.

Dusk was no longer just rising; he was moving forward, gaining speed. As he veered up toward the trees, he slewed from side to side, not knowing quite how to steer himself under power. His whole body suddenly felt unfamiliar to him, and he didn't trust himself to make a landing. He caught sight of Sylph, gawking at him from the end of the branch. He stopped flapping, fixed his wings, and shakily glided down beside her.

"You flew," Sylph gasped.

"I flew," he wheezed.

For a moment neither of them said anything as he caught his breath.

"It's the speed," he said excitedly. "I just wasn't flapping fast enough before!"

"Before? You've tried this before?" Sylph exclaimed.

He winced, but his secret was out now. "Well, just a few times."

"On the Upper Spar, right?" she said. "I knew it! I knew you were doing something weird up there!"

"I was trying to copy the birds, but it wasn't working, because they don't need to flap as quickly as I do!"

Sylph hunched forward eagerly. "Show me!"

"Not here," he said. He was worried one of the search parties would hear or see them, and come to investigate.

They glided back into the forest a ways, and settled on a roomy tree.

Dusk inhaled and closed his eyes, trying to summon up the exact sensation of flight. He found it easier if he demonstrated with his sails.

"Down and forward, like this, stretching, then you've got to flex them—"

"Bending at the elbows and wrists?" said Sylph, watching intently.

"Yes. And then, look, right away you're bringing them back, tilted upward. Way up over your head. And then you start all over again."

"That's it?" Sylph said, unimpressed.

"That's it."

"Shouldn't be a problem."

"You have to flap fast," Dusk told her, a little annoyed. If she was going to be so cocky about it, maybe he didn't want her to fly after all.

"How fast?" she asked.

"As fast as you possibly can."

"Right." And with that Sylph jumped.

Clear of the branches, she started pumping her sails up and down. She worked hard, but her strokes were sluggish, her sails billowing with every downstroke. Churning the air furiously, she was slowly but surely going nowhere but earthward.

"Make your sails taut!" Dusk said. Despite his irritation with her, he didn't want to see her fail. If she could do it, it meant others could do it, and he wouldn't be alone. He wouldn't be a freak. "Flap faster! Remember to flex on the upstroke."

It did no good, but she persisted, falling all the while. From his branch Dusk could hear her sharp cries of exertion and frustration.

When finally she gave up and glided back to the tree's lower branches, she made no attempt to climb up to Dusk. So he glided down to her.

"Why wasn't it working?" Sylph panted.

"I don't know. You flapped as hard as you could?"

"Yes!"

"You'll get the hang of it," he said confidently, hoping to mask his own doubt. "I didn't get anywhere my first few times."

"I'll give it a try later," Sylph said.

"Good."

"We should probably head back."

Dusk nodded. The possibility of finding a saurian nest didn't seem very enticing at all anymore. The most exciting thing he could imagine had just happened to him, and the memory of his first flight throbbed in every muscle and sinew of his body.

On their way back to the sequoia, Dusk didn't know if he should fly again. He didn't want Sylph to think he was showing off, trying to make her feel bad. But his shoulders and chest and arms felt different now. The urge to flap was overwhelming, and he was desperate to make sure he could do it again, that it wasn't just some freakish accident.

In midglide he took his first stroke. Down went his sails. Their wind buffeted his face. He shot forward, lifting. Then he flexed his elbows and wrists, half folding his sails, angling the leading edge upward, and raised them with all his might. And then, within seconds, he did not need to think anymore. Instinct, long denied, took over.

He was careful not to streak too far ahead of Sylph, circling back so he could practice his turns. They were tricky, and he was unused to traveling at such speeds through the branches. A couple of times he nearly brained himself.

Landing was another challenge, because he tended to come in too quickly at the best of times. Now, under power, he was even more uncontrolled. For the time being, he merely settled back into a glide to lose speed, and landed as he'd always done. It didn't feel right, but it was something he could work on over time.

How had he tolerated all those months of gliding? It was so inefficient, so limited, the earth always pulling you down. Flying, all those restraints were cut loose. He could rise and fall as he chose. It was as if his body had been patiently waiting for him to realize the full extent of its abilities. It was sheer glee.

Exhaustion was the only price he had to pay. He could only fly for a little over a minute before he was gasping and had to rest. He hoped that, in time, his stamina would improve.

"I want another try," said Sylph. "I've been watching. I think I can do it now."

"Let's see," said Dusk. "I can't be the only one who can do this. It's just like the thermals—no one's bothered to try it. If I can do it, others can do it!"

With a whoop, Sylph launched herself into the air and started flapping. When Dusk flew, he'd noticed his own sails only as a blur. Watching his sister, he could easily count every one of her strokes. They were not nearly fast enough. Once again, she fell, jerking wildly down and down. She landed dejectedly.

"I can't make my sails move any faster," Sylph said, her voice breaking.

Dusk fluttered down to her, but she refused to look at him. His elation cooled.

"First you see in the dark," she muttered, "now this."

"I'm sorry," he said.

"I'm your sister! I should be able to do this too!"

"I don't understand it either."

"Oh, I do," she said after a moment. "You're different, Dusk. Always have been. But this—flying—makes all the other things seem tiny."

"There must be others who can—"

Sylph cut him off. "No other chiropter has ever flown, Dusk."

"Not that we know of anyway."

"It's not right."

Her words stung, because the same thought had worried him. Still, he was not ready to concede anything yet.

"Just because something's unusual or new doesn't make it wrong," he insisted.

"I don't know about that," she retorted, turning angry eyes on him. "All I know is that flying is something birds do."

"And winged saurians," he pointed out.

Suddenly he remembered the dream he'd had last night. *I give you my wings,* the dead saurian had told him. It was just a dream, but it still made him feel a bit sick.

"Chiropters were made for gliding," Sylph said.

"I'm not sure I was," said Dusk. "My sails never glided that well. They always wanted to flap. Always!"

It was the first time he'd ever admitted it, and the secret, after being clenched inside him for so long, came out in a triumphant cry.

"Like I said, that's what makes you different. It's unnatural." Sylph paused, as if wondering whether to say something. "It's like you're not even a chiropter."

Dusk's heart thumped. "Don't say that. I *am* a chiropter!" In his fear he almost shouted it. He did not want to be so different. The very idea terrified him.

In that moment he wished he could undo everything. If only he hadn't landed on the ground. If only that wretched bird hadn't been foraging nearby and scared him half to death. If only he hadn't flapped.

"Is "different" wrong?" he asked Sylph.

She grunted. "Dad is going to be really angry."

"You think?"

"He's the leader of the colony. Do you think he wants a son who flaps around like a bird?"

Dusk swallowed.

"And remember what Mom said. Behave like the colony, or risk being shunned by the colony."

"You can't tell anyone about this," Dusk said urgently. "Promise me, Sylph."

"Don't worry," she said kindly. "I promise. I'll keep your secret."

Carnassial prowled the forest.

After his first kill, he'd been overtaken with a shame almost as overwhelming as the pain that had twisted his guts. On the bank of the stream, he'd vomited up part of his feed, and then returned to the prowl, promising himself he would never do such a thing again. Patriofelis was right: it was barbaric.

But a day passed, then another, and the memory of that warm paramus flesh never left him. It lingered in his mouth, tingled his salivary glands. The surfaces of his teeth could not forget the ecstasy of tearing. His mind became a weary battle-field, his thoughts clashing again and again until he was exhausted.

It was unnatural; it was natural.

He could not do it again; he *would* do it again.

Even in his sleep, he was tormented by visions of hunting, which brought equal measure of remorse and elation.

Now night was falling and he was deep in the forest, his pupils dilated. In his head echoed two words.

I must.

He was far from the other felids; but he had to be certain there were no other beasts watching.

He barred his mind to all other thoughts and doubts.

He ground his teeth; his nostrils flared.

There.

A small groundling rooted near the base of a tree. Carnassial approached stealthily from behind. It was not a he or a she. It was an it. It was neither son nor daughter, father nor mother. It was prey. It was his to devour.

A twig snapped under his paw, and the rooter looked over his shoulder and saw him. Their eyes locked. At first the rooter's squat body registered no alarm. It was common to see felids in the forest, and all manner of beasts crossed paths peaceably. But this time, the rooter must have sensed something other than simple indifference in Carnassial.

Carnassial saw it tense, ready to flee.

"No!" it squealed.

Carnassial ran forward, then sprang. It was an ugly fight.

The rooter thrashed with all its strength, scratching and biting, twice wrenching itself free from Carnassial's jaws and trying to drag itself away on wounded legs. But each time Carnassial seized it again, clamping its throat tighter. The kill took much longer than Carnassial had expected. It was a sweaty, dirty, loud business. When the rooter's body was finally limp, Carnassial was worried their noise must have been heard.

Panting, he hauled the carcass into the thick cover of some tea bushes. His breath came in ragged little bursts. He listened for a moment, but heard nothing nearby. And then he could wait no longer. His blood pounded through him and he was almost whimpering with need. He pushed the rooter's face down, so he would not have to look at its dead eyes, and tore into the soft flesh of its belly. He knew he would have to feed quickly, for the rich, intoxicating smell of the guts would spread through the forest quick as a breeze.

He ate like a creature who'd starved for days, heedless of everything else.

When he lifted his head for breath, Panthera was watching him from the other side of the bushes, not five feet away.

"What have you done?" she whispered.

Her nose quivered with the smell; her whiskers twitched in agitation and her ears pricked high. Her astonishment made him realize how he must look: his face a mess of clotted blood, strings of flesh snared between his teeth.

"We are meant to do this," he said quietly. "Try some."

She took a step back.

"Panthera," he said, wounded by the fear and revulsion glimmering in her eyes. "This is the way of the future. This is how we will rule."

She turned and ran.

CHAPTER 7

Way of the Future

Waking early, Dusk's muscles hurt so much he wondered if he really was meant to fly. When he breathed in, his chest throbbed hotly and his shoulders jolted with pain. Flexing his sails made him wince. He lay very still, listening to the start of the birds' dawn chorus, the first solitary notes carrying through the forest, then multiplying like echoes. Usually their music filled Dusk with a sense of wonder and well-being; he liked to imagine the birds were singing the day to him, conjuring the sun. But this morning he felt heavy with worry.

He should be happy. Yesterday he and Sylph had returned

to the tree well ahead of the others, and rejoined the new-borns, their absence completely unnoticed by the harried Bruba. They'd had their adventure and escaped punishment. And as evening came on, the search parties had returned one by one to the clearing, each bringing the same news. There was no sign of saurians or nests. The mood in the sequoia was joyous. Dusk was relieved the island was safe, and delighted that his father had proven Nova wrong.

But none of this seemed important.

He could fly.

He closed his eyes and remembered the thrilling sensation. Yet right now he felt about as buoyant as a stone. Should he tell his parents he could fly? Was he supposed to go his entire life hiding it? He glanced over at his mother and father, their eyes still closed, and wondered what they would say.

"Come on," said Sylph, shifting beside him. "I'm hungry."

Stiffly he followed his sister. Launching himself into the air, he had to restrain himself from flapping. He gave a little moan of pain as he unfurled his sails, made them rigid, and began hunting. His empty stomach yowled, but he felt listless.

"Are you all right?" Sylph asked as their paths crossed.

"Just sore," he muttered.

As the sun appeared, the clearing became more crowded. Dusk's hunting was lackluster. Something was smoldering beneath his low spirits, and he realized it was anger. Every muscle in his shoulders and arms wanted to flap, and yet, he was denying himself. He could fly, so why didn't he? Why should he be so afraid to be what he was?

"You're not going to do anything stupid, are you?" Sylph

asked worriedly as she glided past.

He banked away, fuming.

He tried to catch a swamp moth and missed.

"Not doing too well, are you, furless?"

It was Jib, sailing just above him.

Dusk ignored him. He sighted a dragonfly, wheeled too sharply, and his prey shot over his head, climbing.

Jib's mockery battered him once more.

"Let me show you how it's done, furless," Jib said, swooping down on the dragonfly.

Dusk couldn't bear it. His sails exploded into action and he was flapping hard, climbing and banking at the same time, his hunting clicks guiding him straight to the dragonfly. He snatched it from the air, a mere second ahead of Jib.

"*That,*" he shouted, "is how it's done!"

Jib was too surprised even to cry out in indignation. He tumbled through the air for a moment, regained his glide, and stared up at Dusk, incredulous.

Dusk landed on a branch, heart pounding triumphantly. No dragonfly had ever tasted better. But his glee was short-lived. He noticed that all the chiropters nearby, some gliding, others crouched on the branches, were staring at him. They gazed at him like something alien that had plummeted from the sky. Sylph hurriedly set down beside him.

"What have you done?" she hissed. "What about keeping it secret?"

"I . . . I just couldn't help it," Dusk said.

Sylph, who had never feared being loud or argumentative or annoying, looked stricken.

"This is going to be really bad," she said.

Dusk's throat felt dry, and he almost choked on the last bit of dragonfly.

"How did you do that?" he heard someone shout.

"He flew!" someone yelled. "Icaron's son flew!"

"You *flapped*!" Jib exclaimed, climbing the trunk toward them. "What kind of freak are you?"

"Chiropters can't fly!" someone else said.

"This one did! I saw it. He flapped."

"He's some kind of mutant!" That was Jib again, on the same branch now, with an unfathomable look blazing in his eyes. Was it envy, or fear, or hatred?

More and more chiropters were crowding around him now, and Dusk didn't like it. Why hadn't he controlled his temper? His split-second mistake was going to get him in more trouble than he could imagine. Some of the chiropters didn't merely sound surprised; they sounded angry, and Dusk started to feel afraid of what they might do. A musk of aggression wafted past him. When he caught sight of his father gliding toward the branch, relief welled up inside him.

"What's going on?" Icaron demanded, his nostrils twitching as he sniffed out the ugly mood.

The chiropters on the branch made room for him, all talking at once.

"He flapped!"

"Dusk flew!"

"We all saw him!"

"He flapped like a bird!"

Dusk waited in agony as his father drew closer.

"Is this true?" Icaron asked.

Dusk nodded.

As miserable as he felt, at least the burden of keeping his secret had now been lifted.

"Show me," Icaron said gruffly.

Dusk dutifully shuffled to the edge of the branch. He had a quick, sad memory of his father teaching him how to glide, and then jumped, unfurling his sails, and soaring up into the air. He could hear the rumble of shock and amazement from the watching chiropters.

For a moment, he considered flapping even higher, disappearing altogether so that he wouldn't have to return to face his father's anger and shame. He could find some new place to live and become odd and smelly and bug-ridden. But that would mean leaving his mother and father and Sylph and his home and everything he loved, and he knew he could never do that. He would have to face his father. He sighed, banked, and came in for a landing on the branch.

Walking through the hushed chiropters toward Icaron, Dusk stared at his claws.

"How long have you been able to do this?" he heard his father ask.

"I just found out yesterday."

He didn't know exactly what kind of punishment would be meted out, but he could only imagine it would be severe. *You are not a bird. You do not flap. Chiropters glide, not fly.* Would they drive him out?

"I'm sorry," he murmured.

"I think this is extraordinary," his father said.

In disbelief, Dusk looked up at him, and saw that his face was not compressed in anger and disapproval, but opened wide with wonder. The other chiropters had gone suddenly quiet, and were watching their leader carefully.

"You do?" Dusk asked.

"Really?" Sylph said, startled.

"Spread your sails," Icaron said to Dusk. "Let me have a look at you."

Dusk did as he was told, and his father moved closer and silently examined the underside of his sails.

"When you flap," Icaron asked, "where does the strength come from?"

"From the chest and shoulders, I think."

Icaron nodded. "Yes, see, it's here. Your chest is larger and stronger than normal. Your shoulders too. They've always been that way, since you were first born. You'd need a lot of muscles to flap your sails as quickly as you do."

Dusk was unable to stop himself from sliding his gaze over to Sylph and then Jib. Stronger than normal. A lot of muscles.

"He can't be the only one who can do it, then," said Jib boldly.

"Try it," Icaron invited him. "I've never heard of another chiropter who could fly. I don't think we have enough muscle power."

"There must be others," Dusk said to his father.

"I don't think so, Dusk." Icaron shook his head, looking again at his son's sails. "It really is remarkable. When you flapped on your very first glide, I had no idea, no idea at all . . ."

"This is so unfair," Sylph sighed, and climbed away up the tree.

The other chiropters were beginning to disperse now too, carrying on with their hunting or grooming. Dusk caught a few wary looks, and heard some sour mutterings about how it wasn't right, and who would want to fly like a bird anyway?

"So is it all right?" Dusk asked. "To fly?"

"Why not?" his father said. "I think it's a wonderful skill."

Dusk still had trouble believing his father's reaction. He seemed genuinely excited, and it helped cleanse Dusk of the corrosive anxiety he'd felt.

"Just make sure you stay below the Upper Spar," Icaron told him. "The birds won't welcome another flyer in their territory."

All morning Dusk flew, gleefully swooping and climbing through the clearing. An intoxicating freedom soared through his body.

Anywhere: he could go anywhere.

He was catching more prey than ever before. He was so much more maneuverable now. Best of all, he would never have to face the long, wearying climb back up the tree. He looked pityingly down at the other chiropters hauling themselves up the trunk.

He found he still tired quickly. Ten minutes was the longest he could stay aloft before needing a good rest. But since his hunting was so much more efficient, he figured he was still saving time overall. With more practice, he was sure his muscles would get stronger, and keep him airborne longer.

The news of his flying blew through the colony quicker than a gale. He caught sight of a few newborns, including Jib, trying desperately to fly. None of them had any more success than Sylph, and when their parents caught sight of them they were angrily told to stop.

At midday, when the sun was at its brightest, and the drone of cicadas was almost deafening, Dusk found Sylph back at the nest, resting in the shade. He settled beside her and began grooming. She did not offer to comb his back.

"You know what really gets me," she said. "If I'd been the one to fly, Dad wouldn't have let me."

"What?"

"You know it's true," she said, her ears twitching. "If it were me, he'd just see it as something else I did wrong."

"Sylph, that's not true. He'd have been just the same."

She turned to him, and Dusk was startled by the disdain in her eyes.

"Think what you like," she said. "It doesn't change the truth."

She glided off into the clearing.

Dusk stared after her, hurt and then angry. She was jealous, plain and simple.

But her words echoed in his head all afternoon, and he wondered if there was some truth to them. Would his father have been so surprisingly generous with Sylph? Was Dad making a special exception just for him?

As he flew through the clearing, everyone stared. The looks were not all nice. Though some were wide with wonder, many were closed with wariness. He didn't like so many eyes on him. It embarrassed him. Sylph would've been different; she would've loved all the attention. It would have been impossible to get her out of the air.

"You're in my way!" a chiropter snapped as Dusk climbed steeply in pursuit of a lacewing.

"Sorry," said Dusk, veering to one side before hurtling up to intercept his prey.

"That was mine!" his brother Borasco shouted angrily.

"Sorry," Dusk said. "I didn't see you."

"Pay more attention then! Anyway, you can't go catching prey from below. It's not done. It's stealing someone's food away! Work from above like the rest of us."

Dusk apologized yet again, but he certainly had no intention of catching prey only from above. What was the point of flying then? Still, he could see how irritating it would be to have someone forever pinching your bugs out from under you.

Maybe he should he feeding outside the prime hunting grounds. It was much less crowded, and he wouldn't be in anyone's way. He sighed. Sylph was already angry with him, and if he wasn't extremely careful, she wouldn't be the only one.

That night, he woke to the sound of his parents' low voices. They had moved off a little ways down the branch, but Dusk could hear them quite clearly if he pricked his ears high. Beside him, Sylph slept deeply. His stomach swirled: It must be serious if Mom and Dad were talking in private in the middle of the night.

"You know what would have happened to him back on the mainland," his mother said.

"I know very well. The colony would've driven him out."

"Or killed him," his mother added.

Dusk felt cold with fear. They were talking about him! He worried his parents would hear his nervous breathing.

"That's why I showed the colony he has my complete approval," Dad said. "If they think their leader approves, they will approve. We need to protect him, Mistral."

"You wouldn't have been so tolerant of our firstborns, Icaron. You would have forbidden them."

Icaron's tone was amused. "Perhaps, but the years of peace and plenty have obviously mellowed me. And it *is* an amazing thing, Mistral, you have to admit."

"Others won't be so kindly disposed toward it," his mother replied. "Some will be envious; more will simply see him as a freak." Dusk heard her sigh. "He'll have trouble finding a mate."

Dusk relaxed a bit. Was this all his mother was worried about? He wasn't in the least bit concerned. Most chiropters didn't find a mate until their second or third year. Anyway, he wasn't even interested. It wouldn't be such a tragedy if he never found a mate. He had his mother and father and Sylph—though he supposed Sylph would go off to live with her mate when it was time.

"He's very odd-looking," his mother said sadly. "I love him, and it shouldn't matter, but when I look at him, he just doesn't look like all my other children. It's like he belongs to some other species."

Dusk didn't know how much more he wanted to hear, but he couldn't stop eavesdropping now.

"He is ours, as much as the others are," Icaron said gently.

"And he has something none of the others do. He can hunt faster, scout the forest more effectively, fly high and describe the world around us. He can see any predators coming from a distance, and warn us. Doesn't that make him a desirable mate?"

"Yes, of course. But sometimes it's not good to be too different. We are drawn to creatures like ourselves. That's just the way of things."

"I chose you as my mate," Icaron said.

"Yes, but my difference is invisible."

Dusk's ears pricked even higher. What was his mother talking about?

"Everyone can *see* Dusk's differences," his mother went on. "But you're the only person who knows mine. And you agreed it was best kept secret."

Dusk heard his father sigh. "Perhaps I was wrong. What shame is there in having night vision?"

"Me too!" Dusk burst out before he could stop himself. He scuttled across the branch toward his shocked parents. More quietly he said, "I can see in the dark too!"

"You can?" his mother said weakly.

Dusk nodded. "With my hunting clicks. I can see everything with them. Is it the same with you?"

"Yes," she said with a chuckle. Then her brow furrowed. "How much have you heard?"

"A bit," he said awkwardly.

She came and nuzzled him. "I love you as dearly as all my children. I'm sorry if it sounded otherwise. And now I learn we have even more in common. Echovision."

"Is that what you call it?"

"Why didn't you tell us sooner?" his father asked.

"I was worried you'd be ashamed of me," Dusk said. "Because I was different enough already."

"We've never been ashamed of you," said his mother. "I just want you to have all the best chances. That's why I think some things should stay hidden."

"But you told Dad about your echovision."

"He's the only one."

"It was a huge asset as a saurian hunter," Icaron said. "Your mother could see greater distances, and in the dark too. The saurians had quite poor vision, especially at night. Your mother could guide us right to the nests without being seen."

Dusk looked at his mother with renewed admiration—and relief too. At least with this strange skill he was not alone.

"Why can we do this?" he asked.

"I don't know. Maybe my own mother or father had the same ability. But they never talked of it. And I never confided in them."

"You were afraid you'd be shunned?"

"Yes."

"But maybe there are others who can do it too," said Dusk hopefully. "They're all just afraid to tell, like we were."

"That may be," said Icaron.

"It would be better if everyone just told," Dusk blurted out. "Then nobody would have to worry about being different."

Mistral nodded ruefully. "The urge to be the same is very strong. It runs through our veins."

"But it also seems," said Icaron, "that within each of us are the seeds for change. Why and when they flourish, no one knows."

Dusk stared off into the dark clearing. He felt a bit bewildered by all the new things he was learning. He'd had enough for now. Part of him wished he could glide back in time, before the saurian had crashed into their world. But the bigger part thrilled at his new self.

"I was worried I might be a saurian," Dusk admitted.

"Dusk, you weren't really!" his mother said, aghast.

"Just a bit," he said sheepishly. "My sails. They look a lot like the saurian's wings. Hairless. And we can both fly."

"I watched you being born," his father said fondly. "And I can assure you, you did not hatch from an egg."

"Are you sure there was no one else in the family who ever flew?" Dusk asked.

"You're the first," Mistral told him.

"But maybe not the last," Icaron said. "Who's to say one day all chiropters might not fly and see at night? Perhaps you're a forerunner."

"Don't fill his head with such thoughts," Mistral chastised her mate. "For now he should keep his echovision secret."

"Sylph knows," Dusk confessed.

"Well, let's hope she keeps it to herself. It's obviously too late to conceal the flying. I still worry you'll be shunned for it."

"I won't tolerate it," said Icaron firmly. "Not while I'm leader. We should none of us fear being different. This entire colony only exists because a small group of us dared to be different. Twenty years ago we broke the Pact, and set ourselves against not just one colony, but the entire league of beasts.

Our differences can sometimes make us great, and lead us to a better future."

Carnassial returned to the prowl, head high. He was not ashamed; he would not come slinking back like some disgraced beast.

He had stayed away for almost two days, deep in the forest, uncertain what he should do. Had Panthera revealed his secret? Was Patriofelis already in a rage? He'd wondered if he should flee and find new hunting grounds for himself. But that would feel too much like an admission of guilt, a defeat. He had done nothing wrong.

As he neared the heart of the prowl, the sun was almost at its peak. Lazing after their morning feeds, the felids watched him from the ground and branches. There was no thrill of admiration in their gazes this time, and they would not meet his eye. He caught the musk of their tense anticipation.

They knew.

His step faltered when he spotted Panthera, padding in his direction. His heart lifted. She did not stop to speak to him, but as she passed she whispered, "It was not me who told them. Others saw you and reported it to Patriofelis. I wanted you to know that."

She carried on without even a backward glance.

Carnassial girded himself as he came upon the poisonwood tree, and saw Patriofelis lounging in its lower branches. When the leader saw Carnassial, he stood, but did not descend to greet him.

"You return to us," the felid leader said.

"Yes."

"And is it true, what we have heard?" Partriofelis demanded.

"It is true," Carnassial admitted evenly.

"You have killed a fellow beast. Have you no remorse?"

"We kill all the time. Grubs and insects."

"These things are unimportant. They have no feelings!"

"They flinch as they're killed. They want life too. We just don't honor it."

Patriofelis snorted impatiently, unimpressed with Carnassial's arguments. "You have killed another beast. This is not the way of things!"

"The saurians fed on us. We must feed on others if we're to survive."

"So you've said before." Patriofelis paced his branch in the poisonwood tree. "But that would bring anarchy to our world. If we all hunted one another, we would have even more bloodshed than when the saurians preyed on us."

"As it was meant to be," said Carnassial.

"No. I forbid it." Then for a moment, the leader's voice softened. "You were a beloved member of the prowl, Carnassial. No one hunted better and fought harder to fulfill the Pact. Return to us. Return to us and renounce your unwholesome cravings."

"I will not," he said. "My cravings are natural, and right."

"Then this can no longer be your home."

"Not with you as leader," said Carnassial, feeling his muscles compress, his sinews grow taut. "Perhaps it is you who should change."

"No, Carnassial, it must be you."

Carnassial lifted his left hind leg and urinated copiously on the ground, marking his territory.

"Come down from your tree," he said, "and let us see who is the more fit to lead."

"That would be a poor test to determine a ruler's fitness," said Patriofelis.

From the surrounding branches a dozen of the strongest felids dropped to the ground, surrounding Carnassial, protecting their leader.

"Go!" shouted Patriofelis. "Find some new home for yourself, far away!"

Carnassial crouched and snarled, and for a moment the other felids faltered. He knew them all. They'd played and groomed and hunted together, and none of them alone was a match for him. But they rallied, and set upon him. He was knocked to the ground, scratched, pummeled and kicked. Claws raked his belly and flanks. Jaws clamped and pulled at his flesh.

He whirled and fought back, enraged that he should be so outnumbered. He hoped Panthera was not watching this humiliation. He knew he could not win such a fight. He staggered up and pelted, turning to snarl and spit at his pursuers. They did not come close enough to fight, but advanced slowly, forcing him away from the prowl.

Alone, he turned and limped into the forest, his wounds bleeding, his head blazing with fury and pain.

CHAPTER 8

Teryx

"Icaron, I need to speak with you."

It was Nova, gliding down to land on their roost as twilight deepened. Dusk looked up from his grooming, then over at Sylph and his mother. Nova certainly sounded grave.

"If this concerns the colony, let's speak in private," said Icaron.

"It concerns your son," said Nova. "He should be present."

Dusk glanced worriedly at his father. What had he done? He could only assume it had something to do with his flying, but he'd been so careful to hunt away from the others so he

123

wouldn't annoy them. And he'd never flown above the Upper Spar into bird territory.

"All right," said Icaron calmly. "Tell me what this is about."

"Many of us are disturbed by your son's flying. It must stop."

"Must?" said Icaron, bristling. "That is a word only I can use."

"It is causing unrest and unhappiness. The other families see it as unwholesome. He is making a mockery of our kind. We have never flapped. It is not in our nature. He tries to be something he is not."

"He is my son," said Icaron. "He is what he is."

Dusk felt an overwhelming gratitude to his father.

"The birds will not like it, Icaron."

"Will they not? I don't see it as any concern of theirs."

"They will not like to see a beast in the air, around their nests, around their roosts."

"Dusk will stay away from their nests; I trust him to use his good judgment."

"Some are saying he is cursed."

"What?" Dusk exclaimed in surprise.

His father glanced at him, cautioning silence with his eyes.

"They think he was tainted by the winged saurian that died in our clearing," Nova went on. "They say it has infected him somehow. It has changed him, and now he flies."

Once more Dusk felt the reek of the saurian's last breath on him. A hot flash of panic bloomed in his chest. It was like something from his dream. He'd never quite been able to banish the idea that the saurian was somehow the cause of his new abilities.

"That," said Icaron contemptuously, "is the worst sort of superstitious nonsense. There is no taint, no infection. I expect you, as an elder, to do your best to put an end to such rumors—not to nourish them."

"There will be resentment," muttered Nova.

"Ah! Now we get to the truth of the matter," said Icaron. "Many seemed eager enough to try flying on their own. The clearing has been filled with flapping. It's only their failure that brings these cries of freakishness."

"I can see you are not willing to bend on this matter."

"Not at all. My son has a special gift. Why should he be ashamed of it? Why should he not use it to his advantage?"

"It may be to his advantage, but not to ours as a whole," said Nova. "That should be your chief concern."

Dusk was amazed she had the strength to speak to his father that way. He almost admired her, for he couldn't imagine himself uttering more than a squeak when confronted with a face so stern. He saw his father's muscles tense.

"This colony has always been my first and dearest concern," Icaron said. "And when I see its well-being truly threatened, I will act. Was there anything else you wanted to say?"

"I have said everything," Nova replied, and started to climb back to her roost. She was almost as old as Dusk's father, and her limbs seemed weary.

Just witnessing this encounter, Dusk felt spent.

"Are you all right?" his mother asked him, and he realized he was trembling.

He nodded.

"Don't be upset by this nonsense," said his father. "Some

chiropters are always going to be suspicious of anything new—and envious."

"I was afraid this would happen," said Dusk's mother.

"I've been trying to stay out of everyone's way," said Dusk. "And I haven't even gone near any bird nests."

"I don't think Nova speaks for anyone but herself," his father told him, "and maybe a few other disgruntled chiropters."

"Jib and Aeolus have been grumbling about it," said Sylph.

"Newborns who don't know any better," said Icaron dismissively. "I've heard nothing from Barat's family or Sol's. Everything's all right, Dusk."

"Okay," he said, nodding firmly. But he could tell his mother was worried, and he felt far from reassured. He wanted to fly. He *loved* it. But he didn't want to be a freak. Surely, despite what his parents said, there had to be someone else like him, somewhere.

Next morning Dusk was back on the Upper Spar, birdwatching. He still had a lot to learn about flying. He was particularly dissatisfied with his landings, and was hopeful the birds could teach him.

He'd just observed one land in the next tree over, and was waiting for it to take off again, when he had the oddest sensation he was being watched. He looked along the branch, expecting to see Sylph, or maybe Jib or Aeolus, spying on him. Dusk knew they spent a fair amount of time on the Upper Spar, launching themselves into their endless hunting competitions. But there was no sign of any of them. The fur on the nape of his neck lifted. He tilted his head back and saw, directly above him, a bird perched on the next branch up, not two feet away. Dusk hadn't even heard it alight.

It stared down at him with great attention, moving its head in abrupt, precise jerks, as though studying him from all possible angles. Its beak was slightly serrated, like a reminder of long-ago teeth.

Dusk shuffled back so he could see it more easily. The bird gave a little hop but did not take flight. It continued to stare at him with its bold, black eyes. Dusk was unnerved. He'd never been so close to a bird, and he'd certainly never had one express such interest in him.

"Why are you staring at me?" he asked.

"Why are *you* staring at *us*?" the bird countered, its voice an odd musical warble.

"I'm waiting to see you fly," Dusk replied.

"Well, I'm waiting to see *you* fly," the bird said. "You *are* the one that can fly, aren't you?"

"Yes." He saw no point denying it, since the news of his flying had obviously spread into bird territory. He'd envied and admired these creatures his whole life, but never imagined one day he'd speak to one. He suspected it wasn't even allowed. He'd have to ask Dad later.

"Everyone's been talking about you," the bird went on.

"What do they say?" Dusk wanted to know.

"They don't like it. They think it's grotesque. I wanted to see too. It seems impossible. You don't even have feathers on your wings."

"You don't need feathers to fly," Dusk said. "Or wings either. I have sails."

"They look like wings to me."

"That's not what we call them."

"Do you have a name?" the bird asked.

"Of course I do! Don't you?"

"Certainly. I just wasn't sure if you bothered naming each other. You all look pretty much the same to me."

Dusk was indignant. He'd always been told that birds were rude, haughty things, and now he could see why. "Well, maybe you all look the same to us too."

"How absurd!" said the bird.

For a moment neither said anything.

"My name's Teryx," the bird said finally, with what Dusk thought was a conciliatory warble.

"I'm Dusk. Are you a he-bird or a she-bird?"

"He!" said Teryx, with an annoyed flick of his head. "It's obvious!"

"How is it obvious?"

"Just listen to my call!"

Teryx let out a brief trill, and though it was very nice, Dusk didn't know that it sounded particularly male or female.

"It's just a bit lower than the female's," said Teryx helpfully. "And the melody is less complex."

Dusk nodded, as though all this was perfectly clear to him.

"Well, it's no easier for me to tell what sex *you* are," Teryx informed him.

"Male," said Dusk.

"I'll take your word for it," Teryx said.

"How old are you?" Dusk asked.

"Four months. You?

"Almost eight."

"How interesting that birds mature faster," said Teryx.

"Do they?" Dusk said.

"Oh yes, I'm nearly full-size now. But it looks like you have some growing to do yet."

Dusk felt he should object, but he supposed the bird was right. He was still nowhere near the size of his father. Still, it was irksome that Teryx was so much larger than he.

Dusk looked around, hoping no one from his colony could hear their conversation. He didn't want to get into trouble—not that he'd ever been told it was against the rules. Anyway, Teryx didn't seem dangerous, and they were both in their own territory. No one was trespassing. Really, Teryx was quite handsome. His chest was a bright yellow, his throat white, his head gray. Dusk found his face a bit baffling: it was a mask, and all the animation came from his bright eyes.

"You live on the island?" Dusk asked him.

"Oh yes, and I've flown all around it too."

It thrilled Dusk to think of such freedom and speed. And now he had it. His sails could carry him anywhere he wanted to go.

"Have you been to the mainland?" he asked.

Teryx gave an impatient hop. "Not yet. My parents say I'm not ready. Soon though."

Dusk wondered if his own parents would ever allow him to make such a journey. It would be a whole new world over there. But judging from the little he'd heard, it seemed a ruthless and frightening place.

"So let's see you fly," said Teryx.

Dusk thought for a moment. "All right," he said, "if you show me a couple of landings afterward."

Teryx gave a quick nod and chirp. Dusk took that as a yes.

He swooped off his branch, flapping hard and climbing as he picked up speed. He circled a few times in the clearing, making sure to stay below the Upper Spar at all times, and then came in to make a clumsy landing.

Teryx looked down at him studiously. "You are very quick and agile in the air," he said, surprising Dusk with this compliment. "But I can see your landings need work."

"Yes," said Dusk. "Maybe you can show me how."

Watching Teryx take off and land so close to him, Dusk realized how truly different their styles of flight were. Landing, Teryx held his wings high, just fluttering the feathery tips to slow himself down and drop serenely onto the bark. Dusk didn't see how that technique could ever work for him. He always came in much faster. As for the bird's take-offs, Teryx's wings seemed to give him instant lift the moment he launched himself into the air. Dusk needed to beat his sails very hard and fast. He figured he was more maneuverable than the bird, especially in tight spaces, but he couldn't imagine his flight ever being as graceful.

Was it the feathers that made it so much easier for the birds, or just the shape of the wings themselves? He couldn't make out the outlines of any fingers through all the feathers, nor could he see claws protruding. Teryx had those only on his feet.

"Can I have a closer look at your wings?" Dusk asked, and without waiting for a reply, he quickly flapped up to Teryx's branch.

Teryx took a hop back in surprise. "You're in bird territory," he said, his voice sounding slightly strangled.

"Oh." Dusk had completely forgotten. "Sorry. Should I go back down? Are you afraid of me?"

Teryx tilted his head high. "I'm not afraid of you! Even if you are an egg eater."

"Egg eater?" Dusk said in confusion. "I don't eat eggs!"

"Yes you do. Saurian eggs. My parents told me."

"Oh. No, not us," said Dusk, eager to clear up this misunderstanding. "Chiropters on the mainland hunt saurian eggs. And they didn't really eat them, they just wanted to destroy them to stop more saurians from being born. But we don't approve of that. That's why we're here. We didn't *want* to hunt eggs."

Teryx cocked his head dubiously. "But there used to be saurians on this island."

"No," said Dusk. "There were never any here. That's why we stayed. It was so safe."

Teryx just kept shaking his head. "You're wrong," he said. "Saurians once lived here, and my great-grandfather said you chiropters destroyed their nest."

"When?" Dusk demanded.

"Twenty years ago."

"*You're* wrong!" said Dusk, angry now. "What do you know, anyway? You look like you just hatched five seconds ago!"

Teryx hopped forward and opened his beak threateningly. Dusk scrambled back. That beak looked sharp.

"I've seen the bones myself!" Teryx insisted. "We see a lot more than you lazy chiropters."

"So where are they?"

Dusk was far from convinced by the bird's tale, but troubled by his fierce conviction.

"Southeast," said Teryx with a flick of his head. "It's not far if you fly. There's another clearing, not as big as this one, and just beyond that the land dips a bit. Where the trees thin you can see big bones on the ground. Go see for yourself."

"I will."

There was a great thrashing of wings overhead and Dusk looked up in alarm to see another bird coming in for a landing between him and Teryx. It had the same coloring as Teryx, but was quite a bit larger, and the branch dipped with its weight.

"Get away from here," shrieked the bird. "Egg eater!"

"Mother—" Teryx began.

"How dare you invade our territory!" the mother shrilled at Dusk, beating her wings and nearly blowing him off the branch.

"I'm sorry," Dusk blurted, scrambling backward. "I didn't mean to—"

"We've seen you flapping around!" the mother screeched. Her crest flared, revealing violent red feathers beneath. "You have no right! Stop flying, for your sake if nothing else! There are those who would gladly rip your wings from your little body!"

Dusk caught a glimpse of Teryx, cringing behind his mother, head twitching, crest ruffling. He looked as terrified as Dusk felt.

"And stay out of our territory!" the mother bird hissed, lunging at Dusk, jagged beak wide. Dusk jumped, unfurling his sails and spiraling down through the branches of the great sequoia. A quick backward glance told him he wasn't being pursued, and he landed, heart fluttering like a moth. He'd never been attacked by another animal. He felt a flare of indignation: Who was she to tell him to stop flying?

Egg eater!

It was so unjust. His father had come to the island to escape the egg eaters. But these birds still blamed them for things they'd never done.

He didn't know what to do. Tell his mother and father, and he might get in deep trouble simply for talking to the bird. Venturing into their territory was even more serious. He couldn't believe how foolish he'd been. If Nova found out, she'd say she was right and that his flying was going to enrage the birds and bring trouble for the entire colony.

But what if Teryx's story of saurian bones and egg eaters was true? His father should know about it.

Dusk stopped shaking. His stomach no longer pinched and slewed. He could always have a look on his own. Teryx said it wasn't far. That way, if the bird was lying, Dusk wouldn't have to tell his parents at all. He could just forget about it, and remember never to go near birds again. Barbaric creatures.

He would go and find the saurian bones himself—if they were even there to be found.

Dusk had already passed the clearing Teryx had described, and when the land started to dip, he slowed down. The trees thinned. He didn't like being all alone in the forest. It hadn't been so bad when he was with Sylph, but now he felt nervous and vulnerable. Chiropters weren't exactly forbidden to explore; it was just that no one did it much. There was no point. Everything they needed was around the sequoia.

This must be the right spot. He didn't want to go too close to the earth, especially after his last terrifying experience down there. He landed on a branch and peered into the tangle of greens and browns, brightly flecked with flowering vines. Sunlight shafted down, but there were many pools of shadow. His echovision illuminated them, the forest floor leaping into sharp focus as he searched for bones.

He sucked in his breath.

Teryx hadn't been lying. They were coated in green moss, and twined with plant tendrils, and with just his eyes he might have mistaken them for curving branches. But his echovision easily saw the pattern they formed: a series of arcs rising from the earth.

Ribs!

What first appeared to be leaves, plastered against the ribs with rain and mud, turned out to be remnants of skin and scales.

Why hadn't any of the recent chiropter expeditions stumbled on these remains? He supposed they'd all been bound for the coast, and weren't looking for anything in the forest itself. And it would be easy enough to miss the bones unless you knew they were there.

He probed farther with his echovision, altering the strength of his clicks. Beyond the ribs he made out the smooth surface of a large skull, picked clean over the years. And scattered across the undergrowth . . .

Dusk stared for a long time, listening to the streams of his returning echoes to make sure.

They could only be egg shards, thick and leathery on the outside, but smooth and curved on the inside. Strewn among the shards were small bones. A leg bone, maybe. A clawed foot. Two skulls, not much bigger than his own.

There *had* been saurians on this island, and it looked as if their eggs had been destroyed.

But what chiropter in their colony would do such a thing?

He had the answer almost before he'd thought the question. Nova.

He flew back toward the sequoia, his head ablaze with what he'd just seen. He wasn't far from the tree when he caught sight of another chiropter up ahead. With surprise he realized it wasn't gliding. It was trying to fly.

Dusk flew closer, trying to get a better view through the branches, wondering who on earth it could be. It was having no more success than any of the others, flapping clumsily and churning the air and going nowhere. It was always the speed, Dusk thought ruefully; they just weren't able to flap their sails fast enough.

He didn't want to embarrass the chiropter, and was about to detour around it, when he caught sight of the streaks of gray fur along its flanks. The chiropter swiveled unexpectedly in the air and looked straight at him, and Dusk realized who it was. His father quickly extended his sails all the way and glided in to land on a branch.

"Dusk?" he called out.

"Hello!" Dusk called back, fluttering closer. He felt awkward: his father obviously hadn't wanted anyone to see him.

"I wanted to give it a try," his father said cheerfully. "Just to get a sense of how it feels when you do it."

As Dusk landed, he could see his father was breathing heavily. He'd been working very hard, and for some time.

"It's really difficult," Dusk said. "And tiring. I still have a lot of trouble—"

His father gave him an affectionate nuzzle. "You don't need to console me, Dusk. I'm too old and wise to yearn for something I can't have. I'm perfectly content to glide."

"Oh, I know," said Dusk, nodding agreeably. He got the sense they were both pretending. He suddenly felt sad. He'd always seen his father as indomitable. Against all common sense, he had hoped his father *would* be able to fly, even without the right muscles in his chest and shoulders. But his father had been defeated, and Dusk hated that. It also made him feel a little afraid.

"Where have you been?" his father asked him. "I don't like you so far from the tree."

"I know, I'm sorry. But—" He tried to think of the best way to begin. He'd been planning his speech as he flew home, but this sudden meeting had thrown him completely off course.

"I was on the Upper Spar," he began, "and I got talking with a bird."

"You were speaking with a bird?"

"We stayed in our own territories. Mostly," Dusk added, then hurried on. "He wanted to see me fly, and I wanted to see him fly, and then a bit later he called me an egg eater."

"Did he now?" said his father with a gruff laugh. "Well, no doubt they're familiar with what our cousins on the mainland have been doing."

"I tried to explain we were different," said Dusk. "But Ter—" He cut himself off, not wanting his father to know he knew Teryx's name; it would seem like they'd become friends. "The bird said there were once saurians on this island, and that we destroyed their nest."

Icaron looked skeptical. "Birds are hardly the most reliable source. There's never been any friendship between us. They're descendants of the saurians."

"They are?"

"Certainly. Long ago they were feathered saurians who could climb trees. Then they learned to fly."

Dusk was so amazed by this information that it took him a moment to rally his thoughts. "Well, the bird told me there were saurian bones on the island. He told me where I could find them."

Icaron's gaze strayed from his son's face.

"And did you find these bones?" he asked.

Dusk nodded excitedly.

"Describe them to me."

Dusk did his best, trying not to leave out even the smallest detail. His father listened carefully. Then Dusk told him about the shattered eggs and the tiny dismembered skeletons among the shards.

"The bird said his great-grandfather saw a chiropter break the eggs," Dusk said. "And I know who it must have been. Nova! Don't you think, Dad? It's exactly the kind of thing she'd do!"

His father made no reply, and as the silence stretched on, Dusk's pulse quickened. Was Dad angry with him? His mind churned anxiously, and he realized how rash he'd been. He'd just assumed Teryx's story was true.

"These are grave accusations, Dusk," his father said. "If such a thing truly happened, it's a terrible atrocity, and one obviously carried out in secrecy. I don't like to think even Nova could be capable of such deviousness."

"I'm sorry," said Dusk, shamefaced.

"I'll need to investigate the remains myself. They do sound like saurians, but I want to make sure. It may be they're centuries old and died long before we came to the island." His nostrils flared in distaste. "But if someone in our colony did this thing, I'll do everything I can to find out who." He paused. "But until I find out more, don't mention this to anyone, Dusk. Not Sylph, not even your mother."

Dusk nodded fervently, flattered to be entrusted with such an important secret.

Carnassial woke swiftly, his claws already extended, a snarl unfurling in his throat. He was encircled by other felids, their eyes flashing moonlight. No doubt they were sent by Patriofelis, to drive him even farther away from the prowl.

"I will fight," he spat at them, showing his teeth.

The nearest slunk back submissively. "We didn't come to fight," she said quietly.

Carnassial stalked closer, sniffing, and remembered her. She was Miacis, an accomplished saurian hunter. He moved around the other felids, sniffing and recognizing most of them. There were twenty-five in all, males and females both. When he realized Panthera was not among them, his heart gave a quick, hard squeeze of sadness.

"Why have you come?" Carnassial asked.

"We are like you," Miacis told him. "We too crave flesh."

"Ah," said Carnassial, pleased. He knew he couldn't be the only one. Others must have tested their teeth on hatchling saurians and carrion. He'd wondered how many would be courageous enough to admit it. "Does Patriofelis know you've come?"

"No," said Miacis.

"Have you killed yet?"

"No," said Miacis. "We are afraid of being caught and expelled."

"Then you must ask yourselves how great your craving is for flesh," Carnassial said. "I tried to quench mine, but it couldn't be quenched. You must ask yourselves if you're willing to hunt and to kill."

"We are," said Miacis, looking at the other felids.

"But are you willing to leave the prowl forever?" Carnassial asked.

"Surely if we all return united and speak to—" Miacis began, but Carnassial cut her off.

"No," he said. "Patriofelis is old and set in his ways. He lives in the past, and he will not allow our new appetites to flourish in the prowl. He fears war, but that is always the way of the future. There are too many beasts for all of us to feed on insects and plants. Sooner or later, some beast will begin hunting another. And they will get stronger and heavier with that meat. Then they will become the new predator we all fear. I say, let that predator be us. But Patriofelis will not listen to reason."

"Then we can overthrow him," said Miacis.

Carnassial growled. "Patriofelis is well loved, and many will fight for him. We have no hope of winning. Once you hunt and kill, there is no going back." He paused. "Are you willing to leave the prowl forever?"

"Yes," said Miacis, after only a second's hesitation.

One by one the other felids gave their assent.

"And are you ready to accept me as your new leader?" Carnassial demanded.

Miacis looked at the other felids and returned her gaze to him.

"We are," she said.

CHAPTER 9

Outcast

HE DREAMED OF flying above the trees, exultant. Birds watched him from their perches. Every time he glanced down, there were more and more, until the branches seemed made entirely of feathers and wings and beaks. The birds sang to him, quite sweetly at first, but then the music became ominously discordant.

As he woke, the dream images dissolved from his mind, but the bird's dawn chorus remained, carrying through the forest. He listened carefully, and the hair on his neck lifted. There truly was something sinister about it this morning: a low, crowing aggression. Strangest of all, he thought he heard a refrain interspersed with the melody, something he'd never known the birds to do.

"Come and see," the birds sang over and over. "Come and see the way of things."

What was it exactly they wanted him to see?

Across the sequoia, chiropters were beginning to stir, a few already hunting in the clearing. Sylph and his parents awoke, and as everyone made their morning greetings and began grooming, the odd dawn chorus faded away entirely. No one else seemed to have noticed it, and Dusk was ready to think it was just his anxious imagination—the memory of that ferocious mother bird—or some sonic mirage cast by his still-dreamy mind.

As he moved about the dawn-dappled branch, he was pleased to find his muscles were not nearly as stiff and sore as they'd been the previous mornings. His body was getting used to flying after all.

"Will you hunt with me higher up?" he asked Sylph.

"All right," said his sister easily.

Dusk nuzzled her, grateful. He knew it was work for her to make the climb, and that the hunting was not quite as good up there. But he needed her company more than ever. Despite his father's support, Dusk felt a definite chill from the colony. He'd never been the most popular newborn; his odd appearance had guaranteed that. But since he'd started flying, he sensed the other chiropters retreating even further, newborns and adults alike. It was nothing obvious, nothing overtly cruel. Mostly it was new little ways of ignoring him.

If he landed on a branch near other chiropters, they tended to shift away a few steps, as if making space for him, but more than was really necessary. Very few called out a hello. When he drew too close to a group, their voices trailed off, as though a nasty smell had wafted past. If he nudged another newborn while moving along a branch, they sometimes looked uneasy, and he'd caught one or two grooming themselves afterward with fierce attention. This was the one he found most hurtful, because he could tell they weren't doing it to tease him: they were truly afraid they'd been infested with some dreadful parasite.

Maybe it would change in time, but for now Sylph was his only friend. As she started to climb the trunk, Dusk climbed with her.

"What are you doing?" she asked, stopping.

"Just keeping you company." He figured it was the least he could do.

"It's okay," she said. "It'll just take us longer to get up there. I'm faster than you on bark."

"I know, but—"

"Fly, Dusk," she told him, sounding almost irritated. "You can fly, so fly."

"You sure?"

"If I could fly, believe me, I'd fly!"

"All right, thanks. Thanks very much."

He fluttered alongside her among the branches, trying not to pull too far ahead. Jib called out to them as they passed his family's perch.

"You coming hunting, Sylph?"

"Dusk and I are going up high," she called back.

"The hunting's not great up there," Jib said. He didn't even look at Dusk. "I'm going to find Aeolus. Sure you don't want to come?"

"No thanks," said Sylph coolly.

"Go with them if you like," Dusk said as they continued up the sequoia.

Sylph shook her head. "I don't like the way he talks to you."

"He doesn't talk to me at all anymore. It's a nice change, really."

"You know what I mean."

Dusk said nothing, marveling at his sister's loyalty. He'd never understood her friendship with Jib, but they'd been friends for most of their young lives. He didn't want to spoil anything for her, especially since she was being so kind to him. He wished he could tell her about the saurian nest he'd found. The secret rattled inside him like a swallowed stone.

He alighted on the Upper Spar and saw with surprise that Aeolus was already there, crouched at the far end.

"Hi!" Dusk called out as he landed. "Jib's looking for you down—"

"Dusk," his sister called from below. "There's something . . ." Her voice trailed off, but its frequency was enough to send a shiver through him.

"What's wrong?" He leaned out over the edge of the Spar and looked down. Sylph was near the trunk, staring at something out along her branch. It was some kind of large, dark leaf he'd never seen before. It certainly didn't belong to the sequoia.

He stared at it harder, letting his echovision brush its surface. The leaf was unusually thick and had a texture that looked almost like . . . fur. His mouth was suddenly parched.

Sylph's thick voice came to him, as if from far away. "Dusk, you don't think it's . . ."

There could be nothing more familiar to him, yet it was so horrifically out of place here, draped all alone against the bark.

It was a chiropter's left sail, severed from its body. The arm bone had been wrenched from its socket, and was protruding slightly from the ragged edge of the torn membrane.

He looked over at Sylph, who had crept closer to examine it. Their eyes locked, and then he pulled himself back to the Upper Spar, trembling.

"Aeolus?" he called out.

The chiropter did not move. Dusk stepped nearer. His heartbeats thudded slow and hard in his ears. Aeolus did not look right. His body seemed strangely thin and shriveled.

Dusk stopped. He needed go no farther to see that Aeolus was dead, and that both his wings had been ripped off.

From the branches overhead, the birds were suddenly singing again, hundreds of them shrieking out the refrain of their malignant dawn chorus.

"Come and see! Come and see the way of things!"

Yelps and growls welled up from the crowd of chiropters gathered around the newborn's body. Aeolus had been carried down to his family's nest, and an almost suffocating odor of fear and fury now filled the morning air. Dusk found his heart beating as it never had before. Swept up in the collective rage of his colony, his jaws clenched and unclenched and a low snarl rose from his throat. His hair bristled, from his neck to his tail.

Aeolus's parents crouched closest to the broken body, along with Barat, who was the newborn's grandfather. After examining Aeolus, and speaking quietly with the parents and the other elders, Dusk's father looked up and addressed the colony, his strong voice cutting through the din.

"The wounds were made by the beaks of birds," Icaron said. "There can be no question of that. Aeolus was not hunted for food. His sails were deliberately amputated. This was an act of murder."

"Why?" came an anguished cry, first from one and then from dozens of throats.

"But why?"

"Why would they do this?"

Dusk felt sick. The purpose of the birds' ominous dawn chorus was horribly clear to him now: it had drowned out Aeolus's cries of pain.

He watched his father closely, saw him about to speak and then falter. Nova reared back on her legs, sails spread to attract attention.

"The birds wanted to send us a message!" she shouted. "They have taken away this newborn's sails, his ability to move through the air. They are saying the sky is theirs and theirs alone."

Dusk took a breath and still felt as though his lungs held no air.

"It makes no sense!" Barat said angrily. "We've never intruded on their sky. How have we threatened their dominion over it?"

"As gliders, never!" said Nova. "But as flyers, we might!"

A strange murmuring enveloped the colony, sounding like a low wind that could quickly build to a gale. Dusk thought of Teryx's mother, the fury in her face, telling him not to trespass on their territory. He pictured her sharp beak. Could she really have had such murderous intent? He pressed himself closer to the bark, wishing it would absorb him.

"But Aeolus couldn't even fly!" the newborn's mother wailed.

"I know," said Nova. "But perhaps the birds thought he was someone else."

Dusk could feel eyes seeking him out, finding him, boring into him. He forced himself to stare straight ahead, looking only at his father. His face felt hard and brittle. Had he somehow caused Aeolus's death?

"We must kill one of their own!" exclaimed Barat. "A life for a life!"

There was a roar of approval from the colony.

"That might bring more attacks," said Icaron firmly.

"It was not a newborn of your family!" Barat retorted.

"I know, my friend. But that's why I'm more able to make a cold, rational response."

"I want justice, not cold reason!" cried Barat.

"I know it gives you no comfort right now, but it's what serves all of us best."

"How does it?" Barat demanded. "If we do nothing, we're

giving the birds permission to kill again. They will have no fear of abusing us. They'll think us cowards."

Dusk glanced over at Nova and saw her bright eyes moving from Barat to Icaron with great interest. No doubt she was glad to see another elder finally disagree with their leader.

"We've lived with the birds peaceably for twenty years," said Icaron. "We have never been friends, but we've tolerated each other. For some reason they may see my son's flying as a threat—to their territory, to their food supply perhaps. We both eat insects. Their actions are monstrous, and unforgivable, but I see no gain to be made by taking revenge."

"You're wrong," Nova said tersely. "I agree with Barat. We cannot overlook this. Sol, what do you say?"

Dusk could see Sol inhale uneasily.

"I agree with Icaron," he said. "Retaliation rarely leads to an easy peace."

Icaron turned a fierce face to Nova. "You are mistaken if you think our voices have equal weight! Mine is the only one that carries authority. Do not think a vote can change that."

"It is your son's flying, Icaron, that has brought this upon us," Nova said. "It should never have been allowed. It's unnatural."

"You will take no action, then?" Barat demanded.

Dusk felt ill, watching his father endure these attacks.

"I will indeed take action," Icaron said. "Though it may not satisfy you, Barat." Dusk saw his father's gaze turn on him, and in his eyes was a terrible remorse. "I will make sure that the birds never again feel their territory is being threatened."

* * *

"The birds don't want you to fly, Dusk," his father said gently.

"I know," he said.

It was late afternoon, the sun's gentle light slanting through the forest from the west. This was the first time in the long, grim day that they'd had a chance to meet as a family in the privacy of their nest. Aeolus had been carried down to the sequoia's dying branch, where his family looked upon him one last time before leaving him to the insects and elements.

"You must stop," Icaron said.

Dusk simply nodded, too guilty to object. Maybe it was pride that had made him want to fly—to be better than the others. But he did love doing it; he loved the exultation and freedom of it.

"Well, I don't think it's fair," objected Sylph. "Why's everyone so angry at Dusk? He didn't kill Aeolus. It's the birds everyone should be angry with. Barat was right, we should—"

Dusk saw his father's eyes spark. "I won't tolerate this nonsense." His voice was almost a growl. "Haven't you heard what I've been saying, Sylph? We can't control the birds' actions. If we want to keep the peace, to avoid further deaths, it's simplest for Dusk to stop flying. Fair has nothing to do with it."

"I know it won't be easy, Dusk," his mother said to him. "But your father's right. It's for the best. The flying must stop."

"I crave it," Dusk said quietly. Despite his feelings of guilt, he could not quell his sadness. He had flown; he had risen.

"It's too dangerous, for you especially," Dad said grimly. "If the birds did mean for you to be their victim, the next time they may not make a mistake."

Dusk shivered, thinking of the shriveled Aeolus on the branch.

Icaron looked kindly at him. "Do you remember when I took you up the tree for the first time?"

"Yes."

"You didn't even want to jump."

"I was very afraid."

"But then you jumped, and your sails filled, and you realized that you were made for the air. More than any of us knew. I'm not asking you to forsake the air. You're a fine glider, Dusk. Very fast. You remember the pleasure of it, don't you? Go back to gliding, hone those skills, and try not to think about flying. It will get easier as time passes."

"I'll try, Dad."

"You'll promise me?"

"I promise."

The next morning when he hunted, Dusk's sails wanted to flap—it was almost second nature now—but he would not let them. He held them rigid, sweating with the effort, gliding down and down, landing, clawing his way slowly up the trunk. He missed a great deal of his prey. He was slower and less nimble now, and that night he went to sleep hungry.

Over the next few days, things got worse. After Aeolus's death, most of the other chiropters would not even look at him. He felt invisible. All his mother's worst fears were coming true. Before, he was just a freak; now he was a troublemaker. Even though he'd stopped flying, it seemed no one wanted anything to do with him.

Sylph remained his only companion—and he was poor company. He didn't have much to say. He kept thinking about Aeolus and the birds. It would've taken quite a few to hold him down while they pecked off his sails. He still could not imagine Teryx doing such a thing. But maybe Dusk was simply wrong. Birds came from saurians, his father had said. Did that make them like the saurians: fierce hunters of beasts?

On the third day after he'd stopped flying, Sylph asked if he wanted to go hunting. He shook his head.

"You go ahead," he said.

"Are you feeling unwell, Dusk?" his mother asked.

"I'm fine. I'm just not hungry."

"I'll see you later then," Sylph said, and eagerly hurried off.

Hunting with her yesterday, he'd seen the way she kept glancing wistfully over at Jib and his group. When she stayed with Dusk, no one else would come near her or talk to her. Dusk knew she must miss her friends, but she was too loyal to leave him alone. He didn't want her to start resenting him.

His mother came close and nuzzled him.

"I know this is hard for you," she said.

Dusk tried not to feel angry, but he was. "I was good at flying."

"I know, but it really is for the best. You'll see."

"Do you still use your echovision?" he asked her.

"There's not much need for it during daylight, but yes, sometimes I use it when I need to see more clearly."

"You didn't have to give that up."

"Nor do you. But only because no one knows about it. Flying's different."

"I gave it up, and everyone still loathes me. Why shouldn't I fly?"

"You know why."

"I hate the birds," he muttered.

They were the ones who'd done this to him. Every time he glided, he imagined them looking down and tweeting smugly about how they'd beat him, how they'd taken away his wings.

"The other chiropters will forget before long," his mother promised. "They're just scared and angry right now. You won't always be shunned. Now, off you go and catch another sphinx moth with that lightning-bolt glide of yours."

Dusk chuckled; his mother's closeness and familiar smell were comforting. But his anger hadn't entirely left him. The truth was, he didn't even want to glide anymore. He felt clumsy and sluggish in the air. After flying, it seemed like such a defeat. He wouldn't give the birds the satisfaction.

As everyone else in the colony hunted, he stayed behind on the tree. He ambled along the familiar branches, feeling sorry for himself. If his fellow chiropters wanted a freak, he'd become a freak. He'd scuttle about gleaning bugs and nibbling at seeds. It would never satisfy his hunger entirely, so he'd doubtless become thin and eccentric and scare little newborns by muttering nonsense.

It was raining lightly, and though the tree's enormous canopy kept most of the branches dry, in places water dripped down along the needles in perfect round drops and filled small fissures in the bark. Dusk paused to drink before working his way out along some of the sequoia's longest branches. They stretched out far enough to form a bridge to the next tree, and from there Dusk made a game of seeking out more branches that could carry him through the forest even farther from the sequoia. He wanted to be alone.

As he went, he came upon some pink clearwing moth larvae boring into the bark and ate them. They were very sweet and juicy, and much fatter than the average flying insect. Maybe he really could abandon the air altogether.

He was always conscious of the birds overhead, a looming, sinister presence to him now. Their song no longer sounded beautiful. Through the gaps in the branches, he caught sight of large groups hurling themselves up into the sky, wheeling, suddenly invisible as they turned on their wings, then contracting back into a tight dark mass. Several birds shot off in the direction of the mainland. He wondered if they were planning some hideous attack on all the chiropters now, and would lash down upon them with beaks and talons.

Dusk ventured no higher in the tree. He had no desire to get any closer to bird territory. Near the end of a branch he found a mushroom orchard, the translucent stalks growing from the mossy bark. He was astounded by how straight and tall the mushrooms stood, when their stalks were so wispy. Their pale heads bloomed at eye level, the edges faintly serrated and finely dusted with some kind of powder that caught the light.

The newborns were told never to eat mushrooms. Many were poisonous, his mother had said. But he'd also overheard some older chiropters saying they weren't truly poisonous, but made the eater see things no one else could. Dusk sniffed. It didn't sound so different from seeing in the dark with his echovision. Newborns were told all sorts of things. He'd been told not to flap, that he couldn't fly. But he could. Maybe there were too many rules. He felt bitter and reckless.

He sidled up to the mushroom and cautiously licked its edge, then sucked at the tip of his tongue. It was certainly unlike anything he'd ever tasted, dark and moist, with a strain of something ethereal. He took another lick, this time crumbling a tiny bit of the mushroom's fringe with his teeth. He liked the taste, but now felt worried. He probably shouldn't eat any more, just in case.

He waited for a little bit, but nothing seemed to be happening. Thirsty, he moved to a small pool in the bark. He lapped, making the sunlight on the water's surface flex and sparkle.

He settled down beside the pool, still waiting to see something unusual. But all he saw were redwood branches. The wind swished gently through the forest. Dusk blinked.

He realized that nothing was moving in the breeze. Not even the skinniest branchlet swayed. Up in the sky, the clouds did not shift, and yet the sound of the wind was slowly building. He looked down at the pool of water and its surface was as smooth and fixed as hardened resin. Hanging in the air inches before his nose, a dragonfly floated, its wings motionless.

Everything was frozen except him, and what was most surprising of all was that he felt no alarm. Heavy lethargy soaked through his limbs. He sank against the branch, sails spread, claws digging into the bark—though he felt not even a hurricane could shift him now. Lifting his eyes skyward, he saw that night was coming on, faster than any sunset he'd known. In a matter of seconds, the brightness between the branches was extinguished—and still the sound of wind rose, though he felt nothing gusting against his fur.

Complete darkness came suddenly and the world went silver, though he wasn't aware of using his echovision. He couldn't be, for the sweep and depth of his sight was impossible. He saw everything all at once, and not in quick flares. The trees stretched their branches into a sky that was suddenly pulsing with stars. Dusk gave a cry as some of them started growing bigger and brighter, moving slowly into new positions. The spectral wind grew until it resolved itself into the rhythm of beating wings. Dusk's first thought was the quetzal—but not even its vast wings could generate such a sound.

The stars throbbed, making Dusk wince. The hurricane of wingbeats grew. In one great gust, all the branches overhead were swept away and there was nothing now between him and the sky. He felt terribly naked and defenseless as the glowing dome of the night enclosed him. He wanted everything to stop.

The stars blazed with renewed vigor as they began to move once more. The brightest of them formed an outline of vast wings, flapping, and the sound of the wind came from these.

"YOU ARE NEW."

The immense voice came not just from the stellar wings, but from the very earth too. Dusk felt its vibration through the tree and his own body.

"YOU ARE NEW."

Dusk stared, terrified. The wings were big as the night.

With every flap he felt he might get blown away, along with the entire earth, though no air buffeted him.

"BUT THERE ARE OTHERS," said the voice.

What are you? Dusk wanted to ask, but his throat and mouth would not move.

Then the wings banked and swept all the stars into new constellations that formed moving images.

A sleek four-legged creature raced through a forest. Its jaws opened, and became so enormous that Dusk could see its strange sharp-ridged teeth, made for shearing.

Dusk shut his eyes. He'd had enough. He didn't want to see any more. But even with his eyes clamped tight, his view of the immense night sky was exactly the same. It was as if his eyelids had been torn away.

The stars spun and the four-legged creature became one that sat tall and upright on its rump, and seemed to run on its hind legs.

Again the stars realigned, and now there was a frightful mosaic of giant beaks and gnashing jaws.

Things grew: stellar plants and trees soaring upward.

Then the giant pair of wings again, beating the sky. On their final downstroke the wings shattered and became billions of small creatures, wings thrashing, streaming from the stars toward Dusk, who cowered on the branch. From the open mouths of these winged creatures came high-pitched clicks, and as they hurtled closer, Dusk realized they all looked like him.

"THERE ARE OTHERS," said the titanic voice once more.

When Dusk finally opened his eyes, the day was back.

Branches rustled in the breeze. The pool of water glimmered. The dragonfly continued on its way. Dusk unlocked his claws from the bark. He was drenched with sweat, and his heart raced. His mouth tasted terrible.

He retched several times until the contractions in his stomach eased.

"That," he panted, "is the last time I lick a mushroom."

He must have slept, because the next thing he was aware of was his sister's voice in the distance. Confused, he looked around. It took him a few seconds to remember where he was. He listened harder. It was definitely Sylph—she was hard to mistake; even whispering she was louder than anyone else.

Dusk thought he made out a couple of other voices now too. They were quite a ways above him. What were they doing away from the sequoia? He started climbing after them, peering up through the branches, hoping to catch a glimpse.

There was Sylph, and with her—of course—was Jib, and another newborn called Terra whom he didn't know very well, one of Sol's children.

He didn't call out greetings; there was something secretive about the way they moved, quick and nervous, as though their destination were forbidden. But what might it be? Up, there was only one thing. Birds. Sylph knew better than to go into their territory after what had happened to Aeolus.

Dusk was never fast on bark at the best of times, and he was still weak from his mushroom experience. But just as he was about to lose sight of them altogether they all paused, silent on the underside of a thick branch. Dusk kept going, hoping to close the distance between them. What were they doing?

Then he saw the nest. Its woven underside was resting on the branch they clung to. There was no sign of adult birds nearby. Maybe they were off getting food for themselves, or more material for their nest. But they wouldn't be long returning. Sylph and the others peered up at it intently, then scuttled onto the branch, claws gripping the twig walls of the nest, heading for the rim. Dread seized Dusk's heart.

He'd promised he wouldn't, but he did.

He flew.

He had to stop them before it was too late. Flapping hard, he climbed swiftly. He dared not call out and risk attracting a bird's attention. Sylph had reached the rim, and then Dusk lost sight of her as she disappeared with her friends over the side. He beat his sails more quickly, and circled over the nest.

Inside, Sylph, Jib, and Terra looked up in terror, thinking him a bird.

There were three blue eggs, and Sylph and her two friends were gathered around one, their claws against the shell, ready to crack it.

"All of you, get out of there!" Dusk cried.

"Shut up, Dusk!" hissed Jib. "They'll hear you."

"Sylph, leave the eggs alone!" he told his sister, breathless.

Sylph looked from him to her friends, as if uncertain what to do.

"Hurry up and smash it!" urged Jib, trying to dig his thumb claw into the shell.

Dusk dropped into the nest and reared up in front of Jib, flaring his sails in the other chiropter's face.

"Get out now, or Icaron will hear about this!"

"They killed my cousin!" Jib spat.

"And they'll kill lots more of us if you do this. Now get out before the mother pecks off your sails! I think I hear something coming!"

He was lying, but he was desperate, and it seemed to break Jib's resolve.

"Let's get out of here!" he said, and they all started clambering up the sides of the nest. At the rim, they launched themselves, gliding away swiftly. Dusk flapped and lifted off, following Sylph and hoping fervently they had not been spotted by any birds.

When they were within sight of the sequoia, Jib and Terra veered off, leaving Dusk and Sylph on their own. She landed on a branch and he set down beside her. She whirled on him.

"You embarrassed me!" she said.

"You *should* be embarrassed!" he told her. "Do you have any idea what you were about to do?"

"Yes, and we would've done it if you hadn't shown up. There probably wasn't even a bird coming, was there?"

"No, but I had to stop you somehow. Was this your idea?"

"Sort of."

"Sylph!"

"Well, Jib and I thought it up. Dad wasn't going to do the right thing. He's lost his nerve! Nova wouldn't have let the birds get away with this."

"Well, she's not leader," Dusk snapped, "and never will be."

"Jib says she would've been leader if it weren't for Dad."

"What're you talking about?"

"It was Nova's father, Proteus, who first thought of leaving the Pact. The whole thing was his idea. And he was the oldest too. So he should've been leader. But Dad made himself leader instead. That's what Jib says."

Dusk felt sick. "What *Nova* says, you mean. I don't believe anything from her."

"Maybe you should! And maybe we'd be better off with her as leader."

"Don't you dare say that!"

He was startled by his own fury, and Sylph must have been too because she flinched. For a moment neither said anything.

"If you'd broken that egg," Dusk told Sylph more calmly, "the birds would've retaliated, and things would just have got worse. You're not going to try this again, are you?"

She glared at him.

"Sylph, promise me, or I'm telling Dad everything."

"Fine," she snapped. "I won't do anything. But I don't see why we should be the forgiving ones."

"You don't have to forgive them; just don't retaliate."

"You sound like Dad," she scoffed.

"He's trying to do his best for us."

"Is he? What about you? You could fly, and now he's forbidden it. Doesn't that make you angry?"

"Yes. But not at Dad."

This wasn't completely true, but he knew his resentment was unfair. Dad was just trying to keep the peace, and the price of peace meant taking away something precious from his own son.

"When are you going to realize that Dad isn't perfect," Sylph said. "He's wrong sometimes, Dusk, and he's too proud to admit it. He was wrong to abandon the Pact, and he was wrong to punish you instead of the birds!"

"No—"

"If I were you," his sister said passionately, "I wouldn't stop flying. It makes you as big a coward as Dad."

And then she glided away from him.

At first, the prey was completely unsuspecting.

Carnassial surprised many groundlings, pouncing upon them before they could even bolt. But even a single kill—the frenzied sounds and smell of it vaulting through the humid air—was enough to make all the nearby beasts wary. And day by day the hunting became more difficult, as news of Carnassial and his meat-eating prowl outpaced them through the forest.

Padding stealthily through the twilight undergrowth now, Carnassial sensed everything grow watchful and quiet. The groundlings were hiding. Up in the trees, the beasts climbed higher, concealing themselves behind foliage.

After a lifetime of eating plants and insects, Carnassial found hunting hard work. Sometimes it took an entire morning or evening to make a kill. The beasts they did manage to run down tended to fight back hard now. They clawed, bit, and often escaped. Carnassial thrilled at the challenge, but he worried that his weakest hunters might desert him, foolishly thinking they could return to Patriofelis and their old lives. Some in his prowl, like Miacis, were natural hunters, sly and cunning as they stalked their prey, and relentless when they struck. But a few hadn't yet managed to catch anything at all, and had to rely on the scraps of others. Carnassial watched and took note of the weak and the strong.

Yesterday the hunting had been particularly meager. They'd resorted to their old foods to keep their bellies full. But every time Carnassial ate a grub or root he felt ashamed. He wanted meat. They would have to become better hunters, especially now that the beasts were becoming more and more vigilant.

Carnassial leaped up into the low branches of a tree and, as he suspected, heard the scrabble of claws on bark higher up. His teeth clenched hungrily, his eyes vanquished the shadows. He would make a kill. He was an agile climber, and though he could not scale a sheer trunk for long, he could leap from branch to branch, his hooked claws giving him ample purchase.

Above him, Carnassial caught sight of a blunt-nosed ptilodus, a white stripe running down the reddish brown fur of its back, from head to tail. It wasn't alone; there was a whole family of them, all scurrying toward the trunk, squeaking in terror.

Carnassial leaped onto the higher branch and gave chase. In dismay he watched as they disappeared into a small hollow in the tree's trunk. He came close, and pressed his face against it, and reached in with his paw, only to be nipped hard. He pulled back, spitting and fuming, and paced the branch, wondering what to do next.

His eyes lifted, and he saw the dark outlines of birds

settling for the night, preening. One sat on a nest.

His mouth filled with saliva. It had been a long time since he'd fed on eggs.

He'd never attempted to hunt birds; they could simply fly away.

But their eggs could not.

He climbed the tree. The mother in the nest set up a shriek, flapping toward him, but Carnassial did not falter. He was hungry, and he would eat meat tonight. He reached the branch and leaped down its length toward the nest, swatting and snapping as the bird strafed him.

"Stay away! Stay away!" she wailed.

The mother was in a fury, scratching him with her claws, pecking at his head, but he was bigger. He bounded into the nest.

"Egg eater!" shrieked the mother. "Egg eater!"

She raked him with her claws. There were three eggs. The shells were much thinner than the saurian eggs, and cracked easily under the weight of just his paws. But he only had time to eat one of the unhatched chicks before more birds joined the winged maelstrom over his head. Even he could not keep them all at bay.

He leaped from the nest and down to the next branch, his wounds stinging.

"There are many who will come to eat your eggs before long!" Carnassial howled back at them. "The world is changing!"

"Beware," the mother bird shrilled in outrage. "Beware, beast! The hunters too can be hunted."

Carnassial snorted with derision and continued down the tree. Now that the saurians were gone, he was the only hunter of any consequence. And he would continue to hone his skills and eat meat—and reign, as he was meant to do.

CHAPTER 10

A Change in the Tide

S YLPH WAS AVOIDING him. She didn't even ask if he wanted to go hunting anymore; in fact, she'd hardly spoken to him since he'd caught her in the bird's nest. He hadn't told Mom and Dad; he'd kept her secret. But she was far from grateful. He kept waiting for her to come and tell him he'd been right, and thank him for stopping her. He'd saved her from the worst mistake of her life, but somehow she still managed to be angry with *him,* and glide off with her mangy little friends.

Dusk missed her terribly. All their lives they'd never been far from one another, gliding together, jostling in the nest, grooming at day's beginning and end. Without her near, he felt he was only half living. He found it infuriating that she was disgusted with him for not flying. What did she expect him to do?

Mom and Dad seemed fed up with him as well. The first few days he'd refused to glide, his mother had been kind and sympathetic, but now she just shook her head sadly, as if she didn't know what would become of her poor, odd son. This morning Dad had barked at him to grow up and stop sulking—and then had pushed him off the branch. Dusk had glided, but only for a few minutes, fuming the whole time. Dad had no way of knowing what it was like to be able to fly, and then not.

He wanted to avoid the sequoia altogether now, but that was just another thing he wasn't allowed to do. Mom told him to stop venturing off into the forest. Everyone was nervous about the birds now, and Dusk saw a lot of parents keeping a closer eye on their newborns. Icaron had even declared the Upper Spar off-limits for the time being.

So Dusk wandered the sequoia, eating aphids and larvae. Being among the colony, yet ignored by everyone, made him feel lonelier than when he was truly alone. But it was amazing the things he overheard while crawling along the underside of a branch, or resting concealed in a fissure in the bark. The tree was alive with chatter, mostly about his father and the birds.

". . . saurians at heart, that's what they are . . ."

". . . been waiting for a chance like this for centuries . . ."

". . . wouldn't have stood for this ten years ago . . ."

". . . getting old, that's why . . ."

". . . he's just inviting the birds to do it again . . ."

Even though he was angry with Dad, every time he heard something said against him, he felt a double flare of outrage and sadness. It wasn't just Nova complaining about their leader anymore.

His mind felt like a small cave reverberating with too many echoes: the destroyed saurian hatchlings deep in the forest; Sylph climbing into a bird nest; a vast winged creature in the stars. He longed to tell someone about his vision, but he dared not mention it to Mom or Dad. If they heard he'd nibbled a mushroom, they'd probably never let him leave the nest again.

If he was smart he'd just forget the whole incident. A poison mushroom had given him a nightmare—that's all it was. But its vividness made it impossible to forget. In his mind he still saw the hot swirl of stars birthing a million winged creatures. They'd had the bodies of chiropters, but naked sails, just like him. *"You are new,"* the voice had said.

It made his heart pound just to think about it. He wasn't sure he wanted to be new, not if it meant he was no longer a chiropter. He didn't care if there *were* others like him. He just wanted Dad and Mom to tell him he was their son, and that he belonged. He'd have to try harder to fit in.

But he could never change the way he looked. And could he ever suffocate his desire to fly? Maybe he could sneak off and do it somewhere no one would see. He'd stay low so not even the birds could spot him.

Ignoring his mother's wishes, he left the sequoia, passing

from tree to tree until he was well out of sight. When he found a good spot he crouched, ready to launch. In his mind he saw Aeolus's amputated sails; his father's grave face, asking him to promise. He sagged against the bark, groaning with frustration.

Something shimmered in his peripheral vision, and Dusk looked around in surprise. On the branch above him he caught sight of a yellow-feathered chest, the underside of a white throat, a beak. A bright eye flashed.

"Teryx?" Dusk said uncertainly.

"Good—it *is* you," Teryx warbled with obvious relief. He hopped into full view. "It was hard to find you, especially when you're not flying anymore."

Dusk snorted. "Of course I'm not flying! After what you did to our newborn."

"I didn't do it," Teryx chirped indignantly.

"Well, your fellow birds, then," Dusk said. He couldn't stop looking at Teryx's beak, wondering just how much damage it could inflict. He'd never quite been able to imagine him doing anything so brutal. But maybe he was wrong.

"There are many birds in our flock who hate chiropters," Teryx said.

"But why?" Dusk demanded.

"They think all beasts are murderers for hunting saurian eggs. We too are egg layers, remember. And when they saw you flying, they were furious. They don't want you near our skies. Who's to say you won't suddenly decide our eggs are prey?"

Dusk was about to object, but he remembered Sylph and her friends clambering into the nest with murderous intent.

Still, that was different: retaliation, not hunting.

"Was it me they meant to kill?" Dusk asked hesitantly.

"Yes. And they still think they succeeded. But when I saw the body, I could tell the markings were different, and I knew it wasn't you. I didn't say anything, in case they were determined to keep trying."

"It was a friend of my sister's."

"I had nothing to do with it. Believe me," Teryx said. "We're not all so bloodthirsty."

Dusk remembered the terrible dawn chorus the birds had sung after they'd murdered Aeolus.

"Your mother seemed pretty bloodthirsty when she chased me off."

"She's protective," said Teryx. "Any mother would have done the same. After all, you were in our territory."

"You're in mine now."

"I know, but I came to tell you something." Teryx's head jerked from side to side, as though checking to make sure no one was watching. "There's something dangerous coming."

Dusk's heart kicked. "On the island?"

"On the mainland."

"Is it saurians?"

"No. Felids. A large group of them, migrating up the coastline."

"What kind of creatures are they?" he asked. He'd never heard of felids.

"Beasts," Teryx told him.

Dusk exhaled in relief. Fellow beasts. "Why would they be a danger?"

"They're hunting other beasts," Teryx said.

"But that's not allowed!" Dusk exclaimed. "Is it?"

"They're attacking birds too. They've been eating eggs out of our nests. I think that must be one of the reasons my flock killed your newborn. They're worried you chiropters might start doing the same."

"But we've never tried to eat your eggs!"

"I know," said Teryx. "But my flock is scared. And you should be too. These felids are monsters."

"Are they big?" Dusk asked, trying to steady his voice.

"Bigger than us."

"But we'll be safe on the island," Dusk said hopefully.

"Not if they decide to cross."

"It's really hard, though." Dusk remembered what his father had said. "The sand bridge doesn't last for long. They probably wouldn't even spot it."

"It depends on how vigilant they are," the bird replied.

"It's fine for you," said Dusk, suddenly feeling resentful. "All you have to do is fly away if they come."

"You can fly too."

"I'm forbidden, thanks to your lot. Anyway, I'm the only one who *can* fly."

"We can't take our nests with us," Teryx pointed out.

"That's true," said Dusk, regretting his outburst.

"I told you because I want you to be ready. In case they come," Teryx said. His head flicked about nervously. "I should go now."

"Wait. Why are you telling me all this?"

"Yesterday I saw you stop the others from killing the eggs."

Dusk stiffened. He'd been hoping desperately that no one had seen.

"Don't worry," Teryx chirped quickly. "I didn't tell anyone else."

Dusk swallowed. If the birds had found out, there surely would have been more attacks, maybe even a war.

"They were friends of the chiropter who got killed," Dusk said, feeling he needed to explain. "They wanted revenge, so they decided to act alone. Our leader didn't tell them to do it."

"I understand. Thank you for stopping them," said Teryx, and he fluttered up and disappeared among the branches.

"Dad, I spoke with the bird again," Dusk told Icaron quietly.

It was near midday, and he'd found his father alone in the nest.

"You sought him out?" Icaron asked sharply.

"He found *me*," Dusk said quickly. "I never left our territory. He flew down to tell me they'd seen something dangerous coming toward the island. A group of beasts called felids."

"I know them well," Icaron said, without any sign of concern.

"You do?"

"Of course. They're active members of the Pact. They're our allies."

"Oh." Dusk felt both relieved and a bit ridiculous. "But the bird said they were hunting other beasts."

His father grunted dismissively. "No beast has ever eaten the flesh of others, except as carrion. I wouldn't pay any attention to this bird. We've seen what treachery they're capable of."

"But Teryx—"

"You know his name?" Dad's voice sounded angry.

Dusk nodded silently, cursing himself for this slip.

"And does he know yours?"

"Yes," murmured Dusk.

"That was foolish, Dusk, very foolish. And what else does this bird know about you? Does he know you're the leader's son?"

"No! I don't think so anyway. I never told him."

"How do you know he wasn't sent by his elders to spread panic and confusion among us?"

In his father's face and posture was the same bullying fierceness Dusk had seen when he sparred with Nova or snapped at Sylph. Dusk felt himself shrinking.

"I didn't think—" he began feebly.

"Who's to say the birds aren't trying to scare us off the island altogether?"

Dusk was mortified. He'd never even considered these things.

"I expect more of you, Dusk," his father said, more gently now. "Birds are notorious liars."

Dusk swallowed. "He didn't lie about the saurian bones."

Icaron's eyes flared again and for a moment Dusk cringed, afraid he was going to be bitten. But then his father sighed and looked away. "True enough, but I think his aim was to kindle paranoia in our colony. It wasn't kindly meant. As for this latest piece of information, ask yourself, Dusk, why a bird would want to help us, especially after what they did to Aeolus?"

"Maybe he was just . . ." He trailed off, wanting desperately to explain how Teryx was thanking him for saving the bird nest, but knowing he couldn't without getting Sylph in a great deal of trouble.

He sighed. He supposed his father's theory might be right, but he still didn't think Teryx was lying. If Teryx had wanted to hurt the colony, he could have told his flock about Sylph's attack on the nest, and created a hurricane of trouble.

"I just thought it was best to tell you," he said humbly, unable to meet his father's gaze. "In case the bird was telling the truth."

"You were right to tell me, Dusk. But ignore what the bird says. This island has kept us safe for twenty years. The water recedes for a very brief time twice a day. Not many beasts would notice, or attempt a crossing."

"But if they did—"

"Right now, the only creatures that should concern us are the birds. Other beasts have never been a danger. The felids are friends. I've never known them to be anything but honorable and peace-loving."

Dusk wasn't sure it was wise to completely ignore the bird's warning. He caught himself wondering what Nova would say, and felt disloyal.

"You don't need to worry so much," his father said, and nuzzled him.

"I just wonder if the colony should know," he blurted.

"Trust me, we can spare the colony any more anxiety.

You're shrewd, Dusk, but you're still a newborn. You can't know everything. One day perhaps, but not yet."

Dusk knew he was being gently rebuked, but still felt a grateful rush of reassurance. His father was leader, and had been for decades. Of course everything would be all right.

That afternoon Dusk glided in the clearing. He was hungry, and tired of scrabbling for bugs on the bark. Most of all he was tired of being a skulking recluse. He didn't want to lick any more poisonous mushrooms and hear voices and see the stars shifting. What he really wanted was for life to go back to normal—or as normal as it could be after all that had happened. It was good to be in the air again, and maybe he didn't need to fly. He'd try to forget all about it.

He hunted for a while, trying not to care that the other chiropters still steered clear of him. Perhaps that would change in time. He caught some food, including a rather interesting-tasting snipe fly. When he first saw his sister he thought she was going to ignore him. His heart warmed when she pulled alongside.

"Thanks," she said. "For not telling."

"I did actually," he said.

She looked at him in shock. "What?"

"Just now. You're in a lot of trouble. Dad's waiting for you at the roost."

Her dismay made her stutter. "But you . . . you said you weren't going to—"

"I didn't tell," he admitted, unable to torture her a second longer. "Your secret's safe. Just having a bit of a joke."

"That was mean!"

"Well, you've been mean to me."

"How?"

"Avoiding me."

"*You're* the one who's been avoiding *me*, always off lurking in the forest."

Dusk sighed, seeing her point. "Well, I'm done lurking."

"Good."

Dusk didn't feel like they needed to say anymore, and they went their separate ways, but he felt lighter than he had in quite some time.

When he returned to the roost later in the afternoon, he was pleasantly tired, and his belly was full. Mom and Dad were already there, and Sylph joined them before long. As they set about grooming themselves and each other, Dusk felt that somehow things were right with his family again, despite all the secrets they kept from one another. Maybe every family had secrets—though he doubted anyone else's could be as numerous and complicated as his own. There was, however, one question he did want answered.

"Dad," he asked, "how did you get to be leader?"

He saw Sylph look up, and locked eyes with her for a second before turning his attention to their father.

"Back on the mainland," Dad said, "when we broke with our colony, we needed someone who would lead our four families."

"But wasn't Proteus the oldest?" Sylph asked innocently.

"He was indeed," Mistral replied. "And he would've made an excellent leader. Without his guidance, I'm not sure the rest of us would've had the confidence to break with the Pact."

"Oh," Sylph said. "So why wasn't he leader?"

"I wanted him to be," Icaron replied, looking at her closely, as if sniffing out her motivation for asking. "All of us did. But he refused. He said he was too old, that we needed someone stronger and younger to take us through difficult times. He asked me to be leader. To be honest, I wasn't eager for such a responsibility, but Sol and Barat urged me as well."

Dusk smiled triumphantly over at Sylph. Jib's story had made it sound like Dad had bullied and cheated his way into being leader, but he hadn't even wanted it! Maybe now Sylph would be a little less critical of their father.

As night came on, the family settled down alongside one another in their nest. Dusk felt so contented that he was half asleep before he noticed something was wrong. The cloudless sky glowed faintly with the day's last light, and a gentle breeze scented the clearing—but there was no dusk chorus.

"The birds aren't singing," he whispered to Sylph.

"Maybe there's a weather change coming," she said drowsily. "That sometimes makes them go quiet."

Dusk sniffed and sipped the air. It didn't smell or taste like bad weather on the way. He could only remember one or two times in his whole life that the birds hadn't sung at dusk, and the silence unnerved him now. He looked over at his father, who returned his gaze calmly.

"Go to sleep, Dusk," he said. "Everything's all right."

He didn't think he'd able to sleep, but he did—

And woke later, the clearing awash in silver moonlight, and

everyone on the sequoia asleep but him.

The sky was still clear, with no sign of a weather change. Dusk hoped there'd been some harmless reason for the birds' silence, but he worried it had something to do with the felids on the mainland. Were the birds too wary to sing? Were they in hiding?

From far away came a noise Dusk had never heard before. It was the type of small sound that he imagined could only be heard at night, when noises seemed to carry so much farther. He turned his face toward it—a strange, low chirping, though not something he'd ever known a bird to make. There was an answering trill of chirps and then no more. Only the drone of insects reached his ears.

The fur on the nape of his neck bristled. What if there was something on the island? What if those carnivorous felids had crossed over? Did felids chirp? It seemed unlikely.

He wanted to wake Dad and ask him to send out sentries, but he knew it was futile. His father would say there was no need. The birds were just trying to scare the chiropters and drive them off the island.

Slowly he crawled away from his family, out along the branch toward the clearing. A full moon blazed down, illuminating the forest.

He flew. He hadn't forgotten how. The knowledge resided in his muscles and nerves and awoke instantly with his first flap. Sails a blur, he rose through the empty clearing. The moon gave him all the light he needed.

He would be the colony's sentry. He was small and invisible in the night, and he could fly away at any time. He almost wished there *were* some threat on the island; then maybe they'd see how brave and useful he was, and shun him no longer.

Within seconds he'd passed the sequoia's summit. His stomach gave a small, giddy plunge as the silver horizons soared out around him. He wheeled, orienting himself. For the first time in his life, he could see the entire island, and it seemed shockingly small. He'd spent his entire life here, on this little hump of forest.

He'd never seen the mainland before, a glowing wall of trees that ran forever to the north and south. That was where his father and mother had come from. The world was immense, and showed no signs of stopping.

With his echovision, Dusk saw birds roosting in the high branches, asleep. His dark fur made him part of the night sky. He flew in the direction of the chirping sounds, toward the east shore of the island, and the mainland.

He tasted the air, alert to new odors. He listened hard, occasionally unleashing lightning bolts of sound into the forest to see if there was anything lurking in the branches or undergrowth. He didn't know what he was looking for. He wasn't even sure what felids looked like. He assumed they were four-legged, furred. The dense vegetation could conceal almost anything. And he wasn't prepared to go lower. He liked being up high, out of harm's reach.

He was surprised by how quickly the trees ended, and suddenly he was soaring out over water. Shards of the moon reflected on its surface. The island was still encircled, separated from the mainland. It was safe. Nothing could come across. He made a slow pass, wondering if it was high or low tide—and then he saw the bridge.

It was just as his father had described it, a pathway of sand connecting the mainland to the island. It was very narrow, and getting narrower even as he watched. Water lapped at its edges, washing over it altogether near the shore as the tide rose.

Dusk gave a chuckle of relief. The path couldn't be visible more than a few minutes at a time. What beast would see it unless they came right to the water's edge? And why would they? The mainland shore was steeply rocky: it would be a difficult climb down, and an even harder one back up.

As he banked toward the island, he sent down a volley of echoes. The water was a sheet of pale silver, the sandbridge a speckled path of even more intense light, etched with paler patterns. Dusk frowned, dipping lower and casting out a tighter burst of sound. The sandy path flared once more in his head.

On the path's soft surface were countless footprints of a four-toed paw.

There were so many that they all melded together, dissolving even as they filled with lapping water.

They all pointed toward the island.

CHAPTER 11

The Massacre

CARNASSIAL STALKED ON silent paws through the under-growth. His pupils, fully dilated, drank in the night, rendering the forest in luminous purples and grays. The moon was bright. It was a perfect time to hunt. All around him, great trees towered overhead. Every few steps he paused, ears pricked, his paws alert to any vibrations in the ground. Trailing behind him on either side, the rest of his prowl kept pace, guided by the occasional hunting chirps he made high in his throat.

This island would be a perfect hunting ground. It was cut

off from the mainland and the beasts here wouldn't have heard of them. Carnassial and his prowl could fill their bellies on easy prey. And after they'd lost the advantage of surprise, the water would keep the beasts from escaping. As the hunted became more wary, the hunters would become more skilled. It would prove an excellent training ground.

All around him Carnassial heard small groundlings rustle through the undergrowth, going about their night's business. He was not interested in them right now. In his nostrils was the scent of carrion. He'd picked it up almost the instant he'd set foot on the beach. It lured him deeper into the forest. The smell excited him; its strength meant it came from a large animal. It meant easy food. But even more important, the carrion might be a lure for other scavenging beasts, and Carnassial and his prowl could lie in wait, and observe what kind of creatures lived on this island.

Up ahead was a clearing drenched in moonlight. The smell was stronger, and Carnassial proceeded more cautiously, knowing that even the rasp of a leaf against his fur might alert other creatures. He sniffed, lapped the air with his tongue, and found the source.

At the edge of the clearing, a giant wing dangled lifelessly from a redwood. It seemed so out of place in the forest that Carnassial had to stare a few seconds, just to make sure it was really there. It was a quetzal wing. He crouched low in the scrub, chirping for his prowl to do the same. He slithered on his belly for a better angle, and saw, silhouetted by moonlight, the quetzal's bony head, decomposed to its skull, the eyeballs long since claimed by insects. Carnassial crawled slowly forward. The meat of the saurian's body had already been stripped. All that was left were the membranous wings and the cartilage, rotting and sending up the stink that had lured Carnassial. There was nothing left worth eating, and his stomach yowled indignantly.

He peered across the clearing at a massive sequoia. He'd never seen a tree with such a thick trunk. His eyes lifted higher. Even the branches were huge, especially in the tree's midregion. If the moon hadn't been so bright, he probably never would have noticed them: the hundreds of dark little shapes nestled in the niches along the sides of the mighty branches. One of the forms stirred in its sleep, flaring its sails briefly.

Carnassial gave a low chirp and Miacis drew alongside.

"Chiropters," he whispered to her.

His glands tingled painfully as saliva seeped over his molars, lubricating them for shearing. It was all he could do to restrain himself from charging up the tree, but he was familiar with these creatures, and knew he needed a plan if his prowl were to be successful on this hunt.

He breathed his instructions to Miacis.

Her lips pulled back and he could see her teeth wetly gleaming.

"Good," she said.

Dusk flew for the sequoia with all the speed he could force from his spent muscles.

Clouds were beginning to scud in front of the moon, and he worried he wouldn't be able to find his way home. But then he saw a single tree rising ghostly silver above all the others, and knew that must be his sequoia. The tallest in the forest; that's why his father had picked it. Closer now, and he saw the clearing open up. Angling his sails, he plunged down into it.

He'd been gripped with fear that he'd return to a massacre, but all was silent as he spiraled past the mighty branches toward his family's nest. His pulses of echovision showed him nothing but chiropters nestled in the bark, asleep. He'd meant to start bellowing warnings the moment he was close enough, but now felt unsure. Everything seemed so normal. Did he want to start a panic? All he'd seen were footprints. How did he even know they belonged to felids?

At the very least he'd have to wake his father, there was no question. He landed near their nest, almost gagging with breathlessness. The moon and stars were obscured by clouds now, and it was very dark. He hurried to Icaron, nudging his gray-streaked head.

"Dad? Dad?"

For a moment, the nearness of his parents, their scent, the familiar bark beneath his claws, made his fears seem ridiculous.

His father stirred and opened his eyes.

"Dusk, what's wrong?"

"Something's crossed over to the island," he panted.

"Where have you been?"

"I went to the bridge."

"Have you been flying?" his mother said, rising.

Dusk glanced over and saw Sylph was awake now too,

blinking and looking a bit bewildered.

"What's going on?" she asked.

"I saw footprints in the sand," Dusk said. "Lots of them."

"Describe them," his father said.

Dusk did, and saw his parents exchange glances.

"A bird has been filling Dusk's head with nonsense about a felid attack."

"You never told me any of this," Mom said.

"I saw no need. The bird was just trying to make trouble."

"Dusk has been talking to birds now?" Sylph asked.

"You shouldn't have gone off alone at night," Dusk's mother scolded him. "And you know you're not to fly! What did this bird say to you?"

"The bird claims," Icaron explained with deliberate calm, "that a group of felids has been marauding the mainland, attacking birds and beasts."

"So were they felid prints I saw?" Dusk asked.

"Possibly," said Icaron, "but I'm not convinced there's any reason for alarm."

"The felids have always been peaceful," Mistral said, but Dusk thought she sounded worried.

"I'll tell the elders in the morning," Icaron said. "We should let everyone know there may be felids on the island. We've led a sheltered life here, and I don't want any of our families to be afraid."

From the branches below came a chiropter's shriek.

Something flashed past near the trunk. Dusk caught sight of a long body and tail before it disappeared higher up the tree.

"There's something in the sequoia!" a voice shouted.

"Don't be afraid!" Dusk heard his father call out. "They're fellow beasts and mean you no harm."

A second creature leaped up onto their branch, near the trunk, and Dusk froze. The beast paused for the briefest of moments, just long enough to turn a blunt face straight at Dusk. Its eyes flashed light and Sylph screamed. Then it crouched and was gone, bounding higher.

"Dad?" Sylph quavered. "Are those felids?"

"Yes," said Icaron.

"What are they doing?" Mom breathed, her voice tight.

"I'll speak to them," said Icaron, "it's all right."

A third felid streaked past, then seconds later a fourth. From overhead came a growing chorus of surprise and alarm. Dusk was shaking so hard he worried he would slide off the branch.

"What is that?" someone cried from above.

"Look out!"

"Where'd it go?"

"I can't see!"

"It's coming!"

"Jump!"

Then the screaming began, the kind of terrible, high-pitched sound beasts make only when they are in peril or frightful pain. Dusk looked at his father, hoping for some impossible explanation. Vicious snarls raked the darkness.

The felids were hunting.

The maelstrom of noise intensified and boiled closer. Claws scrabbled furiously on bark; parents cried out the names of their children. From the clearing Dusk heard the whisper of sails filling as chiropters leaped blindly into the darkness to escape. His nostrils flinched and his eyes watered as the air was shot through with a thick musk exuded by the felids in their frenzy.

His father was shouting something at him, but Dusk could scarcely hear him, he sounded so far away.

"Dusk, Sylph, get ready to jump!"

Near the trunk, a felid had pulled itself onto their branch, and this time it did not move on. It was long and sly, twice his father's size, with a gray, black-spotted body and a long tail banded with white. Sharply pointed ears folded back against the sweat-matted fur of its head. Its jaws seemed small until they opened and became huge, rimmed with thin, sharp teeth at the front, and thicker ones at the back.

"Dusk!" his mother shouted, but he could not turn away.

"Dad, come on!" he wailed to his father.

"Go, Dusk!" Icaron said.

He watched in awe as his father reared up on his hind legs and flared his sails, seeming to double in size.

"Stop this!" he roared at the felid. "We are allies! This must stop!"

Amazingly, Icaron's voice carried above the din, and for a strange moment, the snarling and shrieking seemed to fade away. The felid at the end of the branch tilted its chin in surprise, ears twitching. Dusk felt Sylph tugging at him, but he could not leave his father.

"We are all united as beasts!" Icaron shouted. "We have survived the saurians together. We have shared the earth in peace."

"Are you the leader, then?" The felid's low growl seemed to emanate from his belly.

"I am Icaron, the leader of this colony. What is your name?"

"Carnassial." The felid's lips pulled back as he answered, revealing large, four-crested teeth at the rear of his jaws.

"And where is the leader of your prowl?" Icaron demanded.

"I am he."

"Then you must know Patriofelis."

Dusk saw the felid flinch in distaste.

"We have parted company with Patriofelis."

"He is a wise ruler."

"He has doomed himself to extinction. The world has changed, but his appetites have remained the same. Ours have not."

"Does Patriofelis know you are hunting fellow beasts?"

Carnassial made no reply.

"I implore you to stop," Icaron said. "Stop this barbaric thing, and let us live in peace. It has always been the way."

"No more," said Carnassial—and he sprang.

Icaron jumped backward, but the felid caught him in his paws, and brought him crashing down against the bark.

"Dad!" Dusk cried out.

"Fly! Fly!" his father shouted to him, even as he thrashed to free himself.

Dusk saw the felid's jaws part, saw the wet flash of teeth in the dim light, and then his mother shoved him hard and he was falling off the branch. He unfurled his sails and flapped. The air was filled with frantic chiropters, gliding across the clearing to the safety of the far trees.

"Mom! Sylph!" he cried.

"Stay with your sister," he heard his mother shout, and realized she'd remained on the branch to help his father.

Hovering, he looked back at his parents, furiously tangled together with Carnassial. What should he do? He heard his sister anxiously call out for him, and he swiveled and flapped after her. He was shaking so hard he felt he would come apart at the joints. He staggered through the air, casting out sound to see better, and caught up with Sylph.

"Where's Mom and Dad?" she panted.

"They're . . ." He didn't know how to say it. "They're fighting with the felid."

Her voice trembled. "I can barely see, Dusk."

"I'll be your eyes," he told her. "We're almost across the clearing."

All around them were other chiropters, trying to stay together, calling out to one another in the pitch dark. Dusk wished he could shut out all their chittering, for it was a terrible echo of his own frenetic thoughts.

What do we do once we land?

Where should we go?

Where was safe?

The shrieks from the sequoia were growing fainter, but with every flap of his sails, Dusk felt a wrenching grief. Mom and Dad were still there. He was a coward. He'd left them fighting the felid all alone. But he was scared, more scared than he'd ever imagined, and it was a struggle not to flap higher and higher and take himself away from the forest and the felids altogether.

But Sylph was beside him and he needed to help her see, for the trees were looming before them now. With his echovision he lit the nearest redwood and searched the weave of silver branches for an easy landing place. There was a smear of movement off to one side, and when Dusk sang out more echoes, he saw a long body pressed flat against the bark, triangular ears jutting from its skull.

"There's a felid in the tree!" he bellowed. "Don't land!"

At the same instant, Dusk heard chiropters screeching high above him from the same redwood.

"They're up here too!" a strangled voice shouted.

Dusk suddenly realized what the felids had done. They'd climbed not just the sequoia but all the surrounding trees, so they could lie in wait for the escaping chiropters. Then they could drive their prey from tree to tree until they were caught.

"Turn away!" Dusk shouted.

"Where? Where are they?" a chiropter cried near Dusk's left sail.

With his echovision he saw the felid lunge to the end of the branch, jaws ready. In the confusion some chiropters just kept sailing on.

"Turn back!" he told Sylph, then flapped hard, flying past her and trying to pull ahead of the other hapless gliders.

"There's a felid, dead ahead!" he shouted to each of them as he passed. He had only a few seconds. An elderly chiropter continued to sail straight for the tree. Maybe he was deaf, or just too scared and confused to comprehend the gale of shouts and screams that now filled the clearing.

"Hey, stop!" Dusk shouted once more. "There's one in the tree!"

The chiropter was already flaring his sails to land, and when he finally glanced back at Dusk in alarm, it was too late. Though he tried to bank away, he'd lost too much speed. He stalled, falling toward the branch. As Dusk watched helplessly, the felid rose up on its hind legs and snapped the old chiropter, thrashing, into its jaws.

Dusk veered away. Some of the other chiropters had swerved to land on nearby branches and were desperately scrambling out of sight. Others had managed to turn around completely and were sailing back for the sequoia. Sylph was among them. He caught up to her.

"Dusk, is that you?"

"It's me."

"We need a safe place to land."

"We'll be fine," he said. "We'll be fine."

Dusk's stomach tightened, knowing they were sailing back toward more waiting felids.

"Can you see Mom and Dad?" Sylph asked piteously.

Frantically he began taking sonic glances of the sequoia, trying to find them. There was too much frenzied movement: images drawn in lightning strokes. He picked out his family's branch, but saw no sign of the felid, or his parents. What had happened to them? Dad would have fought his way free, with Mom's help. He was strong and fearless, he couldn't be killed. And his mother, she had long sight; she could see the felids coming; they'd both be fine. But where were they?

He pulled his gaze back to Sylph's glide path, seeking out

a likely landing site. He had to concentrate on keeping the two of them safe. Higher in the branches he caught sight of one felid, feeding intently on a dead chiropter. It was an unrecognizable tangle of guts and flayed skin. Dusk could smell the carnage from here: blood and feces and urine and sweat sickeningly intermingled. The thought that the chiropter might be one of his parents overwhelmed him with nausea, and he retched in midair.

Dusk looked lower and saw another felid, prowling the branches, waiting. They were clever beasts, not just hunting for themselves, but herding prey for their fellows.

"We're going deeper into the forest," he told his sister. "There's too many of them in the sequoia."

Sylph's glide path was already worryingly low, and Dusk knew he couldn't take her very far before she'd need to land. He flew in front, probing the darkness with his sonic sight, swinging away from their home, where chiropters still scrabbled half blind along the branches, throwing themselves into the air. Dusk guided his sister into the forest and to a safe landing site.

As they touched down on the branch, Dusk heard a terrified squeal, and spotted a group of chiropters cowering together in a deep furrow in the bark.

"It's all right," he whispered. "It's just Dusk and Sylph."

There were five of them, and as they looked up he recognized Jib and four other newborns, all separated from their families.

"There's no room for you," Jib hissed at Dusk. "Go away!"

"I don't think you should stay here," Dusk said. "If one of

them passes, they'll sniff you out, and you're trapped."

"You just want our hiding place," Jib said.

"We should fight them," said Sylph angrily, "not hide. If we all fought together—"

"You don't know what you're talking about," snapped Dusk.

"We're not so weak," Sylph said. Even now she was so hot-tempered he was worried she'd do something rash.

"We need to get away from them."

"You sound just like Dad," she retorted. "Always running away."

"You saw it attack!" Dusk hissed at her. "You saw its teeth."

Sylph said nothing, her flanks heaving.

"We need to hide." His voice shook. "And wait."

"Come with us," Sylph told Jib and the other newborns.

"My parents told us to wait here for them," said one of them.

"They said they'd be right back," said another.

"The felids will kill you if they find you here," Dusk said.

"Dusk can see in the dark," Sylph said. "He can see them coming. He'll keep you safe."

Dusk was not sure he could do anything of the sort. His stomach was still slewing about inside him, and the urge to retch was almost overwhelming. He was amazed at his sister's confidence in him. He sent out quick barrages of hunting clicks and scanned the branches all around, making sure nothing was slinking closer.

From the sequoia, the sounds of carnage still wafted through the night. How long had this been going on? Forever, it seemed. He desperately wanted to find Mom and Dad, but knew it was far too dangerous to go creeping back to the tree. He wished Dad could tell him what to do. Instinctively he wanted to keep moving. He didn't like where they were. It was far too open and vulnerable to attack.

"We're going deeper into the forest," Dusk decided.

"But how will our parents find us?" Jib asked, sounding scared for the first time. "I'm staying right here."

The other newborns weakly muttered their agreement.

In his echovision Dusk caught a smudge of movement.

"Something's coming," he rasped.

He sent out another quick volley of sound and spotted a felid chasing a chiropter, headed in their direction. The chiropter finally jumped and glided away, and the felid paused, tasting the air with its tongue. Its eyes flashed as they turned toward Dusk. He flattened his body, holding his breath, hoping his body looked like bark.

The felid took two slow, deliberate steps, head low, nostrils flaring and contracting.

"We have to go," he whispered to Sylph. "It's coming this way."

"Come with us," Sylph urged the other newborns one last time.

Dusk didn't wait. Moving as quickly as he could, he unfurled his sails and leaped off the branch, flapping for the next tree. He looked back at the felid, no more than twenty feet distant. It bounded toward them.

"Sylph, now!"

His sister followed, and then, to his surprise, Jib and the

other newborns scrambled from their hiding place and sailed after her. Seconds later the felid pounced down onto the branch, a snarl uncoiling from its throat.

"Follow me!" said Dusk, knowing he needed to lead them, for they couldn't see far in the dark. He glanced back, and in horror saw the felid jump after them. It was surprisingly agile in the air, using its bushy tail to steer. Down it came onto the next tree, barely skidding on the branch. Dusk hadn't thought it could jump so far.

Flapping, he steered the newborns away. The trees grew so close together here that the felid pursued them easily, running from one branch to the next, jumping whatever gaps Dusk tried to put in its way. The strength and speed of the felid's legs was easily outpacing the chiropters' powerless glides. It would soon overtake them.

Peering back once more, Dusk saw the felid touch down on a slender branch that bent steeply, spilling the felid off. Spitting, it landed clumsily on a lower branch, but quickly recovered, and was soon back on their trail. Dusk could hear its panting growing louder, a whine of anticipation echoing in its mouth.

"It's getting closer!" Jib yelled.

"Split up!" yelled another newborn.

It was a natural impulse, but Dusk knew it would cost one of them his life. He had another idea.

"Wait!" he said. He kept casting around desperately with sound, and finally found what he was looking for: a small clearing, and on the other side, a branch that tapered to a very thin end.

"There!" he shouted out to them. "Land right there near the end! It's too skinny for the felid!"

When Sylph touched down beside him he felt the branch tremble. That was good. One after another the other five chiropters clutched the bark. The branch bobbed slowly up and down with their weight.

Dusk turned back and saw the felid pause on the other side of the clearing. It could make the jump across, but it seemed to realize the branch was too narrow and wouldn't take its weight. It crouched, head swaying.

"We're safe," Dusk panted. "It won't jump."

They all clung hold, staring fearfully at the predator.

The felid looked carefully all around, then hopped down onto some lower branches.

"What's it doing?" Sylph whispered.

"It's giving up," said Jib.

"I can't see it anymore," one of the other newborns said.

Dusk tracked it with his echovision. Below, the felid jumped across the small clearing.

"It's in our tree now," Dusk said. The felid bounded swiftly toward the trunk and began to haul itself up with its claws. Dusk could see this was hard work for the felid. It wasn't adept at long, vertical climbs. But finally it reached their branch, which was thick enough near the trunk for the creature to take a few steps out. Its eyes blazed starlight. One of the newborns screamed. The felid was no more than twenty feet away.

"Sail!" Jib cried.

"Wait!" Dusk urged him. "It can't come any closer!"

The felid sniffed, and made an excited chirping sound in his throat.

He won't come, Dusk thought. *The branch is too thin.*

The felid came. It took two careful steps and paused, feeling its balance. The branch bounced up and down. Dusk and Sylph and all the other newborns pressed against one another, edging as close as they dared to the end. Dusk studied the felid's feet: there was no way it could come any closer without teetering off. Its claws were fully extended, stabbing into the bark. It took one more step, nearly lost its balance, and then stopped, breathing heavily. The branch swayed dangerously.

Dusk could smell its hungry breath from here, heavy and sickly with meat. It had already eaten tonight. Dusk had a sudden fear that it would speak to him; he did not want to hear its terrible snarl of a voice.

The felid took a step back, and Dusk hoped it was giving up. But then the predator sank its claws deep into the bark and began to stand, then crouch, stand, crouch, making the branch rise and fall, ever more quickly, until it was whipping up and down.

"Hold on!" Sylph shouted.

The felid was trying to shake them loose! Dusk had to dig in hard to stop himself being flung into the air. The nighttime world blurred dizzyingly. How long would the felid keep it up?

"Sylph?" he said, his voice warbling. "Are you okay?"

She grunted, too scared to form words.

"Whatever you do, don't let go!" he told her.

Up and down the branch lashed. It was so frightening, so maddening, that part of Dusk wanted to let go and fly free. He hoped none of the others felt the same deadly temptation.

The branch slowed. Vision swimming, Dusk looked back at the felid. It was panting, saliva clotted at the corners of its maw. From its throat it released a shriek of frustration that nearly jolted Dusk from the branch.

"Clever," the felid said in a low growl. "I'll be back for you."

It leaped down through branches, working its way toward the sequoia in search of better hunting.

For a while no one said anything. Dusk readjusted his claws in the bark, listened to his heartbeats slow.

"I thought he'd never stop," he said, mouth parched.

"Fine for you," grumbled Jib. "You could just fly away."

"But he didn't, did he," Sylph said.

Dusk said nothing, guiltily thinking of all the moments when his body had wanted to fly away.

"And the skinny branch was his idea, too," Sylph said fiercely. "He saved your lives."

"It was just lucky," Dusk said. "I wasn't sure it would work."

"Really?" Sylph asked, aghast.

"Well, I was pretty sure, but how do I know how heavy a felid is?"

Sylph did not speak for a moment, horrified. "Well," she finally said, "it worked, and that's the important thing."

"How many of them are there?" Jib asked.

Dusk shook his head. "I don't think anyone's had time to count."

"Feels like hundreds," whispered a newborn, shuddering.

"They have light in their eyes," said Sylph.

"They can hunt at night," Dusk said. "They see better than us."

They fell silent again. Dusk scanned the trees with sound, and saw more and more clusters of chiropters gliding and running from the sequoia, heading deeper into the forest. But he didn't see any felids in pursuit this time. He listened and heard hardly any shrieking or snarling. Could it be over?

"It's quieter now," he said. "I'm going to find Mom and Dad."

"Don't go," said Sylph; and he'd never heard her sound so pleading. "We can't see without you."

He noticed that the other newborns, including Jib, were staring at him beseechingly, but were too proud to beg him to stay.

He waited with them, in anguish, until a large group of chiropters glided past, one of them whispering repeatedly for Jib.

"I'm here, I'm here!" Jib called back, almost too loudly.

Looking at him, Dusk saw not an obnoxious bully, but a frightened newborn, overjoyed at hearing his mother's voice. It was a sound he himself was craving.

Jib's parents landed on the branch and made a fuss of their son.

"Have you seen Icaron?" Dusk asked them. "Icaron or Mistral?"

"No, I'm sorry," Jib's mother told him, and it was the first time a chiropter outside his own family had looked at him with any tenderness. "It was so dark, and everything was so confusing."

"Stay here with Jib's family," Dusk told Sylph. "I want to see if I can find them."

"You're sure?" Sylph asked, still not wanting him to go.

"I need to," he said, emotion choking his voice. He didn't want to leave Sylph either, but she was safe now. She had some adults with her. He couldn't banish from his mind the image of the felid attacking Mom and Dad, jaws and claws whirling. He needed to know they were all right. Sylph looked at him and seemed to understand.

She gave a quick nod. "Okay."

"I'll come back."

He cast around thoroughly with his eyes and ears before taking flight, and then flapped cautiously through the branches, toward the sequoia. He passed many chiropters, calling out softly for their mothers and sons, daughters and fathers.

"Have you seen Icaron?" he whispered, fluttering overhead. "Icaron or Mistral?"

Most shook their heads, some gave vague answers; others ignored him altogether, too stupefied with fear and sorrow to hear him or form a reply.

Nearing the sequoia, he gave it a wide berth, wanting to have a good look before he came any closer. He was wary of all the trees around the clearing, knowing they too might contain felids.

He was exhausted, but he wanted to stay airborne, even if

he was more noticeable that way. The idea of landing and being easy prey for the felids was too horrible. He wanted to be able to move, in any direction, in a split second.

Except for a ghost of moonlight, it was completely dark now, and Dusk flew almost entirely with echovision. The world was a pulsing silver image that etched itself again and again in his mind's eye.

He decided to take a risk and fly into the clearing. Blazing in him was the need to find his parents. Even if the felids saw him, they couldn't do anything about it. He was well beyond their reach.

He fluttered up the clearing, keeping far away from the branches. The sequoia teemed with felids. They seemed to be everywhere. He started counting, and was surprised when he came to only twenty-six. Surely there'd been more than that! Maybe it was only their large size and deadly speed that had made them seem so many.

They were done hunting. He realized that within seconds. Many of them were still feeding on their prey. Dusk could not look. Others, having already eaten their fill, were stalking lazily along the branches, or were curled up somewhere licking the blood from their paws and muzzles.

They had taken over his tree.

They showed no signs of moving on. A few of them even looked on the verge of sleep, their startling, wide-mouthed yawns making slits of their glowing eyes. They could go to sleep without a second's fear, and Dusk hated them. They'd killed. And now they were stealing his home.

At the outer fringes of the tree Dusk spotted a last, small

group of chiropters rushing along a branch toward the forest. With his echovision, he studied every one of them, but didn't find his parents. A felid glanced down at the fleeing chiropters from above, and then turned away, uninterested. Its belly was full, and it had no desire to hunt.

Dusk spiraled higher, watching the felids, listening. Deep, satisfied purrs emanated from their throats, making his ears flinch with revulsion. On his family's branch lounged Carnassial, the one who had attacked his father. Dusk recognized him from the sharp angles of his face. His long sweaty body was sprawled over the very bark that he and Sylph and his parents slept on every night.

Carnassial turned and addressed a nearby felid.

"It will be excellent practice," he said, "and their flesh is sweet."

"Your strategy was excellent," said the second felid. "Will it work again?"

"They seem a witless bunch," said Carnassial lazily. "They glided back and forth as if they couldn't bear to be separated from their beloved tree. But it would be better for us if they grew wilier. It would hone our skills."

"They'll provide us with food for many, many nights," said the second felid contentedly.

Suddenly Carnassial was on his feet, his eyes flashing in Dusk's direction.

"There's something out there."

"In the clearing?" his companion asked.

"Look," Carnassial said in amazement. "One of them flies!"

Dusk had thought himself invisible in the dark, but he had

clearly underestimated the felid's night vision. Heart pounding, he veered out of the moonlight and into deeper shadow. Even though he knew he couldn't be caught, the mere idea of that creature looking at him was terrifying.

"It's a bird, isn't it?" he heard the second felid say.

"No bird. A flying chiropter," said Carnassial. "See how the world changes?"

Dusk wanted to ask him where his father was, half considered it, but he couldn't bear speaking to this monster. And what if his answer was the one he most dreaded?

"You have a fine tree, chiropter!" Carnassial shouted up at him. "But it's ours now. Fly off and tell your fellows to find a new home."

Dusk could bear it no longer, seeing his beloved sequoia squatted on by these creatures. He could scarcely smell the tree's natural fragrance for the stink of them, and the reek of blood. He didn't like their large moonlit eyes on him.

He dipped into the forest and steered a watchful course around the clearing, back toward where he'd left Sylph. He flew past ragged groups of chiropters, still making their fearful exodus from the sequoia. He spotted one large group assembling on a branch after their glide. At the forefront was Icaron. Dusk streaked joyfully toward him.

"Dad!"

He landed beside his father, who whirled at the sound of his voice.

"Dusk! Dusk, you're all right!" He began sniffing and poking his son's back and flanks to see if he'd been injured.

"I'm all right," Dusk said.

His father wasn't; he saw that instantly. Icaron's left shoulder was slick with blood, and the edge of his sail was badly torn. Looking at the wound sent a sympathetic flash of pain across Dusk's own body. There was something else changed about his father that had nothing to do with the wound. Dusk couldn't quite understand it. Wizened, was the closest he could come to describing it. His father seemed wizened and parched.

"Are you okay, Dad?" His voice wavered.

"Yes. The felid gored me, but it'll heal. Is your sister all right?"

"She's fine. She's waiting with a group of other newborns. I was just heading back to her. Where's Mom?"

Dusk looked around at all the other chiropters warily climbing past them up the tree. He turned back to his father and felt a sudden and terrible weakness sweep through his body. He could not speak at all. But he understood at once why his father looked so dreadfully transformed.

CHAPTER 12

To the Coast

THE NIGHT WAS half over before the colony was fully reunited, deep in the forest, in the shrouded branches of another redwood. Dusk's father had posted sentries all around the tree in a broad perimeter. It was an awful time, almost as bad as the massacre itself, as frantic chiropters tried to find their missing mates and children and parents. Most were lucky; too many weren't. There were names that Dusk heard called out over and over until it became a kind of torture to hear them, and he pressed his head to the bark, trying to block the sounds. All he could think about was his own mother, and how he would never hear her answering cry again.

He and Sylph huddled together alone, whimpering and shivering and staring into the distance. Dad wasn't with them. He was leader and, despite his own grief, he'd had to go off to console and reassure the other families too. Dusk was still struggling to make himself understand that Mom was truly dead. There were split seconds of forgetting, when it seemed impossible, and then he'd have to tell himself it really had happened, and grief would smother him all over again.

"She had echovision like me," he murmured. "She should've seen them coming. She should've been one of the survivors."

But she had tried to help Dad, and Carnassial had seized her instead. Dad had fought to free her, but it was no use. This was what his father had told them earlier.

"I wish he'd died instead," Sylph said, her voice barely audible.

"Sylph!" he said, astonished.

"This is his fault. It is, Dusk, and you know it. You told him what that bird said. He should've warned everyone. Then we would've been prepared. Mom might still be alive."

The thought of Mom beside him, right now, was too much to bear, and he started sobbing again.

"Dad shouldn't have kept it to himself," Sylph fumed. "If the elders knew . . ."

"You can't tell them," he said.

"Why not?" She sounded dangerous.

"You know why. They might blame Dad. They might even

try to overthrow him."

"Maybe that's a good thing."

He knew she didn't mean it, and decided it was safest to make no reply. He didn't want to fuel her anger. He could feel himself bending to his sister's opinion, and it frightened him.

"Dad's pretty badly hurt," he said.

He wanted Sylph to say something reassuring—that their father was strong and would heal quickly—but she was silent.

The moon had set, and the clouds had parted to allow some starlight onto the branches. Dusk watched as his older brother Auster glided down toward him and Sylph. He landed and nuzzled them both.

"Are you two all right?" he asked.

It seemed an absurd question. How could they be all right? But Dusk nodded, grateful for this show of kindness.

"It's hardest for you two," Auster said. "But you'll be fine."

"Is Dad going to be okay?" Dusk asked.

"Of course. There's no one stronger."

Not long afterward, Dad returned to the branch with the three other elders. They settled a ways off and spoke in muted voices, but Dusk could still overhear.

"We're safe for the moment," his father was saying. "The felids' vision is excellent in near dark, but they're not usually night hunters. The full moon made their attack possible. They won't hunt during the day." He paused. "But we must leave before the next sunset."

Dusk looked at Sylph in shock. Leave for where?

"You're suggesting we leave the island?" Nova said.

"My son flew through the clearing after the massacre,"

Icaron said. "The felids have moved into our tree. Dusk over-heard them talking. They mean to stay on the island and feed on us until we're all killed."

There was a brief silence after this devastating news.

"But our home," said Sol, sounding stricken.

"As long as we're here, they will hunt us," said Icaron. "At twilight they'll come again. And the night after. And the night after that. We lost thirty-eight tonight. How many more are you ready to lose? Are you willing to lose your own mates, your own children? I don't want to leave this place either, but I see no other choice."

"Another tree," Barat suggested hurriedly. "The felids can't climb vertically for any distance; they're heavier than we are, and their claws can't bear their weight for long. If we could find a tree with branches that only grew high up, the felids couldn't reach us."

"Even if we found such a tree," said Icaron, "the forest is so dense, the felids could simply jump across from a nearby tree."

"We've become spoiled on the island," Nova said. "We've not known predators for a long time. We were wrong to cut ourselves off from the mainland. If we'd maintained scouts there, we wouldn't have been surprised by the felids."

Dusk glared at Nova, hating her. How could she bring this up now, after what everyone had suffered? What was the point?

"But we shut our eyes and ears to the larger world," Nova went on, "and lived in blissful ignorance. We paid for it tonight."

Now Dusk shifted uneasily. Nova couldn't have known about Teryx's warning, but her criticism of Icaron was unnervingly pointed. He glanced at Sylph, knowing what she must be thinking. Dad had ignored the felid threat, and left the colony vulnerable. Dusk waited for his father's angry rebuttal, but surprisingly none came. He wondered if Dad was just too exhausted and stunned. Or maybe he himself felt Nova was right, and was too guilty to deny it.

"Perhaps we could learn wiliness again," Sol suggested hesitantly. "We could remain on the island, but seek out secret places to live. Our smallness can be an asset. We can hide and be vigilant. We certainly won't be taken by surprise again. That's what cost us so dearly tonight."

Dusk listened carefully to his father's reply but could detect not a glimmer of guilt or remorse.

"But the felids will always have the advantage, Sol. They are faster than we are on the trees."

"But we can glide."

"They can jump. We're near blind in the dark, remember. Their eyes let in more moon and starlight."

"But to abandon our island—" Sol said.

"No, Icaron's right."

Dusk blinked in amazement, for it was Nova who'd spoken.

"This island's been our safe haven for twenty years, but it's been invaded now. The felids truly mean to exterminate us; we must leave before they stage another massacre."

No one spoke for a moment; no doubt Dad too was startled by this show of support from Nova.

"But what makes you think it will be any better on the mainland?" Sol demanded. "We've been gone a long time; things may have changed more than we know."

"These felids are rogues," said Icaron. "Their leader, Carnassial, told me as much before he attacked me and Mistral." His voice faltered as he spoke his mate's name, but he went on hoarsely. "They've splintered from Patriofelis's prowl and come here to commit their atrocities in secret. I can't believe all felids have turned flesh eaters. It'll be safer for us on the mainland."

Dusk felt heartsick. The island, the sequoia, was his birthplace—as it was for practically every chiropter in the colony. All his memories lived here, sheltered under the canopies of the redwoods, whispering among the branches.

"It will only be temporary," Icaron told the elders confidently. "On the mainland we'll send word to Patriofelis, and he may be able to deal with these miscreants. Or Carnassial may simply abandon the island once we leave. It will be ours again before long. Now, go and spread the news to your families."

"I don't want to go," Dusk whispered to Sylph.

"It's the right decision," said Sylph, but her voice was small and it was obvious to Dusk she was just trying to be brave. "Nova's right."

"It was Dad's decision," said Dusk firmly.

Their father walked over wearily and nuzzled both of them.

"Are we really leaving?" Dusk asked, trying not to look at his father's wound.

"I'm afraid so. I have to go tell all our family. I'll be back soon. You two need to rest."

As he watched his father leave them, it was all Dusk could do to stop himself whimpering. He didn't want to go to sleep. Sleep was supposed to happen on the sequoia, in the deep furrows of their nest, with Mom and Dad and Sylph and him all together and warm. How could he rest here? His heart raced in panic.

"It's okay, Dusk, he'll be back," his sister said.

She settled down beside him, pressed up tight. He pressed back. It was comforting, but it also reminded him how diminished they were as a family. He and Sylph didn't speak, just lay very still. After a while he stopped trembling. He didn't know if she'd already fallen asleep. It wasn't until his father returned and lay down against them that he felt safe enough to let sleep take him.

The night slowly seeped away, leaving a colorless sky above the forest canopy.

Dusk was not glad of the dawn. He felt like he'd hardly slept at all, waking again and again with a start among unfamiliar branches. When he did lurch back into sleep, his slumbering mind churned. He saw things that were completely unremarkable: insects on a branch, a mushroom, his mother frowning—and yet in his dreams they were charged with doom, and woke him up as if he'd glimpsed a monster, his heart racing.

Throughout the night he'd been aware of activity in the branches, as sentries came on and off duty, and sleepless chiropters talked. Sometimes a newborn cried out and his parents would chitter softly to reassure him.

"How's your wound?" Dusk asked as his father stirred beside him.

"Already feels better," he replied.

It did not look any better to Dusk, but he said nothing more, wanting to believe his father.

"I must ask you to do something," Icaron said to him gravely.

Dusk waited, his stomach aswirl.

"As a father, I don't want to ask, but as a leader I must. We'll be traveling for the coast soon, and I need you to fly on ahead, and scout a path for us."

"Yes," said Dusk, glad of the chance to be useful, and proud that his father thought him brave and capable enough for the task.

"No one else will be as fast or long-sighted as you," said Icaron. "But you must promise to be careful."

Dusk nodded.

"Now, I've got to go and start organizing our journey."

As their father left, Sylph looked at Dusk. "At least you get to fly again."

It was true, but Dusk felt no joy at all.

It took a good part of the morning to organize the colony. Dusk busied himself feeding, though his stomach felt ill. He kept needing to pee. The thought of flying on ahead worried him very much. He was frightened of being spotted by a felid; more frightened simply of being alone. He wanted Dad and Sylph close to him right now.

He was only starting to feel the full terror of last night. At

the time he'd been too busy and frantic just trying to survive.
Now he couldn't believe he'd managed to do anything at all:
flap, think up escape plans.

Shortly before midday they were ready to leave. The felids
were most likely lounging in the sequoia. That was what his
father said. During the day, especially the hottest hours, felids
avoided exertion. They slept and groomed themselves. This
would be the best time for the chiropters to make their exodus to the coast.

"We'll have sentries keeping watch on our flanks, and in
the rear," Icaron told Dusk. "We'll advance behind you. The
moment you spot any felids, fly back and tell us immediately.
Are you ready?"

"Yes."

Dusk set off. He caught himself peering through the trees,
hoping for a glimpse of the sequoia in the distance. He saw
nothing, though he still felt a constriction in his throat. For a
moment his vision blurred. He would never see his mother
again. But he promised himself that one day he'd gaze again
upon his birthplace. He pulled his eyes away from its direction, found a branch, and landed so he could survey the
forest.

He waited until the colony came into view behind him and
then, as his father had instructed, flew ahead a little farther.

As the day wore on, the light shifted through the forest.
The chiropters' journey was slow, and Dusk had to reign in his
impatience. They could only glide so far before landing and
climbing up for another launch. It didn't help that everyone
had started out exhausted, and the day's heat was building to

its peak. Frequent halts were called so they could feed and drink.

Dusk saw no felids, but the birds had returned to the forest. He was aware of them overhead, and in the sky, flitting about. He hoped Teryx would see him and come and speak to him. The forest seemed so serene right now that he couldn't help wondering if it really were necessary to leave the island. Maybe there was some way they could stay, and just be more vigilant. But he needed only remember Carnassial snaring his father in his paws, and his mother leaping in to help her mate.

As long as the felids remained, they could never be safe here.

The forest finally ended and the ground sloped down to a rocky beach. Across the water, the mainland rose. Dusk had seen it just yesterday, though from a greater height. Now, from the trees at the forest's edge, it seemed more imposing, a great wall of rock and dark vegetation that thrust up much higher than their island. It was midafternoon. The tide was still high.

Sylph was off hunting, but Dusk stuck close to his father. He wasn't hungry right now anyway. Dad seemed tired. The blood from his wound had congealed and stiffly matted his fur. Mom would have licked the wound clean, groomed his fur neatly back into shape. Was his father in a lot of pain? Dusk didn't want to ask, not in front of so many chiropters. Now of all times, it wouldn't do for Dad to appear weak.

Icaron sniffed and tasted the air.

"Do you remember the crossing?" he asked the three elders who crouched beside him on the branch.

"We had the wind behind us, as I recall," said Sol. "It hastened us."

"And we launched from the tallest trees," Barat added. "Was it those ones, up there? I think so."

"Even from that height, we needed the wind behind us," said Nova. "And there were some whose glide paths didn't take them safely across."

Dusk peered up into their tree. It wouldn't give them much height to work with.

The elders seemed to be thinking the same thing, for Sol said, "Is it enough to get us across? I'm not sure it is."

They all stared down at the water.

"When will it draw back?" Barat wanted to know.

"Will it be the same time as yesterday?" Dusk asked.

Nova glared at him, and Dusk averted his eyes, knowing he had no place in this discussion. He was forgetting himself. All his life he and Sylph had overheard things they weren't meant to. Because they were Icaron's newborns, they had often skulked around when he was discussing colony matters. Other newborns would have been scolded and sent on their way; and sometimes Dusk was too. But mostly he was allowed to be nearby—especially if he wasn't so rash as to speak out.

"I'm sorry," Dusk said quickly, bowing his head. "It's just that I saw the water drawn back yesterday, and if it happens at the same time, it'll be after sunset."

"Good," said Icaron, turning to the elders. "When we first crossed, we studied the water for several days, do you remember? It drew back twice a day—though then it was not at sunset. It must change over time." He looked at his son.

"And you saw the bridge?"

Dusk nodded. "I think it was over there. A thin strip of sand."

"It didn't last long," said Sol.

"No," agreed Barat.

Nova turned her head to and fro. "I feel no wind."

"Dusk," said Icaron, "can you fly above the trees and tell us the direction of the wind?"

"What of the birds?" Nova asked. "What if they see him?"

"We have greater worries," said Icaron. "Dusk's skills are too valuable to us now. Go on, Dusk."

Dusk leaped eagerly into the air, sails pumping, and spiraled up until he'd cleared the tallest tree on the coast. He circled, testing the air, waiting for it to flatten his fur. But the wind was calm today. He returned to Dad and told him.

"It may change," Icaron said. "It often does late in the afternoon."

"But will it change in our favor?" asked Barat.

Dusk studied the distance between the island and the mainland. The water sparkled. In his mind, he tried to plot the glide path from the trees. It was not encouraging. Most of the time his gaze plunged into the water, well short of the shore. If the sand bridge were exposed, they might be able to land on that, but then they'd be grounded, and slow, and it would be a long scuttle to the mainland. And if they missed the bridge—he shivered as he imagined water soaking into his fur and dragging him down.

"We won't make it without a wind," said Barat, "and even so, that's unlikely to get us up into the trees."

"That slope's rocky; it will be no easy climb," said Nova.

A discouraged silence settled over the elders. Dusk watched his father, waiting for him to pronounce a decisive remedy.

"We must hope the wind shifts," Icaron said. "We have until sunset. Then we must make the best of it."

"We could wait a day, to see if the wind changes," suggested Barat.

"Then we invite another massacre," said Icaron. "We go tonight."

Dusk shifted awkwardly. The crossing would be easy for him. All he had to do was flap. He looked back at the sunlight dancing broken on the water. Would the long day's heat gather and rise as it did in their clearing?

"Dad," he said quietly, "what about thermals?"

His father nodded, understanding. "Go see."

Dusk launched himself out over the water, not flapping this time, but holding his sails rigid. He aimed for the sun's brightest glare. But when he reached it, there was no sudden lift. He flew higher and tried a few more likely places without success. It seemed the water did not store and release the heat as well as the land. Dejected, he banked back to the island.

From his lofty height he spotted a rocky clearing not far from the beach. They hadn't passed through it on their way to the coast, but it looked sizeable. An idea suddenly occurred to him. Skimming the treetops, he flew to the clearing.

Instantly he felt the sun's heat against his belly. He circled, testing the air, and then felt a shove beneath his sails. He would've given a whoop of joy, if he hadn't been so afraid of the felids hearing. Strong thermals soared from the bottom of the clearing. He rode one, wanting to see how high it would take him. In the calm air he wafted up to the treetops, then beyond.

When the lifting power under his sails evaporated, he turned himself to look at the mainland. Quickly he plotted a glide path. They could make it! He was sure of it. If the chiropters rode the thermals to this height, they'd make it across, and not just to the shoreline. They'd be able to land midway up the trees.

Below him, at the edge of the clearing, something shifted in one of the trees. He wheeled, dropping a bit closer and sending out a volley of sound. His echoes returned a picture of a felid crouched tensely on a branch, peering through the forest in the direction of the coast. Just by the hunch of its head and the angle of its ears, Dusk knew it had seen something—his entire colony! Had it been following them all along, tracking their movements? Were there others prowling nearby, just waiting to attack?

As Dusk watched, the felid leaped swiftly down the branches to the ground. But it did not streak toward the coast as Dusk had most feared; it turned and ran in the opposite direction, deeper into the forest, back toward the sequoia.

CHAPTER 13

The Crossing

"THERE WAS A felid in the trees!" Dusk gasped to his father and the elders. "He saw us, all of us, I'm sure of it!"

"Where is he now?" Nova demanded

"He ran back into the forest. Toward the sequoia."

"A scout," Icaron said. "He's gone to tell the others. We have to leave now."

"What about the wind?" Sol said.

"We can't wait," Nova said.

"Dad, there are thermals in the clearing back there," Dusk said, and hurriedly explained his discovery. "If we ride them high enough, we can glide to the mainland."

"We've never done such a thing," said Nova. "Who's to say the rest of us can do it?"

"Sylph's done it," Dusk said. "If she can do it, everyone can do it." He fervently hoped he was right about this.

"I don't like it," said Nova. "The shortest route is from here. If we go back to the clearing, we just increase the distance."

"That's true," said Icaron, "but if my son's right, the extra height we gain from the thermals will let us sail across more easily."

"It's fine for your son," said Nova. "All he need do is flap."

"I won't flap my sails," said Dusk, feeling both guilty and indignant. "I'll do it the same as everyone."

"You'll do no such thing," Icaron told him harshly. "You will use all your skills and strength. There's no shame in it," he added, looking fiercely at Nova.

"We should wait at least until the sand bridge appears," Sol insisted. "Just in case."

"That would be ideal," Icaron replied, "but if we wait, the clearing will lose its heat, and there might not be enough hot air to lift us."

"What about the birds?" said Barat. "We'll be seen."

"We must risk it," said Icaron.

"I just thought of something else," Dusk said boldly. "If we leave now, before the water's drawn back, it means the felids can't follow us."

Icaron nodded. "Dusk is right. Well done."

"This is not a decision to be made by a newborn," snapped Nova.

"He's not making the decision," said Icaron. "I am. We're going back to the clearing to ride the thermals. Go tell your families. We don't have much time before the felids return."

Carnassial stretched his lithe body along a sun-warmed branch and settled down contentedly, licking his paws. He liked this tree. Its broad branches were generous, and the bark soft against his belly. The tangy fragrance of the sequoia needles made him sleepy.

He was pleased with the efforts of his prowl last night. Almost everyone had killed once, and some twice. The chiropter he'd taken, the leader's mate, had been a bit stringy and tough, but later he'd caught a younger one, whose flesh was much sweeter. His stomach had become accustomed to his new carnivorous diet, and no longer cramped and twisted after he fed.

He had grown; he'd seen it first in Miacis and some of the others. The meat was making them larger and stronger. Carnassial felt it in his chest and shoulders and neck. It was just as he'd hoped. How big would they grow? he wondered. Would they one day become as big as the saurians? No, that was too big. Once you were that enormous, you couldn't move freely through the trees, and you were slow. He only needed to become big enough to dominate all other beasts.

The island was ideal. The chiropters were their captives. There were birds in the trees, and rooters and browsers on the forest floor. He'd ventured out briefly at dawn to have a look. When his felids left the island, they'd be indomitable.

"Carnassial!"

His ears twitched and he peered down over the branch. Across the clearing bounded Miacis, whom he'd instructed to scout the island and keep track of the chiropters' movements. Carnassial wanted to be able to find them tonight. Miacis looked like she'd run quite a distance.

"What is it?" he called down.

"They're gathered in trees along the coast," Miacis said. "All of them, facing the mainland."

"Quickly," Carnassial shouted, leaping to the ground. "Gather the prowl. We can't let them leave the island."

Hundreds of chiropters lurched through the air of the small clearing as Dusk fluttered about, shouting advice and encouragement.

"Almost!"

"Try again!"

"You've got it! Now angle your sails and don't slide off!"

The thermals were numerous and strong, and already a good number of chiropters were rising into the sky. Dusk was relieved to see that most of them, especially the newborns, caught on fairly quickly. A few seemed to have an instinctive revulsion of rising, and shied away from the lifting currents. They were used to going down, not up, and it felt unnatural to them. Sylph surfed from one thermal to another, calling out advice to whoever would listen. Dusk was grateful for her help, since she explained things clearly—and more loudly than he could have done.

Dusk glanced skyward and, with a sickening jolt, saw a large flock of birds wheeling over the island. They splayed themselves across the sky like a constellation of dark stars, and then contracted ominously into a tight black mass. But they were still a ways off, and didn't seem to be drawing any closer.

"The felids must be on the move," Icaron said, gliding past him. "The birds are agitated."

Dusk knew they didn't have much time. Many of the chiropters had cleared the trees now, and would soon start their glide toward the mainland. But plenty still hadn't caught a thermal yet. This was all his idea, and he felt terribly responsible. He spotted a small group of chiropters still gliding fecklessly to and fro across the clearing, and hurried over to them. He steered them toward the nearest thermal. Not everyone was appreciative.

"This was a bad idea," muttered one frustrated chiropter.

"I can do it on my own, newborn," an old male from Barat's family grumbled. "I don't need your help."

Sylph was still sailing about, offering advice, catching lifts on thermals so she wouldn't lose height. She was amazingly determined, but Dusk now wished she'd just ride high and start her glide to the mainland. There weren't many chiropters left in the clearing now.

"They're here!"

The shout came from one of their sentries. At once all the remaining chiropters launched themselves from the trees, and sailed out in search of thermals. Icaron was among them.

"Sylph! Dusk! Time to go!"

"Go on!" Dusk told Sylph. "I'll catch up with you." To the sentries he called out, "There's a strong thermal right over here!"

They glided toward him, and he helped steer them into the hot air. Up they shot! Now, where was Dad?

From out of the trees came the felids. Some bounded into the middle of the clearing and turned their faces skyward. Others leaped into the branches and started climbing.

Dusk saw his father and flapped over.

"Dad, slip into this one right here!" he said.

His father tried, but hit it too obliquely and was deflected. He circled round, losing height fast. Dusk glanced down at the ground and saw, not thirty feet below, Carnassial staring up at them, snarling.

Dusk fluttered around his father, fighting the urge to give advice. Even now, his father would not welcome it.

Again Icaron flew into the thermal, and gave a grunt of pain as his wounded sail was buffeted from underneath. He lost his balance and slid off, circling ever lower.

"Dad, you've got to—"

"I know!" his father snapped. "I'll be fine. Just go."

Dusk could not go. He needed to get his father aloft. The trees were already filled with felids. If Dad didn't catch the thermal soon, he'd hit the ground. Beneath them, Carnassial rose onto his hind legs and leaped straight up. The felid fell back, twisting, far short of them, but Dusk was still alarmed by the height of his jump.

"There's another thermal over here, I think," he said, but his father was stubbornly trying for the same one. He glided in, flared his sails, and caught the hot air. He began to rise.

"Got it," he muttered, wincing as he rose. Dusk flapped alongside him.

"I was worried," Dusk said.

"No need to worry about me."

Up into the clearing they rose, leaving the felids spitting in fury below.

Carnassial stared in amazement as the last of the chiropters floated skyward. How was this possible? He'd never known a chiropter to do such a thing. It was unnatural. He ground his teeth, pacing in frustration. Then he noticed that Miacis and the others were watching him, waiting.

In fewer than fifty long strides he reached the coast. Overhead, the dark trail of chiropters slanted toward the mainland. All his prey. He ran along the beach, looking for the sand bridge they'd taken yesterday. The sun's blaze off the water half blinded him.

"Where is it?" he roared.

"It's not time yet," said Miacis at his side. "Not until after sunset."

That was not for several hours, and by then the chiropters would be long gone. He whirled on Miacis, teeth bared.

"Why didn't you tell me earlier they were on the move?"

"Your orders were to follow them," Miacis replied evenly. "I never thought they meant to leave the island."

It hadn't occurred to Carnassial either, but he needed someone to blame, so he lunged forward and bit Miacis on the ear. She cringed, more in shock than pain. A slow trickle of blood matted her fur.

Carnassial turned to the rest of his prowl.

"We don't need the chiropters," he spat. "There's plenty of

prey for us on this island—on the forest floor, in the trees. I've seen it. Let the gliders go. They're not worth the effort."

Dusk's jubilation was short-lived. As he and his father rose, the air was filled with hundreds of other chiropters, most still lifting on the thermals, others starting their glides to the mainland. But the large flock of birds that had been whirling over the island now seeped toward them.

"Don't flap," Icaron said tersely.

Dusk wondered if it was too late. Maybe the birds had already seen him flapping in the clearing. But he had no wish to antagonize them further. Fearfully he watched as the birds massed high overhead, churning like a storm cloud. The thermals carried the chiropters ever closer.

"Egg eaters!" came a bird's shriek, and then it was picked up by the others.

"Egg eaters!"

"Egg eaters!"

Dusk was afraid they would swoop down toward them, but they stayed high, crying out their ridiculous accusations. More and more chiropters tilted themselves into their glides, eagerly putting distance between themselves and the birds. Dusk and his father were bringing up the rear. Dusk's heart pounded painfully. He kept watch on the mainland, waiting for the moment when he too could begin his descent.

Almost there.

The birds swirled angrily. He could feel the turbulence of their wings.

Finally he and his father slipped out of the thermal, sails

angling to ride the wind. It felt strange now to be moving through the air without power. Before him the other chiropters slanted toward the coastline. Long-legged birds strutted in the rocky shallows, dipping their beaks into the sun-shattered water, pulling up weeds.

Dusk felt a rush of air across his tail and back, and something sharp scraped his shoulders. Three birds shot overhead and banked sharply, their lowered claws sharp in the sunlight. They were coming back, straight at him and Dad.

"Egg eaters!" one of them screeched.

Instinctively Dusk angled his sails to dive—as did his father. The birds soared over once more, battering them with their wing strokes, raking them with their claws.

"They're trying to drive us lower!" Icaron said.

In shock, Dusk recalculated their glide path. They'd still make it to the trees. Just. But if they fell any lower they'd be lucky to reach the base of the rocky cliffs.

"Dusk, fly higher."

His father could not do the same.

"We'll be all right," Dusk said.

More birds were streaking past them, toward the rest of the colony. They easily overtook the chiropters, whirling around them, gouging them with their claws and beaks, smacking them with their wings. In panic Dusk watched as chiropters veered off course, or worse, plunged below their planned glide path.

Halfway across, Dusk heard a chorus of cries and turned to see three birds flying at them from the side. This time Dusk was ready. He flapped his own sails and swerved to meet them, baring his teeth and making the worst and loudest sound he could manage. It came out a strangled scream, the likes of which he'd never heard. The birds were so startled they veered away to miss him.

Dusk didn't know how long a respite he'd earned—long enough to reach the mainland was all he needed. He hurriedly flapped back to Dad.

"We'll make the trees," he gasped.

"You're very brave," his father said.

Dusk had little time to savor his father's compliment. Ahead of him he caught sight of several chiropters perilously close to the water, still hounded by birds. They hit the surface, and Dusk watched helplessly as they struggled for a few moments before their bulky sails dragged them under. Another chiropter ditched just a few feet from the beach, but managed to heave himself out onto the rocks. A few more were forced down on the shore and started the long, frantic climb to the trees.

"Egg eaters!" screamed the birds one last time before wheeling and heading back to the island.

The mainland was close now, and soon Dusk was sailing over the beach. The trees were coming up fast. He matched his trajectory to his father's, and landed in the middle branches of a redwood. He clung to the bark, panting, all his limbs shaking with exhaustion and relief.

PART II

The

MAINLAND

CHAPTER 14

The Mainland

DUSK LOOKED BACK at the island and saw Carnassial standing hunched on the rocky shore, flanked by the rest of his prowl. Their whines and growls carried eerily across the water, setting his fur on end. Once the tide went out the felids could bound across in pursuit. Dusk wanted to get as far away as possible.

"Will they come after us?" he asked his father.

"I don't think so."

Scattered among the nearby trees, the rest of the colony scuttled and glided, chattering as heads were counted and names called. It was all depressingly similar to last night, when the four families had tried to find out who was alive and who was dead.

"Who has been lost?" Icaron cried out. "Barat, Sol, Nova, who is missing among your families?"

"Sylph!" Dusk called. "Sylph?"

Each second he waited was too long, but mercifully there were not so very many before she appeared, sailing happily toward him.

"We did it!" she said. "It was so easy once you were up high. I almost felt like I was flying. Just a little bit," she added, and Dusk was reminded of how much he loved her, and how he'd missed her during his long, solitary sulk.

"Your idea worked," his father told him, patting him with his sail. "I'm proud of you."

"You saved the entire colony," Sylph said.

"Almost," said Sol, settling beside them. "Three of my family are missing."

"I am sorry, Sol," said Icaron.

"It would have been much worse if not for your son's ingenuity," said Sol. "Thank you, Dusk. This won't be forgotten."

Dusk didn't know how to respond to this praise, so he just nodded mutely. He felt little sense of accomplishment, knowing that chiropters had died following his plan.

Soon Nova and Barat glided down to make their reports. Barat had lost two, and Nova four. Auster came to bring the news that Icaron's family had lost two as well, drowned like the others after being forced too low by the birds. Dusk looked up at them, still wheeling in the sky over the island.

How could they do such a thing? He hated them now, Teryx too. Had the young bird even tried to stop the rest of his flock? Had he taken part himself?

"We must keep moving," Sol said, staring at the felids on the opposite shore.

"I agree," Icaron said. "Farther along the coast we can find a temporary home and monitor the island. When the felids leave, we can return."

"That might be some time," said Nova. "Surely we should try to rejoin our old colony. The mainland's foreign to us now, and much will have changed. We need shelter and advice. It's a three-day journey to the south, no more. All four of us remember the way back home."

"The island is our home," said Sol pointedly.

"I'm in no hurry to seek out our old colony," said Icaron. "It won't have forgotten the four families who were exiled. Are you really expecting them to welcome us?"

Dusk glanced up as a female chiropter sailed low overhead, calling out a greeting. She wasn't from his colony, he knew that immediately. The slope of her face was longer, the angle of her ears slightly sharper. Her fur was a pale gray, and not because of age. All his life Dusk had known only chiropters whose fur was black or brown or copper.

"I seek the leader!" she called out.

Icaron called back and she landed gracefully beside him and the elders. Nova shooed Dusk and Sylph away, but Dusk stayed close enough to hear.

"I'm Kona," the strange chiropter said, giving a curt, formal nod. "I'm a soldier in the family of Gyrokus."

Dusk stared at her, fascinated. He'd never known a soldier. There'd been no need for them in his colony. Kona crouched alertly on the branch, head poised, her eyes moving swiftly from one elder to the next as they introduced themselves. Dusk sniffed tentatively. She had an unusual smell. Maybe all the chiropters on the mainland did. Did they eat different food, or nest in trees whose bark had an odd fragrance?

"My detachment has been guarding the coastline," Kona told Icaron.

Peering up into the trees, Dusk now caught sight of several other gray-furred chiropters perched attentively on the ends of high branches.

"We watched your crossing," Kona went on. "Were any of you harmed by the birds?"

"Nine of us didn't make it across," Sol said. "They drowned after the birds drove them into the water."

A twitch of Kona's ears was her only reaction to this news. Nothing seemed to rile her. Her gaze lifted to the flock of birds only now dispersing over the island.

"Your crossing must have been difficult," she commented. "Especially with no wind to hasten your glide."

"We used thermals to lift us high," Icaron told her. "We couldn't wait for favorable winds. We were escaping from a prowl of rogue felids."

Kona gave another curt nod. "Yes, we've been monitoring their movements."

Dusk looked over at Sylph in surprise.

"You know about these fiends?" Nova asked.

"Certainly. That's why Gyrokus has posted sentries everywhere. We saw them cross over last night. But we weren't aware of any chiropters living on the island. Gyrokus will want to speak with you. Please come with me, and I'll take you to him now."

"Yes, we will come," said Icaron.

Kona was polite but aloof, and Dusk wasn't sure he liked the way she talked to his father. It didn't seem properly respectful. Still, she radiated confidence and discipline, and Dusk couldn't help but find that immensely comforting right now. He was so grateful that the first creature they'd met in this new world was a chiropter, and that they were being taken somewhere safe.

Icaron and Kona continued to speak as Barat and Sol went off to organize their families. Dusk swallowed nervously when he saw Nova turn and walk straight toward him. He doubted she was coming to praise him for helping the colony reach the mainland; her face was far too stern.

"Listen to me," Nova said quietly. "You must not fly here. On the mainland, the chiropters are not as lenient as your father. They have much harsher ways of dealing with *aberrations*."

"What will they do?" Dusk said in a squeaky whisper.

"Beat you, most likely, then drive you away—and us with you. For your own good, and the good of this colony, you must use your sails only for gliding. Do you understand me, Dusk?"

He was cowed by her forcefulness, but not so cowed that he didn't feel indignation at being told what to do.

"I thought that only the leader could—"

"You're right, Dusk," said his father, suddenly beside them. "Only a leader's command needs to be heeded in the colony. But in this case, I must reluctantly agree with Nova. We're strangers here, and I don't want to test the kindness of Gyrokus's colony. We need to avoid scandal, at least for now. Nova, you needn't have harangued my son, I would have asked him to do the same."

"I just wanted to be certain," said Nova coolly.

When the colony was assembled, Kona and several of her fellow soldiers led them deeper into the forest. Icaron and the elders glided up ahead; Dusk and Sylph were well back. It was a relief to be moving away from the felids, even though it also meant moving farther from home. Dusk looked back toward the island one last time, but his view was already blocked by trees.

He was entering a new world. Everything around him seemed illuminated by the light from a different sun. There was much that looked familiar, but already Dusk had picked out vines and flowers and fruits he'd never seen. He sipped the air and tasted pollens and spores they didn't have on the island. As he touched down on a tree to climb higher, his claws skittered, and he noticed how smooth and hard the bark was. This was the mainland, the birthplace of his parents.

His mother would never see it again.

Dusk's sadness for her was a constant echo in his head, and all it took was the smallest thought to set it booming like thunder.

This new forest was alive in a way he'd never known. He was used to being the only beast in the trees, but here, many creatures shared the branches. Dusk caught sight of numerous small, wiry animals with skinny tails and quick eyes.

On the ground, every crack of a twig made his heart quicken. This was the homeland of the saurians, and for all he knew, they lived here still. He'd seen their bones; he knew how large they were. He did spy a worryingly large groundling with tusks curving from its upper jaws. Fortunately it was far too bulky to ever climb a tree.

"Did you see that?" Sylph asked him. "What is that?"

"I don't know," he replied, feeling terribly ignorant.

Why hadn't his parents taught him about all the different kinds of creatures in the world? Even if they were never to see them, it would've been interesting to learn about them.

"They're friendly, aren't they?" Sylph asked.

"Yes," Dusk told her, having no idea whatsoever.

Gliding across a clearing, he saw something that resembled bones, but he wasn't willing to stop and look more closely. The colony was moving steadily forward, and he had no desire to be left behind.

He paused only once, to lick some moisture from a flower, and gave a cry of surprise when its petals closed around him, as if intent on devouring him.

"It's just a plant," Jib said as he passed.

Shadows stole into the forest, reaching out across branches and flowing into one another. It was a clear night, and the moon's light penetrated the canopy. Up ahead Dusk saw a brightening and knew they must be close to a clearing. He wondered if Gyrokus's colony lived in a sequoia, just like them.

Scattered in the branches were several other gray-furred soldiers. They didn't call out greetings, just held their positions as the colony passed, gazing intently into the distance.

"Do they really need so many sentries?" Dusk whispered to Sylph. He was beginning to think the mainland was even more dangerous than he'd imagined. Guards had never been necessary back home. They'd slept on their branches unafraid—until last night, when everything had changed. But maybe the rest of the world had always lived in this state of tense vigilance.

"Do you think they're keeping watch for saurians?" Sylph whispered.

"I hope not. But it's like they're at war," said Dusk. "Or waiting for one."

"They're very organized," Sylph replied, with obvious admiration. "They seem ready for anything."

The colony was fanning out as they neared the clearing, landing and finding space on several mighty pines. This was obviously home to Gyrokus's colony, for the trees were already crowded with gray-furred chiropters. There was a great deal of wary sniffing and chittering as everyone got settled.

Dusk glided toward a free spot with Sylph. The surface of the branch looked like saurian scales, and even though he knew it was just bark, it made him feel ill at ease. With his eyes he sought out his father—just there on the next branch up, with the other elders.

Kona and a phalanx of older chiropters sailed down to meet them. There was something almost menacing about their swift descent in tight formation. They landed beside Icaron and his elders.

A grizzled male stepped forward. He was the largest chiropter Dusk had ever seen, and had the bearing of a warrior. There was a thick pink ridge of scar tissue running across his broad chest. His claws, though gnarled with time, were formidable, and Dusk could easily imagine them slashing at saurian eggs, and maybe even saurians themselves.

"Welcome, welcome!" he cried. "I am Gyrokus, and you are very welcome here." His powerful voice and bearing emanated authority, but there also seemed genuine warmth in his greeting. He went on to introduce his many elders, each of whom stepped forward in turn, nodded curtly, and then stepped back. It seemed his colony was vast, and well disciplined.

"Kona tells me you have suffered mightily on the island," Gyrokus said.

"Yes," said Icaron. "A prowl of felids, led by Carnassial, massacred my colony. Thirty-eight were killed."

Shocked chattering erupted from the branches.

"My friend, I am sorry," said Gyrokus. "This is evil work, worse than anything I've yet heard. We've been watching out for this prowl. Carnassial split from Patriofelis some time ago, and has been marauding the forests. We're always vigilant here, but I've doubled my sentries as a precaution, and so far we've escaped unscathed. I know these felids have killed groundlings and pillaged bird nests. The birds too have become extremely troublesome."

"They attacked Icaron's colony as they crossed," Kona

informed her leader. "They were vicious."

"They think we're egg eaters," Icaron said.

Gyrokus gave a patronizing snort. "The birds are too stupid to understand that we have no interest in their eggs. They haven't made any attacks here yet, but I fear it won't be long. Carnassial's felids have brought chaos to the beast kingdoms. Many have sent envoys to Patriofelis, charging him to put a stop to the carnage, and he's deployed soldiers to hunt down Carnassial. And we've already sent word that we've found his murderous prowl on the island."

"What will these soldiers do?" Nova asked.

"They must kill the rogues," Gyrokus said bluntly. "That is the best solution. We must act brutally to maintain the peace, now that the saurians have finally been wiped from the earth."

Dusk swallowed back a chirrup of surprise, and looked at Sylph, whose eyes were bright with excitement.

"Can it be true?" Barat said in amazement. "Can every nest and egg have been destroyed?"

Gyrokus gave a laugh. "Have you not heard the news on your island? It is true. The saurians are gone forever."

Dusk watched his father's grave face, and tried to imagine what he must be feeling. Wasn't the world a better, safer place without the saurians? But how could his father be truly glad of it—the fulfillment of a plan he'd thought so wrong?

"A glorious victory!" said Nova.

"Indeed," said Gyrokus.

"A quetzal did crash in our clearing not many days ago," Sol said hesitantly. "Its wings had the rotting disease."

"A straggler from the coast, no doubt," Gyrokus said with assurance. "Their cliffside nests have all been eliminated. Ironically it was Carnassial who was responsible for destroying the last of the eggs. He was a hero before his appetites became barbaric. But he may not be the only worry for us in the coming days."

Gyrokus's voice was solemn, and it made Dusk's claws dig deeper into the bark.

"You may have heard the same rumors we have," Gyrokus went on. "New breeds of predator birds from the north. And from the east, massive flesh-eating beasts."

Dusk turned to Sylph, shocked.

"We've not seen any such thing yet," Icaron said.

Gyrokus shook his head. "No, and perhaps we never will. Many think they're merely tales invented by frightened minds. But I know this as well: since the saurians have disappeared, all the beast kingdoms are becoming larger. And with greater size comes greater demand for hunting grounds. Territory is fought over more often now. Even creatures with whom we used to cooperate are now becoming quarrelsome. It's as if we've been released from one enemy only to create new ones among old friends."

"That would be truly sad," said Icaron. "Let's hope our better impulses prevail."

"Indeed," said Gyrokus. "But as you've seen, we remain in a state of constant alert. We do not crave war, but we are ready for it. Now, you've all suffered a great deal, and need food and rest. Take it here, in the safety of my colony, and we'll talk more tomorrow."

"Thank you, Gyrokus," said Icaron. "You're very generous."

It was late, and Dusk was exhausted, but he dreaded trying to sleep. The furrows in the pine's bark were not nearly so deep and comfortable as those on his old sequoia. The smell was sharper and less soothing. Settling down on this strange branch brought the stabbing reminder that Mom was gone, and would never be back. But with his father and Sylph close on either side, sleep finally came to him.

He was traveling through a strange forest, and the trees opened into a clearing and across the clearing was the sequoia. Everyone was there, waiting for him, wondering why he had gone away.

"Where have you been?" his mother asked, shaking her head wonderingly.

How was it he had gone so far astray? Home had been so close all along. It didn't matter. Dusk was only too happy to surrender himself to the joy of his homecoming, and settle down on his branch to groom, while Sylph and his father and all the other chiropters began hunting through the clearing.

And then, even in his dream, his anxious mind intruded, and he knew it was all an illusion, a lie. But he was still afraid that something terrible would happen to his home. He wanted to keep it safe and perfect, at least in his dreams, so he urged himself to wake up rather than see it destroyed a second time.

CHAPTER 15

True Natures

IT WAS DAWN, and Carnassial was searching for eggs. It wasn't scarcity that drove him up into the trees: even after the chiropters had fled, four days ago, the island still had plenty of prey. Last night he'd caught several groundlings to fill his belly. But his many years as a saurian hunter had left him with a craving for eggs—the delectable, viscous fluid, the tender flesh of the unborn.

It was proving difficult to find unguarded nests. The birds here were extremely vigilant, and vicious whenever he got too close. He'd already had one rake him with its talons. He would've attacked it, and broken its neck, except that four more birds had quickly come to help the first, driving him back in a flurry of beaks and wings. He'd moved off deeper into the forest.

Beside him in the sinewy branches of a copperwood slunk Miacis. She'd become his frequent hunting partner, and he was glad of it, since she was proving to be, after him, the most accomplished in the prowl. He wondered idly if she'd one day consent to be his mate. The thought gave him little pleasure, for he still thought often about Panthera, even though she was lost to him forever.

He stopped and sniffed. It was eerily quiet in this part of the forest. He hadn't heard a bird or seen a nest in some time. But his nostrils picked up a telltale scent of mud, saliva, and dried grass. He looked all around. There.

At first he thought the nest was abandoned, it looked so forlorn, crumbling a bit on one side. He glanced at Miacis and nodded. They stole forward, listening, tasting the air. There was no sound of nearby birds. Carnassial reached the nest and peeked inside.

The shape of the eggs made him hesitate. They were perfectly round. He'd never seen such eggs. Their shells were white, which was common with bird eggs, but these were considerably larger. He licked his teeth greedily. The nest itself was the typical greasy braid of grasses and twigs, virtually identical to the others he'd poached from. Yet these eggs did not seem to match the nest.

"They could almost be saurian eggs," said Miacis softly.

A dreadful thrill coursed down Carnassial's spine, flooding

him with both fear and excitement. He missed his days as a saurian hunter. It was not so long ago he'd been able to satisfy his craving for meat and still remain part of the prowl. He thought of Panthera, her scent, and felt the familiar clench of longing in his chest.

He sniffed one of the spherical eggs, then lapped at it with his tongue. Its shell tasted strange. He drew back and invited Miacis to taste it as well.

There was no warning. Hooked claws sank into Miacis's back and she was jerked off her feet, thrashing and screaming. Carnassial looked up in horror to see a winged creature lifting her into the air. It hovered, huge wings beating almost silently, and then its beak opened and plunged into Miacis's neck.

Carnassial tensed, not knowing whether to flee or attack. Within seconds Miacis was beyond help, her torn body limp in the creature's talons. Carnassial scrambled backward, never taking his eyes off this thing. It dumped Miacis onto the branch and landed atop her, eating her, fur and all.

Carnassial had never seen anything like it. Its powerful wings had made it seem huge, though its actual body was not so much bigger than his own. At first he assumed it must be a saurian, for it seemed covered in mottled scales, and from its head jutted two horns. But as the creature folded its wings, Carnassial saw they were feathered, and what he thought were scales on its broad chest was densely layered brown and white plumage. Those weren't horns protruding from its head, but some kind of thick tufts, angling angrily up over each large eye. It was a bird, but a type he'd never encountered. A predator.

It watched him, swiveling its head to follow his wary retreat through the twisting branches. Those malevolent eyes made Carnassial shiver, for they were like frozen things, but gave the piercing impression of seeing sharply, and for a great distance.

The bird had killed Miacis, his strongest hunter. It had torn her asunder as though she were nothing more than a sodden pile of leaves. Before he turned to leap to the forest floor, Carnassial saw a second raptor drop silently down to join the first. It gave two mournful, resonant hoots, and from deeper in the forest Carnassial heard several answering calls.

He bolted.

When he reached the sequoia, most of his felids were already in the clearing, and Carnassial sent out an alarm yowl to summon the others. Within minutes his entire prowl was assembled.

"We must leave the island," he told them, without offering any explanation.

He ran, leading his prowl toward the coast. The forest was haunted with the calls of the raptors, slow but deliberate.

"What are those sounds?" Katzen asked nervously.

"Killers," Carnassial said tersely.

The felids pounded through the undergrowth. It was impossible to tell where the hoots came from. The other birds were silent, as though afraid their dawn chorus would attract deadly attention. Carnassial's eyes warily swept the branches overhead.

Breaking from the trees onto the beach, he rejoiced to see that the water had drawn back, and the sand bridge had reappeared.

"We can cross," he said, leading the way.

But he had hardly set foot on the sand when he saw, advancing toward them from the mainland, dozens of felids. At the forefront was Patriofelis, and at his side was Panthera.

Waking, Dusk couldn't explain the calm hopefulness he felt as he lay against the bark, not yet ready to stir. He was content just to look around and breathe in the early scents of the forest. Even his grief for his mother was muted momentarily. Maybe it was the gentle dawn sunlight through the branches, or the familiar sight of other chiropters already slanting through the air, hunting. Maybe it was simply that he felt safe. His father had already gone off somewhere, but Sylph still slumbered beside him.

When he could no longer ignore the grumblings of his stomach, he stood and launched himself off the branch. As he hunted, several gray-furred newborns called out hellos to him. Gyrokus's colony was surprisingly friendly. Dusk had been nervous around them at first, especially since half of them seemed to be soldiers, constantly engaged in various drills and sentry duties. But they didn't seem to mind sharing their trees with a strange colony, and were pleased to answer any questions Dusk had. They were obviously proud of their home, so proud that they didn't have the slightest curiosity about where Dusk had come from. He was just as happy not to talk about it right now, his memories were so weighted with sadness. He was simply grateful to be accepted, despite his strange appearance. Gyrokus's chiropters didn't seem bothered by his furless sails or jutting ears. And of course he made sure not to fly, and risk becoming a freak all over again. Even his own colony had been nicer to him over the past few days. Several had actually thanked him for getting them across the water.

After catching his fill of insects, he saw his father talking to Gyrokus with Sol and Barat. Wanting to know what they were discussing, he came in to land a ways off, but their conversation had reached an end, and they were already dispersing. He called out to Dad.

"You've eaten well?" Icaron asked.

Dusk nodded, and wondered if his father had. He tried not to let his eyes stray too often to his father's wounded shoulder. At least it looked like it had been freshly cleaned, though he wasn't sure it was healing over yet.

His father nodded toward the lower regions of the tree. "Down there," he said. "You see them? Those are ptilodonts."

Dusk caught sight of the small sinewy animals, moving nimbly through the branches. They had long tails that could wrap around a twig to give them extra support and balance. They chattered animatedly with one another.

"And on the ground," his father said, "do you see that one?"

Dusk had spotted something like that when he'd first arrived on the mainland, a lumbering giant with a dark coat, spotted white.

"Those teeth . . ." Dusk said nervously.

"Tusks. Not for hunting," Dad reassured him. "Watch. See how he digs up the earth with them. He's looking for grubs or tubers. He's not a meat eater."

"Must be good for defending himself, though," said Dusk,

wishing he'd had such fearsome things the night the felids attacked their colony.

"There's Sylph," Dad said, seeing her glide past. He called out and beckoned her to join them.

"I like it here," said Sylph as she landed. "Everyone does. Are we staying?"

"We'll return to the island, once it's safe," said Dad.

"But that might take a long time," said Sylph. "We'd stay here until then, wouldn't we?"

"Gyrokus would need to invite us first," Dad told her.

"Would you say yes?"

"It would mean I couldn't fly," Dusk said quietly.

"Oh. I hadn't thought of that," said Sylph. "But isn't it better to stay here with everyone else than to find someplace off by ourselves?"

Dusk knew exactly what she meant. It was reassuring to be surrounded by all of Gyrokus's vigilant soldiers, even if they were a bit arrogant and aloof. Maybe it was plain selfish of him even to be thinking of flying right now.

"You'll fly again, Dusk," his father promised him. "Once this upheaval has ended, and we're back on our own."

"It's not like my own colony even wanted me to fly," Dusk said.

"They should let you do whatever you want," said Sylph. "If it weren't for you, we couldn't have escaped the island."

"Your sister is your most outspoken ally," Dad said, looking at Sylph kindly. "She has a loyal heart."

"I'm just outspoken in general," Sylph said, but Dusk could tell she was happy to win her father's praise. Dusk breathed in and almost didn't want to exhale. He didn't want this good moment to pass away from him. It was so pleasant being together, just the three of them, without any elders nearby. But it also made him feel his mother's absence more keenly. Would he ever be able to look at his father and sister without thinking someone was missing?

The urgency in Sylph's voice jarred him. "Dad, is that a—"

Dusk followed his sister's gaze to the ground. A sleek four-legged creature effortlessly leaped onto the lower branches of a neighboring tree and proceeded to bound higher. Dusk heard startled screams, and his sails flared instinctively, his body ready for flight.

"It's a felid!" Sylph gasped. "It's coming up!"

"Don't be afraid!" Gyrokus called out loudly from the clearing. "This felid is our friend, and he comes at my invitation."

In amazement, Dusk watched as Gyrokus glided toward the felid and landed beside it, just one branch below him and Sylph and Dad.

"Welcome, Montian," said Gyrokus heartily. "Welcome!"

"Hello, Gyrokus." The felid's low purr made Dusk's jaws clench.

"Icaron, come and join us," the powerful chiropter leader called up. "Your elders too."

Nervously Dusk watched as his father glided down to their branch, calling out for Sol and Barat and Nova. Within a few moments his elders were around him. The felid sat upright on its rump, its forelegs extended. This image of civility was such a stark contrast to his memory of the ravening beasts on the island that Dusk could scarcely believe they were the same species. Peeking down, he and Sylph listened as Gyrokus introduced Icaron and his elders to Montian.

"I have news that I hope will please you," the felid purred. "Patriofelis's soldiers are confronting Carnassial even as we speak."

Gyrokus gave an approving snort. "Excellent. And how does Patriofelis plan to resolve this problem?"

"Carnassial has chosen his own prison," Montian said, "and Patriofelis means to keep him there. An alliance of beasts will organize a permanent watch on the mainland to make sure Carnassial's prowl never leaves the island."

"But that's our home!" Dusk blurted before he could check himself.

"Dusk, silence!" his father said sharply. He turned back to the felid emissary. "This is not the solution we'd hoped for. We had meant to return to our home as quickly as possible."

"Patriofelis has decided that the island is an ideal place to isolate Carnassial until he and his prowl die from starvation."

"They won't starve there," said Icaron. "They'll live on and breed. It would be better to put a stop to them now."

Montian looked at Icaron calmly, almost insolently. He lifted his front paws, one after another, from the bark, licked them, and put them down again. "You are advocating murder?"

"Carnassial has already murdered; he must be accountable for his actions."

"Surely Patriofelis's solution is better than spilling more blood," said Montian.

Dusk couldn't stop himself hating this felid. Even if Montian wasn't personally responsible for the massacre, it was his kind who'd murdered Mom, and here he was trying to make Dad and the chiropters look bloodthirsty. It was disgusting.

"I understand your anger," Montian went on, "and I am truly sorry you and your colony have suffered. I can only say that Carnassial's prowl are outcasts, and share nothing in common with the other felid kingdoms. But if we are to kill our own kind, does it not make us as bad as Carnassial?"

"No," said Icaron, "because he has broken the law first. He's a liability to all the beasts. Patriofelis's solution isn't just, and it punishes my colony by robbing us of our home."

"I agree," said Montian, "that your colony suffers unfairly, but Patriofelis felt the solution was best for the common good, all things considered."

Dusk could see the fur on his father's neck bristle, as was his own. He hated being dictated to by these creatures.

"This is Patriofelis's decision," said Montian. "I am only conveying the news of it."

"Thank you, Montian," said Gyrokus. "We understand. Convey our best regards and thanks to your leader."

The felid nodded at Gyrokus and Icaron, then sprang away down the tree. Dusk let out a breath, his heart still pounding in anger.

"That was no way for allies to behave," Icaron told Gyrokus.

The battle-scarred chiropter merely grunted. "You must remember that the felids are our most powerful allies. We need their friendship. It's best we don't anger them."

Dusk narrowed his eyes at Gyrokus. This gruff chiropter

leader hadn't said anything to support Dad in front of Montian. He hadn't even seemed that upset by the news. It wasn't fair that Carnassial was allowed to take over their island, their tree. He loved that tree, every knobbly surface of it.

"They should send their soldiers in and kill them," Sylph whispered beside him, and Dusk couldn't help agreeing with her, no matter how brutal it sounded.

"It seems our home is permanently lost to us, then," said Icaron.

"You will find a new one," Gyrokus said. "Here, if you wish."

Dusk blinked.

"My elders and I have spoken on this at some length," Gyrokus continued. "You've suffered a great deal and you're in need of a home. You'd be very welcome to join my colony. Very welcome indeed."

"This is an extremely generous offer," Sol said.

Dusk caught Sylph looking over at him, smiling.

"I thank you, Gyrokus," Icaron said. "I must of course discuss this with my elders."

"We're honored by your invitation," Nova told Gyrokus warmly.

"As am I," said Barat.

"My family as well, would welcome this place as our home," said Sol.

Dusk was surprised at the speed of the elders' decision. He knew he should've felt more grateful, but he didn't. It was one thing to imagine staying here a little while, but forever? A place where he could never hope to be himself, to fly. He couldn't do it. He *needed* to fly.

"The more numerous we are," said Gyrokus, "the stronger we'll be! If war ever comes we will be all the mightier. Join us and prosper with us." He looked at Icaron. "You would, of course, be an honored elder among us."

But not leader, Dusk realized with a start.

He hadn't thought that far ahead. Joining another colony didn't just mean a new home, it meant a new leader. He felt sick. He watched Dad, trying to guess what he was thinking.

"The decision is yours, my friend," Gyrokus told Icaron.

Dusk waited, sensing that his entire colony, scattered about in the branches, was also holding its breath, hoping.

"The safety of my colony is my gravest concern," Icaron said, "and I know they would find an excellent home here. Give me some time to consider your kind offer, Gyrokus."

Dusk felt relief, but heard Sylph's sigh of frustration, a sigh that seemed to whisper faintly through the branches.

"Of course," said Gyrokus. "Take all the time you need. It is a large decision you must make—a daunting one, I'm sure, for a colony that has led such a secluded life."

"The island was our home for almost twenty years," Sol said.

"Twenty years!" said Gyrokus in amazement. "I had not realized it was so long."

Dusk noticed a new attentiveness in the grizzled leader's eyes.

"Tell me," he asked, "before you came to the island, where was your original colony?"

"Not so far from here," Icaron replied. "To the south. Our leader was Skagway."

"I remember him. He would have died not long after you left. He was killed hunting saurian eggs."

"He was a brave hunter," said Icaron.

Gyrokus looked steadily at Icaron for a moment before asking, "Why did you leave?"

Dusk swallowed. Would his father lie and say it was to find new hunting grounds? What truthful thing could he say that wouldn't reveal they'd been driven out? He looked at Nova and saw her ears flick anxiously.

Icaron said evenly, "I left with three other families because we chose not to hunt saurian eggs."

Dusk could hear the surprised murmurings of Gyrokus's chiropters as this news seeped through the trees.

Gyrokus opened his mouth, as if tasting the air, then exhaled slowly. "Icaron. Yes. I wondered why your name was familiar. You were all expelled as traitors."

"Conscientious objectors," Icaron said.

"A name changes nothing!" said Gyrokus sternly, and Dusk flinched. Would his father rear back and flare his sails, as he'd done when Nova contradicted him? No. Everything was different now. His father wasn't leader here.

"A name changes nothing, you're right," said Icaron. "But we weren't traitors. We served the Pact well until we felt we could serve no longer. We had no wish to desert our colony, but, as you say, we were expelled for our beliefs."

"Because they harmed all of us," said Gyrokus.

"Many of us have regretted our choice," Nova blurted out.

"Icaron doesn't speak for all of us."

"A leader speaks for *all* his colony," Gyrokus barked at Nova. "Let me hear no more from you!"

Dusk was amazed at Gyrokus's ferocity—not even his father would have been so easily angered.

"You shirked your responsibilities to all beasts," Gyrokus said, turning back to Icaron. "And to your own kind especially. And now you return to a safer world that you did nothing to achieve."

"The world does not seem so safe," Icaron replied. "Former allies just murdered almost forty members of my colony."

"Perhaps if you hadn't hidden yourselves away on the island, isolated and forgotten, you would not have been so vulnerable! They preyed on you because they thought no one would ever notice!"

"Is he saying we deserved to be slaughtered?" Dusk whispered angrily to Sylph.

"Sounds like it," she muttered.

"Could we ever welcome you into our colony?" Gyrokus asked with chilling calm. "Who's to say you wouldn't abandon us again in our next time of need?"

"Our newborns had no part in our decision to repudiate the Pact," Nova insisted. "Don't punish them for our decision."

"Every generation of newborns has no doubt been reared on your deformed principles," said Gyrokus disdainfully. "You are all tainted."

"Would you turn us away in our time of need?" said Barat.

Gyrokus said nothing for a moment. "I am not so unkind," he said. "But if I'm to accept you into our colony, I must have you renounce your past, and then I may know that you are trustworthy."

"You would have me admit my wrongdoings?" said Icaron calmly.

"It's a simple thing, and only right," said Gyrokus, and some of his hearty warmth returned. "My friend, you obviously care deeply for your colony, and that's an excellent quality in a leader. Now you need to care for them by giving them a new home, a safe haven. Join us. But first, tell me and all assembled that you regret your traitorous decision to abandon the Pact, and I will know that I can trust you."

"Just do it," breathed Sylph.

Dusk could feel her desperation rising up from her fur like vapor from hot bark.

"I will do no such thing," said Icaron. "I cannot."

Dusk felt a fierce throb of pride.

"Then I cannot help you," said Gyrokus, his voice hardened with anger. "Be on your way. Wander far. No chiropter colony will accept you once they know who you are and what you've done. I'll make sure of that. You have made refugees of yourselves."

"This is unjust!" Nova exclaimed, and at first Dusk thought her outrage was directed at Gyrokus. But she whirled on Icaron. "You're sentencing all of us to your fate, because of your foolish ideals."

"They're not foolish ideals," Sol said angrily. "And they aren't Icaron's alone. I share them. Barat shares them. You once held them dear."

"We were offered a home!" said Nova.

"We don't need someone else's home," said Icaron. "We'll find our own." He turned to Gyrokus. "I thank you for sheltering us. We will be on our way immediately."

Carnassial watched as Patriofelis advanced across the sand bridge with his forty-five soldiers. He wondered how they would fare in combat. They were strong, but they had never hunted; they had never *torn*. Would they be willing to attack and kill their own kind? For that matter, he wondered if his own prowl would.

Patriofelis's cohorts reached the island and fanned out across the beach, blocking the bridge. Carnassial's eyes lingered on Panthera. She wouldn't meet his gaze. Her presence here made it obvious she felt no loyalty toward him, and yet he was still glad to see her.

"Carnassial," said Patriofelis. "So this is where you have fled."

"We didn't flee anywhere," said Carnassial. "We're seeking a new homeland."

Patriofelis seemed to be taking a tally of his numbers. "Where is Miacis?" he asked.

"Dead."

Carnassial could hear a whine of surprise from among his own prowl.

"What happened to her?" Katzen asked.

Carnassial ignored him, his eyes narrowed hatefully at his old leader.

"Dead!" Patriofelis repeated loudly so all could hear. "What a shame to lose one of your strongest. What a perilous life you've chosen. But you were right in one respect, Carnassial. The world is changing, and becoming more dangerous. There are rumors that new creatures are approaching from the east, and no one knows if they will be friend or foe. The birds have become more aggressive too, no doubt due to your savaging of their nests. We beasts must stand united. And you, sadly, have become a dangerous liability to any new alliance. We will not allow you to throw our world out of balance."

"We've committed no crime," said Carnassial. "We feed like any other creature, only our prey is not the same as yours. Who's to say what is right or wrong? Our craving for meat is as real as yours for grubs or seeds."

"No more of this talk," Patriofelis said disdainfully. "I come to offer you one last chance of amnesty." He addressed the felids ranged behind Carnassial. "Any of you who choose to return to the prowl, come forward now. It's not too late. All will be forgotten and forgiven, and we can carry on in harmony with the other beasts."

"He asks you to deny yourselves," Carnassial told his felids. "He asks you to deny your natural appetites. Would you be content to serve such a leader?"

"My offer is open to you as well, Carnassial."

Carnassial growled dangerously, and saw Patriofelis and his cohorts flinch.

"I reject your offer!"

"That is unfortunate," said the old felid, "since the alternatives are far less pleasant. If you persist in your abominable ways, this island will be your home for the rest of your lives. The beasts will not allow you to roam the world, murdering.

You are exiled here, Carnassial. You and all your deviant prowl."

Mere hours earlier, the prospect of a life on the island would not have seemed so dire. Now, with the sudden appearance of the predator birds, it was likely a fatal punishment.

"We will not be bound by your laws," Carnassial spat.

"We'll be watching the island. Any who set foot on the mainland will be killed."

"You'd kill your fellow felids, Patriofelis?"

"Yes, to prevent even more killing."

"I doubt your resolve," he said mockingly.

"That is unwise," Patriofelis said. "Now, who among you wishes to renounce your past crimes, and rejoin your true prowl? Come forward!"

Carnassial surveyed the members of his prowl. From the trees behind them he heard a mournful hoot, and an answering call. Katzen glanced at him furtively and then quickly stepped toward Patriofelis.

"Well done, Katzen, you've chosen wisely. Are there no more?"

To Carnassial's surprise and shame, five more of his felids crossed over.

"How your numbers dwindle," Patriofelis said.

Carnassial looked at Panthera, who still would not meet his gaze. As the day's light strengthened, the sea water lapped impatiently at the sand bridge.

"For the rest of you," Partiofelis said, looking pointedly at Carnassial, "the best I can wish for you is a quick death."

A vast shadow fell across the old felid leader, and seconds

later, feathered wings enveloped his head and torso. A ghastly scream issued from Patriofelis as he bucked and twisted, trying to throw off the predator. But Carnassial knew those claws and how deep they bit, and the bird held tight.

Panthera bounded to her leader's side, sank her teeth into the raptor's tail, and pulled. The bird swiveled its head, facing almost backward, and lunged with its hooked beak. Panthera fell back as the raptor lifted Patriofelis off the ground and flapped into the forest.

The air was suddenly filled with wings as more birds came slanting down at them. The felids scattered in terror.

"Come with me!" Carnassial shouted to his prowl.

In the ensuing chaos, he saw a chance. The sand bridge was within reach, only just now disappearing under a skin of water. He shoved and snarled and snapped his way through Patriofelis's remaining guard. Suddenly leaderless, the soldiers panicked, some retreating across the sand bridge, others racing for the cover of the island forest.

"Go!" he shouted to his prowl. "Cross!"

He let his felids go first along the sand bridge, protecting their rear should any of Patriofelis's soldiers try to attack from behind. The birds rained down on them. In horror he saw one drop toward Panthera. She twisted nimbly out of the way, but the predator still sank a set of claws into her haunches. She cried out, twisting and clawing at the bird that hovered above her, battering her with its wings.

Her companions were too terrified to offer any help. Carnassial did not even hesitate. He ran back and launched himself at the bird, knocking it off Panthera. On the ground

he sank his teeth into its neck. Blood and flesh and greasy feathers filled his mouth. The bird swiveled its mottled, horned head and impaled him with its terrifying eyes. Its beak opened and gored his right foreleg before he could spring away, yowling. The bird lifted off, shrieking its own pain, and flapped back to the forest.

Carnassial looked at Panthera, and this time she met his gaze.

Birds still wheeled overhead, dropping down on the few felids that remained out in the open. Panthera said nothing, but followed Carnassial as he leaped onto the submerged sand bridge and started splashing toward the mainland. The water slapped against his knees and was achingly cold, but at least it numbed the pain in his foreleg. Up ahead, the last of his own felids slogged their way across. Some were already scrambling up the rocky shore to the heights above. He kept glancing back to make sure Panthera was still behind him. She was, and each time he glimpsed her he felt stronger.

Halfway across, he looked up and saw a dark shape soaring down on them.

"Into the water!" he shouted, hoping Panthera would trust him.

He threw himself from the bridge. In the moment before his head went under he saw a pair of wickedly angled claws overshoot his skull, and felt the wind from the bird's great wings. And then his entire body was submerged. Cold pounded at his temples. He thrashed his legs and came up, gasping, his fur sodden. Panthera churned the water beside him, and they hauled themselves back up onto the sand bridge, not even taking the time to shake themselves dry. They struggled for the mainland, knee deep in water now, their limbs numb.

At the shore, Carnassial dragged himself shivering onto the rock, and craned his neck to check for any more raptors. He saw a few circling the island's beach, but no more over the water.

With Panthera at his side, he scrabbled up the steep slope to the trees and there found his felids assembled in the low branches, growling uneasily at eight of Patriofelis's guard.

"Back to the island!" barked Gerik, whom Carnassial could only guess had assumed control.

"We will not," said Carnassial quietly.

Gerik saw him for the first time, and involuntarily took a step back.

"We have our orders," he said.

"Your orders were to kill any who left the island," Carnassial reminded him. "Who will fight me? Will it be you, Gerik?"

He remembered playing with Gerik when they were new-borns, the hunting and fighting games that had prepared them for adulthood. Carnassial was the smaller of the two now, but he doubted Gerik's courage, especially with so few reinforcements. Most of his warriors were still cowering on the island, unable to cross until the evening. Gerik was out-numbered, and he knew it. Carnassial watched as his con-fused eyes slid to Panthera.

"Why do you stand beside him, Panthera?" he demanded.

She said nothing.

"You can't keep things the way they were, Gerik," Carnassial told him. "Your leader's dead. There are birds that can kill us now. Patriofelis said there might be new beasts who can do the same. The old alliances will soon be meaningless. My prowl can't be the only one to have discovered a taste for flesh. Live the old way if you want, but don't hinder us. We'll do what we must to stay strong and live."

"No," said Gerik.

"You can join us," Carnassial said.

The other felid took a step back, shaking his head in revulsion. "I will not. And I will not let you pass."

He leaped.

Carnassial was ready, and threw himself at Gerik. They crashed against each other and skidded across the earth, clawing and biting. Gerik was heavier, stronger, and unwounded, but his bites lacked deadly intent. Carnassial saw his chance and sank his teeth deep into Gerik's left haunch, ready to tear. He felt his opponent falter. Carnassial didn't want to mortally wound a fellow felid, but he would if necessary. Gerik seemed to sense this, and went limp. He lay still, whimpering in submission. It was hard for Carnassial to release his jaws, for his blood pounded, and the desire to fight pumped through every one of his veins. He finally let go and stood glaring down at Gerik, whose eyes rolled fearfully.

"Get up," Carnassial told him. "Go. And don't come after us."

Gerik scrambled to his feet and led his soldiers away along the coastline. Panthera stayed behind.

"Will you come with us?" Carnassial asked her.

"I always feared you," she said. "Your craving for meat: I saw it as destructive, unnatural."

With a pang, he remembered her expression of horror when she'd caught him eating his kill back in the old forest.

"And I feared I might wake up one morning with such cravings," she said.

"And have you?"

"I have."

Carnassial growled softly with delight. "Come with me," he asked her again, his heart thumping.

She stepped closer and licked at his wounded foreleg.

"Yes," she said.

CHAPTER 16

Tree Runners

"ISN'T IT OBVIOUS," the pointy-nosed beast said angrily, "that there isn't enough food for so many mouths?"

Dusk looked on in dismay as the irritable creature told Icaron and the elders that they couldn't make their home here. When they'd first come across this little patch of forest, the trees hadn't looked occupied. But only minutes after they'd settled on the branches and surveyed the hunting grounds, a huge clan of pale-furred alphadons had materialized as if from thin air, hopping through the boughs, using their long, skinny tails to swing themselves from twig to twig.

"Surely this forest can accommodate both of us," Sol said. "Your diet is fruit and seeds—"

"—and insects," the alphadon interrupted, its wet pink nose twitching. "Which your lot will pilfer from the air, leaving none for us. Now move on! This is our territory."

"In the past we weren't so ungenerous with one another," Icaron said.

"Take a look around you, chiropter," said the alphadon. "The world's a crowded place now. If you want to eat, you've got to protect what's yours."

"I'd like to bite its tail," Sylph whispered to Dusk.

Dusk wasn't so sure he'd risk it, given the alphadons' high state of agitation. He'd thought them meek-looking things when they first appeared, but now they began to crowd in on the chiropters, their narrow mouths parted slightly, hissing. Nuts and pinecones suddenly began to rain down on them, hurled by alphadons higher in the trees.

Dusk looked over at his father, and saw him shake his head in resignation.

"We set sail once more!" he called out to his colony, and the air filled with hundreds of gliding chiropters.

It had been three days since they'd left Gyrokus, three days of searching for a new home without any success. Not all the beasts they'd encountered had been as unpleasant as the alphadons, but the message was always the same: they were unwanted.

Dusk glided beside Sylph. He wished he could fly, but Dad had asked him to wait, worried that his flapping might make the other beasts hostile—though Dusk couldn't imagine them getting much more hostile than they already were. He did what Dad asked anyway and, as he labored up tree after tree, tried to remember his father's promise that he would fly again, just as soon as they found a home of their own.

"We should've stayed with Gyrokus," Sylph muttered as they slogged up another trunk.

Dusk looked over at her sharply.

"I'm not the only one who thinks so," she said. "And I'm not just talking about Nova. I hear things. Plenty of chiropters are getting tired of this."

Sylph would know. Since leaving Gyrokus's colony, she'd been spending more time away from him and Dad, gliding and hunting with other newborns, including Jib. Once, Dusk had even seen her talking briefly to Nova. He couldn't help feeling his sister was being disloyal. With Dad's wound still not healed, and things so uncertain, Dusk wanted her close by.

"We're *all* tired of it," he said. "But Dad's going to find us a new home."

"We had a perfectly good one offered to us."

"Dad did the right thing."

"He should've just told Gyrokus what he wanted to hear," Sylph whispered. "Even if he didn't mean it."

"Was that Jib's idea?" Dusk demanded. "Or maybe Nova's?"

"They're just words," Sylph persisted.

"They're not just words. They mean something."

"Do they?"

"Dad and Mom did something great when they left the Pact. It made them different. It made them . . . better. It did."

"What's it matter now anyway?" Sylph said impatiently. "The saurians are gone. All that's over. Isn't it more important to have a safe home for the entire colony right now?"

"If Dad had said he was sorry, everyone would think he really had made a mistake. They'd think he was weak. How could anyone respect him after that? How could he respect himself?"

Sylph sniffed. "Yeah. He just thought of himself, as usual. His pride ruined it for the entire colony."

"Dad was willing to give up being leader!" Dusk reminded her angrily. "That's not being proud, Sylph!"

His sister fell silent.

"We'll find someplace else," he told her, "someplace better."

But he was beginning to worry this new world didn't have any room left for them. They weren't the only creatures looking for a new home, either. Over the past few days he'd noticed many other groups of migrating beasts, their eyes fixed on some distant point that would finally offer them a hunting ground and safe haven.

He looked up ahead at Dad, leading the way with Auster at his side. Dusk had noticed they'd been spending more time together lately, and at night were often engaged in quiet conversation. He'd tried to listen in, but they always managed to be out of earshot. He was jealous of all the attention his oldest brother was suddenly getting, but it also worried him. What were they talking about?

Dusk carried on, gliding and climbing with the rest of his exhausted colony. They were headed north. Dad had said there was no point trying to reunite with their ancestral colony. They'd only be rejected once again. They needed to forge on, try to find a place far from any other chiropters, a place where they were unknown. "A place where we can escape the sins of our past," Dusk had overheard Nova mutter bitterly.

The long day wore on. When the forest changed, it happened so gradually it was some time before Dusk—or anyone else—realized they were suddenly the only creatures in the trees.

At first it felt pleasantly familiar, just like being back on the island, but then Dusk began to find it eerie. The quiet was broken only by the occasional twitter of birdsong, the buzz of insects, and the rustle of leaves in the breeze.

Icaron called a halt, and the colony settled among the branches, some grooming, others seeking out water or food. Sylph went off to hunt. Dusk glided over to his father. He'd never been far from him since they'd left the island. Whenever he was out of sight for long, Dusk felt panicky. He wasn't sure whether he was afraid something would happen to himself, or to his father.

Every night when Dusk slept, he hoped that his father's wound would be healed by morning. But it never was. On good mornings it looked the same, on bad ones, worse. Right now Icaron's eyes looked swollen and red. His fur had a sharp odor that Dusk didn't like. Over the past two days, his pace had slowed noticeably and he'd been calling for more frequent rest stops.

Dusk knew better than to ask him if he was all right. His answer was always the same, and Dusk found the lie harder and harder to bear. Dad needed to rest more if he was to get better, and that seemed impossible right now.

"This looks like a good place," Dusk said hopefully. He didn't understand why it wasn't more crowded, but right now he didn't really care. There were plenty of tall trees, and lots of bugs by the look and sound of it.

A small, dark shape dashed out of sight in a nearby tree. Dusk heard a patter of footsteps, and what sounded like whispering. His fur tingled. He looked at his father, and saw that he too was watching and listening.

From the corner of his eye Dusk saw something move in another tree. He jerked his head around. It was swift on the branch, and gone almost before he could focus on it. He had the impression of something running not on four legs, but on two. A second later, the creature emerged from behind the trunk, and hurried out along the branch in plain view.

It was a beast, silver-furred, twice the size of a chiropter. Its hind legs were longer than its front ones, and though it did in fact move on all fours, it gave the unnerving impression of walking on its hind legs alone. The creature paused and sat back on its haunches, its hands together, fingers intertwined. A bushy tail swayed from side to side. Dusk had never seen such large eyes on any beast: huge dark moons with brown irises and large pupils. Large white-tipped ears slanted out diagonally from its head.

And suddenly all the trees around them were filled with more of these creatures, appearing as from nowhere, lining the branches and watching the chiropters. They did not seem at all aggressive, just curious, but Dusk could not help noticing that his colony was completely surrounded.

"They're tree runners," his father told him, and then called out a greeting.

From the branches, one of the spry creatures scampered eagerly toward Icaron. There followed the usual cordial sniffing.

"I am Adapis," the tree runner said. "Welcome to our home."

"Thank you. I'm Icaron, the leader of this colony."

The tree runner peered inquisitively at the wound on Icaron's shoulder, and seemed quite excited by it. "It's become infected. But I can heal it. Will you allow me?" Before waiting for an answer he turned back to several other tree runners who'd edged closer. "Gather the ingredients! This needs tending to."

"You're very kind," Icaron said.

Dusk didn't know how this creature could possibly heal Dad's wound. Wounds healed on their own, or didn't. All you could do was keep them clean. What more could this tree runner do? But Dad seemed to have confidence in his claims.

"Please tell your colony they're welcome to hunt here," Adapis said. "I think you'll find we have plenty of insect prey."

Within minutes, the other tree runners had returned, bits of bark and leaf clutched in their hands.

Sylph glided down beside Dusk.

"What's going on?" she whispered.

"They say they can heal Dad's wound."

In amazement he watched as Adapis took a thin piece of

bark in his two hands and shredded it. His five tapered fingers were marvelously nimble. Dusk had never seen any animal hold or tear something so easily. Adapis fed the bark into his mouth, and chewed while taking hold of a dried leaf and crumbling it into a small pile. He then spat the bark onto the leaf dust and, with his dextrous fingers, mixed it all together before scooping it back into his mouth for another quick chew. His preparations complete, Adapis stepped closer to Icaron and proceeded to spit the green paste onto his wound.

"Do you think that's really going to help?" Sylph whispered to Dusk in consternation.

Dusk winced. The green slime drizzling from Adapis's mouth looked a lot like the foul pus that was already scaled around Dad's wound.

"Don't worry," Adapis said, looking over. "The paste will defeat the infection, and help the gash to heal more quickly. You must trust us. We know a great deal about what plants can do."

"It soothes already," said Icaron, closing his eyes and sighing.

"At sunset we'll clean the wound again and apply more."

"Thank you, Adapis," Icaron said.

"Most important, you need rest. You and your colony may stay here as long as you like."

After so many days of tamping down on his fears, Dusk felt himself tremble with relief and gratitude.

Dad quickly fell asleep. Normally he never slept during the day, and Dusk realized how tired and ill he must have been lately, forcing himself onward.

"Let's hunt," Sylph said.

Dusk was hungry, but he felt strangely nervous leaving Dad's side. All his life he'd assumed his father's watchful eyes were always upon him, making sure no harm came to him— or to the colony. Now those eyes were closed, and he looked so vulnerable that Dusk felt he should watch over him.

"He'll be here when we get back," Sylph said. "Come on."

Dusk told himself he was just being foolish, but he left reluctantly.

The hunting was excellent. If anything, the insects were even more numerous than on the island, and it took little effort to catch them. It seemed the bugs here hadn't had much experience with airborne predators.

Certainly the tree runners didn't seem to eat them, prefer-ring the fruit and seeds that grew in the trees, and especially the grubs and roots they dug from the ground with their clever hands. They really did seem to have a great knowledge of all the plants in their forest, and Dusk saw them mixing things together and crushing them into a paste before eating them. He felt a little in awe of them. Imagine knowing all that; imagine being able to make things with your hands.

He glanced over at Sylph. It was good to have her gliding at his side. He'd missed her.

"Why've you been staying away so much?" he asked her as they climbed a trunk.

"I don't know." She paused. "I was angry with Dad, for not letting us stay with Gyrokus. And then I just couldn't stand it anymore, seeing him so weak, and getting weaker. I didn't want to watch. I was afraid he was going to die."

Her rear claws slipped on the bark, and Dusk realized she was shaking. He climbed alongside her and pressed his face against her cheek and shoulder.

"It's all right now," he said. "They're making him better."

Her voice was so quiet he barely heard it. "I want Mom back."

It was only four words, but they brought a whimper to Dusk's throat too. He'd tried hard to lock away his thoughts of her, because they only caused him pain, an actual physical ache in his torso, reminding him he would never be near her again.

"I hate them," Sylph said savagely, "the felids. They took everything."

"We'll find a new home," Dusk said.

"I don't want another home," she said, "I want our old one back."

"One day."

"I want things back the way they were."

"Me too."

He was used to her outspoken anger, but not her raw grief, and it stirred in him a fierce desire to make things right—and an equally fierce frustration at his own powerlessness.

Sylph took a big breath and kept climbing, obviously not wanting to talk anymore. Dusk followed, and realized that, on the branch overhead, three tree runner newborns were watching them with wide-eyed curiosity. One of them called out a hello and introduced himself as Strider. Dusk was glad of the chance to talk to them. They were so kindly-looking that his initial shyness had all but evaporated.

"I wish I could glide," Strider said.

Dusk chuckled. "I wish I had hands like yours."

"Really?" said Strider, staring at his left hand as if he'd never seen it before.

"You can hold things really well," said Dusk. "It must be very useful."

"I suppose so. But you can sail through the air. That's almost as good as flying."

Dusk looked quickly at Sylph to make sure she wasn't going to blurt anything about how he actually *could* fly.

"Can I see them, your wings?" Strider asked politely.

"Sails," Sylph corrected. "Haven't you ever seen chiropters?"

"Maybe once," said Strider uncertainly. "But I don't think they stayed very long."

Dusk obligingly spread his sails. With keen interest Strider studied the ridges of his arm and fingers on the undersides.

"They're like hands," Strider said excitedly, "but just with really long fingers and skin across them." He glanced from Sylph back to Dusk. "But how come yours are different from everyone else's?"

"Are you some kind of freak?" one of Strider's companions asked.

"Shut up, Knoll," Strider told his friend.

"I'm just different," Dusk replied.

"I'd rather have sails than hands," Strider decided.

Dusk smiled at the tree runner's good-natured impetuosity, but he himself couldn't imagine being anything other than what he was. He only wished he didn't have to hide what his sails could really do.

"Is it true you just eat bugs all the time?" asked the third newborn, speaking for the first time.

"Pretty much—why?" said Sylph warily, as though anticipating an insult.

"Doesn't it get boring?"

"There's a lot of bugs out there, Loper," Strider said, as though his friend were a bit simpleminded. "They probably eat hundreds of bugs every day."

"Thousands, actually," said Sylph.

Loper looked a bit queasy at this news.

"We eat seeds and plants too," Dusk added, not wanting to appear unworldly.

"Have you ever tried this one?" Strider asked, holding up a slender green leaf, which he must have been concealing behind his back. The leaf was finely veined, with a slightly serrated edge. There was a glimmer of mischief in his eyes.

"I don't think so," said Dusk. "No."

"You should try it," said Knoll. "Pass it over, Strider."

Strider glanced around furtively and took a tiny nibble before passing it to Knoll, who did the same. Loper chuckled and chewed off a bit as well.

"What is it?" Dusk asked suspiciously.

Strider's whisper was barely audible. "It's tea."

"That grew all around our old forest," said Sylph, a bit wistfully.

"But did you ever *try* it?" Knoll asked. His eyes seemed a little bigger than before, and his toes were drumming on the bark.

"It's not something chiropters ever eat," Dusk admitted.

"What a shame, what a shame," said Strider, talking quickly. "It's really good."

"Our parents don't like us eating it," Loper admitted. "They say it makes us too irritated."

"Too *agitated*," Strider corrected.

"Hard to get to sleep," Knoll added, his eyes skittering all over the place. "But it's pretty fun while it lasts."

All three tree runner newborns were now bobbing up and down on the branch, as though unable to keep their bodies still.

"Try some," said Strider, jiggling the leaf in front of Dusk.

Dusk hesitated, remembering the incident with the mushroom. He didn't want any more scarifying visions.

"I'll have some," said Sylph. She leaned forward, and snapped up a piece of the leaf. The tree runners all looked at one another, openmouthed with surprise.

"That was *a lot*!" said Knoll.

"You probably shouldn't have taken that much," said Strider.

Sylph shrugged. "What am I going to do, start flying?"

Strider and his friends chortled giddily. Dusk looked at his sister in concern. She was flapping her sails hard.

"Maybe I'll just lift right off!" she said. She turned to Dusk. "Maybe all I needed was some tea leaves!"

She was certainly flapping quickly, and Dusk wondered if this was still a joke, or whether she truly was trying to fly. For a moment he wanted her to soar off the branch, so she could join him in the air. But her efforts now were no more successful than her early ones, and he felt a stab of sadness. The tree runner newborns, however, thought this was all uproarious, and were bouncing up and down on the branch, urging her on.

Before long, though, his sister seemed to tire of flapping and contented herself with pacing frantically along the branch. The tree runners were springing up and down, seeing who could go the highest.

"Try some tea, Dusk," Sylph said to him. "It really perks you up."

"No thanks," he said.

Sylph looked all around as if something had just occurred to her. "How come it's so quiet around here?" she asked the tree runners. "It's just you living here. Everywhere else it was so crowded."

"Lots of creatures pass through," said Knoll, "but no one stays long."

He sprang up, caught the branch overhead with his nimble fingers, and swung back and forth before letting go.

Dusk noticed that Strider looked like he had a secret, but one that he was eager to share. The tree runner lowered his voice, though he was still talking rather loudly.

"There's a monster in the forest," he said.

"That's just a story," said Loper, blinking.

"No, I've seen it."

"You never told me that!" Knoll said. "When?"

"Well, I heard it. Once, at night," Strider insisted quickly.

Dusk looked at Sylph, whose ears lifted in amusement. He wondered if the tree runners were normally this talkative, or if it was just the tea loosening their tongues.

"What kind of monster was it?" Sylph wanted to know,

restlessly furling and unfurling her sails.

"Big," Strider replied confidently. "It sounded very big. It scares most creatures away, but it never bothers us."

"It didn't scare us away," Sylph said.

"Well, it doesn't live that close to us," said Strider, sounding more uncertain now. "No one's ever really seen it. Anyway, that's why not that many creatures live around here. They got scared off. But we know it's safe."

Dusk wondered if Strider knew what he was talking about, and decided not. Probably he was just reciting some story the adults told their newborns to keep them from wandering off. Surely if there were a real monster in the vicinity, the tree runners wouldn't have such a large and contented colony here.

"And if you aren't scared, maybe you can live here too," said Strider before taking a running leap at the next tree and bounding away with his friends. "I *like* chiropters!"

Dusk was touched by his innocent sincerity. The tree runners' home really did seem like an ideal place, and he couldn't help wondering if this might become their home as well.

When Carnassial made his first kill on the mainland, he offered it to Panthera. He stepped back and watched her expectantly. She sniffed the carcass, pawed it briefly, and then without any hesitation expertly tore through the fur and skin, shearing the bloody meat from the ribs. Carnassial's tail flicked in surprise.

"This is not the first time you've eaten meat," he said to her.

She licked clean the fur around her mouth.

"No. After you left, I hunted several times."

"And you were never caught?" he said in astonishment.

Panthera purred in amusement. "I was more careful than you. I went farther afield. I didn't want to be expelled."

"You wanted to remain in Patriofelis's prowl?"

"I wasn't as courageous as you—or as rash. I liked the safety of the prowl, and I thought I could continue to satisfy my appetites in secret."

Carnassial looked at her with a new respect, but also some wariness. Just where did her true loyalties lie?

"And would you have killed me," he demanded, "if Patriofelis had given the order?"

She broke his gaze. "None of this would've been necessary if you'd stayed with us. You could have lied to Patriofelis and appeased him. Then we'd have had more time to win support within the prowl. We might have forced Patriofelis to change—or overthrown him. Then you'd have been leader of hundreds, instead of just dozens."

"Such deviousness isn't in my nature."

"Is it deviousness, or shrewdness?" she said.

"I showed myself for what I was, and accepted the consequences. Those who had the same strength followed me. That is how to build a mighty prowl."

"Perhaps I don't belong with you, then," said Panthera, her eyes flashing at the rebuke.

Carnassial had never seen such spirit in her, and it annoyed him—and intrigued him greatly.

"That is your decision to make," he told her.

She came to him and pushed her head against his.

"You are my only leader now," she said.

Carnassial led his prowl north. There were seventeen of them. His wounded foreleg was slowly healing, though he still limped. With Panthera at his side, he felt a boundless strength and confidence.

Prey could not have been more bountiful. The world was indeed changing: he'd never known such large movements of beasts through the forests. Many seemed to be seeking better hunting grounds; others claimed to be fleeing for their lives. With so many creatures around, it was easy for Carnassial and his prowl to make their way unrecognized. Even after they'd been seen to kill, all they had to do was march on for half a day, and once more they became anonymous.

With every day, Carnassial cared less and less about concealing their appetites. Let everyone know who and what they were. No one would dare stop them now, especially after news spread of Patriofelis's failure to exile them. They were the feared.

"What do you think will happen to the old prowl?" he asked Panthera.

"With Patriofelis dead, it will disintegrate. Gerik's no leader."

Carnassial snorted his agreement. "They'll disperse. Maybe some will cross paths with us and ask to be let in." He looked at her carefully. "Do you regret leaving?"

"No," she said.

He'd seen her hunt now, and as he suspected, she was excellent, though there was more he could teach her. Watching her feed gave him such delight—and relief too. She was one of them.

"That bird back on the island," she said. "What was it?"

Carnassial's fur bristled. "I'd never seen it before. It was new."

He'd been watching for it ever since, especially at dawn. He remembered its huge eyes, and wondered if they could pierce the night. But he hadn't seen its kind again, though just once, far away, he thought he'd heard its eerie and mournful hoot.

"They killed us easily enough," Panthera said.

"They took us by surprise," Carnassial replied proudly. "It won't happen again. We'll be watchful. I could kill one with ease."

She lifted her ears questioningly, but he would not retract his bold statement. The mere existence of these birds was a persistent dark cloud in his mind. Where had they come from? Sometimes, before sleep, he thought about their beaks and talons and silent wings, but he felt confident that they were no match for his muscle and claws and teeth.

For most of the morning the land had been rising gradually, and his prowl was beginning to slow as they neared the top. Carnassial exulted in the long journey. It reminded him of the days when he and Panthera had hunted saurian nests, traveling miles and miles to find them.

At the hill's crest, they all paused. Before them, the land dipped away into a valley. At the bottom, a creek bubbled through dense undergrowth. That would be fertile foraging for small groundlings, Carnassial thought. On both slopes were ample trees, many of which bore fruit that perfumed the air. He caught sight of many tree dwellers. The bark looked soft, good for gripping with claws, and the branches were inter-laced, making arboreal trails for all his felids.

Carnassial stared at the vista, transfixed. He felt a content-ment he'd not had since he'd destroyed the last saurian nest. He felt at peace, and completely in control of his life. There was water here, shelter, and plenty of prey.

"This," he proclaimed, "is our new home."

CHAPTER 17

The Feast

Dᴜʀɪɴɢ ᴛʜᴇ ɴɪɢʜᴛ Dusk woke to a distant cry. His entire body tensed, ready for escape. His stomach felt sick. Shakily he crawled to the edge of the branch, trying to remember where the sound had come from. *There's a monster in the forest.* Strider's childish statement suddenly seemed terrifyingly plausible.

He cast out long streams of sound, but caught no signs of movement among the trees. He listened, hoping he wouldn't hear another shriek, closer than the first. The forest was silent now. He settled back down, his pulse slowing. Sylph was still asleep, as was their father. Looking at their peaceful faces, he eventually dozed off.

When he woke it was morning, and his father was stirring beside him.

"How are you?" Dusk asked.

"Better," Dad said, and this time, Dusk believed him. He certainly looked more rested. He'd cleaned away the hard green crust of the poultice, and the wound itself seemed smaller, and much less angry.

"Adapis left the ingredients for me," Dad said, nodding at the pile of crumbled leaves and bark. "Would you prepare it?"

Dusk nodded and with some trepidation started chewing the bark. Its taste was bitter but not unpleasant.

"How do you think they learned all this?" he asked, his mouth full.

"Accidentally, some of it. They eat lots of different plants. Over time I suppose they discovered ones that could heal."

Dusk mixed the bark with the leaves, chewed again, and drizzled it onto his father's wound. Icaron gave a grateful grunt.

"Thank you, Dusk."

Dusk spat out the rest, and licked a dewy leaf to clean the taste from his mouth.

He was so glad his father was improving that he didn't feel like mentioning the scream in the night. No one else had been woken by it. It was probably just some night animal protecting its territory or fighting over food. Things always sounded louder and more frightening at night.

He went off hunting, and when he was sure he was out of

sight, he flew. He didn't want the tree runners suddenly turning against him, after they'd been so hospitable to his colony. But he needed to fly.

His spirits lifted with every beat of his sails. His father was healing; the colony was safe for now. Before long they'd have a new home—maybe right here. He hunted as he flew, snapping insects from the air. Landing on a branch, he looked around. It was a beautiful forest; the trees' bark was smooth and the color of pink sand, shaped as though by waves. Sunlight lapped at the leaves and heated patches of the forest floor. He'd lost track of how far he'd flown from the others.

A powerful smell of scat suddenly wafted up to him, making his nostrils flinch. The particular scent was unfamiliar to him, though judging from its intensity, it was relatively fresh. He dropped from the branch, flapping lower. He didn't have far to go before he found it: a pile of long grayish droppings at the base of the tree. Their considerable size scared him. No small animal had left these.

Off to one side of the scat he saw the mangled carcass of a groundling, picked nearly to the bone. Anxious, Dusk looked all around, but saw no sign of the predator.

He turned himself in the air and flew back to tell his father.

"Do you know of a large predator in the area?" Icaron asked Adapis. "My son saw some scat."

Dusk watched Adapis for his reaction. He was attentive, but seemed untroubled.

"What did it look like?" Adapis asked Dusk.

He described it as best he could.

"You must have been quite a ways from our trees," said Adapis.

Dusk nodded. He'd been flying, and it was hard to calculate the distance.

"We keep to our part of the forest for a good reason," Adapis said firmly, though not unkindly. "There are larger beasts deeper in the forest, some of them meat eaters, but for some reason they've never ventured into our territory. Don't stray so far next time."

"I won't," said Dusk.

Adapis turned to his father. "Have you ever eaten this fruit?" he asked, holding out a small berry in one of his hands. It was still amazing to Dusk how easily the tree runners could grasp things. It always made him feel clumsy.

Adapis placed the berry on the bark before them, and Dad lowered his head to taste it.

"Try it, Dusk," his father invited him.

Dusk had seen this purplish berry growing from a sturdy vine all over the forest. Fruit was not something chiropters ate much of, but it was juicy and sweet and quenched his thirst. He took another nibble.

"It's very good," he said enthusiastically.

Adapis chuckled. "Perhaps something you can incorporate into your diet?" Excitedly he added, "We will prepare a feast! Let us introduce some new foods to you. Doubtless we can learn a great deal from each other."

"There are too many of us, Adapis," said Icaron. "It's very kind of you to offer, but it would be too much work."

"Not at all, not at all," Adapis insisted. "Let us do this for you. To welcome you. Maybe we can convince you to make our forest your new home. We'd happily have you as friends and allies. The world is large, and there is plenty for all of us."

All that day and the next, the tree runners were in a state of high excitement, busily harvesting fruit and seeds from the trees, and grubs and roots from the forest floor. Dusk watched, fascinated by their labor. They transported all their food to what they called their feasting tree, which was quite a ways from where they nested. This tree had a great many low branches that were flat and wide, and on these the tree runners set out their food in long lines. Newborn tree runners would draw close, hunger in their eyes, only to be shooed away by their elders.

"Are we going to have to eat all that?" Sylph asked, gliding past with Dusk.

"I've never seen most of those things," Dusk said. "But see those purple berries over there? I tried one yesterday and it was really good."

Sylph grunted, unconvinced.

"Don't eat too many bugs today," one of the tree runners called up to them. "Save your appetite for the feast tonight!"

"What if we don't like the food?" Sylph asked.

Gliding past, Nova overheard her. "Shush," she replied sharply. "We must eat. We don't want to insult our hosts. It's a sign of great hospitality, the likes of which I've never seen. After being spurned by our own kind, these strangers are offering us a new home."

* * *

Late in the afternoon, the tree runners had almost finished their preparations, and set about calling the chiropters to the feasting tree. Dusk caught sight of Strider and his friends sitting forlornly near their nests.

"Aren't you coming to the feast?" Dusk asked.

"Not invited," said Strider.

"None of the newborns are," added Loper.

"That seems a bit unfair," said Dusk.

"Exactly what I said," Strider agreed. "They didn't listen."

"It's not really for the tree runners at all," said Knoll sadly. "It's all in your honor."

"Let's go find some tea leaves," Loper suggested, and the idea seemed to cheer them all up.

"Enjoy the feast," said Strider to Dusk.

Dusk glided off toward the feasting tree. When he arrived the branches were already filling up with chiropters. He climbed high, wanting a better view so he could find Sylph and his father. He looked down on the splendid display of fruits and seeds and leaves spread along the branches. Knoll was right: very few tree runners seemed to have been invited.

Dusk saw Adapis scampering about, overseeing the final arrangements. The tree runner started climbing toward him, but stopped several branches below to speak with two other tree runners. He obviously hadn't even seen Dusk. The intent angle of the tree runners' heads as they leaned close made Dusk instinctively draw back into the shadows. He wasn't supposed to see this. He listened hard, but only caught the last sentence.

"It's time to invite her," said Adapis. "Come with me."

Dusk got the sense this female must be important, but he'd never heard anything about a special guest. There was something secretive about Adapis now. His fingers waggled nervously and his eyes seemed even wider than usual. The three tree runners set off—but not in the direction of their own nests. They were heading deeper into the forest. Dusk's heart thumped. He'd assumed this guest was another tree runner, but it seemed that wasn't the case. Who was she? Unseen, Dusk followed them.

Gliding, he was virtually silent, flapping only when necessary to maintain his height. Adapis and his two companions ran purposefully through the trees. They knew where they were going. After half an hour, Dusk heard something large stirring in the distant forest, and a cloying smell of meat and excrement wafted on the breeze. He almost wanted to call out a warning to Adapis, but the tree runners surely must have noticed the stench, and were in fact moving straight toward it.

"She's just up ahead," Dusk heard Adapis say to his companions.

On a branch about twenty feet above the forest floor, Adapis and the other two tree runners finally stopped and sat on their haunches, staring down. Dusk glided as close as he dared, but the dense foliage still blocked his view of what the tree runners beheld. Adapis's hands twisted nervously.

Something spoke.

"You are ready for me?"

The voice was unearthly, a kind of throttled shriek that made Dusk's fur spike.

"Yes, the feast is almost ready," Adapis said.

"It is an ample feast, I hope."

"Indeed it is."

Adapis, he noticed, never took his eyes from the creature. Occasionally he winced, and his nostrils flinched, no doubt at the odor this creature belched forth. Were they really inviting her to their feast? No one would be able to eat with such a stench in the air. Dusk craned his neck, trying in vain to get a glimpse of this she-creature.

"The last one was meager," the malodorous creature screeched.

"I am sorry it displeased you. This one, I promise, is much more lavish. I am sure you will enjoy yourself."

"For your sake, I hope so. Remember, you are safe only as long as you honor our agreement."

"Of course."

"You feed me. I protect you."

"Come just as the sun sets. We will be ready then."

"I will come."

The hideous voice said no more, and Adapis wasted no time turning away and leaping for home. Dusk retreated behind his screen of leaves, flattening himself against the bark. He'd wait a few more moments for the tree runners to pass, and then fly back to the feasting tree. He'd get there first if he flapped hard. His father would be able to make sense of this.

He peeked out through the leaves to check on the tree runners, and something grabbed him from behind. He flailed, craning his neck to see what held him. It was Adapis's two companions, each clenching one of his sails in their nimble, clever hands. He hadn't expected them to be so strong.

"Let me go!" he hissed, struggling in vain.

Suddenly Adapis was before him, holding a berry in his hand.

"You've been very troublesome," he said.

"I didn't mean to be," Dusk replied, thrown by Adapis's hurt tone.

"We've been inviting a very special guest to the banquet."

"Who was that?" Dusk wanted to know.

"Another honored guest. Here, you must be thirsty."

Dusk jerked back, but Adapis pushed the berry insistently against his face. Juice drizzled down his fur. He clenched his mouth shut, heart thrashing in his chest.

"Very well," said Adapis. He placed his free hand across Dusk's nostrils, pressing hard.

Dusk whipped his head from side to side, trying to dislodge those strong fingers, but they wouldn't budge. The berry oozed against his clamped mouth. He did not want it. But he was suffocating. When he could stand it no longer he opened wide to take a suck of air, and in that split second, Adapis shoved the berry into his mouth and held his jaws tight with both hands. Dusk had to swallow, or choke.

He swallowed.

Adapis released his grip.

The taste of the berry was cloying, and he gagged a bit, spitting out as much as he could.

"Give him another to make sure!" one of the tree runners said.

"That will be enough for a newborn," said Adapis.

"What was that?" Dusk demanded, afraid he'd been poisoned.

"It's something your whole colony will be enjoying at the feast," said Adapis. His huge eyes widened, and he looked sorrowful. "I am sorry, Dusk. Everything has changed, you see. We do what we must to survive. Unwholesome things, sometimes."

"What?" Dusk said, feeling confused and oddly heavy. "What do you mean?" His voice crackled and he was sobbing. "I want to go back to Dad and Sylph. . . ."

At this Adapis looked away, as though ashamed.

Despite Dusk's terror he was so enervated that all he could do was collapse against the bark, panting, feeling darkness bound toward him.

He clawed himself out from under the weight of sleep. He wrenched open one eye, then the other. Light slanted low through the trees. Looking around, he did not know where he was. His heart kicked, and his memory began to flow, at first like a listless creek, then a torrent. Something terrible in the forest; tree runners pinning him down; Adapis forcing a berry into his mouth. He felt a sudden violent swell of nausea, and vomited several times against the branch. He staggered back, revolted.

Was it morning already? His panicked mind told him the light was coming from the west. Sunset, not sunrise. *Come just as the sun sets,* Adapis had said. There was a monster in the forest, and she was coming to the feast. He had to warn his colony.

He quickly took his bearings and leaped into the air, aiming for the feasting tree. Pain jolted through his sails where they'd been wrenched by the tree runners. Every beat was an effort and he hadn't gone far before he had to land, struggling for breath. He was unbelievably weak, his muscles still saturated with the berry's enervating juices.

Again he threw himself into the air, but most of his progress was downward. He simply could not muster the power to beat his sails. He whimpered with fury and frustration.

The ground was not far below him and in the dying light he saw a dense green clump of plants. Tea. He flew to it immediately, landing hard on the ground and tore a leaf from the stalk. He chewed it hastily. It was bitter and made his eyes water, but he ate another for good measure. The effect was almost instantaneous. His heart picked up speed, and a restless tremor jittered through his limbs. His head cleared. He wanted to *move*.

His sails churned and lifted him off the ground. He felt taut and alert. The sun had almost set and darkness was clotting between the trees. He used his echovision to plot his course, veering around branches and cascades of vines. His breath came raggedly, but he pushed himself harder still. He sniffed and listened as he flew, wary of the monster. Had she already passed this way?

In the sharp, silvery world of his echovision, everything looked so different that he almost overshot the feasting tree. He wheeled and spiraled down. On the broad lower branches he made out the dark shapes of his colony. It took him only seconds to realize none of them were moving. There was not a single tree runner in sight.

"Dad? Sylph?"

Cautiously he fluttered closer, sniffing for his family's familiar scent. But in the air hung the sickly perfume of the same berry that had plunged him into sleep, exhaled through every chiropter's slack mouth.

They were not dead, just unconscious—and completely helpless—sprawled among the remains of their poisonous feast. Dusk's skin felt clammy beneath his fur as he finally realized what was happening.

"Wake up!" he shouted as he clambered over the chiropters, trying to find his father and sister. Some of them stirred, muttering indignantly.

"Sylph!"

He found her slumped in a cluster of other newborns. He nudged her head with his. She shifted but did not wake.

In the forest, something crackled.

Dusk went rigid. He stared into the darkness. It was truly silent now. The usual night throb of insects was missing. Then came a second crackle, and a third. The slow, deliberate pauses in between made him realize he was hearing the advance of some enormous two-legged creature.

"Sylph," he barked into his sister's ear. "Wake up!"

He bit her, and she gave a furious cry, jerking up.

"Did you just bite me?" she demanded angrily.

"Start waking everyone up. Be as loud as you like! Bite them if you need to, just wake them up!"

"Where were you?" she asked, frowning in confusion. "You weren't at the feast, and . . ."

"Never mind, Sylph! Something's coming. Where's Dad?"

"Over there, I think."

More footsteps crackled through the forest, and Sylph looked at him, unblinking.

"It's big," she murmured.

"Hurry," he told her. "And get everyone awake to help you."

Dusk hurried across the branch, intentionally stepping hard on every chiropter in his path, hissing at them to wake up. Nova, Sol, and Barat slept near his father. He butted his head against Dad's, calling out to him again and again. He knew that his voice likely carried well into the forest, but he couldn't help that now.

"What is it?" Icaron said after a moment, his voice thick.

"Dad, something's coming to eat us!"

His father shook himself and stood, blinking. "Where?"

Dusk tilted his chin.

The silence was as heavy and congealed as the darkness. Dusk sniffed, but he was upwind and smelled nothing.

"Are you sure, Dusk? Where are the tree runners?"

"Long gone. I saw Adapis talking to a creature in the forest. I tried to come back and warn you sooner, but they caught me and put me to sleep. Just like they did you."

Icaron frowned, struggling with his memory. "We were feasting and—"

His father glanced around in alarm, saw the dark forms of all the sleeping chiropters, many now awake and moving sluggishly.

Two more footsteps crackled through the darkness, the loudest yet. Then silence. Whatever it was, it was close. Dusk remembered the scat he'd seen, the size of it. His insides churned.

"Wake everyone!" Icaron bellowed. "Tell them to climb high! We're in great danger!"

He turned and set about rousing the other elders. Dusk fluttered over to the next branch and began waking more of the colony, trampling, nipping, shouting at them, doing whatever was necessary to wrench them from their unnatural slumber. The more he woke, the more helpers he had, but most of them were badly weakened by the berry's poison, and Dusk worried they'd not be quick enough to reach safety. The tree runners had cleverly laid the feast out on the lower branches, some no more than four feet off the forest floor.

"Get to the trunk!" he shouted. "Climb as high as you can!"

Unexpectedly the breeze shifted, and Dusk's nostrils twitched at the reek of decayed flesh. Others must have smelled it too, for he saw many chiropters turn their heads and flinch.

Massive footsteps thundered through the night.

Dusk froze, unable to look away. Branches and ferns and bushes thrashed as the monster burst into view.

He did not know what she was—bird, beast, or saurian.

Walking erect on two vast sturdy legs, her feet were those of a bird, three thick, taloned toes in front, and one wickedly hooked claw at the rear. Her gigantic head seemed too big for her body, with a broad lethal beak. Her muscular torso was densely haired, but the wings were practically nonexistent—nothing more than little feathered stubs, surely incapable of flight. A thick array of ragged tail feathers sprouted from her rear. She stood ten feet high, her head well above the branches where the chiropters had been slumbering. A long scar ran across her right leg, and she limped as she ran, her appalling smell cresting before her.

For a second she hesitated, craning her neck to take in the chiropters, who surged in terror along the branches and trunk.

"You were to be *sleeping*!" she shrieked, and galloped toward them.

Dusk looked around desperately, trying to find Sylph and his father, but all was chaos now as terrified chiropters clambered over those who still slumbered.

The monster reached the low branches and attacked. Her powerful shoulders heaved forward, neck stretching, beak agape. When she reared back, two chiropters were impaled on her hooked beak, and then flicked inside by a muscular gray tongue. The monster's head swiveled, eyes flashing violet. Wet air hissed from the slits in her beak.

Again and again she struck, snatching up chiropters, sleeping and awake, from the branch. Nothing seemed to slake her furious appetite. She wanted more. She wanted them all. The trunk crawled with chiropters heaving themselves higher; others, trapped on the branches, leaped and glided earthward, hoping to hide in the undergrowth.

"Climb high!" he heard his father shouting off to his left. "It can't follow! Climb high!"

Dusk wanted to fly to safety, but not before he'd made sure Sylph was all right. The monster lifted her left foot onto his branch, gripped it with her talons, and snapped it in half. Unconscious chiropters tumbled to the earth. Dusk flew clear

and caught sight of Sylph, sails spread, gliding to the forest floor. He dropped down and landed beside her. The monster's legs were not five feet distant, towering over them.

"Hurry!" said Dusk, scrambling with her over the earth toward the trunk of the nearest tree.

For the moment, the monster's face was turned away from them as she plucked up the unconscious chiropters and shook them down her throat. Dusk and Sylph reached the trunk and started climbing.

"Just fly," Sylph hissed at him.

"I'm fine." He struggled to keep up.

The monster exhaled noisily. Glancing back, Dusk saw her glaring at the feasting tree. Its lowest branches were all but empty now. With relief Dusk saw that most of the chiropters, sluggish though they were, had managed to climb beyond the reach of that deadly beak.

"This is no feast!" the thing shrieked.

She turned, and was still. In the near dark, Dusk couldn't be sure what she was looking at. He sang out sound, and his echoes illuminated the monster. Her head was turned straight toward him, eyes blazing. She blurred as she lurched at them.

"Keep climbing!" he cried to Sylph, and jumped into the air, sails unfurling.

He needed time for Sylph to get higher.

"Hey! Look here!" he shouted at the monster, flapping to meet her.

The creature's head jerked to and fro, trying to fix him as he fluttered past erratically. Suddenly she lunged. He wasn't prepared for her reach. The beak hurtled toward him, and

Dusk braked, rolling to the side. The creature's rancid breath crashed over him and the beak clipped the tip of his left sail, snapping him around.

He crashed against the thing's neck. Her oily feathers were dense and for a moment his claws got tangled up in them. The monster whirled, trying to impale him. Dusk tore his claws free, thrashed his sails, and leaped clear. The monster's own stubby wings fluttered as she screeched in frustration.

Dusk took no more chances. He circled high above her head, hurling insults until the creature's jaws foamed with fury. She jumped for him, but was too heavy to go far. When he thought Sylph was high enough to be out of harm's way, Dusk flew back to the tree. She was safe. He settled beside her, out of breath.

The monster careened back to the feasting tree, searching for any unconscious chiropters she had missed. She tilted back her muscly neck and gawked up at the survivors beyond her reach, then let loose a terrible high-pitched trill that made Dusk's ears vibrate in pain.

"Where's Dad?" Sylph asked.

"He got clear. I think he did. We should get over there."

"Adapis!" the monster shrieked. "This was not a feast! You promised me a *feast*, Adapis, *and you will provide me with one*!"

"Adapis was going to feed us to that thing?" Sylph exclaimed.

Dusk winced and nodded. "We were the feast."

Below, the monster finally gave up trying to climb the feasting tree and went shrieking off in the direction of the tree runners' nests. Dusk felt his stomach tighten. He thought of Strider and his friends. Surely they couldn't know about this terrible thing their parents did.

"I hope it eats them all," Sylph muttered darkly.

"Dusk! Sylph!"

It was Dad, calling from high in the feasting tree.

They climbed a bit farther and glided across to him. Dusk was happily folded into his father's sails, alongside Sylph. Dad was alive. Dusk didn't know how many had died tonight, but the three of them were still alive.

"What was that thing?" Sylph asked.

"A diatryma," Icaron said, voice hoarse with exhaustion. "A flightless bird."

"A bird that can't fly?" Sylph said, amazed at the very idea.

"She protects the tree runners," said Dusk, remembering the conversation he'd overheard. "That's why their forest is so quiet. She scares away all the predators. But the tree runners have to give her food."

"Why can't she feed herself?" Sylph asked.

"Her leg. She limps."

Icaron nodded. "The diatrymas need speed to chase down their food on the grasslands. She must've come into the forest hoping for smaller prey she could catch by stealth. But she's a clumsy thing among trees. Without Adapis to bring her prey, she'd starve."

Dusk shuddered at the fiendishness of the whole arrangement. He remembered Knoll saying that lots of animals passed through the forest, but never stayed long. He wondered how many Adapis had lulled to their deaths.

"They seemed so friendly," Sylph said, clearly unable to understand how any creature could do something so terrible.

For the first time Dusk noticed the blood on his father's fur. His old wound had torn open.

"Dad, your—"

"I know. I'll worry about that later," he said. "We can't spend the night here. The tree runners are strong, and who knows what other treachery they're capable of. We've got to move."

From the branches around them came the whimpers and moans of terrified chiropters. Icaron raised his voice so all could hear.

"I know you're exhausted," he called out. "I know you've suffered. But we must leave this place now. Think of the new home that awaits us. Twenty years ago, when I was expelled from my colony with Sol and Barat and Nova, we feared we'd never find another home. But we discovered the island. Now we're homeless once more. But I promise we will soon have a new home, and it will be bountiful and safe. Think of that tonight as we travel."

Icaron turned to Dusk and said, more quietly, "There's enough moonlight if we travel high. You and Sylph stay close to me. And, Dusk, we may need your echovision to guide us safely through this night."

With Panthera at his side, Carnassial emerged from the cool of the hillside caves to begin the twilight hunt. As the rest of his prowl emerged, he stood looking over the valley with immense satisfaction. It had been a good choice for a home. As was his custom now, he carefully scanned the tree-tops and skies, listening for the mournful hoot of the predator birds. But there was no danger overhead.

Instead it arrived on foot.

Carnassial did not even smell the creatures before they burst into view. He was so startled by their sheer size he thought they must be saurians. But their speed, and their fur, told him they were beasts—bigger than he'd ever seen. Their hindquarters were striped black and white, and their upper bodies were an earthen color, tapering to dull black around their powerful muzzles. They ran on their toes without planting their feet, and their legs were taut with muscle. Jutting like fins from the sides of their elongated skulls were sharply spiked ears. There were six of them, and they immediately spread out to trap as many felids between them as they could.

One faced Carnassial. It was four times his size. A pair of oversize canines projected over its lower jaw, all the better to grip its prey. But it was the ridged teeth farther back that made Carnassial's sinews tighten. He sensed how easily they could crush bone and tear flesh. He could smell the meat on the beast's humid breath.

Still, he would not back down. He had already fled his territory once because of an invader, and would not do it a second time. He was glad to see that some of his prowl had already made it up into the trees, and were poised on overhanging branches, hissing and yowling, ready to jump. His other felids remained on the ground, tensed, set to attack at his command. Panthera crouched beside him, hackles raised.

"This is our territory," she spat.

When the creature spoke, its throat and mouth seemed unaccustomed to forming language. Its words were barks.

"We—seek—Carnassial."

"You have found him," he growled suspiciously. How did they know of him?

He didn't let his astonishment dull his fight instinct. He was taut and ready. He watched them all carefully.

"You are Carnassial?" the creature grunted in seeming disbelief. "A saurian killer?"

"It was I who killed the last of them," Carnassial hissed.

"No," barked the beast. "They live."

"It's not possible," Carnassial said, amazed and insulted both. He and Panthera had scoured the earth; they had found and destroyed the last nest. He'd once been known as a hero among beasts. He glanced at Panthera and saw she too was incredulous.

"If there were any left, we would've found them," he told the giant before him.

It coughed out its words. "You—will—kill—them—for—us."

"Will I?" said Carnassial, his muscles uncoiling just a bit. It seemed these creatures did not come to hunt, but to ask for his help. But the beast clearly disliked his boldness, and took a single, menacing step closer.

"You must!" it said.

"How did you hear of me?" Carnassial asked, determined not to be intimidated by this monstrous thing.

"Felids told us of the Pact."

Carnassial couldn't help wondering under what circumstances this beast had talked to the felids. Perhaps just before ripping out their entrails.

"Who are you?" Carnassial wanted to know.

"Danian."

"And what are you?"

"Hyaenodons. We are many. We eat flesh."

"As do I," Carnassial replied.

Danian snorted, as if amused at the idea of such a small creature hunting live prey. "We seek new hunting grounds. But saurians live where we would settle."

"You're powerful creatures. Surely you could defeat these creatures by yourself."

"The adults are sick. They will die soon. But there is a nest."

"And you've been unable to find it," said Carnassial.

"You are small and stealthy. You will find it."

Carnassial could see that the hyaenodons had no chance of hunting nests successfully. The saurians would easily spot them coming and attack with all their strength. Clearly Danian was not so powerful that he didn't fear them. For the first time Carnassial noticed a large raised scar on his back. Had it been inflicted by a saurian?

"We can be of use to one another, then," said Carnassial. These beasts could barely speak. They were likely imbeciles, but terribly powerful ones.

"Who is to say there is only one nest?" Panthera mused aloud.

Carnassial glanced over, about to contradict her, but her piercing gaze silenced him.

"The saurians may be more numerous than any of us thought," she continued. "Carnassial and I can certainly find any saurian nest and destroy it. But if we do this thing for you, Danian, we will expect something in return."

"Life," said Danian.

"Yes," said Carnassial quickly, now understanding Panthera's cunning scheme. "I propose a permanent alliance between your pack and my prowl. We will not feed on one another. There is plenty of other prey in this new world. We will protect you from the saurians. You will protect us from any other predators. Are we agreed?"

Danian licked his fearsome teeth. "Agreed," he said.

CHAPTER 18

A New Order

Dusk dreamed of a tree with no low branches, taller even than their old sequoia. It stood alone, so that the felids wouldn't be able to jump across to it. But even as he gazed at it in his dream he knew it wasn't good enough.

We need other trees to glide between for hunting, he thought.

You don't, a dream voice told him. *You can fly.*

I know, he thought, but the other chiropters can't. Anyway, there wouldn't be enough food. The bugs like it best when there's lots of trees.

As he said this, more trees grew up beside the first, equally tall, and without any low branches.

Yes, he thought, delighted, not just at the sight of this perfect little forest, but at the fact he'd conjured it into being himself. He could control something. This vista, he realized, bore a startling resemblance to the one the stars had made for him when he'd tasted the poisonous mushroom.

A hill, and on it a tree, growing from the earth like a shoot from a seed, becoming a sapling, then thickening into a great strong trunk that branched into the sky.

This is the home you're looking for, the dream voice told him.

Yes, Dusk thought. It's perfect.

It was still night when Sylph woke him. Dusk felt he'd scarcely been asleep, his mind glutted with images and urgent messages he couldn't quite decipher.

"I think Dad's really sick," she said. She looked scared, and her voice trembled.

Panic seized Dusk. It had been two days since they'd fled the tree runners, and his father's wound had become infected again. He moved his face closer to Dad's, and felt the heat emanating from his fur. Muttering and flinching, Icaron slept fitfully. Dusk felt small and useless.

"Go wake Auster," he told Sylph. "He'll know what to do."

When Auster arrived he looked closely at Icaron and sighed wearily.

"How can we help him?" Dusk asked.

"We can't fight the infection for him," Auster said quietly. "That's something only he can do."

Dusk ground his teeth. "What about the stuff the tree runners used?"

Auster shook his head. "How do we know it was actually helping him?"

"Yeah," said Sylph. "Why would they bother making him better if they were just going to feed him to that thing?"

"To make us trust them maybe," said Dusk. "Or maybe the diatryma didn't like wounded prey."

"We've never used bark and leaves," said Auster. "It's never been our way. I don't even know the ingredients."

"I do," said Dusk impulsively. "I watched."

"You're sure?"

"The bark anyway. I'll go look."

"It's still too dark to see properly," Auster told him.

"I can see in the dark."

Auster stared at him, then nodded. "Go find some. Sylph and I will stay with Dad. Be careful."

Dusk flew by echovision alone. He steered clear of branches where other beasts slept. Since leaving the sinister quiet of the tree runners' forest, they had reemerged into a world of beasts vying for territory. Finding an unclaimed space simply to spend the night was difficult enough.

He'd seen the tree from which Adapis had stripped the healing bark—a dark twisting trunk with skinny branches and enormously broad leaves. There was no color to his echovision, so he searched for the tree's outline alone, his mind churning anxiously. What if he couldn't find it? What if it didn't grow anywhere else? The tree runners were so clever. But how could they be capable of such barbarity? Maybe it was *because* they were clever, and they'd realized that they could trade others' lives for their own.

He spotted it. Landing on the trunk, he sank his claws deep and sniffed to make sure. With his teeth he gouged the bark and then tried to peel a strip back. It was difficult to get his jaws close enough, and he cursed his clumsiness, wishing he had the tree runner's hands, just for a few moments.

There. A thin strip pulled free. It was enough, wasn't it? Adapis hadn't used any more than that. Clenching it between his teeth, he pushed off and flew. He'd never known what kind of leaf it was that Adapis crumbled into the bark paste, and only hoped that it wasn't important. The bark would have to be enough.

When he got back, his father's eyes were open but seemed unfocused. Auster and Sylph looked on in silence.

"I've led poorly," Icaron murmured. His flanks throbbed with his breathing.

Dusk glanced fearfully at Sylph. She said nothing.

"You've led well," said Dusk, biting off pieces of the bark for him and Sylph to chew. He wasn't even sure if his father heard him, or if he was still locked in feverish dreams. Dusk was afraid of what Dad might say next. What if Dusk didn't know the right things to say to comfort him? Hurriedly he started working the tough, bitter bark between his jaws, mulching it.

"The island spoiled us," mumbled Dad. "We're ill-suited for this new world."

"You've taken care of us all," Auster assured him.

Icaron grunted, and Dusk wondered if he was disagreeing.

But when he spoke next his thoughts had meandered.

"No such thing as paradise," Dad said, slurring the words. "Dangerous to think so."

"Rest," said Dusk. "Please rest. Things will be better in the morning."

It seemed an absurd thing to say, a childish thing, but it was all he could think of.

"I think it's ready," Sylph said. She moved over Dad's wound and drizzled the slime onto it.

Dad flinched, and seemed to rouse from his half slumber. He twisted toward his daughter and bared his teeth, as though Sylph were a malevolent tree runner. She shrank back in shock.

"What's this?" Icaron demanded, craning his neck, tasting the slime and spitting it out.

"It's the healing bark," Sylph said. "We found some—"

"Poison!" Dad said. "Trying to poison me again."

Dusk caught Sylph's eye and shook his head. Dad wasn't making sense. He was delirious.

"It worked before, Dad," Dusk said.

His father turned and stared at him a long time, before finally seeming to recognize him.

"Dusk," he said.

"The infection's come back," Dusk told him. "It might help."

"No," he said.

"Dad—"

"No! I won't have it on me. It's poison." He seemed exhausted by his recent movements, and sank back against the branch.

"He's asleep again," said Auster after a moment. "Do it now."

Dusk and Sylph crept forward and drizzled their paste onto the wound. Dad twitched and muttered, then made a loud exhalation. He began shivering, though it was a warm night, so Dusk lay down beside him, pressed close. Sylph snuggled up on the other side.

"There's nothing more to do now," Auster said. "Come get me when he wakes again." He gave an approving nod. "You two are very capable."

Dusk watched Auster return to his own family. He'd liked having an older brother nearby, and felt abandoned now. He closed his eyes, squeezing hard, and whispered to his father, "Rest. It'll be better tomorrow."

Something rasped against the bark. Dusk opened his eyes in fright. His father was no longer beside him.

The darkness was just beginning to leech out of the sky. Dad was hauling himself away along the branch. Dusk hurriedly woke Sylph and they caught up with him. His father's eyes were no longer dulled and confused, but fierce with purpose.

"Dad, come back and rest," he said, though instinctively he knew what his father was doing and where he was going. He felt his throat constrict.

"Go wake Auster," he whispered to Sylph.

"There's no need for that," Dad said calmly.

"Go find more of that bark," Sylph urged Dusk.

"No," said Icaron.

He'd crossed over to the next tree now and kept going, seeking out more distant branches.

"Don't go," Dusk said. They were the only words he could clutch from the tumult in his head. His father paused and looked back at his son.

"I must go."

Dusk knew it was the way of all creatures—some instinct that took them away from the living when they knew death was imminent. His father was leaving to die alone, and fear and anguish reverberated through Dusk's body. He looked numbly across at Sylph.

Dad limped along, and Dusk and Sylph followed mutely, not knowing what else to do. They were shadows, the three of them, moving through a kind of limbo that was neither night nor day. The birds had not yet sounded the first note of the dawn chorus. When his father paused to rest, Dusk and Sylph paused with him, letting him set the pace of this dreadful journey. Finally he seemed satisfied with where he was, and settled himself into a deep furrow in a branch. It reminded Dusk a little of their old nest in the sequoia.

His father shut his eyes tight, as if concentrating. His tattered breathing seemed loud in the still of the forest.

"There's something I must tell you," he said, looking straight at Dusk.

Dusk waited, not knowing what he was about to hear, whether it would be lucid or incoherent. But his father's voice was calm, and his eyes clear.

"The saurian nest you discovered on the island, do you remember?"

Dusk nodded. It seemed so long ago, and not at all important now.

"Nova didn't destroy the eggs," his father said. "I did."

"What's he talking about?" Dusk heard Sylph whisper beside him.

But he didn't turn to look at her. He just stared at his father, unable to speak.

"All those years ago, when we abandoned the Pact and the other chiropters drove us out, my dearest wish was to find a safe place for all of us. The island seemed ideal. When we first arrived we explored and saw no sign of saurians. We found the sequoia—and what a tree it was, a perfect home for a new colony. But later that same year, when I was off alone, patrolling the island, I spotted two saurians. They must've crossed from the mainland, maybe for the same reasons we did. Maybe they were banished; maybe they were just trying to find a good nesting place. The saurians were old; I could see they had the rotting disease on their flesh. They wouldn't live long. But in their nest were four eggs."

Dad paused, taking long, slow inhalations. Dusk felt breathless.

"I knew their kind," his father continued. "They weren't flyers. Winged saurians would have posed little threat to us. These were land hunters, meat eaters; and they could climb trees. Barat, Sol, your mother and I—we all had newborns, just learning how to glide and hunt and take care of themselves. It changed how I felt about things. When I saw those saurian eggs, I didn't want them to hatch. I didn't want my own children to be their prey. I did the thing I'd sworn never to do again. I destroyed the eggs."

"But . . . you lied to me," Dusk said. For some reason it was all that his mind could grasp right now, and he felt terribly hurt. "When I told you, you seemed so shocked, and you said you'd find out who did it. But you knew all along."

"I'm sorry, Dusk."

Dusk stared at the bark. All his life there was no one he'd trusted more than his father.

"Did Mom know?"

"I told no one. But some birds saw me do it. I could hear them shrieking overhead. I hoped they'd forget with time, but obviously they passed the story down to their hatchlings."

Dusk lifted his eyes. His dad was watching him. "All the things you said, though, about how wrong it was—"

"He did it to keep us safe," Sylph said sharply. "Can't you understand that, Dusk? He wanted to keep all of us *safe*!"

Dusk flinched at his sister's exasperation.

"No, Dusk is right," Dad said quietly. "You're not to rebuke him, Sylph."

Sylph sagged visibly, and Dusk saw some of the old resentment flare in her eyes.

"What I did was a terrible betrayal of my beliefs," Dad said remorsefully. "But I did it nonetheless. And it makes me a hypocrite. What makes it worse is that I don't even regret doing it, even though I knew it was wrong." He nodded sadly at Dusk. "When you have your own children, maybe you'll understand and forgive me."

His eyes were beseeching, and Dusk wanted to help him, but wasn't sure how, he was so overwhelmed by the whirl of thoughts in his head. His throat would scarcely let his words escape.

"Dad, it's okay," he breathed. "You took good care of us."

Icaron's flanks rose and fell quickly, and he nodded. His breath had an unearthly odor that made Dusk instinctively want to draw away.

"I don't want you to die," wailed Sylph.

Dusk watched in amazement as his sister pushed her head against Dad's, trembling helplessly. "We won't have anyone!"

"You have each other," said Icaron with surprising sternness. "You," he said, looking at Sylph, "are spirited and strong." Dusk thought he heard his father chuckle. "You may drive others to their deaths, but you will live. And you," he said to Dusk, "must help the colony find a new home. Fly high. See far."

"I will," said Dusk.

When they all made their final good-byes, the words seemed blunt and small and utterly inadequate. Dad said nothing more to them after that. Still, they would not leave, and only when he bared his teeth and snapped weakly at them did they scuttle back a few steps. But Dusk would retreat no farther.

Icaron turned his back on them. He looked like a newborn nestled in the bark.

His body shuddered occasionally, and Dusk heard his father mumbling to himself, and realized he was reciting the names of all his children, from first to last. The whistle of his breath became fainter. Dusk wanted to draw closer, to lie beside him and give him some company to the end, but something prevented him. His father's death was hovering all around him, and Dusk feared if he moved too close, he'd be enveloped in its wings and carried away. He watched and waited. When he thought the night would never end, he heard the first clear notes of the birds' dawn chorus.

"Is he dead?" Sylph asked.

"I don't know." Hesitantly he moved forward to Dad's right flank, and touched his sail to his fur. It was cool.

"Dad," he whispered to his ear.

There was no reply, no movement. His father's eyes were half open, but sightless.

"He's dead," Dusk said.

Sylph hunched down against the branch, as if bracing against a strong wind.

"We're orphans," she said.

For a long time they said nothing. Dusk felt numb and empty. He did not fear diatrymas or felids anymore: the worst thing in his life had already happened, and nothing else seemed frightening.

Insects were already beginning to settle on Icaron's body, and Sylph scrambled close and angrily shooed them away with her sails. It was futile. The flies came in greater numbers, settling around his nostrils, on the surface of his dull, misted eyes. Dusk did not want to see his father like this.

"Come on, Sylph, we should go."

She kept swatting at the flies in a fury.

"Sylph!" he said sharply, tugging at her with one of his claws.

"It was only you he cherished," she shouted. "His eyes were

always on you. I could never make him proud. But you with your stupid deformed sails—that was more impressive to him!"

Dusk sighed. He could no more stop her rage than he could a squall.

"Why should I care?" she said darkly. "He betrayed all of us."

"How can you say that?" Dusk demanded.

"He broke his own rules, he killed the eggs. Don't you see what that means? He was *wrong* all along. When it came right down to it, he killed the eggs—because he knew it was the *right* thing to do! And he couldn't even admit it!"

"He was ashamed, Sylph."

"No, he was too proud. He wanted everyone to think he was the perfect, noble leader. He could never admit he was wrong. He'd rather keep secrets and lie to everyone. He'd rather turn down a new home with Gyrokus, and make his whole colony suffer."

"He made a mistake, one mistake twenty years ago! It doesn't mean his beliefs were wrong."

Sylph grunted. "I wonder what Nova would think."

"You can't tell her. Sylph, please."

"You're just as bad as him. Keeping secrets. What's it matter now?" She looked miserably at her father's body.

"Dad was a good leader. He tried his best. If you tell Nova, she'll twist it all round and they might . . ."

"Think badly of him?"

"Yes. And they'd be wrong."

"Fine," she muttered, "I won't tell. But you have to promise you won't keep any more secrets from me."

"I promise. We need to watch out for each other. Let's make a pact. We'll protect each other always. All right?"

"All right," she said after a few moments. "But I wish I could fly too."

"Me too," Dusk said. "I really do."

They did not want to return to the colony just yet, and as the dawn chorus built, they began to groom each other. They didn't speak, but in their heads echoed memories of happier days.

"Where's your father?" Nova asked when they finally returned to the tree.

"He died, just before dawn," Dusk told her.

He'd expected grim delight to show in her eyes, but was surprised to see genuine shock. Barat and Sol were mute. Nearby chiropters overheard the news and sent it wafting through the branches.

"This is dire news for all of us," Sol said.

"We will go on," said Nova. "When one leader dies, another rises."

"It must be Icaron's eldest, then," said Barat.

More and more chiropters gathered around, filling the branches. Auster struggled through the crowds.

"Is it true?" he asked, looking bewildered. "Is he dead?"

"The leadership must pass to you, Auster," said Sol.

"The role of leader," Nova remarked, "is one that Auster may not wish to take on in such extraordinary times."

"That is the way," said Barat firmly. "Leadership passes by birth to the eldest male. If there's no male, it passes to the eldest female."

"Very true," Nova said. "But everything is different now. We're homeless, and in an unfamiliar world. No one here has even set foot on the mainland, except those of us who left it twenty years ago. And among them, I am the eldest."

Sol gave a hollow laugh. "Are you saying you should be our new leader, Nova?"

Dusk's heart beat faster; he felt he was witnessing a nightmare but was powerless to rouse himself and end it.

"I am saying," Nova went on, "we are best guided by someone with experience, who remembers the mainland and its creatures."

Furious, Dusk looked over at Sylph, but saw she was nodding. How could she be so disloyal? Nova had berated their father at every opportunity. She'd coveted his position for years, and now, only hours after his death, she was trying to wrest power from their family.

Dusk turned to Auster, and saw both indignation and uncertainty in his face.

"Auster," Nova went on, "I was born here; I know this landscape and those who live and hunt in it. I do not want to steal from you. I'm only asking your permission to lead the colony safely to a new home. And then the leadership will be restored to you, as is your right. Will you allow this?"

She spoke with such sincerity and respect that Dusk was momentarily confused. Did Nova really mean what she said? Could Auster say no?

"Nova's right," said Sylph suddenly. "She should lead us for now."

"It's not your decision, newborn!" Auster said sharply.

"Barat, Sol, what's your advice?"

Sol sighed. "You'll make a fine leader, Auster. But this would be a perilous moment to begin. If you agree to let Nova lead us temporarily, Barat and I will make sure that she relinquishes power once we've reached safety."

"Barat?" Auster asked.

"My advice would be to join us as an elder. Nova's strong and able; I trust her to lead well during difficult times, and honor her promises."

Dusk's thoughts were at war. His blood urged his brother to refuse and lead; but he too was scared, and his reason told him they needed an experienced leader now. He didn't trust Nova, though. How he wished his father were alive.

"I agree, then," said Auster. "Nova, I give you permission to lead us."

"Thank you," said Nova. "I will bring us all safely to a new home."

Dusk could sense the relief of the assembled chiropters, comforted to have a new leader, even one who'd been so hostile to his father. Dusk could not look at Nova as she addressed the colony—his father's colony.

"We've learned that we can't trust other creatures," said Nova. "We've been lulled by false kindness. We must rely on ourselves now. We've lost many, but we're still numerous enough to create a new and great colony, once we find our home. And I promise you all, we will find it soon."

As the other elders went off to speak with their families, Auster remained behind with Sylph and Dusk.

"I wish you'd woken me," he said.

"There wasn't time," said Dusk. "Dad wouldn't stop, and we didn't want to lose him in the dark."

"I'd like both of you to nest with my family now," Auster said. "Would you like that?"

Dusk looked at Sylph, and they nodded at the same time.

"Thank you," Dusk said.

"You've both been very brave," said Auster. "Now, can you show me where our father is? I'd like to see him one last time before we move on."

As Carnassial and Panthera watched in amazement, Danian and his pack brought down a tusked rooter nearly twice their size. The six hyaenodons worked together, one jumping on the rooter's back, while others attacked from both sides, some tearing at its soft underbelly, others clamping their jaws around its neck.

Carnassial's blood pounded at his temples, as though he himself were in on the hunt. The musk of Panthera's blood-thirsty excitement hung heavily around her.

For two days and nights, they'd been traveling northward with Danian's pack. The rest of the felids had stayed behind in the valley, awaiting Carnassial's return. The pace the hyaenodons set was exhausting, but Carnassial didn't falter; he did not want to appear weak. Though constantly wary of his brutal companions, he still felt strangely content. Panthera was at his side once more as they embarked on a saurian hunt. It was something he'd thought would never happen again.

Wherever they went the hyaenodons blazed a trail of panic.

Most beasts had never seen such ferocious predators, and fled at first sight. But not everyone could escape in time, especially the larger, slower groundlings.

Sprawled defenseless on its side, the rooter kicked once more and then was still. Danian released his suffocating hold on its throat and slit the beast open from sternum to navel. Its insides uncoiled across the earth.

Danian looked up at Carnassial in the branches. "Eat," he called out. "Be strong."

Panthera was about to go, but Carnassial growled. "No," he told her quietly. "We hunt our own food. We won't be beholden to them. We must be equals."

"You're right," said Panthera.

"We can learn from them," Carnassial said. "The way they worked together to bring down bigger prey; our prowl could do the same."

She nodded.

He tried not to look at the bounty of meat below, but he could hear the hyaenodons' noisy feeding. They seemed to eat everything—even bone and teeth—and leave nothing. They were rapacious. When they'd gorged themselves, they urinated all over the carcass, claiming it as their own, even though they had no intention of eating the rest.

Carnassial knew he had to be very careful with these creatures. If he angered them, if he was no longer useful to them, they could rip him asunder in a heartbeat.

Danian was strong, but weak-minded. He was impressionable. As long as Carnassial could make the hyaenodons believe there was still a threat from the saurians, he could be useful to them. He could guide them. He could make them do his bidding.

Not long ago Carnassial had thought he could rule the world with strength; now Panthera had helped him realize that cunning might be the more powerful weapon of the two.

CHAPTER 19

Chimera

DUSK LIFTED THROUGH the upper branches and into the sky. The forest spread in all directions. The sun hot on his sails, he spiraled higher, until the horizons began to curve. Off to the south he saw a flock of birds contracting and expanding as they flew off somewhere. He felt conspicuous up here, his dark body a blot against the bright sky. But he needed a big view now.

Higher he went.

Far to the west was the pale blue line of the ocean. He looked for their island, but couldn't find it. He spun himself around to the north, which was the direction his father had been leading his colony. In the distance the forest gave way to broad grasslands, and beyond them the land rose, and on the slope he saw trees. Maybe it was some trick of the light or his height, but they seemed immense, tall and broad and mighty.

He inhaled sharply. With eerie accuracy, the panorama before him matched the silver landscape he'd seen in both his vision and his dream.

Angling his sails, he made a fast descent, looking all around for birds. Near the canopy a few spotted him from their roosts and sent up a chorus of consternation, but he fluttered past them quickly, down through the branches to where Nova waited for him along with Barat, Sol, and Auster.

"What did you see?" Barat asked.

Dusk told them breathlessly. "They look exactly like the trees we need. None of them has low branches. No felid could scale their trunks."

"Surely this can't be known from such a great distance," Barat said dubiously.

Dusk couldn't tell them about how he'd already seen these trees—he'd be dismissed at once, and maybe rightly so. It seemed outlandish. But he couldn't extinguish his certainty that they were *meant* to travel to these trees.

"What about the grasslands?" Barat said. "Are there enough trees to make a glide path? Or would we have to cross on foot?"

"On foot, I think," said Dusk. It hadn't even occurred to him, he'd been so excited by the trees in the distance. But of course Barat was right. On the plains, the trees were few and far between, and most of the journey would have to be made across the earth. He'd only been thinking of himself as a flyer. He waited for Nova to rebuke him.

"I don't like it," said Auster. "On the ground we'd be too vulnerable to attack. I say we pick another route."

"But if the trees are perfect," Nova began, "then the journey might be worth the risk."

Dusk looked at her in surprise.

"Your skills are a great asset to us," she told him, and he felt an unexpected gratitude and pleasure at her compliment.

"In hours you could cover a distance that would take us days and nights," Nova went on. She appeared to be considering something. "These high trees you saw—fly there and see if they can truly be a home for us."

"Really?" Dusk asked, his delight tinged with a sudden trepidation.

"Are you strong enough to make such a journey?" Nova asked.

"Yes," he said, after only a moment's hesitation. He'd never flown so far, or been so far away from the colony. "I'm strong enough."

"Make sure the trees are safe, and that no other creatures have already laid claim to them," Nova instructed him. "See everything, especially on the grasslands. Find out what kind of beasts forage there, and if there are predators."

"How long will it take you?" Sol asked.

Dusk conjured up a memory of his high vista, tried to guess at the distance. "If I leave now, I could make it there by nightfall, I think. And then I'd return tomorrow by evening."

"Good. We'll wait here for you. This forest seems safe enough for now."

"It's a sound plan," said Barat.

"Are you sure you want to do this?" Auster asked Dusk kindly.

He nodded.

"Then go," said Nova. "And bring us back good news."

He found Sylph hunting. "I'm going," he told her excitedly, and he described the trees he'd seen from on high. "I've seen them before," he added tentatively, because he had promised to keep no more secrets from her. He told her of his mushroom vision and subsequent dream. "I think these trees are the same ones, Sylph. Do you think I've gone insane?"

"I don't know," she said.

"They're going to be our new home, I just know it!"

She nodded. "How far is it?"

"I'll be back tomorrow night."

Sylph sagged against the bark. "I wish I could come."

"Me too. I—" He trailed off.

"What?" Sylph said.

He lowered his voice. "I don't trust her."

"Nova?"

Dusk nodded. "She always thought I was such a trouble-bringer, with my flying, and Aeolus being murdered by the birds."

"Give her a chance," said Sylph. "She's wise. I know you always took Dad's side, but Dad wasn't always a good leader—just let me finish. He could have told the colony about the felids after the bird warned you, but he didn't. He nearly let the tree runners make a feast of us."

"No one suspected them," said Dusk. "I didn't hear Nova say anything! She thought we'd found a new home."

"Maybe so. But we've lost a quarter of the colony. If he'd made different choices, it wouldn't be that way."

"He made the best choices he could," Dusk said stubbornly.

Sylph chittered in exasperation. "Nova will lead well."

Dusk sighed. "Maybe you're right. I wish you could come with me."

"It's just one night, right?"

"Probably." It would be the first time he'd ever spent a night away from his colony. Loneliness groaned through his bones.

"Be careful," Sylph said. "Fly fast."

He'd never flown for such a long time at one stretch, but now he pushed himself, and after a while something happened. His heart seemed to find a new rhythm, and his breathing slowed and deepened. It was still hard work, but he felt he could keep it up.

He flew above the forest canopy, near enough that he could quickly take cover in the trees if any birds attacked. He kept watch higher in the skies too, hoping that the last of the quetzals truly had died out.

Swarming above the forest were a fair number of insects, but he mostly ignored them, not wanting to waste time or energy darting off course. He kept his nose aimed at the distant hills. The vast trees there still seemed impossibly far away, and for a moment he was frightened. How could he possibly travel so far, and alone? But it was good finally to have a firm destination, after all the uncertain days deep in the forest.

Below him, the trees began to change. There were types he hadn't seen before, great twisted things with bark so craggy and sharply ridged the trunks looked like they were made of hooked beaks jutting down. Still other trees were a dead color, and looked like they'd flake away if you sank your claws into them. Their flowers and leaves released new fragrances. When the forest canopy began to thin, the shrubs and ferns grew denser. Muddy pools became more numerous, until finally there were hardly any bits of boggy land between them. Swampy trees thrust up everywhere, trailing great swaths of moss. Dusk carefully kept track of the trees, making sure there were always enough for the chiropters to glide between.

Something long and green stirred the water below him, and Dusk caught sight of a knobby back and tail before it disappeared entirely beneath the swirling surface. He swallowed, glad he was not a groundling.

Up ahead the swamp became forest once more, but only briefly before giving way to the grasslands. Here, at the border, Dusk circled the trees and picked out a safe branch before landing. Exhausted, he lapped dew off leaves, and when he'd slaked his thirst, he backed against the trunk so nothing could creep up on him. He gazed out across the grasslands.

There were numerous trees, but they were widely spaced, and Dusk knew there was no way his colony could glide from one to another. They would have to cross this sea of grass largely on foot. He tried not to feel too discouraged. The grass was tall, and would offer some cover. He hadn't known it grew in so many different colors and textures. The feathered tips glowed brilliantly in the late afternoon light, leaning gracefully as the wind shifted them. For a while Dusk just stared, content to let his mind empty.

He must have slept, or half slept, for his ears were still alert. A snort from below startled him awake, his sails twitching. He peered down through the branches. At the base of the tree, a beast snuffled among the plants. It was easily ten times his size, Dusk realized, perhaps five feet long, with a long tail. Its coarse brown fur was striped with black. When it lifted its blunt head from the grass, he saw with relief that it had been grazing, for bits of leaves and grass dropped from its jaws as it chewed. Its intelligent eyes fixed on Dusk, then turned away without a trace of concern. Obviously this creature knew all about chiropters, but Dusk knew nothing about it.

The creature gave a soft whinny, and moments later a second beast cantered in on long legs from the grasslands. This one's short hair was dappled brown and gray; it blended in well with the undergrowth.

Dusk marveled at their feet. They had five long toes that had no claws but ended instead with a flat layer of what looked like bone. They thudded softly on the ground with every step.

Together the two creatures grazed, their soft mouths nuzzling and pulling at the grasses. Occasionally they exhaled in a kind of humorous wheeze. Dusk liked looking at them.

They seemed gentle, and were clearly intelligent, for he noticed that they never had their heads down at the same time. They took turns watching.

Dusk wanted to talk to them. Since they were plant eaters, they could hardly be dangerous. Of course, the tree runners were plant eaters too, and they'd turned out to be diabolical. But Dusk decided to take the chance.

"What are you watching out for?" he called down.

"Diatrymas," said the brown and black creature, scarcely looking up.

"Ah," said Dusk. "I've seen one of those."

"Where?" Both creatures looked about in consternation.

"Not right now. Sorry. Back in the forest there was one."

"In the *forest*?"

"It was wounded. There was a group of tree runners feeding it."

"Ghastly," said the dappled beast.

"Mostly they keep to the grasslands," said the other, eyes sweeping the tall stalks. "They're fast."

"Are there many?"

"Yes," said the dappled creature.

It took a moment for Dusk to work up the courage. "What are you?" he asked.

"Equids," said the first. "I'm Dyaus, and that's Hof."

"Thank you," said Dusk. "Those toes on your feet are—"

"Hooves."

"Is that what they're called? Are they very hard?"

Dyaus tapped a hoof against the earth, and it made a satisfying *clop*. "Hard enough to run on."

"Do you know the other side of the grasslands, to the north?" Dusk asked.

"A little."

"Are there felids there?"

"Some, I suppose. They've become numerous since the saurians died off."

"Do they eat flesh?"

"What?" Hof said in surprise.

Dusk told them about Carnassial and the invasion of his island. Dyaus and Hof looked at each other, aghast.

"The felids here have never bothered us."

Dusk was relieved to hear that. It meant his father was right: that Carnassial was a rogue, acting on his own.

"But we've seen hyaenodons," Dyaus said. "Big predators from the east. They came through the grasslands not so long ago. Luckily they seem to have moved on."

"As if we needed anything to make our lives more difficult," grumbled Hof morosely.

"Maybe they'll devour those flesh-eating felids of yours," said Dyaus cheerfully.

The idea gave Dusk some satisfaction but little comfort. He was trying to find a safe homeland for his colony, and didn't want to think about more predators.

"Why are you interested in the north?" Dyaus asked.

Dusk did not know whether he should tell them about his colony's plans. They seemed friendly and harmless, but he didn't want to take any risks.

"Are there any other predators around here?" he asked instead.

"Apart from the diatrymas you mean?" Dyaus said thoughtfully. "Back there, to the south, there's the swamp saurians. They're about the only kind of saurian that survived the Pact. They never stray far from the water. They hide underneath, just their eyeballs sticking out."

"Then they lunge," Hof added with grim enjoyment. "Once their jaws lock, they can't be pried apart. They could carry off one of us easily. Wouldn't even think twice about it. We never go near the swamp. You're lucky to live up in the trees."

A small movement in the tall grass caught Dusk's eye. From his high vantage point he saw, thirty feet away, a massive, hooked beak protruding from the stalks.

"There's a diatryma!" he called down to the equids.

The giant bird came hurtling toward them, amazingly fast despite its ungainly body. The two equids ran, swift and graceful on their hoofed feet. The diatryma's shriek made Dusk's knees weaken, and he was not even the one pursued. The flightless bird was many times larger than Dyaus and Hof, and could easily disembowel them with a shearing chop from its beak.

Dusk shot pulses of sound after the three creatures, and could tell from the returning echoes that the equids were the quicker, though not by much. He fervently hoped their stamina matched their speed. They rapidly disappeared into the tall grass.

The sight of the diatryma left Dusk shaken. If his colony meant to cross these grasslands, they'd have to be extremely careful, and travel only at night. Surely the diatryma, like most birds, slept then. The chiropters' coloring and small size would be their only advantages. And Dusk, with his echo-vision, could guide them in the dark.

He only had one more hour of daylight, and wanted to get going again. Among the trees he hunted quickly, always keeping his eyes and ears alert to the sounds in the forest. Other small beasts foraged around him, but he never let himself speak, or get too close, to any of them.

He probably shouldn't have talked to the equids either, but he was lonely, and longed for company. Gone from his colony half a day, and already lonely. He'd never realized how much he relied on their physical proximity—the smell and heat of their bodies giving him comfort and confidence. Alone, he felt frightfully vulnerable, like something soft without its protective shell.

Fed and rested, he launched himself over the grasslands. He made sure his course never took him too far from a tree, in case he had to rest.

He caught glimpses of numerous four-legged groundlings—all ones he'd seen before, and none of them flesh eaters. But he also spotted another diatryma. It hunkered in the grass, long neck folded so its head just grazed the tops of the stalks, giving it a view while remaining hidden. Its black eyes flashed in the light and Dusk knew it was watching the grass for any sudden movement that would signal a creature moving beneath. He flew on with a shudder.

Sometimes the tall grass gave way to russet stubble and open plain. It was far from flat. Even from above he could see it had a rise and fall to it. In a muddy pool he saw a creature he thought at first must be a swamp saurian. But it wasn't green or knobbed. It was fat, with short hair of tan and white. The beast seemed content to stand in the murk, dunking its head beneath the surface and reappearing with its mouth seeping with wet weeds.

All across the grasslands Dusk spotted bones, scoured to a blinding white by the sun and elements. Some were so huge he could hardly imagine the size of the creatures they once formed. These, he was sure, belonged to the saurians. What had happened to make them all sicken at the same time? And why not the beasts as well?

The sun neared the horizon. Birds wheeled, ready to find their roosts. Their dusk chorus began to carry through the air from all directions. Though it sounded a little different from what he was used to, he still found it comforting. It had been such a steady, predictable part of his life: the birds singing the night to them.

For the first time in days he thought about Teryx. He'd been kind, even if the rest of his flock hadn't. And the equids had seemed kindly too. In the past days he'd come to look on everyone as an enemy, someone who might trick or eat him. Surely this new world couldn't be as bad as that.

The sky began to lose its color but Dusk flew on, fighting the instinct to find a safe place to roost. If he could only reach the great trees on the far hills, everything would be all right. He'd sleep there, and have the morning to explore. That would still leave enough time to make the return journey tomorrow, and be back with Sylph and his colony by nightfall. He hoped Sylph wasn't too lonely without him. She was a survivor. She'd be just fine.

Night came. The throb of insects had replaced the birds' chorus. A layer of mist unfurled across the grasslands as the world contracted into darkness. Dusk fought panic. He reminded himself that he needed neither sun nor moon. With sound he could summon the world to him, etched in silver.

To the west was the black sea and its unbroken horizon; to the north was the silhouette of hills against the starlit sky. As he flew, he began shooting out sound after every breath. From the darkness of his mind bloomed the grasslands and the constellation of insects that were coming alive. The night was every bit as clear and bright as the day! After a while he started enjoying himself. It was exciting, but also strangely soothing. He felt safe, invisible. Just him and the night.

He was much better now at catching his echoes while in flight. At first he'd collided with them and seen only a blur, but now he seemed to have his sonic bursts and hearing and breathing in sync, though he had no idea how he managed this. It worked, and that's all he cared about.

He rested briefly on a tree, careful to pick branches that were uninhabited. He gleaned some dopey insects and lapped water pooled in the bark. He flew hard, the night air cooling him. The grasslands rose to meet the hills, and he rose with them. Higher he went, his shoulders now sluggish with fatigue, but he would not stop until he reached the trees.

He felt himself drawn forward by some homing instinct he did not understand, the silvery image of the dream tree flaring in his mind's eye. He was very close. He was so tired that he did not know whether he was having another vision or whether he had finally reached his destination. His eyes showed him only blackness, but when he cast out another burst of sound, the trees, suddenly, were before him. It seemed impossible he had actually reached them.

He made one circle, too weary to explore his surroundings right now. He landed, murmuring just enough sound to make sure there were no other creatures sleeping nearby. He found a deep niche in the bark, pressed himself into it, and fell hard into sleep.

But his mind was not ready for rest, and even as he slumbered, he imagined he was still flying. His mouth was parched; his stomach was cavernous with hunger. But he would not bother hunting now. Pain gusted through his arms and shoulders. He thought he might die. When he looked up into the sky he felt an enormous sense of well-being. The stars shaped themselves into giant wings and enveloped him, and this time he wasn't afraid.

Dusk opened his eyes.

He was certain that another creature was nearby. The sky was just showing the first signs of coming dawn. Though the moon was still out, he was so well nestled into the bark he felt all but invisible. He looked around but saw nothing on his branch. He tilted back his head.

Directly above him was a chiropter, hanging upside down from a branch by its rear claws. It was a female; he could tell by her scent. Her sails were wrapped about her. Dusk stared up at her curiously, for it was not the custom for chiropters to hang upside down, though he had seen a few launch themselves that way. He felt dejected. Perhaps this tree was already claimed by another colony, and they'd refuse to share it. Dusk wasn't sure if he should even call out a greeting.

The chiropter was grooming herself. Dusk wondered why she was so active this early in the morning. Most chiropters would still be sleeping. She dropped from the branch and went gliding off between the branches.

Then her sails lifted high, and she began to flap swiftly.

She was flying!

Before he could stop himself Dusk cried out in surprise, and she banked sharply.

"Who are you?" she asked, soaring back toward the tree. Just before she landed, she made a nimble aerial flip and gripped the underside of the branch with her rear claws, swinging upside down, and peering straight down at him.

Before she furled her sails, he saw that they were virtually hairless, and that the moonlight shone through them, silhouetting the bones of her arms and fingers.

"They're the same," he muttered in amazement. "As mine. Your sails . . ."

He felt a gentle barrage of hunting clicks against his face and fur. She was looking at him with sound.

"Who are you?" she asked again.

"Dusk. You can fly!"

"Show me your wings!" she said excitedly. Her dark eyes were quick and lively.

"They're not wings, they're sails," he said, spreading them.

She dropped down to his branch and came closer on all fours.

"No, they're *wings*," she said, nudging him with her nose.

Dusk's heart raced. "Chiropters are born with sails," he said. Somehow he knew what she would say next, and he both dreaded and craved it.

"Yes, but you're not a chiropter."

"I am. My mother and father—"

She shook her head. "You were *born* from chiropters, but you've made the change."

"The change?"

"You've become something else. You're new."

Dusk felt himself shaking.

"Don't be afraid," she said kindly. "You're not alone. There are others."

"How many?"

"Plenty. We have a colony not far from here. All flyers."

"How does this happen?" he demanded, his voice hoarse. "Why did it?"

She flicked a wing. "No one knows. In my colony there were three of us who could fly."

"Three!"

"Our skeletons were different. We had stronger—"

"Chests and shoulders?"

"Yes, and wings without fur."

"I thought I was the only one. A freak."

"Not a freak. We've become something different, that's all. But it meant we had to leave our colony."

"You did?"

"Haven't you been driven out too?" she asked.

"My father was leader."

"That might explain it," she said. "But why are you all alone?"

"They sent me ahead to find a new home."

"Sent? Or banished?"

"Sent," he said, a sudden coldness pulsing down his spine.

"We were all banished," she said. "We were resented. We could hunt faster, eat more, and see at night. We would never have found mates."

"But we're still chiropters," said Dusk.

"We have a new name for ourselves," she said. "Bats."

"Bats?"

"Our leader's name is Bat-ra. She was the one who started the colony. She was the first."

"I worried I was the first," Dusk admitted.

She chuckled. "She's much older than you. We were all lucky to find her. She gave us a home, so it made sense to name ourselves after her."

Bat. It was short and fast, like something shooting through the air.

"I'm Chimera," she told him.

He just wanted to stare at her. Her sails—or wings—might have been his own. Her fur was dark, like his, but with different markings. She had streaks of white around her face and throat. And her ears were pointier and larger.

"I was always trying to flap," he told her. "From the very first."

"Me too!" she said. "It was such an effort to keep it secret. I had to go off into the forest to practice flying."

"I did the same thing!" All at once he was telling her about everything that had happened to his colony. The story had been reverberating in his mind for so long that setting it loose in words was a tremendous relief.

"Your family sounds more accepting than mine," Chimera said. "Your father especially."

"He let me fly—at first anyway. I think he was proud of me."

"Come with me and meet all the others," she said. "You belong with us now."

"I can't," he said, startled by how easily she seemed to claim him. "I have to go back and tell my colony about this tree. It's not yours, is it?"

"No."

Dusk let out a breath.

"Where is your colony?" Chimera wanted to know.

"On the other side of the grasslands. They're waiting for me."

"But how will they cross?"

"On the ground mostly."

She shook her head. "It'll take a long time. They'll be hunted. Have you seen the diatrymas?"

"Yes. But we're small. We can hide. We can cross at night."

She sighed. "They'll be in terrible danger, and you with them."

"Well, that's the way it has to be," he said. "I'll bring them all back here. Do you live far from here?"

"Just on the other side of the hills. Do you see those three stars there? Follow them, and you'll find us."

He felt a pulse of excitement. It was so good to be talking to someone like himself.

"You're not going anywhere?" he asked her urgently.

She laughed. "No. We're staying where we are."

"Then I'll find you when I come back."

"I hope you do. Good luck."

He felt a bit desperate as he watched her go. Part of him wanted to call out, to follow her. But his own colony needed him.

The sun had just cleared the eastern horizon, spilling red light over the tree. He flew around and around it. It was massive, with many branches, and its bark emanated a pleasant smell that reminded him of the island. He couldn't see any other creatures living in the mighty boughs, and though a dawn chorus was starting to carry across the sky, he spotted no bird nests in the tree's upper reaches. It seemed the tree was waiting just for him. He dipped down to examine the base. The trunk towered at least forty feet before the first branches jutted out. There was no way even a clever felid like Carnassial could scale such a trunk, especially since the bark was somewhat harder and smoother than the sequoia's.

With growing anticipation, Dusk flew among the surrounding trees. There were about a dozen in the cluster, and they too towered high before sending out limbs. An abundance of insects filled the air between them. Were there any nearby trees the felids could use as a bridge? Dusk flew above the canopy, looking straight down, measuring the distance between tree limbs. The closest were nearly twenty feet distant, surely too far for even the nimblest felid to jump.

He landed. The view would be invaluable. From up here Dusk could see out over grasslands to the forest beyond, where his colony waited.

He'd found the perfect tree, the perfect home. He wished Dad and Mom could have seen it.

He unfurled his sails and looked at them. Wings. He closed his eyes and sang sound over them and saw how they blazed silver in his mind, the texture of his skin sparkling like the sea. He tried to see them as natural, and not something freakish.

Bat.

That's what she'd called herself—and him. He resisted the name. All his life he'd thought of himself as a chiropter. Take that away, and didn't you also take away some part of who he was? It was like saying he wasn't Icaron's son anymore.

He thought of Sylph, depending on him, and set off at once, eager to return, the bearer of good news.

A stiff wind battled him most of the way back, and it was getting dark as Dusk neared the forest where he'd left his colony. Exhaustion weighted his wings. He sniffed, surprised at himself: he'd automatically thought *wings* instead of *sails*. The two words had been echoing softly in his head the entire journey, as though battling for supremacy. He felt a little frightened at how easily the new word came to him. But words didn't change things, did they? Or maybe they did. Maybe words, once thought or spoken aloud, had a kind of power, and made things permanent.

Now that he was about to face his colony, his courage faltered. How could he tell them about Chimera? How would he explain that, in fact, he might not even be a chiropter, but something called a bat? If they thought him freakish before, what would they think of him now?

He'd never forgotten what Jib had said to him back on the island, about how he would've been driven out of the colony if it weren't for his father. Would this now give Nova all the reason she needed, especially with his father gone?

But maybe she'd be so pleased with him for finding a new home that she'd overlook his differences. He'd served the colony well. They couldn't expel him after all that had happened. Anyway, once they reached the new tree, Auster would be leader, not Nova, and his own brother would never banish him.

You haven't changed, he tried to console himself. *You're the same as you always were.*

But he'd always been different. And now he knew there were others like him. It was both a comfort and a worry. It meant he really was a new kind of creature, and there was no avoiding it. He decided to tell only Sylph for now. Later, once things were more settled, he'd tell the rest of the colony.

This was the place. He remembered the tall tree, its summit scorched by lightning. He dived down through the canopy, swerving deftly between branches.

"It's Dusk! Hello! I'm back!"

All that greeted him were the usual sounds of the twilight forest: the warble and chirp of birdsong, the mounting thrum of insects.

"Hi! I've got good news! Auster? Sylph?"

All the branches were empty.

CHAPTER 20

Abandoned

ON THE BARK, the scent of his colony was faint but unmistakable—the scent he'd grown up with. Smelling it now, without a single chiropter in sight, he felt a crushing sense of abandonment.

Nova had said they'd wait. Sylph had promised.

He fought back his panic. Maybe they were just a little ways off, hunting. Or maybe they'd found a better set of trees. He flew off again in ever-widening circles, calling out for his colony all the while. No return cry came.

He crumpled, breathless, on a branch. Which way had they

gone? He could fly faster than they could glide, but how would he know which direction to choose? And even if he did find them, what was the point?

Despite everything that had happened to him and his family, he'd never felt defeated until now. He'd been discarded by his own colony. Nova had tricked him. She'd never had any intention of traveling to the distant tree he'd spotted. She'd just wanted him gone. Probably she was hoping he'd be killed on the way.

He couldn't stop himself whimpering, and he must have been sending out small pulses of sound because in his mind's eye he saw little sonic flares of the empty branches around him. The sight made him all the more desolate. Just emptiness. Nobody there.

Except—

Something blurred in the fringes of his echovision.

He opened his eyes and whirled around hopefully.

Running toward him along the branch was a felid, eyes fierce, jaws wide. It pounced.

Dusk threw himself off the branch. The felid leaped after him. Dusk felt the frantic heat of its breath against his tail and legs. He opened his wings and beat furiously, lifting clear. Looking down, he saw the felid steering through the air with its bushy tail and landing on a branch. It spat and snarled up at him.

Dusk stayed aloft, scanning the surrounding area. He knew how the felids hunted, and he didn't want to be driven to a new kill zone. But his frenzied glances showed him no more predators. He landed high up, where he had a clear view of the felid. He recognized this one.

"Carnassial," he said.

The felid's ears twitched. "I don't like it when my food talks to me," he growled.

"I'm not your food," Dusk said indignantly, still checking all around in case this was a trap.

"You're the one who can fly," Carnassial said, pacing the branch. "From the island."

"How did you get off?" blurted Dusk.

Carnassial purred smugly. "Ah. So you heard they tried to imprison me there. The soldiers weren't up to the task. The island no longer pleased me, so we left."

Dusk said nothing, he was so surprised—and filled with hope too. If the felids had left the island, that meant it might be theirs again.

They could go home!

"If you were thinking of returning, I have sad news," said Carnassial. "A new type of predator bird has claimed your island."

"Diatrymas?" Dusk said with a shudder.

"No. These were flyers, very vicious and strong, with talons and beaks that could easily kill one of my own."

Dusk's hope vanished. If these birds were rapacious enough to drive out the felids, it would hardly be safe for the chiropters.

"Were there many?" he asked.

"Many. They'd massacre your kind."

Dusk grunted bitterly. "Just like you did."

"Of course I did. It's in my nature."

"Not all felids are meat eaters."

"Not all chiropters can fly. Which is more unnatural?"

For a moment Dusk did not know what to say. "What I do doesn't harm anyone," he replied, but he thought of Aeolus, murdered by the birds.

Carnassial stretched on the branch, his craving for prey seemingly evaporated.

"Before long, you yourself may turn to meat."

"No," said Dusk.

"We felids aren't the only beasts who do it." Carnassial sniffed and tasted the air. "Where is your colony?"

"They've abandoned me," Dusk said. He saw no reason to lie. "They think they'll have better luck finding a new home without me. They've decided I'm a freak."

"Interesting," said Carnassial, "that both of us were exiled because of our natural inclinations. For simply being what we are."

Dusk disliked having anything in common with this creature.

"Where's your prowl?" he asked, feeling anew how bizarre it was to be talking with this monster. Carnassial had murdered his mother, and had given his father the wounds that eventually killed him. Yet here they were, cloaked in the coming night, a safe distance between them, prey and preyed upon.

"Far away," said Carnassial. "I'm traveling temporarily with new allies."

Dusk felt his stomach lurch. "What new allies?"

"Flesh eaters, much larger than myself. Look there."

Dusk followed Carnassial's gaze, down through the branches to the forest floor. A powerful, four-legged beast had just pounced on a shrieking groundling and was shearing its flesh.

"Hyaenodons," said Carnassial. "You see, there are other beasts who eat meat. But you needn't worry about them. They're groundlings. Stay in your trees and you'll not come to harm."

Dusk resented Carnassial's reassuring tone. He didn't believe for a second that this felid had any concern for his well-being. But it was as if they'd silently agreed to a short truce.

When he next spoke, Carnassial's voice was a conspiratorial whisper, as though he didn't want the hyaenodons to hear.

"There's no perfect world," he said, reminding Dusk uncomfortably of what his father had mumbled just before he died. "There's no homeland safe from predators. There will always be predators, and ones bigger than you and me. We must make use of whatever skills we have to survive. Freaks like us might have an advantage. Your ability to fly may be your salvation. I used to think my hunter's teeth and strength gave me an advantage." He gave a small, self-mocking growl. "Now I know I must be smarter and quicker to excel."

"I don't wish you luck," Dusk told him.

"Keep your luck," said Carnassial. "You will need it more than me."

Dusk was frightened by the hungry look sparking once more in Carnassial's eyes. He launched himself into the darkening forest. He didn't care where he was going; he was intent only on leaving the felid and his beast allies far behind. He felt sickened by their conversation.

When it became too dark to see, he navigated by echoes alone until his weariness overcame him, and he landed. He wrapped himself in his wings. Should he simply go back to the mighty tree on the hill, and find Chimera and the other bats? At least there he'd have a home.

But what about the pact he'd made with Sylph, to take care of each other? It seemed she'd already broken it. But part of him couldn't believe this. His sister had the most loyal of hearts. If she wasn't here, there must be some good reason for it—and one, he hoped, that wasn't terrible. Tomorrow he'd think more clearly. Tomorrow he'd know how to find her.

For the second night in a row, he slept alone, huddled in a strange tree.

"Dusk!"

Even in his dreams, he wondered if it was just the wind. But when he heard his name called a second time, more clearly, his mind began prising him out of sleep.

"Dusk!"

He woke and saw his sister gliding right past his branch, not seeing him. He was so stunned that for a moment he couldn't speak or move. She was like an apparition of his deepest wishes and he couldn't quite believe she was real. Then he threw himself into the air and started flapping after her.

"Sylph!"

She banked and saw him.

"Oh!" she exclaimed. "I was so worried!"

Dusk flew to her and fluttered around her delightedly as she glided in to land. On the branch they nuzzled and embraced each other with their sails.

"Where were you?" Dusk said. "I thought you'd left me!"

"We had to," she explained. "Yesterday afternoon, some of our sentries saw a pair of felids. And they seemed to be traveling with some other scary-looking beasts. We don't know what they were."

"Hyaenodons," Dusk said.

Sylph hunched forward in surprise. "How do you know?"

"Carnassial told me."

His sister looked so bewildered that Dusk couldn't help chuckling. He told her about his surreal encounter and conversation with the felid last night.

"Did he say where he was going?" Sylph wanted to know.

"I should've asked. But I doubt he would've told me the truth."

"I hope he gets eaten by his new friends," Sylph said bitterly.

"I'm so glad you're here," Dusk said.

"We started looking for you at first light."

"I was worried Nova had abandoned me."

Sylph exhaled loudly. "She did."

Dusk squinted, confused. "What?"

"After you left, she held an assembly. She said we should return to Gyrokus and join his colony. Now that she was leader, she'd renounce the past and apologize, and Gyrokus would take us in. She said it was the best thing to do." Sylph took a deep breath. "But she said we couldn't risk taking you with us."

"Because I fly," Dusk said dully.

Sylph nodded. "They'd reject all of us as deviants. Nova said it made her sad to leave you, but her responsibility was to all the chiropters in the colony—not just one."

Sylph seemed to remember Nova's words well, as if she'd gone over them again and again in her head.

"And everyone agreed with her," Dusk said.

"Not *quite* everyone."

"Who's left, Sylph?"

"Sol wouldn't leave, but most of his family did anyway."

"Sol was always the most loyal to Dad," said Dusk.

"And Auster spoke against the plan too. He said it was a betrayal of Dad to go back to Gyrokus. He stayed behind, and so did about half our family. Nova, Barat, all their two families, and everyone else—they left yesterday."

Dusk said nothing. If a felid had sunk its teeth into his shoulder, he doubted he'd have felt a thing. After a while he realized Sylph was watching him in concern.

"Dusk. Are you okay?"

"Jib's gone, I suppose," he said finally.

Sylph sniffed. "Yeah. He's gone."

"So the news isn't all bad."

"He really was a little nit," his sister agreed with a chuckle.

Dusk looked at her gravely. "You must've wanted to go too."

Sylph gazed at the bark for a moment. "You know how I felt about Gyrokus and Dad's decision."

"I know."

"I'm not sure if Nova's decision was a bad one," she said slowly.

"You always did feel some loyalty to her," Dusk said.

She raised her head, her eyes fierce. "Yes. But I'm more loyal to *you*. Nothing could've made me leave."

Dusk nodded, amazed. She'd thought Nova's decision was a good one; she'd wanted a safe home. Yet she'd chosen to stay with him. Even when she was angry and resentful, she'd always stood up for him. Always.

"No one ever had a better sister," he told her.

She frowned. "Even if I thought going back to Gyrokus was a good idea, the way Nova did it wasn't right. Lying and sending you off like that, after everything you've done. She'd probably be mulched up in the gut of a diatryma if it weren't for you! I'd rather be homeless than live in her colony now."

"You don't have to be homeless," Dusk told her. "I found us a home."

"Really?" she said. "Those trees you saw?"

He nodded. "They're perfect."

It was a much-diminished colony that Dusk guided through the forest and swamp. There were fewer than a hundred of them now. Still, when he was reunited with them he'd been overcome with joy and relief—and surprise, for they greeted him so warmly. There was such comfort simply being among his own kind, enveloped in the scent and closeness of their bodies.

It took them an entire day to reach the edge of the grasslands, and the sun was floating above the horizon when they finally landed in the branches. Auster immediately posted sentries all around their tree, in case Carnassial and his cohort were stalking them. Crouched beside his sister, Dusk stared out at the distant hills.

"They look a long way away," said Sylph.

"They didn't seem so far when I was in the air," Dusk confessed.

Auster settled beside him silently as he surveyed the landscape in the last light of the sun. He was leader now.

"We'll plot our course from tree to tree," he said. "That way we can rest safely, and then start out again with a long glide. It'll save us some time on the ground." He exhaled quietly. "There's a lot of ground to cover."

"I can be your guide," Dusk said.

"We couldn't do it otherwise," Auster sighed. "We'll need your night eyes up high."

Dusk nodded.

Auster lifted his gaze to the hills and made a satisfied grunt. "It's good to finally have our home in sight."

They spent that night in the forest, and all the next day fed and rested in preparation for the crossing. When darkness fell, they would set out. The diatrymas would be sleeping; the chiropters' dark bodies would be concealed; and though their vision would be poor, Dusk would lead them with his echovision.

He knew he should be off hunting, gathering strength for the coming journey, but he had no appetite. With every passing minute he felt more exhausted with worry. He just wanted to get going. As the sun began to set, the earth cooled. Mist sifted across the grasslands. The moon was big tonight. It would help guide them; but it would also help any nocturnal predators.

Sylph returned from hunting and settled beside him on the branch.

"Maybe this isn't a good idea," he whispered to her. "This crossing. Maybe we should just go back to our island."

Sylph shook her head. "Auster and Sol agreed it was too risky, with those predator birds."

"Maybe Carnassial was just lying, to keep us from going back. Out of spite."

"Anyway, it's so far away now."

"Ten days' journey, that's all."

"I didn't mean just that," his sister said. "After what happened, do you think you could be happy there again?"

"We were born there, Sylph! I loved that tree."

"Me too. But Mom was murdered in our nest. Going back there, I worry I'd think about her too much. Dad too. You said these new trees were perfect."

"I know, but . . . what if I can't do it?" he murmured. "What if I can't get everyone across?"

"You can do it."

"You don't know what you're talking about," he said, suddenly angry. "What if I can't see far enough? What if I make a mistake? What if I tell everyone to go one way and it's the wrong way and they get eaten?"

"You got us off the island—"

"Not everyone. Some died."

"Most lived. And you saved most of us from getting eaten by that diatryma."

"What if I get scared and fly off?" Dusk said. The idea had been haunting him all day.

"You'd never do that," she said. "You've got a loyal heart too, you know."

"But I'm not like the rest of you," he blurted out.

"Yes you are."

"No, I'm something else. I am. I really am." It was not the right time, but it was too late to go back now. He hurriedly told her about Chimera and what she'd said to him—how he wasn't a chiropter at all; how he was really a bat.

"You can't tell this to anyone else, Sylph."

"Of course I won't." She stared into the darkening sky.

Dusk watched her anxiously, wondering what she was thinking.

"I didn't want any of this," he said miserably. "It just happened to me. It could've happened to anyone. I don't even want to be a bat."

"It doesn't matter what you're called," Sylph said firmly. "You're different, we always knew that. But you're still you. You haven't changed."

"The colony will never accept me!"

"They trust you, Dusk."

He looked at her, surprised.

She lowered her voice even more. "They didn't stay because of Auster. They stayed because of *you*. They remember all the things you've done for them. They know you'll take care of them."

"Me?"

"Maybe I shouldn't have told you," she muttered. "You're

going to start thinking you're special."

"Well, I am in line to be leader," he chuckled.

"You and half the males in the colony. Actually I think that's the real reason so many decided to stay."

They settled down side by side, grooming one another, not talking. He could overhear little snatches of conversation, fading and rising, from the other chiropters waiting in the dark branches.

". . . be starting out soon . . ."

"Is your hind leg any better?"

". . . a pool of water along that branch if you're thirsty . . ."

"Don't be afraid; Dusk can see in the dark . . ."

". . . be in our new home soon . . ."

"He'll lead us through the dark, you'll see . . ."

"Dusk?"

Startled from his reverie, he looked over to see Auster and Sol standing before him on the branch.

"It's time to go," Auster said. "Ready?"

"Yes," said Dusk, "I'm ready."

CHAPTER 21

Soricids

DUSK PUSHED THROUGH the tall grass, the stalks so thick and high he saw only what was directly in front of him. Dew beaded his fur. He scuttled around small gnarled plants whose leaves spread overhead like the canopies of miniature trees. Twigs scratched his face. The air was thick with insects and spores and spider gossamer.

They were halfway across the grasslands.

Sylph was on his left, Auster on his right, with the rest of the colony following close behind as they moved swiftly toward the next tree. Over the past few hours, Dusk had realized that walking was much more tiring than flying. He felt clumsy and heavy on all fours. His body craved the air. When he came to a spot where he could fully extend his wings, he took flight.

Fireflies pulsed like stars dislodged from the sky. Wind whispered through the grass. It was good to be aloft again. Quickly he sighted their destination, a lone poisonwood tree rising from the plain. It was still quite far away, and he could tell at once they'd drifted off course again. Down in the grass, without any landmarks, it was frighteningly easy to lose your sense of direction. That's why he was spending a good part of his time up high, keeping the colony on target, and keeping watch for any predators. They'd been lucky so far.

He landed near Auster, and wordlessly steered him in the proper direction. Auster nodded and the rest of the colony silently followed. Dusk fell into step beside Sylph.

A shriek traveled like jagged lightning through the night.

Auster paused and looked over at Dusk. "See what you can see."

Dusk flapped up through the grass once more, spiraling into the sky. He cast around, trying to fix the direction of the noise. A second shriek vaulted over the grasslands, along with several whinnying snorts, and then came the distant pounding of hooves. Dusk's heart thundered against his ribs.

It was the sound of equids, running scared. He was almost certain. But what had scared them? Surely the diatrymas couldn't be active this late at night.

He moved swiftly through the air, heading in the direction of the noise. The moon was now veiled by cloud, and he sent a hail of sound earthward. In his mind's eye he saw each and every stalk of grass, the occasional small dark shape of a scurrying groundling. Suddenly the grass parted and an adult equid and newborn bolted past.

Dusk wheeled, opening his eyes to follow their silhouettes. The two creatures were quickly joined by another adult, and they continued their sprint across the plain. Their hoofbeats faded into the night. Dusk was glad they'd escaped harm, but he still felt clammy with dread. What were they running from?

He didn't have to wait long for his answer. He continued southwesterly, and in less than a hundred wingbeats, caught a glancing echo image of a four-legged creature in the shadows of the deep grass. He circled and sprayed out more sound.

He'd seen this kind of creature only once before, but it was too distinctive to mistake. It was a hyaenodon, and it wasn't alone. There were six of them, striding menacingly through the grass. They stopped briefly, their blunt snouts close to the earth, and the one in front grunted irritably.

"The scent is gone," it said, the words so low and ill-formed that Dusk could barely make them out. "Carnassial."

Invisible against the night sky, Dusk watched with growing dismay as Carnassial and a second felid appeared beside the larger beasts.

"Smell," the hyaenodon instructed him gruffly.

Carnassial dropped his head and belly to the earth and slunk around, seeking out the scent of prey. "Yes," he said, "the equid scent is gone. But there is another here I know well. Chiropters."

"Here? They are not groundlings," said the hyaenodon.

"There must've been many of them," said the second felid. "I can still smell their fear."

"Panthera's right," said Carnassial. "An entire colony must be crossing the grasslands on foot."

Without warning Carnassial peered up into the sky, and Dusk tumbled steeply backward into the night, fervently hoping he hadn't been seen. He banked steeply, and flapped with all his strength back toward his colony.

For a chilling moment he didn't recognize where he was, the plain was so featureless in the dark, but then he oriented himself by the silhouettes of the solitary trees. It took a few low passes before he made out the dark cluster of his fellow chiropters in the grass, and he landed quickly at the vanguard.

"Will we make it to the poisonwood in time?" Auster asked, after Dusk had made his report.

"It won't guarantee our safety," remarked Sol, who'd come up from the rear. "Hyaenodons may not be able to climb, but the felids can."

"We won't reach it in time," Dusk said quietly. Following the scent trail, the felids would soon overtake them. "But I saw a fallen tree up ahead. It's not far, and it's big. It might hide us until they pass."

Dusk waited for Auster's answer. He could hear anxious squeaks and whimpers from some of the other newborns. Even Sylph looked worried. It was what they'd all feared most, being caught in the open.

"If they have our scent, and want to feed, they'll come right to us," said Auster. "We'll be trapped."

"I see no other option," Sol said.

"Can you take us there, Dusk?" Auster said.

Dusk still had the toppled tree's bearing locked in his head, so he led the way. They'd never moved faster. The grass thinned and suddenly the dark bulk of the trunk loomed before them. They approached its jagged base.

Sylph wrinkled her nose. "What's that smell?"

"Scat," said Auster.

"Diatryma scat," Dusk whispered, remembering the smell from the tree runners' forest. He immediately took flight, and circled the fallen tree. There were no nesting diatrymas to be seen. The scat must have been left in passing. He returned to the others.

"It's all clear," he told them.

"We're lucky," said Sol. "The scat will cloak our scent."

"And might scare them off," Auster added.

Dusk nodded hopefully. "Where should we hide?" It was odd, looking at a tree sideways, some of its branches jutting up into the air, others stretching out along the earth, leafless and broken.

"What about inside?" Sylph said. "It looks pretty big."

Dusk hurried over to join her at the tree's severed base. In the tough tissue of the exposed trunk were countless tiny holes bored by insects, but also a larger opening through which a chiropter could just squeeze. Dusk crawled closer and sang sound into the hole, listening hard. His returning echoes took a moment to reach him. In his mind flared an image of a deep cavernous space.

"It'll hold us all," he told Auster.

He knew they didn't have much time. Auster insisted on going first. One by one, the other chiropters squeezed through. Dusk had never been inside a tree, and he found the humid fragrance of the wood a bit overpowering. It was surprisingly spacious, and not completely dark. Pale light slanted through little gashes and insect holes in the tree's bark.

Using his echovision, Dusk studied their hiding place more carefully. It had been hollowed out by rot and an industrious army of bugs, together creating a weird hivelike cavern. From the ceiling hung thick cords of ancient cobweb. Insects teemed over the wood, and Dusk heard many of the chiropters hungrily send out hunting clicks.

"Not yet," Auster told them quietly. "When danger's passed, we'll feed. We need to be quiet now."

Dusk settled down beside Sylph, glad of the chance to rest.

Sol had positioned himself at the entrance, peering out into the night. He turned and shook his head. Nothing yet.

"Do you see that hole over there?" Sylph whispered to him.

"Where?" Dusk's fur bristled. He thought he'd checked for any other ways inside.

Sylph showed him the hole, and he let out a breath of relief. It was in the floor, and went right through the bark and straight down into the ground. It was far too small for a felid, or a chiropter even.

"Where's it go?" Sylph asked uneasily.

He sprayed down sound. The hole went quite deep before dead-ending—or curving off sharply to one side, he couldn't be sure. Echovision couldn't go around corners. There was nothing he could see down there. But when he sniffed he caught a faint animal scent mingled with the pungent smell of bark and earth.

"See if there's any more," he whispered to Sylph.

Scuttling clumsily over the ridged floor he found a second hole, then a third, bored deep.

"Four," Sylph said when they regrouped. "One smells pretty bad."

They found Auster among the chiropters.

"I think there's something living below the tree," Dusk told him.

"Shhhh . . . ." Sol hissed from the entrance, pulling back inside. "They're coming."

Silence throbbed within the hollow trunk as all the chiropters pressed themselves against the dead wood. Dusk's pulse outpaced the passing seconds. Beyond the walls of the tree he heard footfalls, and then an abrupt, guttural voice.

"You've led us to bird scat."

"No," came a soft growl. "It was the chiropters' scent I followed."

"Then where are they?" The same coarse voice.

Something pounded on the bark overhead and Dusk jerked. One of the newborns whimpered and was quickly pulled tight against his mother to stifle its cries. The hyaenodon must have leaped up onto the trunk, and now was pacing impatiently. Dusk hoped the wood was thick.

"I've lost their trail."

That was Carnassial's smoother voice. Dusk heard him sneezing and trying to purge his nostrils of the overpowering stink of the diatryma droppings.

Move on, Dusk thought. *Move on.*

He sought out Sylph's eyes. She was staring fixedly at something, and he followed her gaze. From one of the tiny holes in the ground, a head was poking up. It was wedge shaped, tapering to a pointy nose. Little semicircular ears grew close to its skull. Gray and black fur ran in jagged swaths across its snout. Its oval-shaped eyes were large. The creature advanced a little farther out of its hole.

Dusk stared. The creature was half his size, but looked uncannily like a chiropter. All it lacked was sails between its arms and legs. The diminutive beast was clearly startled, for the hair on its head and neck bristled, and it pulled back into its hole as if tugged from below.

"It's only a soricid," whispered Sol nearby. "Timid little things. Probably scared witless."

From the hole came a series of alarmed squeaks.

Dusk looked worriedly overhead. Would the hyaenodons and felids hear?

"Shush," Sylph said, bending over the hole. "We're not going to hurt you."

More shrill pips and squeaks welled up, not just from the one hole, but from all of them.

"Stupid little things," muttered Sylph.

"It must be their nest down there," said Sol. "They think we're invading."

Abruptly the heavy footsteps overhead stopped. Dusk could not hear Carnassial's voice or the hyaenodon's. Had they finally moved on, or were they still outside, mere inches away, listening hard?

Once again the soricid stuck its pointy little head out and looked around. To Dusk's amazement it came out all the way this time, and crouched, poised on the rim of its hole.

"Don't be afraid," Sol whispered gently, taking a few steps closer. "We'll be on our way very shortly."

The soricid opened its mouth as if to speak, and Dusk saw its teeth. They were small and numerous and very, very sharp. In the pale shaft of moonlight they flashed red. A ghastly hiss emanated from the little creature's throat and it flung itself at Sol, nipped him sharply on the neck, and then danced back.

Sol gave a cry, more of surprise than pain, for the tiny beast's bite couldn't have hurt much. Dusk couldn't even see wound marks. Angrily Sol flared his sails and advanced, but then his legs stiffened beneath him and he collapsed onto his face. He twitched several times, his eyes wide open, uncomprehending.

"Sol!"

Auster hurried to the elder's side. Sol wasn't dead. Dusk could see his flanks rise and fall. He was alive, and awake, yet he couldn't move.

"He's paralyzed!" said Auster, glaring at the little soricid. "Its bite poisoned him."

One after another, eight more soricids sprang from the hole and advanced, hissing, toward Sol and Auster. Bravely Auster held his ground and flared his sails, standing tall. In that moment he reminded Dusk so much of his father. He hurried to his brother's side. He was aware of Sylph coming too, and a few other chiropters. Together they shielded their fallen elder.

The soricids' faces blazed with a mad hunger. They feinted,

shrewdly waiting for the right moment to deliver their paralyzing nips.

"Drive them back into their hole!" Auster commanded.

Dusk advanced with the others, feeling fearless and strong.
He bared his teeth. He hissed. He made himself huge with his
wings. The soricids retreated to the brink of their hole, but
then Dusk heard shrieks from the rest of his colony.

"There's more of them!"

"They're *everywhere*!"

In horror Dusk beheld torrents of soricids flowing from
their many holes. Some chiropters held their ground, spitting
and lashing out with claws and teeth. They were unpracticed
warriors, but they knew enough to avoid the soricids' heads,
and instead aimed for the flanks and hind legs. The chiropters
had size and strength on their side, and when they flared their
sails, the soricids sometimes cringed back—but not always.
They seemed to have little fear, and attacked again and again,
sending chiropters scattering in terror.

The soricids facing Dusk had increased in number, and now
they heaved forward as a mass of jagged fur and poisonous red
teeth. There was nothing to do but fall back. Sol lay defenseless on the ground. Dusk did not want to abandon him, but
he also didn't want to meet the same fate. The soricids
swarmed over the paralyzed elder until Dusk could no longer
see him.

"Everyone out!" Auster shouted hoarsely to the colony.
"Get out!"

Dusk pressed tight against Sylph, whirling round. Panicked
chiropters made for the single exit, climbing over one another.

Nobody cared if the felids or hyaenodons were still outside. The predators inside were just as terrifying.

"This way!" said Dusk, leading Sylph up a wall, desperately trying to escape the tide of soricids sweeping toward them.

From the ceiling a soricid dropped onto Sylph's back. Without hesitating, Dusk reared up and sank his teeth into the creature's flesh. He'd never bitten another beast before, and he felt a feverish surge of excitement and fear. He released his jaws and bit again, deeper this time, and wrenched the soricid right off Sylph. It crashed against the floor, stunned, and Dusk continued to climb, Sylph pulling ahead. If they could just get a clear passage along the ceiling, they might make it to the exit, though it was already clogged with the other chiropters.

In his haste, he hardly felt the bite.

He looked over and saw the soricid at his side, its dreadful red teeth bared, and he knew what had just happened. In terror he imagined the creature's poisonous saliva seeping into him.

Frantically he tried to lick the wound clean, but it was too far down his flank and he couldn't reach it properly. He needed to keep moving, to get outside, but he was starting to feel queasy. The more he tried to move, the weaker he felt. He couldn't even muster the strength to call out to Sylph, now well above him.

A horrible numbness climbed his spine, vertebra by vertebra, clenching the muscles of his legs, stomach, chest, arms, shoulders. The claws on his wings involuntarily contracted, sinking deeper into the wood, and he couldn't release them to take another step. His body dangled rigid from the wall.

Even his eyes were paralyzed. He could only stare unblinking at the advancing soricid and, beyond it, the swarm feeding on Sol's body. He caught a white flash of a stripped leg bone, and then the soricids' bodies closed over it.

Dusk's lungs filled and emptied frantically. His heart flailed in his chest. This was about to happen to him.

He wanted to scream, to bolt, but the soricid's poison would not allow it. He could do nothing but watch his death come. The soricid gave a series of staccato shrieks, and suddenly there were others coming too, summoned to feed. From overhead he heard Sylph calling his name again and again, and he wanted to tell her to get out, but his throat was clamped tight, barely allowing him enough air. He hoped he would lose consciousness before they attacked.

"Get away from him!" he heard his sister screech. He couldn't see her, but felt her rearing up behind him, trying to protect him.

Violent scratchings came from outside, the sound of claws gouging into bark.

A ragged hole was suddenly ripped open in the wall, no more than a wingbeat from his body. A pair of clawed paws thrust inside, tearing away more of the wood and bark. Soricids scattered. The hole was enormous now. Moonlight poured into the trunk briefly, and was then blotted out as a hyaenodon's head plunged inside, jaws wide.

Helpless, Dusk watched the jaws shoot past him, grazing him as they seized two soricids. The tiny creatures managed to twist their upper bodies and necks enough to give the hyaenodon multiple nips on the side of its snout—but then the hyaenodon just gnashed its teeth, cleaving them in two and grinding them into its hungry mouth.

Dusk felt Sylph tugging at him with her claws and teeth, trying to drag him to safety.

"Come on, Dusk, move!" she roared.

The hyaenodon shoved its head even deeper inside, turned, and saw Dusk hanging from the wall, wings dangling. Dusk hoped Sylph had the sense to flee. He urged his legs to move, his wings to flap. Nothing.

He could not even close his eyes.

The jaws shot toward him and he gazed straight into the darkly gleaming maw. Bits of soricid fur and flesh were caught between jagged ranges of teeth. A rough tongue undulated hungrily. Suddenly the jaws were veering off to one side, and the hyaenodon's nose struck him, hard enough to knock him off the wall. He fell, helpless, to the ground.

He could still see the hyaenodon's head, but it was not making an attack; it was slumped awkwardly through the hole in the trunk. Its tongue lolled. An awful gargling noise emanated from its gullet, and then it was only the gory heat of its breath that marked it as alive. It had been paralyzed by the soricids it had devoured.

Within the tree, the legion of soricids shrieked in a triumphant frenzy, and threw themselves upon the hyaenodon's head, pouring out through the hole to lay claim to the rest of its meaty body.

Dusk's right leg twitched violently. The poison was wearing off. His left wing trembled. He felt his shoulders relax, clench, and relax again. He turned his head—

And saw a soricid scrambling toward him, jaws parted, its red teeth glinting.

With a colossal effort he rolled over onto his belly and reared back onto his hind legs, beating his wings. He sent a spray of wind and dust over the soricid and kept flapping. He lifted. There wasn't much space for flying in the trunk. He bobbed erratically between floor and ceiling, trying to evade the soricids. Most of them seemed intent on the downed hyaenodon; others were busy feeding on several other paralyzed chiropters.

"Dusk!"

Sylph clung to the wall above him, and he flew to her.

"I got bitten," he said apologetically.

"I figured. Come on!"

They scrambled along the ridged wall to the exit in the trunk's base. Dusk could see the last of the chiropters squeezing through. But converging on them from the ground was a swarm of soricids.

Dusk flapped with all his might, but he and Sylph weren't quick enough. One of the lead soricids deftly clambered up and blocked the narrow exit. Dusk hurtled down on it. Avoiding its spitting mouth, he clamped his rear claws around the soricid's tail and beat his wings hard. The soricid was surprisingly light and Dusk dragged it off the wood. He carried it high into the air before flinging it away. The exit was clear.

"Go!" he yelled at his sister.

She faltered. "What about the hyaenodons and felids?"

"Just go!" he shouted.

She dashed through the hole and into the night.

The soricids rushed to cut Dusk off, but he threw himself at the hole, furling his wings tight and wildly dragging himself through. No jaws snatched him on the other side. Then he was out, and following Sylph as she scuttled for cover in the shadows of the toppled trunk.

CHAPTER 22

Alone in the Grasslands

DUSK HUDDLED WITH Sylph in a misty tangle of dead branches. From the other side of the toppled tree came the baying of hyaenodons, punctuated by the snarls of felids.

"Where are all the others?" Sylph whispered.

"Hiding like us," Dusk said. He hoped so, anyway.

"Fly up and see," said Sylph.

"You sure?" He didn't want to leave her alone.

"Just do it fast. Find out what's going on."

He left their hiding place and lifted into the air, the night silken against his fur. He wanted to be quick, but the soricid's poison was still ebbing from his body, and his wingbeats were sluggish. He wheeled over the fallen tree.

The paralyzed hyaenodon, its head slumped inside the trunk, was overrun with soricids, busily stripping away fur and flesh. A second hyaenodon was dragging itself away from the tree, followed at a careful distance by a large, patient group of the diminutive predators. Each step the hyaenodon took was slower than the last until it crumpled stiffly to the earth. Despite the furious barking of the nearby hyaenodons, the soricids swarmed forward onto their fallen prey. Carnassial and the other felids stayed well back. But behind them, more tiny soricids boiled up from hidden holes in the ground.

Circling, Dusk caught sight of several small groups of chiropters scattering through the tall grass in different directions. Auster might have been among them, but he couldn't be sure. It was all chaos. How would they ever find each other again? He felt hopeless watching them disappear into the mist, but he dared not shout out and draw attention to their escape.

He flew back to Sylph.

"This way," he whispered, leading her away from the tree.

"Where's everyone else?"

"All over the place," he muttered without stopping. He wasn't thinking clearly; he just wanted to keep moving, to get away from all the predators. It was only a matter of time before the hyaenodons and felids retreated into the grasslands, and started sniffing them out. Leaves and twigs whipped against his face. He quietly sang sound, probing ahead. He watched the earth too, sniffing for holes that might release more red-teethed soricids.

"Dusk, where are we going?" Sylph asked after several minutes.

He didn't stop. "Poisonwood tree."

Sylph looked shocked. "What about the others? We can't just run away!"

"We're not *running away*!" he said angrily. "Do you want to get eaten?"

"But how are we going to regroup?" Sylph demanded.

"Everyone's scattered. We'll all meet up at the tree."

"What if they don't know the way?"

He stopped, breathing hard.

"Auster knows the way; he'll help them."

But he remembered how quickly the colony would slide off course without someone in the air. He tried to think like a leader. What was the best thing to do? His thoughts collided and ricocheted. How many groups had the colony split into? Would they dare call out to each other?

"We need to find them, Dusk," Sylph said. "They need you."

Dusk filled his lungs shakily. He wished his father were here, to tell him what to do.

"I'll take a look," he said finally. "Don't go anywhere."

He lifted, spiraling high to get his bearings. There was the toppled tree, thrusting its dead limbs skyward. And off to the east was the lone poisonwood—the colony's next destination. He dipped as low as he dared and began a slow circle, parting the tall grass with his echovision, searching for the other chiropters. He hoped he'd find them already on their way to the poisonwood.

The mist thickened, and Dusk was beginning to despair when his echoes brought him back an image of a lone chiropter in the grass. He sped closer, and saw there were others, traveling together. He whispered a greeting to them as he glided in, wings tilting, and landed clumsily in the tall stalks.

"Dusk!"

Auster hurried toward him and nuzzled him quickly—and Dusk felt stronger for it. Auster smelled like his father.

"I saw you get bitten and thought we'd lost you," Auster said.

"The hyaenodon saved me. Sylph and I were the last to get out. Is this everyone?"

Auster nodded. "We lost seven. One of my sons was among them."

Dusk remembered the horrible mounds of soricids he'd seen inside the tree, and shuddered. "I'm sorry, Auster."

"But afterward the rest of us all managed to find each other somehow," said Auster. "That was good fortune."

"You're off course for the poisonwood," Dusk told him, and nudged his older brother in the right direction. "It's not so far. I'm going back to get Sylph. We'll meet you at the tree."

"We'll wait for you there," said Auster. "Please be careful."

When Dusk took to the air again he was startled by how much denser the mist had become. The far hills had disappeared and the grasslands too were starting to dissolve. Some of his landmarks were no longer visible. He wheeled, trying to orient himself. The darkness contracted around him.

Dusk flew on, watching as the mist seeped between the

stalks of grass. He was pretty sure he was close now. He didn't want to, but he had no choice: he had to call out.

"Sylph! Sylph!"

Her answering cry pulled him sharply to the left and he started shooting out sound to find her. He'd never known his echoes to bounce back so quickly, and they nearly blinded his mind's eye. All he saw was a pulsing barrier of light.

"Dusk! I'm down here!"

He forced a deep breath into his lungs, and this time altered the strength and speed of his sonic cries. His echoes returned a blurry image of grass and vegetation, and a bright smudge off to one side: Sylph.

"I see you!"

He was just dropping down into the tall grass when something grabbed him. He thrashed wildly, but soon realized it was no animal that held him. His body and wings were tangled in a web. He'd flown through plenty of spiders' webs— every chiropter had—but none with strands this sticky and strong. He ate spiders from time to time, but they weren't his favorite food; often they were venomous, and though he was immune to the poison, it had a nasty taste. He struggled against the web some more, but it was quite useless. He bobbed around a few inches above the earth.

"Dusk?" came Sylph's voice, much farther away than he'd expected. He'd seen her just over to his right, hadn't he?

A chill surged through his veins.

"Sylph!" he said. "Where are you?"

"I'm coming, I'm coming," she said. "Just keep talking."

But he was now too frightened to speak. He croaked out a

barrage of sound and saw the vague shape he'd mistaken for Sylph. It was certainly about her size, but completely motion-less. Suddenly it shifted, standing tall on eight bony legs. Moving with shocking swiftness, the biggest spider he'd ever seen scuttled toward him.

Dusk wrenched his neck, chewing furiously at the web. His teeth seemed almost useless against the tough strands. He managed to saw through only one, and then the spider was upon him. Its abdomen was striped and hugely fat. Its face was amazingly hairy, with many globular eyes glinting darkly. Dusk saw fangs.

The spider lurched toward him and he bellowed, flailing about. He'd already been bitten once tonight, and was in no mood to be bitten again. He shouted and hissed and showed his teeth, trying to convince the spider to back off.

In his frenzy he wasn't sure what has happening, whether he was being bitten or cocooned. The spider darted all around him with savage purpose. Only when he felt his right wing pull free, and saw the severed strands of web, did he under-stand.

The spider was cutting him loose.

Dusk had messed up its web, and the spider wanted him gone so it could get on with catching proper food. Seconds later, he got a firm shove and tumbled down through the mist. He thudded on the ground.

Sylph was beside him.

"What's going on?" she cried. "Are you all right?"

"I got caught in a spider's web," he panted.

"Oh, honestly, Dusk." Now she just sounded angry. "All

that noise about a little web?"

"It was huge, Sylph, and—"

"Where? I don't see it."

Dusk looked up too, but the mist was so thick he could no longer make out the web or the spider.

"Just right up there! The spider was as big as me. Its fangs—"

"You don't seem that scared," Sylph said. "Why aren't we running?"

"Well, it doesn't eat chiropters. It cut me loose and shoved me out."

She stared at him.

"You believe me, don't you?"

"I believe anything now. Did you find the others?"

He told her about the plan to meet at the poisonwood. "The mist is thick," he said worriedly.

"What about your echovision?"

"I can't see very far in this, and it's all blurry."

"Just keep flying and scouting ahead."

"It's really bad, Sylph. I nearly didn't find you just now. I'm not leaving you again."

"Well, let's just do our best."

He took a breath. "I think we should wait for the mist to clear."

"I am *not* waiting here any more," said Sylph, and he saw how scared she was. "The whole time you were gone I kept hearing things in the grass. Sooner or later something's going to stumble along and eat us. I want to keep moving. I want to get to the tree." She started scuttling ahead of him.

"Sylph! Wait!" She didn't stop and he saw there'd be no reasoning with her. "That's not even the right way. Come on."

He caught up with her, prodded her in the right direction, and together they crept on through the mist.

"I smell them."

The scent was faint but unmistakable to Carnassial's nostrils and tongue.

"Eggs," he said. "There's a saurian nest not far from here."

Danian stared at him balefully. "Be sure of this."

Carnassial knew that the hyaenodon somehow blamed him for the two deaths in his pack. Carnassial had led them to the tree, it was true, but he wasn't the one who'd rashly clawed it open and ignited the wrath of the soricids. He'd known many types of soricids, but none with saliva that paralyzed. To make matters worse, in the ensuing panic, all the chiropters had escaped. Carnassial's belly ached with hunger.

"I'm sure," he told Danian.

"I smell them too," Panthera said.

Since fleeing the soricids, they'd been wandering half blind in the deepening mist, across the grasslands that Danian meant to claim as his new home.

Carnassial inhaled the saurian scent hungrily, but it was very difficult to tell where it came from. The mist confused him, sometimes obscuring the smell, other times intensifying it. Then it would disappear completely and he would have to scramble around in circles until he found it again.

He could not fail. He needed to find the nest to prove to Danian how useful he was. Glancing over, he saw that the four hyaenodons were nervous, heads dipped, ears pricked high. Danian pawed the earth. Carnassial felt some of the hyaenodons' fear diffuse toward him. They knew these saurians, knew what they could do, even when sick and dying.

All Carnassial's senses were alert as he paced through the mist, sniffing his way toward the nest.

"We're lost, aren't we," Sylph said.

Dusk grunted irritably. His limbs ached and his fur was soaked with dew. "We should've stayed where we were."

"You said you knew the way."

"Do you know how hard it is to go straight in this?" he demanded. "You move around a plant and already you're a bit off course, and it just gets worse and worse."

"So we're lost."

"Yes, we're lost."

He was angry with Sylph for hurrying them on, and angry with himself for letting her. They certainly should have reached the tree by now. For all he knew they might've walked right past it. Or they might've turned around in a complete circle and now be back where they'd started. He still clung to the hope, ever dwindling, that the journey was just taking longer than expected, that soon they'd arrive at the poison-wood.

"Does the mist feel warmer to you?" he whispered.

"The ground's warmer too," Sylph said.

Dusk slowed down, unsettled. His sister was right, the earth definitely felt warm—even hot in places. He lifted his feet apprehensively.

Sylph gave a sudden cry and hopped almost on top of him.

"It's coming from the ground!" she said.

Dusk stared and saw, dimly in the gloom, a skinny column of vapor boiling up from the earth. The only reason he saw it at all was its dark tinge, making it stand out slightly against the fog. It carried a heavy, earthy smell. As they moved cautiously forward, he spotted several more jets of warm vapor hissing from the soil. With a shudder Dusk imagined some vast, terrible beast beneath them, exhaling.

Before he could banish this premonition from his mind, something surged forward from the mist. A huge skull, flat against the earth, towered over them. He froze, too horrified to make a sound. And then the mist swirled again and revealed the rest of the creature's massive bulk.

Dusk swallowed. It had only *seemed* to move, through some trick of the mist.

"Just bones," he rasped.

"A saurian," Sylph said. "Nothing else could be this big."

It must have collapsed on its belly when it died. Little of its flesh was left. It lay there, the size of a small hill, seeming to steam in the night air. Dusk let his eyes travel its length: the long skull, jagged teeth clenched tight, then its neck, and the huge arch of its spine and ribs, tapering to an undulating bony tail. Its right arm was trapped beneath it, the leg splayed and broken at the femur.

Dusk whirled, ears pricked, staring into the mist behind him. He'd heard something. Maybe it was just the sound of the hot vapor escaping the earth. He sent a sonic cry into the mist, and when his echoes returned he had to fight every instinct to keep himself from flying.

"Get inside the skull!" he yelled at his sister.

Two felids bounded toward them. Dusk and Sylph hurled themselves at the skeleton and squeezed through an eye socket, tumbling down the smooth white insides to the saurian's jaw.

Dusk peered through the chinks between its clenched teeth. Carnassial and his companion leaped onto the skull, and tried to push their heads and shoulders into its various openings. But they were too big, just as Dusk had hoped. Carnassial suddenly thrust in a paw, claws fully extended. Dusk cringed out of reach.

The felid glared at him through an eye socket. "The flyer, come to ground. That was a mistake."

The brutal bulk of four hyaenodons loomed over the skull now.

"Small prey," said one of them in its guttural voice, almost as if insulting the felid.

"I will have them," said Carnassial, pacing the skull, looking for a way in.

The hyaenodon sniffed and lunged forward, and Dusk thought he meant to maul Carnassial, who stepped smartly to one side. But the hyaenodon's target was the skull itself. He clamped his jaws around the eye socket. Dusk watched in horror as the beast's massive teeth slowly came together, crunching through bone, sending white splinters flying.

"Dusk, this way!"

Sylph tugged him around. At the base of the skull was a narrow opening, a kind of protected passageway created by the saurian's neck vertebrae. Dusk squeezed into it, dragging himself after Sylph.

Through the gaps between the spiky vertebrae he saw flashes of Carnassial, keeping pace with them. He felt the felid's hot breath.

As the spine started to arch upward, Sylph slipped out between two of the vertebrae into the cavernous space of the rib cage. Dusk followed. The ground was warm underfoot. Malodorous vapor rose around them. The rib bones curved down from the saurian's spine, the skinny ends embedded in the soil. Dusk looked worriedly at the gaps between the ribs, and with relief saw they were small enough to keep out the felids and hyaenodons pacing angrily on the other side.

Carnassial looked in at him and purred menacingly. "You're trapped inside the bones of an extinct animal, about to meet your own extinction. It seems the world won't be seeing any more flying chiropters."

"There are others," said Dusk.

Carnassial sniffed and turned to one of the hyaenodons. "Bite through and we will have them."

Dusk was amazed at how readily the larger beast followed orders. Powerful jaws closed around the lower half of a rib, crunching an opening that would soon be big enough for the two felids to slip through.

Within the rib cage, the vapor swirled and eddied, momentarily blocking Dusk's view of the predators.

"Let's make a run for it," Sylph whispered.

Desperately Dusk cast around for an escape route. Back toward the saurian's hips the ribs got shorter and the ceiling lowered as the spine curved down and flattened against the earth. Dusk shot out a bolt of sound and saw how the tail vertebrae created a protective tunnel.

"This way," he hissed to Sylph. He heard the hyaenodon's teeth grinding, then a sharp snap, and knew the felids would be inside within seconds. He scrambled into the skeletal tail.

"Where are they?" Carnassial demanded behind them in the mist.

Dusk crawled deeper. The felids wouldn't be able to follow. Right now the gaps between each of the saurian's flared vertebrae were big enough to squeeze though to the outside, but he wanted to put more distance between themselves and their predators before they ran for it. The tunnel seemed to be angling downward, and Dusk suddenly realized they were underground. The gaps between the vertebrae had narrowed, and on either side was only hard-packed earth.

"Dusk, how're we going to get out of here?" Sylph said behind him.

The tunnel was shrinking, and it was getting hard for Dusk to drag himself forward.

"I think it's a dead end," he whispered back to Sylph.

"Back up, come on!" Sylph said, her voice thin with panic.

Wisps of steam played against Dusk's face. He shot out a pulse of sound. "Wait," he said, "there's a hole up here!"

"I'm not going into any hole," Sylph snapped. "We don't even know where it goes!"

From behind them came the sound of bones crunching, then furious digging.

"Keep going!" came Carnassial's voice. "They're hiding inside the tail!"

"Get into that hole!" Sylph cried, nipping Dusk's rump. "Hurry up."

He scrambled toward the hole. Fighting his involuntary disgust, he hauled himself over the rim, claws clutching at soil and rock. Warm mist dampened his face. He sang out sound, but before his echoes even returned to him, he lost his grip and fell.

CHAPTER 23

Birthplace

DUSK PLUNGED THROUGH the hole into an enormous underground cavern. Instinctively he spread his wings, flapping wildly. Twisted strands of rock spiked down from a slick ceiling. He circled quickly back to the hole, just in time to see Sylph fall through with a scream. She automatically unfurled her sails and leveled out into a glide."Dusk?" she called out.

"I'm here," he said, flying alongside her.

Eerie light emanated from the walls. Steam rose from yellowish pools. From the uneven floor grew bizarre rock formations, some as smooth and pale as giant eggs, others skinny as redwood saplings, still others teetering like immense stacked toadstools.

"This way," said Dusk, guiding his sister to one of the taller structures.

They landed on its peak. The rock was damp and chalky beneath his claws. The humid air was unpleasantly warm, and smelled strongly of minerals. Water pattered down on his back and head. He licked some from a puddle, and spat it out, revolted by the foreign taste.

"The felids won't follow," said Sylph, looking back up at the bristling ceiling. "They can't fit through that hole."

What worried Dusk more was how the two of them were going to get out. The cave seemed endless, stretching into darkness in every direction. He might be able to fly up and haul himself out through the hole. But there was no way Sylph could do the same. Anyway, the felids and hyaenodons might be waiting for them. He glanced back across the enormous cavern, and despite the heat, suddenly felt icy cold.

Bones.

They weren't in any shape he could recognize. They'd all been torn loose, cracked and gnawed, and piled in an enormous heap. There were more bones here than could make up any one animal, or ten for that matter.

"Dusk," Sylph said, her voice hoarse with fear. "I see eggs."

He followed her gaze. Near one of the steaming pools, swaddled in grass and rotting leaves, were eight long, leathery eggs. There were so many strange shapes and colors in the cavern that, for a fleeting moment, Dusk hoped she was mistaken. He remembered their laughable encounter with a pinecone, back on the island. But the longer he stared, the more certain he was that Sylph was right. It was definitely a huge, high-rimmed nest, about ten feet across.

A nest meant adults.

Dusk looked around, lifting his ears and listening. There was the constant patter of water on the rocks and pools. There was the whisper of steam. There was the sound of his own breathing and Sylph's.

"Could just one saurian lay all those eggs?" she asked.

"I don't know," he whispered back. "But if they made a lair of this place, there's got to be a big way out somewhere."

There was no point in both of them blundering around, with Sylph needing to land and climb all the time. He could go faster and stay high out of harm's way.

"Stay here," he said. "I'm going to find the way out."

He'd expected her to object, but she just nodded, staring, dazed, at the eggs.

Very quietly he flew to another high stone tower, and took a look around. From his new vantage point he almost immediately spotted a saurian, sprawled on the floor. Its eyes were open, unblinking, and its chest did not rise or fall. In the cave's eerie light, the patches of bright green and violet rot on its scales seemed to glow. It had been dead for some time, judging by the sagginess of its skin and the noxious smell rising from it. Its belly and one of its thighs looked well chewed.

Dusk didn't know what kind of saurian it was. He'd only ever seen a quetzal, and this one certainly had no wings. It was smaller, with slim, agile legs no doubt capable of considerable speed. In its death grimace, it showed all its sharp teeth: definitely a meat eater. His father would have known its name.

Dusk flew on. Half submerged in a steaming pool was a second adult saurian, so horribly bloated it was hard to say if it was the same kind as the first. The body rocked and jerked in the bubbling water, the skin so loose it seemed about to slide off the bones.

He continued deeper into the cave, probing with sound, encouraged when his echoes didn't bounce back at him right away. After a while the ground sloped upward, rubble-strewn, and the darkness seemed less intense. He sniffed fresh air. He flew on eagerly, and finally reached the mouth of the cave.

It was obscured by a dense tangle of tall grass and plants. It didn't look like it had been disturbed for some time. Dusk landed on a branchlet. He and Sylph would have no trouble crawling through this. He could see a bit of the moon, and hear the swish of the grass in the breeze. From the outside, the cave mouth would be invisible to all but those who knew it was there. He wondered how persistent Carnassial would be in his pursuit. Surely there was better prey on the grasslands.

Excitedly he headed back for Sylph.

"We're okay!" he exclaimed, landing beside her. "There's a way out."

"What about saurians?"

"I saw two dead ones. Adults. I think they must've had that rotting disease Dad talked about."

"They must've come here to lay their last eggs," Sylph said, staring down at the nest. "They won't hatch now, not without anyone to keep them warm."

"I'm not so sure. It's pretty warm in here."

Dusk wondered if the saurians had known that the steam from the pools would incubate their eggs, even after the parents died.

"Were they flesh eaters?" Sylph asked.

"I think so. We should get out of here."

Sylph launched herself from her perch, but instead of gliding high, she put herself into a steep dive, straight down toward the eggs.

Amid the dirt and scattered tail bones, Carnassial sniffed at the steam venting from the hole in the earth.

"They're down there," he said.

"We've wasted enough time on small prey," Danian barked.

"I'm not talking about the chiropters," said Carnassial. "The nest is down there. The eggs."

Mingled with the earthen mineral scent was the smell that had been haunting him across the dark grasslands.

Panthera inhaled. "Yes. I smell them too."

"Are there caves near here?" Carnassial asked Danian.

"We know none."

"There should be an entrance, a large one, not far from here," Carnassial said.

He and Panthera bounded off in different directions to search. He lost the scent of the nest, but that didn't matter so much now. He knew what he was looking for, and as the eastern horizon started to pale, his eyes had more than enough light to guide him. It was rare for saurians to make nests in caves, but in his years as a hunter he'd uncovered several underground. He searched on through the rolling grassland. He wanted a slope where he could find a cave mouth.

Panthera found it first. He heard her calling out and ran to meet her at the entrance. He was mightily impressed with her. It was easy to miss, buried behind several layers of dense scrub.

"You can see the vapor rising through the plants," she pointed out to him.

The hyaenodons had followed at a distance, and would not go near the entrance.

"Kill the eggs!" Danian shouted viciously.

"I will," said Carnassial.

With Panthera at his side, he slunk through the tangle of undergrowth and into the warmth of the cave. He knew that most saurians became active only with the sun's ascent. At this hour they'd still be dormant—if they were even still alive. The rotting disease acted quickly, and if Danian had already noticed it on their hides, it wouldn't be long before death took them.

They proceeded deeper into the humid cave, around strange towers of rock and simmering pools. The walls glowed. The smell of the nest was strong now.

"We'll leave two eggs undisturbed," he told Panthera.

She looked over at him, confused.

"We need to leave the hyaenodons with some enemies, or they'll become too powerful. We need to keep them scared. This way they'll need us to find and destroy more nests."

"Once we were saurian hunters. Now we're their guardians." She purred approvingly. "My kittens will be lucky to have such a cunning father."

Carnassial stared at her in surprise. "You're sure?"

"Oh yes," she said. "I can feel them growing inside me."

Despite the hazards awaiting him, he felt suffused with pride and happiness. He nuzzled her and then they carried on in search of the saurian eggs.

"Sylph, pull up!" Dusk gasped, fluttering down beside her.

His sister's voice was clear and calm. "We have to destroy them."

She flared her sails and landed in the middle of the nest. Dusk touched down beside her on the thick plant mulch. The nest seemed much bigger now that he was actually inside it. All around them loomed the saurian eggs. Dusk didn't want to go too close. The eggs were almost twice his size. Still and silent, they radiated a sinister power. On the other side of those thick shells, Dusk knew, pulsed wet, curled lives, just waiting to emerge and feed.

"Sylph, we need to get out of here! What if the felids find the way in?"

She ignored him, awkwardly pulling herself up against the nearest egg, digging in with her claws. Dusk caught hold of her leg and dragged her back. She whirled on him, showing her teeth. Dusk recoiled in surprise.

"I don't think they're even climbers!" he said urgently. "They can't hurt us!"

"Are you sure about that, absolutely sure?"

"No."

"Then we have to kill them."

"It's not what Dad wanted!"

"Dad's gone."

"Sylph, stop!"

"Help me, Dusk! Do you want them hatching and terrorizing us in our new home?"

"I don't think they—"

"I want to do something great too!" she fumed. "You can fly and see in the dark and lead us all to safety, and what have I done? This will be my great thing!"

"It's not a great thing, Sylph," he pleaded, and he felt himself trembling, for it seemed she wasn't intent on destroying just the eggs but their father as well—everything he believed in. "It's not what Dad wanted!"

"He wasn't perfect, Dusk. He wasn't even a good leader toward the end. He was weak, and he hurt the colony! He couldn't even protect his own children."

She managed to dig a claw deep into the shell and drag a long gash into it.

"Don't say that, Sylph!" he said, his anger mounting. "Leave the egg alone!"

"We've got to take care of ourselves!" Sylph raged, sinking her claws into the shell once more. "Because no one else will. Especially not now. The world's an ugly place. The big animals eat the little ones; the clever ones trick the stupid ones. That's just the way it is. We need to kill them before they kill us! You want to be like Dad so much, then do what he did. When it came right down to it, *he killed the eggs*!"

"He regretted it!"

"But he *did* it!"

Dusk thought of everything they'd suffered since the massacre, all the lives lost during their search for a new home. Was everything they'd strived for going to be undone by the hatched saurians? He felt his anger and bitterness harden inside him, like an extra bone. Maybe Sylph was right: the world was an ugly place. It had not been kind to them; why should they be kind to it?

He understood now how his father must have felt, all those years ago on the island. At war with himself, knowing what he'd always believed was right, but knowing also what he most wanted to do: protect himself, protect his colony.

"We can kill these eggs," Dusk said slowly, "but maybe there are other eggs in other nests. I suppose we could kill those too. But we'll never be perfectly safe. What about all the other creatures who hunt us? The felids and the hyaenodons and the diatrymas? We can't kill them all. There's no such thing as paradise—that's what Dad told us. And you said it yourself, Sylph: the big animals eat the little ones; the clever ones trick the stupid ones. Everything needs to eat. No matter how hard we try, something will always hunt us. We can't stop that."

"We see things differently," Sylph said. "These saurians, right here, we can stop. They need to be stopped."

The shell finally cracked under her claws and clear fluid seeped out. Sylph jerked back in shock, as if distressed by the harm she'd caused. She started whimpering. She lifted her claws to gouge the shell again, and faltered.

"I don't know if I can do this!" she quavered.

Dusk moved to comfort her, and from the corner of his eye

caught sight of something that made him freeze.

"What's wrong?" Sylph said.

"Shhhhh."

Beside one of the other eggs in the nest were two large shards. Cautiously Dusk stepped closer. The shards were dry. He stared hard at the egg they lay against. Then, keeping his distance, he crept around it. The far side, hidden from view until now, was broken wide open. It was empty.

He rushed back to Sylph.

"One's already hatched!"

"Where?" she squeaked.

Dusk remembered the half-eaten corpse of the saurian adult. Food.

"In the cave," he gasped. "It's living here in the cave."

A snout suddenly thrust itself from the gash in Sylph's egg, small blood-spattered jaws snapping to break loose more shards. Dusk yelped and tripped over his sister in his haste to move away. A claw broke through the shell, flexing weakly. A high-pitched peeping came from the hatchling's throat.

"Come on, hurry!" Sylph shouted.

She started for the edge of the nest, then stopped, wide-eyed. Dusk followed her terrified gaze.

Poised on the rim of the nest, staring down at them, were two felids.

Dusk hissed threateningly and scrambled backward with Sylph. Behind him, he could hear the hatchling struggling to get free of its egg. Dusk saw Carnassial's eyes flick from him to the saurian, as if he couldn't decide which to attack first. The felid's eyes narrowed with craving; his teeth were wet.

Dusk kept moving back through the nest, never letting his gaze stray from the felids. He could fly away at any time, but Sylph was helpless until she could get to higher ground.

"Get the flyer, Panthera!" Carnassial said.

The female felid leaped with such speed that Dusk scarcely had time to open his wings and hop into the air. Panthera skidded, whirled, and jumped up at him. He didn't fly high, just bobbed about, mere inches above Panthera, taunting her. While Sylph frantically scrambled for the far side of the nest, Dusk kept fluttering just out of reach, to keep the felid focused on him.

In his peripheral vision he saw Carnassial jump into the nest after Sylph. In five bounds he was upon her. Dusk cried out in anguish, and in that split second, Panthera pounced and caught him with both paws. His wings crumpled as the two of them tumbled down in a heap. He struggled to escape but felt the full weight of her powerful body atop him.

He couldn't see Sylph anymore, did not know what has happening to her. He tried to cry out, but Panthera had already closed her jaws around his throat and was clamping down, cutting off his air.

His vision flared and then narrowed: a tunnel getting ever smaller. At its end, he saw a head peer over the nest, a narrow, sharply tapered head with quick bright eyes. It plunged toward him. Dusk heard a cry, as if from far away, and felt himself heaved up into the air for a moment before falling free of Panthera's screaming jaws.

Back in the nest, he leaped to his feet, and whirled to see a young saurian with Panthera flailing between its teeth. It gripped her tightly across her belly and lower back. Dusk guessed the saurian was only a few weeks old, but already it was twice the size of the felids, a born predator grown strong on the corpse of its parent.

"Panthera!"

Dusk spun around and saw Carnassial release Sylph and launch himself at the saurian. Dusk didn't wait a second more. He flew over to his sister, who was coughing and shaking violently.

"I'm okay," she said.

They clambered out of the nest and rushed to the nearest rock tower. While Sylph climbed the soft sides, Dusk flew to its summit. The saurian still had Panthera in its mouth, though she no longer struggled. Carnassial flung himself again and again at the saurian, but was deflected by its stubby three-clawed hands. His shrieks carried not just the fury of the hunt, but a terrible desperation and sorrow.

Dusk quickly plotted their escape route. Sylph climbed up beside him and, without even a moment to catch her breath, glided after him toward the next stone tower. Their path took them right over the nest, and when Dusk glanced down, he saw the deadly saurian's head jerk up, intently tracking him and his sister through the air.

They landed, and wasted not a second before launching again. He led Sylph from one tower to the next, toward the cave mouth. Light filtered through the screen of dense vegetation. With a start Dusk realized it must be morning. They landed high amid the tight weave of branches, and immediately started squeezing their way through.

Behind them Dusk heard the sound of a surprisingly light-footed gait. He looked back into the cave, but his eyes were no longer accustomed to the darkness. Instead he shot out a volley of sound, and with his echoes saw the slim body of the saurian taking swift, agile leaps toward them.

"It's coming!" he cried, plunging ahead with Sylph.

Just before they emerged on the outside, he saw, through the thinning undergrowth, the four hyaenodons, crouched on the ground. They were well back from the mouth of the cave, but watching it with all their attention.

"Down there!" Dusk said, plotting a glide path for Sylph that would take her into the cover of tall grass. Maybe the hyaenodons wouldn't notice.

Branches crackled as the saurian forced its way through behind them. Squinting, Dusk sprang into the early daylight, Sylph at his side. Their dark bodies must have stood out easily, for he saw two hyaenodons stand and start running toward them—but then freeze.

Dusk glanced back over his wing to see the young saurian crash through the vegetation. It paused, blinking and looking all around at the world beyond its cave, seemingly for the very first time. Its snout, Dusk noticed, was spattered with gore.

The hyaenodons began barking, hackles raised, their tail hair spiking. But they did not draw closer.

The saurian cocked its head, a strange, almost birdlike gesture, but made no move to retreat.

And then Dusk could see no more, because he was surrounded by the tall grass and braking with his wings as the ground rose to meet him. As fast as their exhausted bodies would allow, he and Sylph scuttled away from the sound of the baying hyaenodons.

Dusk flew above the grass, keeping watch as Sylph labored along the ground. In the distance he'd spotted the poison-wood tree, but he knew it would be at least an hour before they reached it. The sun had just cleared the horizon. He didn't like being out in the day, but they had no choice now. He could only hope Auster and the rest of his colony were still waiting.

Galloping across the plain toward him were two equids. Worriedly he looked behind them, but saw nothing in pursuit. They ran simply because they could, for pure joy, and as he watched them Dusk felt his spirits lift. When they came closer he recognized their markings. It was Dyaus and Hof, and he couldn't resist calling out. He was so glad to see creatures who had no interest in eating him.

He dipped down to tell Sylph.

"There're equids coming," he said. "I know these two. I'm going to talk to them."

He flew on ahead, calling out another hello and tilting his wings so they'd spot him more easily.

"Ah," Dyaus said, "I remember you. Dusk."

"Be careful up ahead," Dusk said. "There are hyaenodons and a saurian."

"Saurian?" Dyaus exclaimed.

"We'd thought they were all dead!" grumbled Hof.

"No. There's a nest in an underground cave. We saw eight eggs. Two have hatched."

Hof sighed heavily. "Just something else to endure, I suppose."

"Where are you going?" Dyaus asked Dusk.

"To find my colony," he said, fluttering overhead, "what's left of it. We agreed to meet in the poisonwood." He nodded toward it.

"It won't take you long with your wings," said Hof. "I'd like wings sometimes. Wouldn't that be nice."

"But my sister can't fly," Dusk told him

"Hello," said Sylph, who'd just caught up.

Dyaus looked down at her. "There are diatryma nests on your way," he warned.

Dusk exhaled. "Thank you for telling us." It seemed they weren't finished with perils yet.

The two equids looked at each other.

"I'll take her," Dyaus said. "On my back."

"Really?" Dusk was overwhelmed by this kindness.

"We'll have a race," said Hof, with uncharacteristic enthusiasm. "Who's faster: the runner or the flyer?"

Dyaus knelt down and invited Sylph to climb up his shoulder onto his back.

"Thank you very much," said Sylph.

"Gently with your claws," Dyaus said. "Now hold on!"

He shot off through the grass, Hof at his side. Dusk heard a cry of sheer delight from Sylph, and then he was flapping as fast as he could after the equids. What would have taken them an hour on the ground took only minutes now. The poisonwood grew swiftly bigger. The equids outstripped him and reached the tree quite a ways ahead of him. Dusk flapped harder, fervently hoping the colony had made it there safely and was still waiting.

Blinking sweat from his eyes, he stared hard at the tree, and was finally close enough to make out the dark shapes of many chiropters moving in the high branches. His heart leaped.

"There he is!" he heard someone cry out. "I see him now!"

"There's Dusk!" someone else shouted.

"Dusk and Sylph are back!"

"He made it!"

"They made it!"

And suddenly the air around the tree was filled with gliding chiropters, calling out greetings and cheering Dusk on as he returned to his colony.

CHAPTER 24

A New Home

No tree had ever seemed this high.

Dusk labored up the massive trunk, sinking his claws into the soft, reddish bark. He could have easily flown to the summit ahead of everyone else, but he didn't. He wanted to climb this tree alongside Sylph and Auster and the rest of his colony. He wanted them all to arrive at the same moment.

They'd set out from the poisonwood at sunset, and it had taken them the entire night to cross the grasslands, climb the hills, and reach the base of the tree. Exhausted, they'd started their ascent in darkness, but before long the dawn's light had ignited the tree's high canopy and slid down the trunk to meet them, warming their fur, easing their aching muscles. Steam lifted from the luminous bark, and Dusk felt his weariness lift away with it.

Mighty limbs thrust out from the trunk on all sides. Auster led them higher still. The fragrance of needles and sap scented the air. Insects glittered in the sunlight. Dusk sank his claws deep, pulled himself up, dug in again. The colony climbed silently, intent, with every second knowing they drew closer to their destination. Dusk felt himself speeding up, and realized everyone else was too. His labored breathing became part of a single sound, the entire colony inhaling and exhaling. Finally Auster called a stop.

"Here," he said.

As the chiropters gathered on the nearest branches, Auster gazed at the vast tree spreading around him, and then out over the grasslands.

Dusk looked too. Up here, high on the slope, in the branches of their new tree, they seemed to float above all dangers. The hyaenodons and diatrymas—and perhaps even saurians—stalked the plains, but they could not reach his colony. Dusk knew that no haven was perfect, but right now he felt safe and at peace. He wondered if this was how his father had felt when he'd discovered the island.

"I can imagine no better home," Auster said, turning to him. "Thank you, Dusk."

* * *

He was amazed how quickly life returned to normal. Within days new nests and hunting perches were claimed. The chiropters groomed and glided, and fed as they'd always done. The first newborns, carried in their mothers' bellies during the frightful journey, were birthed.

But even though the familiar daily rhythms of the colony had resumed, there was sadness too, and plenty of changes. When Nova and Barat had left, they hadn't just divided the chiropters in half; in many cases they'd taken away the friends and siblings and children of those who'd remained loyal to Icaron and Auster. Other families had seen their members killed by predators. Dusk still wasn't used to how small the new colony seemed.

The leadership of Sol's family was taken up by his son, Taku. And Auster quickly named two new families, and appointed elders from them. Dusk wasn't sure it made the colony seem any bigger, but it did make things more like home, and he could see that four families and elders were better than just two.

He was glad, though, that he and Sylph were still part of Auster's family. It made him feel closer to Dad and Mom. He and Sylph still slept in Auster's nest, but it was a little more crowded now, since one of the recent newborns was the leader's new daughter. Dusk was an uncle yet again.

There was one other important change.

Dusk was allowed to fly.

"Your sails saved our lives more than once," Auster had told him. "I see no reason why you shouldn't use them to their fullest."

But apart from Sylph, he still hadn't told anyone else about Chimera—about his true nature. He didn't want to ruin things. He wanted to belong.

He was hunting when he saw her again, her dark wings fluttering as she skimmed the treetops, dipping and wheeling to snatch insects from the air.

It had been two weeks since they'd arrived at the tree, and not a single day had passed when he hadn't thought about Chimera and her colony on the other side of the hills. Every day he'd watched for her, hoping she'd come, *terrified* she'd come. The mere sight of her now was so overwhelming he wanted to flee. He hurriedly landed, crouching low on a leafy branch. Maybe she hadn't seen him.

He peered out through the leaves. She circled, as if waiting. What would Auster and the others think? It was one thing for his colony to tolerate a useful freak—but a completely different creature? He feared being shunned again, but even more he feared his overpowering desire to go to her, this creature who was just like him. He dug his claws into the bark, feeling as if he were resisting the pull of gravity itself.

Others had seen her now. As the chiropters glided between trees, hunting, several cried out in surprise, a few even gave an alarmed hiss. Did they think she was some kind of malignant bird? Couldn't they see Chimera was just like him?

When she started calling out his name, Dusk knew there was no point hiding any longer. He shuffled out along the branch.

"Dusk?" Sylph said, landing beside him. "Is that her? The bat?"

He nodded.

"Are you going to talk to her?"

"I suppose so," he answered weakly.

He launched himself into the air, climbing.

"You made it!" Chimera said, fluttering toward him. "You led them to a new home!"

"Some of them," he said. "Not everyone wanted to come."

As before, he couldn't stop looking at her, marveling at their similarities.

"Did everyone cross safely?"

When he shook his head, she made a sympathetic murmur. "It must've been awful on foot."

They landed side by side on a high branch. Below, Dusk could make out some other chiropters, including Sylph, watching him. The distance between him and his sister made him suddenly sad. He remembered the time—it seemed so long ago now—that he rode the thermal up the clearing, and looked down at her from his lofty height. The bewilderment and indignation on her upturned face! Back then she'd been able to follow him at least. But was there any way of closing the gap between them now?

"Bat-ra's been asking about you," said Chimera.

"Really?"

"Of course. She wants to meet you. She wants you to come to us."

Dusk said nothing.

"Are you afraid?"

"This is my home," he told her firmly.

"Are you sure?"

"They've accepted me," he said, wanting with all his heart to believe it.

"I'm sure they're very *grateful* to you. For now," she added pointedly. "After a while, they'll forget everything you did for them, and you'll just be an oddity again. Did you tell them about me and the bats?"

"Only my sister."

"Why not the others?" she asked.

"You know why not," said Dusk. "I was worried they'd expel me. But maybe I was wrong."

"We'll find out soon enough," Chimera said with a touch of mischief in her voice. "Now that they've seen me, they'll know there're others. They'll know you truly are a different beast."

"They're letting me fly," Dusk told her, feeling a bit desperate. "They don't mind anymore. Auster said the colony treasures me."

"They should! But Auster won't rule forever. Your next leader might not be so tolerant."

Dusk thought of how Nova had abandoned him.

"Your colony does sound very just," said Chimera. "Mine wasn't like that. But, Dusk, you must know that even if they respect you, you'll never truly be one of them. How could you? You're different."

"Does it matter?"

"Bat-ra says we all crave what's most like ourselves. It's in our nature."

He felt it, this sense of yearning, so strongly it almost made him sick. At the same time it terrified him. If he embraced it, didn't it mean that he was abandoning his colony and what he'd once been? Icaron's son. Sylph's brother. He felt as though he were being wrenched apart.

"Even if you stay here," Chimera said gently, "no one will ever mate with you."

His mother had said the same thing. He certainly hadn't forgotten how, back on the island, the other chiropters had avoided him, as though he might infect them. Even now, he sometimes sensed they weren't entirely comfortable being close to him. They never snubbed or ignored him anymore; they seemed genuinely to like him. But they kept their distance, like they were struggling against some involuntary revulsion.

"Well, I don't *have* to mate," he muttered, feeling embarrassed.

"You're still too young, anyway," Chimera said. "But everyone wants a mate eventually."

Right now he was more worried about what would happen once Sylph found her mate. It probably wasn't so far off. She'd always been popular. She'd have her own nest, a new companion, and then newborns to look after. He'd still see her, of course, but it wouldn't be the same. After spending his entire life side by side with her, he'd be lonely.

"Bat-ra says we should be proud of who we are," Chimera told him. "It wasn't easy. We'd all been shunned and exiled. But we have all these amazing abilities that no other beasts have. If you lived with us, you'd never have to feel ugly or ashamed, or like an outsider. You're one of us, Dusk. You belong with us."

When she said it, he felt a surge of excitement. He wasn't sure he'd ever truly had it, that feeling of belonging. He'd been tolerated. Maybe now he'd even been *accepted*, but was that the same as *belonging*?

"It's going to be hard for you," Chimera said kindly. "With me and everyone else in our colony, our decisions were made for us. We were expelled. We were *told* we weren't chiropters. But you've got to decide for yourself. Are you a chiropter or are you a bat?"

"I still don't know," he said.

"Do you remember the way to us?" she asked.

He nodded.

"I hope you'll come."

Dusk watched her fly off, and felt panic tighten in his chest. What if he never saw her again? What if couldn't find his way to the other bats? He was completely upended. He sighed heavily and fluttered down to Sylph.

"They want me to join them," he said.

"What are you going to do?"

"I'm not going," he said. "My home's here—isn't it?"

"You know it is. You found it for us."

"She kept saying I was one of them, but I don't know anything about them. Just because I *look* like them, does that mean I belong with them?"

Sylph said nothing.

"They'll never be my parents, or my sister."

"No," Sylph agreed.

"Maybe they won't even think the same way we do about things."

Sylph sniffed. "It's hardly like all chiropters think the same way. Look at Nova and Dad. Look at you and me."

He felt sad when she said that, but she was right. They'd talked a lot about what happened in the saurian hatchery, and Sylph still thought destroying the eggs was the right thing to do. She even hoped Carnassial had survived to finish the job.

"Well, we think differently," Dusk admitted, "but it doesn't matter. We're still brother and sister, and we made a pact to take care of each other. I'm not going anywhere."

"You want to go," Sylph said simply.

"No."

"You *want* to go."

"Do you want me to go?" he demanded in exasperation.

She shook her head silently.

"I want to go," he breathed. The wild calling was beyond understanding, keening through his veins.

"Go and see," Sylph said. "Go find out what they're like."

"I just need to see what it's like to be with them."

"And if you're not sure, you can always come back."

"I'll come back," he told her.

"Good," she said, and nuzzled him.

Poised on the edge of the branch, ready to take flight, he faltered.

What if, once there, he changed, and forgot everything he'd been before? What if he could utter the word *chiropter* and think "them" instead of "me"? What if he never came back?

"I'm afraid to go," he said, and then Sylph shoved him hard off the branch.

Dusk was so surprised he plunged a few seconds before opening his wings and pulling up. He banked sharply.

"You pushed me!" he cried out indignantly.

"Believe me," she said, "no one wants to make the first jump. Isn't that what Dad used to say?"

He hovered for a moment, looking at her. "Thanks, Sylph."

Then he flapped harder, rising up through the branches, and into the darkening sky.

AUTHOR'S NOTE

After writing three books about bats, all set more or less in our own time, I became interested in the long-ago origins of these fascinating creatures. I wondered how long they'd been soaring through the skies of our world. How and when did they get their wings and learn to fly?

The oldest bat fossil we have is about 50 million years old, and reveals a creature that looks almost identical to a modern bat. So it's possible that the earliest bats were flying around as far back as the reign of dinosaurs, more than 15 million years before. Some scientists think that bats evolved from small shrewlike mammals that lived in trees and glided on membranes stretching between their elongated arms and legs.

In *Darkwing*, I tried to imagine what these pre-bats might have been like. Dr. Brock Fenton, a world-renowned bat expert at the University of Western Ontario, patiently answered many of my questions, and shared with me his theories on how bats might have evolved the ability to echolocate. I am very grateful for his generosity and expertise. Ultimately, Dusk and the other pre-bats in my story—I call them chiropters—are fictional creations, and not the result of rigorous scientific research.

As the last dinosaurs died out, mammals started to become much more numerous and varied, perhaps because their main predators were disappearing. Since we have no fossil record of a pre-bat, we have no way of knowing exactly when they evolved into modern bats. For the purposes of my story, I chose the early Paleocene epoch, 65 million years ago.

All the characters and creatures in my book are based on real species, most of which lived during this epoch—give or take a few million years. Carnassial was inspired by an early mammalian carnivore called *Miacis*, which might have looked a bit like a modern pine marten. Miacis was an agile predator and had evolved uniquely shaped teeth (called carnassials!) that allowed him to shear meat from his prey.

During the same epoch there was also a giant bird called *Gastornis* (or *Diatryma*) that was seven feet tall. Though it couldn't fly, it was a swift runner and a terrifying hunter. The equids in my book were based on a hoofed animal called *Phenacodus*, which scientists used to think was an ancestor of the horse. And the soricids that Dusk and his colony encounter are based on a tiny and voracious species of shrew with red teeth that excreted a paralyzing neurotoxin. I hope never to encounter one at night.

The Paleocene was a fascinating period of Earth's history, full of drama and change, and it seemed an ideal setting for this story of the very first bats—the only mammals capable of powered flight.

DARKWING

A Note from Kenneth Oppel

After writing three books about bats, all set more or less in our own time, I became interested in the long-ago origins of these fascinating creatures. I wondered how long they'd been soaring through the skies of our world. How and when did they get their wings and learn to fly?

The oldest bat fossil we have is about fifty million years old and reveals a creature that looks almost identical to a modern bat. So it's possible that the earliest bats were flying around as far back as the reign of dinosaurs, more than fifteen million years before. Some scientists think that bats evolved from small shrewlike mammals that lived in trees and glided on membranes stretching between their elongated arms and legs.

In *Darkwing*, I tried to imagine what these pre-bats might have been like. Dr. Brock Fenton, a world-renowned bat expert at the University of Western Ontario, patiently answered many of my questions, and shared with me his theories on how bats might have evolved the ability to echolocate. I am very grateful for his generosity and expertise. Ultimately, Dusk and the other pre-bats in my story—I call them chiropters—are fictional creations and not the result of rigorous scientific research.

As the last dinosaurs died out, mammals started to become much more numerous and varied, perhaps because their main predators were disappearing. Since we have no fossil record of a pre-bat, we have no way of knowing exactly when they evolved into modern bats. For the purposes of my story, I chose the early Paleocene epoch, sixty-five million years ago.

All the characters and creatures in my book are based on real species, most of which lived during this epoch—give or take a few million years. Carnassial was inspired by an early mammalian carnivore called Miacis, which might have looked a bit like a modern pine marten. Miacis was an agile

3

predator and had evolved uniquely shaped teeth (called car-nassials!) that allowed him to shear meat from his prey.

During the same epoch there was also a giant bird called Gastornis (or Diatryma) that was seven feet tall. Though it couldn't fly, it was a swift runner and a terrifying hunter. The equids in my book were based on a hoofed animal called Phenacodus, which scientists used to think was an ancestor of the horse. And the soricids that Dusk and his colony encounter are based on a modern-day tiny and voracious species of shrew with red teeth that excretes a paralyzing neurotoxin. I hope never to encounter one at night.

The Paleocene was a fascinating period of Earth's history, full of drama and change, and it seemed an ideal setting for this story of the very first bats—the only mammal capable of powered flight.

Creature Gallery

Chiropter (KIE-rop-ter)

Small tree dwellers that glide between trees, hunting insects with their primitive echolocation. They launch themselves from hunting perches high up in trees. The chiropter does not have wings, but rather sails that are incapable of powered flight.

Felid (FEE-lid)

Lean and quick, the felids are equally at home in trees or on the ground. With their keen night vision and sense of smell, the felids are excellent at rooting out saurian nests and destroying their eggs. Most felids eat insects, vegetation, and carrion, but some have developed meat-shearing teeth and a craving for live prey.

Saurian (SORE-ee-uhn)

Though the saurians have been all but wiped out by natural disaster, a few still survive. Though many are vulnerable to terrible flesh-rotting disease, some are still able to lay eggs in hidden nests. The meat-eaters are feared by all the beasts.

Hyaenodon (hi-een-uh-don)

With its bone-crushing teeth, large size, and raw power, the hyaenodon is an unrivaled hunter. It hunts in packs, and is one of the few beasts who can battle the saurians.

Diatryma (die-uh-try-muh)

A flightless bird that can grow to seven feet in height, the diatryma is fast on the ground, and hunts down its prey on the open grasslands. Its beak and wickedly sharp talons are deadly weapons.

Soricid (sore-eh-sid)

Despite its timid appearance, this tiny shrewlike creature is a voracious eater that spends almost all its waking hours hunting. Its red teeth excrete a neurotoxin that paralyzes its prey and allows the soricid to hunt animals much larger than itself.

Equids (ee-kwids)

These timid herbivores have hooved feet and live on the grasslands. At full gallop, equids can usually outrun the diatryma, which frequently hunts them.

A Q&A with Kenneth Oppel

Why did you choose to write a prequel and not a sequel to the Silverwing series?

Over the years, I've received thousands of letters from readers asking if I'd write a sequel to *Firewing*, the third book in the Silverwing trilogy. Often these same readers would even suggest plots I could use to continue the adventures of Shade and Marina and Goth. The truth was, I wasn't at all sure I wanted to continue their story. Over the course of three books, I felt like my characters had experienced pretty much every peril and emotion possible. I was worried that if I wrote any more about them, it might feel like a rerun. I didn't have an idea that I thought would be original or exciting enough to keep me—or my readers—interested.

But I did have an idea for a story that took place long before Shade was even born.

So I decided to write a prequel.

In *Silverwing*, there are many mentions of the Great Battle between the Birds and the Beasts, which took place millions of years ago, and resulted in the bats being banished forever to the night skies. I started thinking about what caused this war. Just how long ago was it? What was the world like back then? What kind of animals inhabited it? I liked the idea of telling a story that would help explain the history and mythology of the Silverwing world.

The more I thought about it, the more I realized I also wanted to tell the story of the origins of bats, their place in the animal kingdom, and how they came to fly for the first time.

All of your characters have really interesting names. How did you decide upon names like Sylph, Dusk, and Carnassial? Do they have any special meaning?

Names are fun to invent. In general, I try to give my animal characters names that fit with their natures. Dusk, who is a gliding creature and is able to see in the dark, discovers he's really one of the first bats. So I liked the idea of conjuring up that transition from day to night (dusk) and also implying that the world too is changing, moving from one period to another.

I had a bit of fun with Sylph's name. Sylph means a spirit of the air, or a very slender girl. As a glider, Sylph is certainly a creature of the air—but she's hardly delicate and graceful! She's loud and strong-willed and determined, so her name, to me, is also a bit of a contradiction to her nature.

As for Carnassial, his name came from two sources. The first is the word carnivorous, which is very appropriate for him, because he's one of the first meat-eating cats. The second source is a special kind of ridged tooth that can tear meat and is actually called a carnassial tooth. Scientists can learn a lot about animal fossils from the teeth alone. And when they find a carnassial tooth in a jaw, they know the animal was a meat eater. Also, I just like the sound of the world carnassial too—it sounds quite regal, like a prince; and it also sounds a bit like some of the angel names from the Bible, like Cassiel, or Ariel, which have a majestic ring to it. Perfect for my prince of cats.

What do want your readers to learn from Dusk?

When I'm writing my story, I'm not sure I have anything particular in mind that I want my readers to learn. I'm just trying to tell a gripping story. It's only in the final stages of writing and rewriting, that I begin to see what the book might be about on a thematic level. Certainly, I think Dusk learns a great deal in the book—some of them very hard things for any young person to learn. He learns that people can be very suspicious and intolerant of difference; that his father isn't perfect, and has actually made some terrible mistakes in his past and present. He learns how treacherous and unfair life can be, but he also learns about loyalty and sacrifice and tolerance too.

You have three children. Has having kids influenced your writing?

I'm sure it has. Having your own kids makes it easier to see, once more, the world through the eyes of a child. What's important to them, what they love, what excites them, what frightens them, or bores them. Whenever I've finished a first draft of a novel, I read it aloud to my kids, and it's really helpful for me, because I can tell when they're enjoying it and when they're not, and I keep these things in mind when I'm rewriting. Kids may not be able to articulate clearly why they like or dislike something, but they are always very honest critics!

You have also written three books—*Airborn, Skybreaker,* and the soon-to-be-published *Starclimber*—about a teenage boy, Matt Cruse, and his adventures aboard airships. What's the deal with Kenneth Oppel and flight?

People sometimes ask me why so many of my books deal with flight—four books about bats and the three novels that are set aboard airships. I'm not sure I have an easy answer. It's not like I love flying myself. In fact, for a long time I was a very nervous flyer. I'd get very tense and quiet and notice every motion and sound and smell aboard the plane. Nowadays, maybe because I fly fairly often, I'm not as nervous, though I still find modern air travel cramped and boring.

What I love is the idea of flight.

As humans, we can't fly on our own. We need machinery around us. We'll never know how it truly feels to be a bird or a bat that can take flight under its own power. And that makes it a mysterious thing for me. All writers like imagining new people and places and situations. I seem to like imagining flight—and the new world it opens up, the sky.

I used to have lots of amazing flying dreams when I was younger. Sometimes I'd be escaping from something frightening, and I'd suddenly realize I could lift off and fly free. Sometimes I'd just be soaring over a landscape, usually a city, and it was really beautiful and exciting. I've never forgotten the exhilaration of those dreams. So maybe that's why I enjoy writing about creatures and people who can fly.

All of your books have a richly invented history carefully woven into the story. What do you do in order to create these alternate, yet similar to our own, worlds?

Even though my books are fantasy, they're all built on a foundation of fact. With *Airborn*, I was careful to research the real airships of the 1920s and 30s so I could make my fictional ships seem very plausible. And even though the books are set in an alternative past, I researched the historical period on which it was based (around 1910) so I could include all sorts of real details and facts to balance the invented details of my imaginary world. The trick is including enough fact to make your readers believe in your world and trust you—and then they'll be ready to believe in the fantasy elements too.

The same is true of *Darkwing*. The book is set sixty-five million years ago, so it was important for me to research that period so I could describe the trees and ferns and climate, and all the weird and wonderful animals that lived at that time. I wanted my readers to be able to feel and smell the world around them, to see the creatures moving through the trees and in the air. This way, even though the world is totally different from their own, they believe in it and even come to feel at home in it. This was especially important since I had to invent a new kind of animal, a chiropter, that was the ancestor to modern bats. There is no fossil evidence of such a creature yet, so I had to use my imagination and try to come up with something that seemed believable. And after all the scene-setting is done, it really comes down to your characters to make your story convincing. Whether they're humans or animals from the past or present, they have to be real characters your readers care about.

Take a peek at *Airborn* and *Skybreaker*!

Airborn

At the top of the ladder I got one arm hooked round the handhold inside the hatch. But Crumlin had me again by the leg and started pulling. I held tight, the metal handhold digging into my bone, and I knew he'd break my arm clean off. My eyes skittered around inside the ship. I saw an oil can within reach, grabbed it with my free hand, then reached down and squirted the pirate in the face and all over the rungs. Cursing, he let go to wipe his eyes and lost his grip. He fell heavily, crashing in a heap in the engine car. I hauled myself into the ship, lungs burning.

I slammed the hatch shut and locked it with my keys. With luck maybe the pirate would fall asleep and not mess with the engine. I leaned against the hatch to catch my breath.

That was another pirate down. Five left. Just five.

A finger of cold metal knocked against the side of my head.

"Hold up there, lad."

I turned slowly.

Crumlin's pistol was against my skull.

Skybreaker

"Captain, I'm not entirely sure, but I think it's the *Hyperion*."

Without a word Captain Tritus dropped the mouthpiece and once more lifted the spyglass to his eye. For a long time he stared.

There could be no one in the control car who hadn't heard of the *Hyperion*. She was a ship of legend, like the *Marie Celeste* or the *Colossus*—vessels that had set out from harbor and never reached their destinations. The *Hyperion* was rumored to be carrying great wealth. She may have crashed, or been pillaged by pirates. But no wreckage was ever found. Over the years sky sailors sometimes claimed to

EXTRAS

have spotted her, always fleetingly and from afar, and usually on foggy nights. Before I was born there was a famous photograph that was supposed to be of the *Hyperion* sighted over the Irish Sea. My father had shown it to me in a book. It was later exposed as a fake. She was a ghost ship—a good story, but nothing more.

"It's her," the captain said. "By God, I think it's her. Look!" he thrust the spyglass at his first officer. "Curtis, can you see her name?"

"I can't quite make it out, captain."

"You're half blind, man! It's clear as day. Cruse, get over here! They said you had sharp young eyes. Take a look!"

Eagerly I hurried to the front of the control car and took the spyglass. When I worked aboard the *Aurora* I'd spent many hours in her crow's nest, doing lookout duty. I had plenty of experience with a spyglass. Before I raised it to my face, I sighted the ship with my naked eye. I reckoned she was more than three miles away, no larger than a cigarette, pale against the distant darkness of the storm front. Quickly, before her position changed, I lifted the lens to my eye. Even with my feet planted wide for balance, and both hands on the spyglass, it was no easy feat to get a fix on her. Whenever I came close, the *Flotsam* pitched and tossed, and my view would skid off into cloud and sky.

Glimpses were all I caught: An enormous engine pod, its paint stripped away by the elements, glistening with frost. A control car almost entirely encased in ice, light flashing from a cracked window. Wind-blighted letters barely visible on her flayed skin: *Hyperion*.